THE

Four years old and better than ever!

We're celebrating our fourth anniversary...and thanks to you, our loyal readers, "The Avon Romance" is stronger and more exciting than ever! You've been telling us what you're looking for in top-quality historical romance—and we've been delivering it, month after wonderful month.

Since 1982, Avon has been launching new writers of exceptional promise—writers to follow in the matchless tradition of such Avon superstars as Kathleen E. Woodiwiss, Johanna Lindsey, Shirlee Busbee and Laurie McBain. Distinguished by a ribbon motif on the front cover, these books were quickly discovered by romance readers everywhere and dubbed "the ribbon books."

Every month "The Avon Romance" has continued to deliver the best in historical romance. Sensual, fast-paced stories by new writers (and some favorite repeats like Linda Ladd!) guarantee reading *without* the predictable characters and plots of formula romances.

"The Avon Romance"—our promise of superior, unforgettable historical romance. Thanks for making us such a dazzling success!

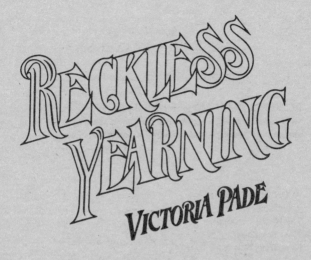

RECKLESS YEARNING

VICTORIA PADE

AVON
PUBLISHERS OF BARD, CAMELOT, DISCUS AND FLARE BOOKS

RECKLESS YEARNING is an original publication of Avon Books. This work has never before appeared in book form. This work is a novel. Any similarity to actual persons or events is purely coincidental.

AVON BOOKS
A division of
The Hearst Corporation
1790 Broadway
New York, New York 10019

Copyright © 1987 by Victoria Pade
Published by arrangement with the author
Library of Congress Catalog Card Number: 86-91010
ISBN: 0-380-89880-2

First Avon Printing: January 1987

AVON TRADEMARK REG. U.S. PAT. OFF. AND IN OTHER COUNTRIES, MARCA REGISTRADA, HECHO EN U.S.A.

Printed in the U.S.A.

K-R   10   9   8   7   6   5   4   3   2   1

To my father for his humor, his
dictionary, and all of his donations

To Mo just for being Mo

To Jeff because he claims to have
been instrumental in writing this book

And to my mother, a woman of strength,
independence, and vitality, who teaches
me more and more how to live life

Chapter 1

July, 1889

"She's a whore's spawn! I want her out of my town tonight! This is the last train for two days, and if she's not on it you'll be on the next one with her!"

It was a midsummer night. Hot. Humid. Brandon Bentley's voice rang loudly from the stationmaster's small shed, and only strangers to Dry Creek didn't know to whom the little town's richest citizen referred.

Lauren Flannery sat on top of her rusted trunk, her head held proudly on a thin neck too stiff to be natural. Her back was ramrod straight, from her high starched collar to her narrow banded waist. She crossed her ungloved hands stiffly in her lap over a small reticule that was too flat to contain more than a coin or two, and stared ahead at the huge black steam engine that was clanking and groaning like a mechanical horse impatient to be run.

People bustled around her, their whispering voices hissing as they passed. But she was aware only of Brandon Bentley's raging voice.

"I don't care if she has to go the whole way to Seattle standing up! Just get her out of here!" Bentley's parting shout was punctuated by the slam of a door that echoed off the iron sides of the train.

Lauren's narrow shoulders imperceptibly drew

back even more, and her pointed chin tilted higher, prouder.

Within seconds, the stationmaster's short, stout body rushed past her, taking such small steps his knees seemed hobbled together. He touched his brimmed cap, but his pea-like eyes were self-consciously averted.

"I'm seeing to it, Lauren!" he called, and Lauren bristled at the fact that his address lacked the respectful "Miss" that would have accompanied the name of any other unmarried woman he knew.

A drop of perspiration fell between her breasts, and she swallowed the rising sense of fear that made the heat all the more uncomfortable. She sensed more than heard the mousey stationmaster's agitated tones over the noise of the train, the hollow echo of shoes on the planked floor, and the hum of voices. How would he get her a place on a train already overcrowded?

Her curiosity won out over her pride, and she turned casually in the direction the stationmaster had gone, one car down. Through the hazy gray clouds of steam billowing from the side of the locomotive's boiler, Lauren saw him talking so fast his second chin rippled against his starched collar. His listener was a man who towered above him in the shadows.

The brass bell clanged its warning, and the conductor's voice shouted "All aboard!" just as a big, black cloud of smoke billowed up from the funnel on top of the engine and spit sparks in golden bursts against the sky.

Lauren saw the big man turn and climb the iron steps up into a box car whose side was painted with the insignia of the Spokane Falls and Northern Railroad. The little stationmaster scurried toward her in his hobbled run, his squeaky voice barely audible. "Come on, Lauren! Hurry it up! I got you a ride to Seattle."

Lauren stood up regally and waited as the man bent to drag her trunk along the weathered boards of the station's floor. She followed behind him, still displaying that unshakable composure.

The stationmaster wheezed, his puffy face red as he climbed backward onto the railed platform of the car, dragging her trunk after him. Lauren waited until trunk and man both disappeared through the door before climbing the steps, one hand holding her faded brown skirt just high enough to allow her feet to move freely.

"Lauren! Wait!"

She turned to see Alan Bentley run to the foot of the steps, his usually impeccable brown hair mussed, beads of sweat tracing a path from his temples down his cheeks.

Lauren smiled wanly, "You shouldn't be here, Alan," she said in a strained voice over the station noises, as the bell clanged its final warning.

"I'm so sorry, Lauren! I never meant this to happen!"

"I know you didn't. It's all right, Alan. I would have had to leave anyway." Up ahead the big box lantern at the front of the engine was being lit.

"I would have married you, Lauren! I would have! I wanted to!"

The stubby stationmaster pushed Lauren aside hurriedly, jumping from the platform just as the high iron wheels made their first rotation.

"It would never have worked, Alan," she yelled over the increasing din of the grating train axle.

His father appeared behind the slight young man. A scowl creased Brandon Bentley's hawkish face as he grasped his son's arm firmly, pulling him farther away from the slowly moving train, away from Lauren.

"Whore's bastard!" Bentley shrieked one last time before the train gained speed and the distance widened. Lauren could just manage to read Alan's last words on his lips; he was telling her to let him know if she needed anything. She watched forlornly as his form grew smaller and smaller.

Only then did she turn to climb the last step to the car's platform. She paused a moment, breathing deeply. She was not sorry to leave Dry Creek behind ... but the thought of what Seattle held for her sent a shudder up her spine.

Chapter 2

Lauren took one step into the bright lantern light of the private car and stopped dead in her tracks. The man facing her was by far the brawniest she had ever seen. He wore a soiled silk shirt hanging free about his hips, the front gaping open to expose a hairy chest and a hard, muscled belly. His big hands were hooked around the front of his pants, the two top buttons of which were unfastened. Lauren couldn't tell whether he was dressing or undressing, but she inferred the latter, and she wondered on what terms the stationmaster had gotten her this berth. She had to make that much clear quickly.

She addressed him in her haughtiest voice. "I don't know what the stationmaster promised you in return for my sharing this car, but my fare was paid for by Brandon Bentley, and that's that."

He glared at her with weary irritation through eyes so black there was no distinction between pupil and iris. "Look lady," his voice was deep and gravelly, as if it rumbled from low in his throat, "I'm too damn tired for a cat fight...or for anything else. You can ride in here or you can sit out on the platform for all I care."

Lauren stepped far enough into the space to close the door behind her. "So long as you understand that

I intend to sit on that sofa for the entire trip to Seattle and nothing more. You needn't even speak to me."

The man sighed in exasperation, "I'll keep it in mind." Then his thick fingers finished the task of buttoning his fly.

Lauren walked around her trunk and sank on to the velvet settee. She pulled a long pin from the straw hat that had seen better days and then set it meticulously on a nearby table. Spotting a speck of dust on the unseasonably long sleeve of her blouse, she flicked at it and then righted the high, stiff pouf at her shoulder. Though it was clean and pressed into sharp creases down the pleated front, the garment showed evidence of careful mending.

Lauren's eyes traveled around the room. She imagined whorehouses were less garish than this purple and gold abomination, which was dominated by a large bed that stood so high it required steps to climb into. Her gaze returned to her traveling companion, who was standing at a small washstand pouring water from a pitcher into a gilt-edged basin.

He had shrugged off his shirt, baring broad, muscular shoulders and a narrow waist that indented just above the low-slung waistband of his pants. He seemed oblivious to her presence as he inspected the black ringed hole in one sleeve by poking an index finger through it. His actions drew her attention to a mean-looking wound at the widest part of his upper arm just as he tossed the shirt aside carelessly and set about bathing his injury in the clean water.

Lauren boldly studied him as his deft fingers performed their task, reluctantly admiring the beauty of his naked back, the swell of hard muscle below a thickly corded neck, the deep indentation of his spine, the slight curve of his firm derriere. Then, realizing the thrust of her thoughts, she primly moved her eyes to her lap where she pretended to brush the station grit from her skirt.

Her head shot up when the man crossed over to her in long, confident strides. He held a faded red bandana out to her. "I can't tie this damn thing myself. If it wouldn't be considered payment, do you think you might consent to perform that minor service for me?" he mocked her.

Lauren took the scarf, her hand small beside his, and silently wrapped the cloth around his arm. It barely circled his bulging biceps. As she knotted the ends, she noticed a large scar rising to his shoulder from well down in the black mat of hair on his chest.

"Apparently you're used to being wounded," she commented, wondering if he was some sort of outlaw.

A low, pleasant-sounding rumble rolled from his throat. "You never get used to being hurt."

"Something you know well, from the look of you," she snapped, noting another jagged scar low across his side.

"I've had my share of scrapes. This part of the country is a long way from being civilized. Or weren't you aware of that?"

"Perhaps it isn't the country that's barbaric but some of its inhabitants." Her steady fingers reached beneath the firmly tied cloth, spreading its folds open to cover the wound more completely. His skin was warm and smooth over the hard muscles, and she was suddenly aware of the clean, musky scent of sweat on his freshly washed flesh. "What happened to you?" she asked, probing without conscience as she let her hands fall back into her lap.

He moved to an open leather valise on the high bed and reached in for a fresh shirt. Just my luck to have some puckered little shrew forced on me tonight, he thought. His annoyance sounded in his voice as he answered, "Some jackass shot me."

"Why?"

"I would have stopped to ask but I had a train to catch," he said cuttingly, which did not ease her suspicions about him one bit.

He pulled on a light chambray shirt, flinching as his wounded arm stretched back, and then rolled up each long sleeve to bare thick forearms covered with black hair. He was totally unperturbed that Lauren watched as he buttoned his shirt, leaving the top two unfastened where wiry hair curled into the hollow of his throat. Then he pushed the shirttails down into the waistband, not bothering to turn away from her.

Lauren's eyes rested on the snug fit of the bull denim dungarees over his narrow hips. She was taken aback at finding her interest centered on the bulge just to the right of his fly and hastily averted her gaze. What had come over her? Strain, she decided. She had been under too much lately and it had taken its toll of her wits. She took a conscious grip on her thoughts as he hunkered down to check the contents of a small cupboard. He rummaged in it a moment and then bounced back up again as if on springs. With a wine bottle and two glasses in hand, he pushed a low wing chair to face the sofa, dropped down into it, and raised two of the biggest, barest feet she had ever seen to the seat just inches from Lauren's side.

"Look," he sighed, ignoring the disparaging glance that fell on his feet and bony ankles just showing below worn denim. "I've had a lousy day. How about we have a drink and start again?"

Lauren hesitated. A small glass of sherry before Christmas dinner and on birthdays was the most liquor she had ever consumed. But her throat was dry, her mouth was parched, and she felt bone weary. It seemed a good idea to accept his peace offering. "Perhaps just half a glass," she agreed, her tone betraying her mistrust.

"Half a glass it is." Cradling the stems between his fingers, he filled them both full of the crimson liquid and then set the bottle beside her hat on the table.

Lauren took the glass he offered, careful that their hands should not meet. He noticed and chuckled wryly to himself. Then he slid low in his chair, running one large hand through his gun-barrel black hair, pulling it straight back, only to have it fall slightly forward again like raven's wings cupping his head. His face was starkly masculine and angular, his nose thin and just a little long. He's a hairy beast, she thought as her glance trailed to hollow cheeks and a sharp jaw, both lightly shadowed with the same blue-black of his hair. The few men Lauren had known had all been so clean shaven as to conceal the fact that they had whiskers at all, and it struck her that she had never encountered a man who was quite so ...male. Perhaps *that* was her problem—simple, natural curiosity. She felt reassured.

"The stationmaster didn't tell me your name." His gravelly voice was in keeping with the rest of him.

"Lauren Flannery," she answered simply, seeing he was bent on studying her now.

"I'm Zach Madox."

Silence fell as he drank his wine and sized her up. She was as scrawny as a prairie chicken and just about as sexless, he thought. Her rich, sable brown hair might have appealed to him if only it weren't pulled so damn tight into that coiled rope at the back of her head. Her nose was pointed and too often, he thought, she looked down it at him. Ah, but her eyes, there was something. Wide, topaz, like a private fireworks display of gold against chestnut. They were clear and bright and reflected a challenge that Zach Madox thought he just might take up. Hell, if he had to spend the night with her he might as well make it interesting.

The stationmaster had begged him, for the sake of

her safety, to get Lauren out of Dry Creek that night. Zach wondered what danger there could possibly be for someone as prim as she in a town tailor-made for priggishness. Looked to him like she'd be an asset in making ice. Then again, maybe she'd frozen the whole town.

"There aren't many reasons to visit Dry Creek, let alone get shot there," Lauren said after a long stretch of silence.

Zach Madox leaned his head back against the brocade of his chair and peered at her from beneath half-lowered lids. "I was there to see your Brandon Bentley."

"I heard he had a guest. And he is not *my* Brandon Bentley." She answered his barb so calmly that Zach couldn't suppress a mischievious grin at such control.

"He wrote to me a few months ago about buying my stock in this railroad. I came here to talk to him."

Lauren's eyes again circled the tasteless railroad car. "Then you own this?" Her opinion was clear.

He laughed. "I own a part of the company, not this particular Pullman. It belongs to a friend."

"And did you sell your shares to Brandon Bentley?"

His chin jutted forward as he scratched beneath it with the backs of four knuckles. She was a nosey little thing. But he answered all the same, "No, he didn't make it worth my while."

"Then he probably shot you," she stated flatly.

He shook his head, one side of his mouth curving up ironically. "Oh, I doubt that. He didn't strike me as a killer," he said facetiously. "He just got me out here on a whim."

"Don't fool yourself! Brandon Bentley is not a whimsical man. He is unscrupulous and uses any methods he must to get what he wants. You were lucky to escape with your life," she said with authority.

"That so? Your Brandon Bentley doesn't sound like a very nice man," he tried again, but his gibe went unacknowledged. "Anyway, as far as he knew, this was a simple business deal that fell through. Nothing to provoke shooting me. Some nearsighted oaf was probably hunting," he said, dismissing the whole thing.

Lauren said nothing, but graced him with a look that said he was foolish to underestimate such a blatantly evil man.

"So, if Bentley is such a villian, why did he pay your way out of town?"

A low, mirthless laugh escaped Lauren. "I believe it's customary to pay for the ticket of the person you are running out of town."

He eyed her up and down again, thinking that her back couldn't be any straighter if she were sitting against a board. "You don't look like the kind of woman who gets run out of upstanding little towns."

"And what kind of woman is that, Mr. Madox?" she challenged wryly over a dainty sip from her glass.

He grinned. She had spunk, he had to say that for her, and he was willing enough to take up the sparring. "The kind that righteous women like you cross the street to avoid."

Her smile was serenely amused; she had drunk nearly all the wine and was feeling unusually relaxed. "You paint a very unflattering picture of me. I must warn you that you are dangerously near to putting your foot in your mouth."

"Am I, now? How so?"

"Brandon Bentley arranged for my untimely departure because of my parentage."

"Your father refused to sell him something he wanted, and you were the weapon of his revenge?" he asked, taunting her with a lopsided grin.

"Hardly. In fact, there's no telling who fathered me. At the time of my conception my mother was the most sought-after woman in the biggest brothel in San Francisco."

His deep boom of laughter bounced off the walls. "Well, I'll be damned." he breathed. "I spent some time in 'Frisco a few years back. What's her name? Maybe I knew her."

"Her name was Kate Flannery, but you wouldn't have known her. She died six weeks ago in Dry Creek after living there for the past seven years." Why was her tongue so loose, Lauren wondered. But she didn't refuse the refill as he leaned forward with the wine bottle.

His black brows formed an unbroken line above eyes that studied Lauren more closely as he settled back again. "You in the business?"

Again she sent him that calm, amused smile. "Does it matter?"

"I imagine it does to you. But I'll tell you one thing, lady—if you're a whore you hide it real well."

"I suppose you expect me to thank you for that." Her smile was tantalizing, seemingly a reflection of her serenity. "Some of the people I've loved most in my life were engaged in that occupation and not a soul who didn't know what they did ever guessed. Appearance is not a reliable determining factor."

"Are you?"

Lauren merely raised her eyebrows, her smile challenged his judgment of her.

Her mouth, he realized, seemed to be set in a smile of perpetual amusement. He stared down at her as if the demand of his piercing black eyes would inspire an admission. It never came.

He shook his head slowly, "So you want me to be-lieve Brandon Bentley ran you out of town because you're a whore."

"People believe anything they want to. Actually, the blackguard drove me out because he judged me unsuitable as a daughter-in-law."

"How did you and your mother end up in Dry Creek anyway? Unless I miss my guess, there's never been a whorehouse in the whole town, let alone one to warrant 'the most sought-after woman' from 'the biggest brothel in San Francisco.'" he said mockingly.

She shrugged. "My mother married Harvey Barton when I was sixteen and his home was there. I came to live with them two years ago when my schooling was finished."

"What kind of schooling?" he interrupted.

"A convent in Stockton, California, and then a finishing school in Boston," she stated simply, knowing he was going to laugh before he did. Rather than acknowledge his amusement she drank her wine and continued with her story. "Harvey died shortly after that and my mother and I stayed on. She wasn't well in the last years, and what little money Harvey left lasted just until her death. That was when Alan proposed, and his father set out to prevent it. His bank repossessed the house, he threatened anyone who might give me employment, and, as a last resort, even threatened to close down the general store if they sold me simple necessities. It was all very effective," she concluded dispassionately, as if she were speaking of someone else's troubles.

"Didn't anybody stick up for you? Not even Alan?"

She laughed, a quiet, refined sound. "He's a powerful man, Brandon Bentley, and a vindictive one. Poor Alan is powerless against him. As for the rest of the townspeople, they were just as anxious to be rid of my sullying presence as was Alan's father."

He twirled the stem of the glass between thumb and forefinger, watching it, a grudging respect for Lauren budding. "So what's in Seattle?" Zach wondered if it was a trick of the lantern light or if her face had paled. Then he saw her back stiffen from its relaxed position, and he knew he had hit a nerve.

"I have a business there. I hadn't planned to work it, but now it's my only option."

"I don't need to ask what it is, do I?" He didn't know why, but he felt disappointed.

"It's a brothel," she answered simply.

"God knows there are enough of them in Seattle."

"Something you're familiar with?"

"Well enough. I live there." He eyed her up and down again, musing. "So, come hell or high water, you're going to take up being a whore."

"It's a living, Mr. Madox," she said sensibly, "and right now I am in need of one."

Zach stared at Lauren as if he were trying to read her mind, and she found his scrutiny unsettling.

"I assure you that you won't find signs of depravity carved into my forehead, if that's what you're looking for," she said sharply.

He only shook his head in answer, wondering what was really going on inside her pretty head. Desperation? She had taken it in stride, he had to give her that. With her mother a whore, she had to know what the life was like. So why did he have the feeling that this little lady was in for one hell of a shock?

His continued silence was unnerving. Lauren finally drained her glass and placed it meticulously near the bottle. Then she turned back to him with too-bright eyes. "I imagine it's quite late, and since you almost seem to be in a trance, perhaps you should retire."

The corners of his mouth began to curve slowly, and he chuckled softly at her attempt at composure even in the face of insobriety. "Perhaps I should," he said carefully, matching her tone. Then his gaze dropped to the sofa on which she sat. It was short, narrow, and hard tufted. "I'm all right where I am. You can take the bed."

"No, thank you." she said, amused by his obvious lack of enthusiasm. "The sofa suits me fine. I would never be able to sleep for fear of that hulking body of yours falling on top of me." Where had *that* come from?

"Is that so? I could fall on top of you on the settee as easily as I could in the bed," he answered dryly.

Lauren braved it through. "Only if you have the power to shrink at will."

He unfolded himself to his full six-foot four-inch height and pulled his chair back to its original place. "The choice was yours, Miss Flannery," he said with deceptive politeness.

He circled the room, dousing lanterns as Lauren watched, and then he mockingly presented her with a pillow and blanket. She thanked him and waited until he moved to the high bed and fell fully clothed onto the velvet coverlet. Only then did she lift her feet to the spot on the settee still warm from his and lie flat.

He heard her settling in, envisioning her lying stiff as a corpse. "I'd sure as hell hate to find you strangled to death in the morning from sleeping in that tight neckband. I figure you could undo just that without driving me wild with desire," he said sardonically.

Her hands did not raise to the high choker collar. "I'm fine, thank you."

A short silence ensued while Zach ruminated on her prudery. "Just out of curiosity, do you mean to run your house with or without participating?" he asked suddenly.

"I mean to do as I please."

His laughter roared out again. "I knew it! It might be a little hard to run a whorehouse from a pedestal. It takes experience to be a good madam."

"Is this something you know well?"

"Could be. One thing I know for sure, there isn't any way for a house to work with a virgin madam running it."

"You make me sound very innocent, Mr. Madox, without knowing a thing about me."

"When's the last time you were even in a whorehouse, Lauren?"

The pause was telling. "I was seven years old." She expected the laughter again, but it didn't come.

"So your mother kept you a long way away from everything to do with the life," he concluded.

"Yes," she answered grudgingly.

Zach shook his head, lifting it to cross his hands underneath. "That's what I thought. One look at you and every whore for miles will figure you've come to reform her. They'll all run for cover."

"I strike you as a pious hypocrite, do I, Mr. Madox?" Still she was unruffled.

"No, but you don't come across like a whorehouse madam either."

"Perhaps I have hidden talents."

His laughter rang out again and this time it nettled Lauren in a way that his suspicions of her lack of virtue had not. "If a more straitlaced woman walks the face of the earth, I'd like to meet her."

"As I said, you don't actually know anything about me, Mr. Madox."

"Maybe not, Miss Flannery," he shot back, saying her name sarcastically, "but I know a whore when I see one and an innocent when I hear one. And you're no whore."

"That, Mr. Madox," she said, wanting to shake his imperturbability, "remains to be seen."

The sound of Zach Madox's satisfied chuckle was the last thing she heard. But in the darkness she frowned, her confidence shaken in spite of the wine.

Chapter 3

Dawn was just a pink and orange blush when the big bell clanged their arrival in a town that could have been Dry Creek's twin city. For any who had slept through that, the screech of iron scraping against iron and the last blustery billow of steam was noisy enough to wake the most diehard late sleeper.

At the sound of the door shutting behind Zach, Lauren shot from the sofa and ran for the chamber pot with an alacrity that would have amused her traveling companion. Then she set about washing her face and hands in what was left of the water in a planked bucket, finishing by rubbing a long, thin forefinger across her teeth.

"We'll be in Seattle in an hour or so," Zach's gravelly voice announced, startling her.

She dried her face with her handkerchief and refastened the three buttons of her high collar before turning to face him.

He stood at the small table, barely managing to set bread, jam and earthenware crockery down before lowering the jar of coffee he held pressed against his stomach with his forearm.

"You must be hungry," Lauren said a bit distractedly, smoothing stray hairs back into the tight coil on top of her head.

17

"I could eat a horse! How about you?"

"I can't afford extravagances until I see what I'll need in Seattle."

"It's my treat. Comes with the accommodations." Her stubborn pride warred with her growling stomach. "Come on, Lauren! The bread's hot," he said, holding up a round crispy loaf enticingly.

"I don't like to owe anything." His use of her first name sounded friendly and familiar, unlike the stationmaster's off-handed disrespect. It comforted her as it made her realize just how unsettled she felt that morning.

Zach smiled through a dark growth of beard. "Call it my payment for your tending my wound last night," he said easily. "Now sit down. How will it look if the new madam passes out from hunger the first time she sets eyes on her house?"

He left her to decide, taking the wooden bucket outside to refill it with water. When he returned, she was sitting obediently at the table, hands folded in her lap. In spite of their short acquaintance, he knew Lauren's is compliancy was something to arouse curiosity. His black eyes watched her as he poured coffee from the mason jar into the two wine glasses and then broke off chunks of bread and spooned jam into the steaming, fluffy white center of each piece.

"Didn't you sleep well?" he asked, but he had the feeling she only half heard him.

"Fine, thank you." Lauren felt his eyes on her and did not like the sensation; they seemed to see more than she was willing to show. "You didn't tell me anything about yourself, Mr. Madox," she countered, staring out the window as she spoke.

"It's pretty boring stuff. And my name is Zach."

"Are you married?"

"Nope."

"Family?"

"None."

"What do you do for a living...besides owning stock in this railroad?"

"This and that. I have a hand in a couple of things."

Lauren nodded her head absently, obviously unaware of his evasiveness. From the frown on her face Zach guessed it wasn't pleasant thoughts that absorbed her attention.

"What's the matter, Lauren?" His gravelly voice was soft, cajoling. "Are you scared?"

She looked at him then, her eyes as wide and alert as if he had suddenly struck too near a secret. "A little nervous," she admitted, a little bemused by his perception.

"It's only natural."

"Yes, I'm sure." She turned back to the window.

"Want to talk about it?"

"No." How could she talk about something she didn't understand herself? All night long his words had played over and over in her mind: the virgin madam. It was ludicrous and Lauren had no desire to be laughed at. She had worked hard to maintain her dignity. Then, as if gates had been opened, one phrase had rekindled all her doubts and fears. She had gone from the clean, secluded life of a convent to a place where she was scorned as the whore's daughter. Now it occurred to her that when she stepped off this train she would be a whorehouse madam...and she would deserve the contempt of the people of Dry Creek. No, it couldn't be talked about.

Since she didn't want to talk, Zach settled for watching her while he ate. She was further inside herself than anyone he had ever seen and he wondered where that almighty cocksureness had gone.

The train jerked to a start again as the sun rose higher. Lauren pushed her food away and continued to stare out the window at the countryside rolling passed.

Better to leave her to sort things out alone, Zach thought and silently cleared the breakfast debris. Then he gathered his shaving gear from his valise.

The sound of water splashing into the china basin drew Lauren's attention back to Zach, and she tried to clear her dark thoughts by studying him at his morning ablutions. He shed his shirt, untied the red scarf from around his arm, and dunked it into the water. Her gaze followed as he lathered the black hair of his chest and beneath each armpit, then rinsed with the same brisk strokes. He used his discarded shirt to pat himself dry and, taking his shaving cup, he twirled the hard-bristled brush in it until lather swelled to the rim. Then he soaped up the black-whiskered shadow on his face and applied the straight-edged razor with deft strokes.

Lauren found the whole process fascinating. She had lived a life oddly devoid of men. As a child she had been kept away from everyone save her nanny, mother, and aunt; in the convent the only man she had had contact with had been a sour-smelling, booming-voiced priest with a bony face and eyes like yellow flames. And there had been Harvey, but he was nothing at all like Zach Madox. In fact, Lauren had never thought of Harvey as a man. Harvey was just Harvey: short, plump, balding, with laughing eyes and an impish smile. But Lauren had never known a man as virile as Zach Madox. Watching him made her devastatingly aware of how ignorant she was of even the smallest aspect of men and masculinity.

She wondered, as she had often in the past, what it meant to be a whore, what kind of life it had been for the two women who had made up her family. How would she run a business that dealt with something about which she was totally ignorant?

As she watched Zach run a brush through his
shiny black hair, she thought that maybe she should
begin here and now. Zach Madox seemed kind
enough. And he was attractive, though the sheer intensity of his masculinity unnerved her. How better
to overcome a fear than by facing it? And certainly
the time was at hand to learn about men.

He took out another faded chambray shirt. The
slapping sound as he shook out the folds could only
just be heard beneath the rumbling din of the train.
She noticed that he didn't flinch when his arm
stretched back into the sleeve, and he left the front
gaping open as he first rolled each cuff above the
elbow. Suddenly the black hair on each forearm appeared intensely personal, even as the sight of his
muscular chest and hard belly seemed more intimate, partially covered as they were by the shirt
front.

What was it like to lie in a stranger's arms? she
wondered. To feel the caress of big, callused hands?
To taste a man's mouth, to test the texture of masculine skin? When had virginity become a burden? Better to give it freely than to sell it, she thought
cynically. And better to a man who stirred something
tingly and fleeting in her, though she didn't understand how or why. At least then she would not go to
her house a virgin madam.

Her decision seemed to have made itself as her
hands rose to undo the three covered buttons at her
collar. Silent steps took her to Zach, her head held
high, her determination evident. She stopped directly in front of and very close to him. He raised his
black eyes abruptly to the calm, brilliant topaz of
hers. His hands stopped short at the button in the
center of his chest and there they remained as he
stared at her, wondering just what the hell was going
on.

Only Lauren's hands belied her composure, their

hesitancy proof of her second thoughts as she
reached tentatively to pull one of his from his shirt
front. She lowered her eyes then, watching her own
hand holding his much larger one.

Zach waited, at a loss to understand what she
wanted of him.

Lauren brought his hand to her lips and placed a
light kiss on the back, breathing in the scent of soap.

"I want you to make love to me," she whispered.

She felt Zach's eyes burn into her but she could
not look at him. Roughly, he pulled her hand to his
lips, hot and soft, and kissed the mounded heel, his
breath searing her wrist. His pointed tongue jutted
out and goose bumps jumped along her arms and
across the back of her neck. Then he held her hand
tightly to his bare chest inside the open shirt front.
The forefinger of his free hand slid like a feather
from the hollow just below her ear along her jawbone and under her chin, raising it gently, slowly,
until she had to meet his black gaze.

There was nothing in his expression condemning
her as immoral. Instead he looked only surprised.
His face lowered so gradually that Lauren was unsure of what he intended until his lips met hers in a
kiss so tentative she didn't respond. She could feel
his breath warm on her cheek and heard a low
chuckle in his throat as his mouth claimed hers
again, his head barely moving in small circles above
hers. She closed her eyes and copied his actions,
though her lips were clamped shut.

Then he pressed his mouth to her cheek and
spoke against it. "Relax, Irish."

Lauren stared at his chin, wanting to be ready for
his next kiss. When it came she met it adeptly, her
lips soft beneath his, open just slightly, her eyes
closed. She leaned into him, her small breasts against
his arm, which rested between them.

Just the tip of his tongue traced the outline of her

lips, and Lauren liked the feel of his mouth, warm and moist against hers, leading her, teasing her. Her nipples tightened into hard little buds and a sudden chill brushed lightly across her skin.

Zach raised her hands to his shoulders, so she could clasp them behind his neck. Then his arm curved around to pull her so closely against his long, hard length that she felt crushed...but in the nicest way. Something rose and hardened at her middle and without understanding it, she felt a curious sense of power. For the first time in her life she felt sensuous.

When his kiss ended this time he pressed her head so that her cheek rested flat against his warm, hair-roughened chest. She breathed in slowly, deeply, and let her body ease into the hard curves of his.

And then he did the oddest thing for a man she thought was in the throes of passion. He laughed.

"I don't want to be the one to make you into a whore, Lauren," he growled. "I won't make love to you just for that. Do you understand me?"

She nodded, wondering how he knew and how she could face him now that he had seen through her.

"You're the damnedest woman."

Lauren eased back awkwardly. But he allowed her only so much distance before his strong arms halted her escape. Her small breasts rose with the deep breath she took to steady herself and quell her feelings of utter foolishness.

"I'm sorry," she said firmly, as if that alone erased her shamelessness.

His grin widened. "You should be." But there was no rebuke in his voice. "A man doesn't like to be used."

She unconsciously reached up one small hand to pull together the open ends of a neckline that showed only a bare hint of her throat as she stared at his chest. "I . . . didn't mean you to know."

Zach laughed ruefully. "Well, at least you don't deny it. I suppose that's something."

This time when she pulled away he let her go. She turned her back on him to button her collar as modestly as if she were concealing stark nakedness, facing him only when she was fastened up to her chin again. "You could consider it a momentary lapse in my sanity," she offered.

"I already figured that. You know, it's bad business to give away what you need to sell."

"It won't happen again."

"That would be one hell of a shame," he murmured regretfully.

"Have a little mercy, Mr. Madox. I've embarrassed myself quite sufficiently today," she said softly.

"Why don't you just admit you're scared and lonely and need a friend?"

"Is that how I seem to you?" she hedged.

"Sure is."

"It doesn't really make any difference, you know."

"It does to me," he said so sincerely she believed him.

"Why?" Her brows arched so high they nearly took wing.

"I'd just like to help you out. And lady, you can use it."

"I was taught to beware of men bearing gifts or offering assistance," she answered tartly, then stared him squarely in the eye again. "I've set my course and I will not be beholden to you or anyone else along the way."

Zach looked at Lauren as if taking a bead on her. "I sure would like to know why you're trying so hard to be something you're not. You'd be a better schoolmarm than a whore."

A hard little laugh answered him. "I made inquiries into that. People with my background are considered to be corrupting influences on children."

He shook his head, sighing disgustedly at the injustice of what she had just told him.

But Lauren saw it differently, "Don't pity me, Mr. Madox," she said with equanimity. "What I will accept from you is to be pointed in the right direction when we get to Seattle. Beyond that, I'm not in need of your services."

"That's not what you said a minute ago," he taunted good-naturedly.

"I was hoping you might overlook the ammunition I laid at your feet," she said calmly, that composure of hers somehow back in place.

"I have to take my pleasures where I can get them." He laughed and shook his head again. "A whore in a high-necked gown."

"I suppose that will be my distinction."

"I suppose it could," he answered thoughtfully. "But I doubt that you'll need one."

"You don't think I'll go through with this, is that it?"

"No, that isn't it, Irish. You're so hell-bent you just might. But if you do you'll be outstanding among whores no matter what you wear. You won't have to contrive at it."

She didn't know if she should thank him or be offended, and so she let it lie.

Chapter 4

Seattle. The city built on seven hills.

In the west, across the gray beaches of Puget Sound, were the snow-capped Olympic mountains; in the east across the royal blue water of Lake Washington were the foothills that rose into the Cascades. On this clear summer day Seattle was the portrait of lush beauty—alive, vibrant, vigorous, roughly hewn.

Beneath a lacy ironwork overhang a group of people waited for the horse-drawn streetcars that stopped there. Men paced impatiently beneath the curved canopy of the black iron grid, and women sat with sleeping babies on wooden benches as children played catch-me-if-you-can around ornate iron pillars with opaque globes at their tops.

Lauren watched them curiously as she waited with their baggage while Zach went in search of a carriage.

A clanging bell soon heralded a streetcar's approach above the noises of hawkers selling their wares, dogs barking after shrieking children, and horses and wagons clattering across the uneven, cobbled pavement.

The waiting area quickly cleared of people as they climbed into the conveyance, paying their nickel fares to a bored driver. It set off down the street bulging with passengers, some barely able to stand on the sideboards and hanging onto ropes dangling from the small overhang. Now Lauren understood why Zach had only laughed at her suggestion that she use public transportation.

Within seconds after the horsecar left, Lauren caught sight of Zach driving a bright red surrey.

"How do you like it? Better than a buckboard, don't you think?" he called out as he pulled to a stop and jumped to the ground in front of her, his handsome face beaming with sly mischief.

Lauren ran a hand through the red fringe hanging from the top, sending the shiny stuff swaying. "I don't suppose I'll get to my house unnoticed in this."

Zach hoisted her trunk onto the floor in back. "I didn't know you wanted to sneak in," he said. "It's good business to announce your arrival. You may as well go in style."

"This is not quite the style I had in mind. A red surrey is a little garish, don't you think?" she said reprovingly like a tolerant, amused schoolmarm, refusing to let him rile her.

Zach shrugged as he piled his own bags on the red, tufted back seat. "I don't think anything is too garish for a whorehouse madam, Irish," he retorted, as he finished loading the baggage. He turned to Lauren, his hands resting on tightly clad hips, waiting.

She shook her head slowly, the corners of her mouth tilted up just slightly. "So this is where it starts, is that what you're telling me?"

"This is it," he concurred, holding out one hand to help her up.

"Then let's get to it, Mr. Madox," she answered in as businesslike a tone as she was able to muster, lifting her skirts just high enough to allow her to ascend.

Zach had to admire her spirit as he handed her up

and settled himself on the seat beside her. He took
the reins, and his gravelly voice asked mockingly,
"Where to, madam? Which of Seattle's innumerable
whorehouses is yours?"

"The house is called Maudie's."

There was a long, heavy pause. "Maudie's," Zach
repeated evenly. Then he shook his head very slowly.
"I should have guessed."

Seattle was a city newly thriving after the destruc-
tion of its business district by fire. A pot of glue boiling over onto the stove in a cabinet shop had set
sixty-five blocks ablaze, razing most of the downtown
area before hand-pumped fire engines could control
it. Even the newspaper in a town as small and far
away as Dry Creek had carried the story, as well as
the prediction that the port city would all but close
down because of the conflagration.

But the people of Seattle were tenacious. They
camped in billowing white tents and they rebuilt
their city with brick and stone, better than before.

But few genteel women had ventured into the
rugged confines of the resurrected city. They were
far outnumbered by brawny, virile men hungry for
gentle company. Many of the ladies of the evening
were Chinese women, who had come with fathers or
brothers or even husbands when the railroad compa-
nies brought the men in as cheap labor, or Indian
women with nowhere else to go. They settled into
seedy shacks or worked the box houses, saloons with
deep, three-sided booths called box seats along the
walls where the baser arts were practiced with a minimum of privacy.

Amidst it all Maudie's was an oasis.

Maudie's offered elegant diversions for those
seeking the kind of discreet entertainment found in
the most sophisticated cities of the world. Rough loggers and gentlemen alike considered it a sort of civic

achievement that such a place had found its way to Seattle.

Zach knew Maudie's well.

"I take it you're familiar with the house?" Lauren queried, interrupting his musings.

He cleared his throat, though his black brows remained furrowed. "I am. It's at the very edge of downtown. We'll be there in a few minutes. But there are some things you should know before we get there."

Lauren's face paled. "It didn't burn down, did it?" She barely breathed the words.

Zach moved uncomfortably in his seat. "It burned, all right, but that isn't the worst of it."

Lauren went very still beside him. "It couldn't be worse than that."

"When did you find out that you'd inherited the place?" he asked, stalling for time.

"Not until after my mother died. Maudie was my aunt. I was going through some papers and found a letter she had written my mother. They had argued bitterly when mother married Harvey. Maudie went to Seattle and, as far as I know, that letter was the only contact they had after that. It was a complete surprise for me to find that she had left me everything in her will. Mother must not have wanted me to accept it because she never said a word. In fact, I was forbidden even to mention my aunt," she finished sadly.

"Maudie died over a year and a half ago." It sounded like an accusation.

Lauren turned her head to stare at him. "Yes, I know. I found her obituary with the letter." She watched him curiously. "Is there something you aren't telling me about my house?"

Zach watched the road ahead. "You could say that."

"Then please come out with it. Maudie's is all I

have." Confusion and suspicion were apparent in her voice. "How badly did it burn?"

Zach drew a deep breath, puffing his cheeks way out and then exhaling slowly. "We have a problem, Lauren."

He turned the surrey down a side street lined with white tents and pulled back on the reins to stop before a three-story brick townhouse. Ignoring Lauren's questioning glare, he jumped down from the buggy and pointed a blunt thumb over his shoulder at the building. "This, Miss Flannery, is Maudie's."

Lauren's gaze went from Zach to the tall structure in front of her. The brick facade was complete save for the empty squares waiting for window glass to be set in. Workmen were carrying lumber inside and the loud banging of hammers could be heard coming from the house.

"I don't understand," she said as Zach lifted her from the surrey. "If this is my house, who is paying to rebuild it?"

Zach's mouth opened to speak, but before the words found their way out, an older man caught sight of them and rushed toward them with a broad, welcoming grin and an outstretched hand. "Mr. Madox! I didn't expect you until tomorrow."

Zach threw a sidelong glance at Lauren as he accepted the man's hand. "Good morning, John. How's it going?"

"Right on schedule. I'm seeing to it, just like you said."

Zach sensed rather than saw the stiffening of Lauren's back as the man continued, "All that fine French furniture you ordered got in yesterday and the mirrors should be here by the end of next week. It's shaping up fine! Maudie's'll be as good as it was before!"

"Yeah, well..." Zach cleared his throat, "I think I'll just have a look around."

"Sure thing, Mr. Madox."

As the man hurried off, Zach took Lauren's elbow and felt the tautness in her arm. "Let's go inside and find a quiet spot to talk."

She turned her head slowly toward him, her topaz eyes wide and bright with anger. "Are we entering my establishment...or yours?"

"That's what we're going to talk about."

Zach led Lauren up a steep flight of stairs that curved to the third level, then down a long hallway to a room at the very back. It was free of workmen, and the noises of construction were remote. It was nothing more than a space enclosed by wooden walls, planked floors, and ceiling; the finishing had not yet begun.

Lauren walked around the room, pausing to stare from the wide slot that would be a window. Then she turned to Zach with an icy glare. "Which of us owns this?" she asked, challenging him.

Zach's black gaze met hers squarely. "That's a complicated issue."

"If you explain it slowly I'm sure I can grasp it."

"I don't know what you have to be angry about. No one ever claimed the place. I was looking out for my own interests," he said reasonably.

"Which are?"

"Along with this house, you inherited a debt."

"I don't suppose I need ask to whom," she said sarcastically.

Zach leaned one shoulder against a wall, crossed his arms over his chest and one ankle over the other, and braced the pointed toe of his boot against the floor. "To me."

"Are you a banker?" she demanded.

"Maudie was a friend," he answered stiffly.

"Then you're the kind of man who befriends

whores. I was wise to be wary of you." Her tone was harsh and judgmental.

A gleam of irritation shone in his black eyes, but he remained calm and kept his gravelly voice even. "The only thing that Maudie's being a whore affected was the way we met. We were friends, no different than if she were a damn duchess."

"How did Maudie end up owing such a good friend money?" she shot at him.

"She borrowed it to buy opium."

Lauren's mouth fell open for only a moment before she regained her wits. "You loaned her money to support an opium habit?" Her voice rang with disbelief.

"Maudie and I were good friends," he said very, very slowly.

Lauren was livid at the thought of Maudie, round-faced and trusting, a slave to a drug. Maudie, who had sewn her crisp white frocks and embroidered them lovingly with tiny flowers. Maudie, who had braided her hair, read her stories, comforted her fears. Maudie, who had spent as many school vacations with Lauren as had her own mother. Who had advised, taught, given her gifts, and loved her every bit as much as if Lauren had been her child.

And Lauren was scared to death at what she might be forced to do without her inheritance.

"I know about men like you," she hissed. "You feed off women like vultures feed off flesh. How many poor wretches work to keep your belly full? To buy your fine silk shirts and that railroad stock you wouldn't sell Brandon Bentley? Maudie wasn't an easy dupe. How did you catch her?"

Her words sparked his temper. He straightened up sharply, his hands going aggressively to his hips. "Now hold on! You can stop right there!"

"Oh, I don't think so! Let's get it all out in the

open since we've already begun. Do you expect *me* to work for you now? Have you been planning that since I introduced myself yesterday? Surely you knew the name of the person whose inheritance you were stealing!"

"Everything was done through lawyers. I only knew you as the niece."

"How many whorehouses can there be waiting to be claimed by an heiress?" she shot back snidely.

"A thousand, for all I know!" He matched her sarcasm. "I didn't put two and two together, dammit. Besides, you didn't act as if it were something that had been pending for the last year and a half. I had stopped even thinking Maudie's 'heiress' would show up. So don't go looking for some kind of conspiracy where there isn't one." He paused a moment to gain control of himself, to give himself time to think and gauge the effect of the idea he was about to propose. "Look, there's a way we can both come out of this all right. I'm willing to make a deal."

"Let me guess. I can become your number-one girl."

"Are you going to listen to me?" His tone was threatening.

"I don't want to hear your vile propositions. It seems to me that you and Brandon Bentley could be bookends. You're both conniving bloodsuckers."

"I'll tell you what, lady," Zach snapped, one finger pointing at her like a spear pinning her in place. "You go down to Skid Row and find a rat-infested shack or maybe, if you're real lucky, a spot in a box house. You can do a little singing or dancing and earn your share of profits from the drinks you sell, and in between you can entertain any man with the price in one of their box seats. I understand the waiters are good about not looking in. See how you like it. And maybe after your bones have been picked a few times, you'll be interested in what I have to say."

Without a pause or a backward glance, Zach walked out the door. And Lauren was left alone and stranded with nothing but her fury...and her fear.

Chapter 5

Lauren paced the rough wooden space in a frenzy, her arms crossed over her breasts. The blood pounded in her head with the rhythm of her heartbeat. Desperation, panic, and red-hot rage warred within her.

Options. There had to be options. Were there? There had to be! There weren't.

She didn't have enough money to last a week in Seattle, let alone pay off Zach Madox to get Maudie's back and then finish rebuilding it. She hadn't even so much as train fare to be able to leave. And the only person offering her anything had just walked out on her.

"All right!" The words were a loud, bitter shout of defeat in the empty room before she turned to follow Zach, hoping to God he wasn't what she had just accused him of being.

She walked briskly down the stairs and out of the house; she would not run after him. As she pushed through the front entrance she was afraid she would find her trunk sitting in the street, with no sign of Zach anywhere. But there he sat on the front seat of the red surrey, his big body taut, his arms folded across his chest, consciously taking deep breaths to control his anger.

Lauren walked over to him with as much pride as long years of practice could muster. She stopped beside the surrey, stubbornly refusing to raise her eyes to him, fighting to find words.

Zach watched her, biding his time, until it seemed she would never speak. "Do you want to hear what I have to offer?"

"Said the spider to the fly." The words jumped out before she could stop them.

"I won't put up with your bitchiness, Lauren," he warned with an edge in his voice. "If I leave again, I'm gone for good. It's in your best interest to be civil, or by God, you won't be left just pretending to be a whore."

"It's only your assumption that it is a pretense." Contrariness just seemed to flow from her of its own accord.

"If you're a whore, Miss Flannery," he said acidly, "then you're the only damn whore in the world who's never been kissed before."

Lauren's chin went up, but Zach knew she had no rejoinder. "There is a better answer to all this, one that will suit us both," he went on. "Do you want to hear it?"

She closed her eyes slowly, loathing her predicament but knowing she had to bite her tongue or lose whatever chance he was offering, "Yes," she managed tightly.

Zach reached down a giant hand to haul her up into the buggy. "Then you're going to hear how it was with Maudie first."

Lauren stared ahead at the horses, squeezing her body as far away from Zach as the narrow seat permitted.

"The last year of her life Maudie was dying, a miserable death no doctor could help. Opium gave her a few hours of peace like nothing else did. When she had gone through all of her own money, she came to see me. She wanted a loan against the house. I couldn't do that, so I gave it to her instead. But like you, it seems, she wouldn't leave it at that. She drew up the papers of indebtedness anyway, signed them, made them legal. I didn't even know about it until she died and her lawyer came to me. He told me I could either claim ownership of this place as repayment of the debt or leave it for her heir to pay. So I waited. When it burned and you still hadn't shown up or notified anybody, I didn't see any reason not to rebuild it and go on from there."

"Rather than lose your investment."

"I'm not a fool, Lauren. I didn't get where I am by sitting still and watching opportunities pass by. I gave Maudie the money freely. *She* decided to do it this way, not me. In fact, had you claimed the place when she died, I probably would have torn up the note."

"And now?"

"Now I have a hell of a lot more invested."

"Then you have claimed ownership."

"Legally it's been set into motion, yes. But the paperwork hasn't been completed." He sighed. "Look, I don't want your damn inheritance."

"Then what do you propose?" She forced herself to keep her tone level.

"I'll finish what I've started here, but I'll release my claim to ownership. You can consider the whole thing a loan, and when the house is finished you can work the place and repay me."

"At what rate of interest?"

"I'll consider your repaying the money I gave Maudie as the interest, since I didn't plan on getting that back anyway."

"Exactly what will I end up owing you?"

"About ten thousand dollars."

The color drained from Lauren's face. A full minute ticked by before she could find her voice. "I'll own Maudie's and you will own me," she whispered, almost to herself.

"Or I'll own Maudie's and you can beat a path out of here right now." He meant what he said.

"A path to nowhere."

"A good whore can work anyplace." His words were sardonic.

Heavy silence engulfed them as Lauren considered his offer, realizing he was handing her back the future she had expected when she came to Seattle. Finally she turned to him, her features tight, her voice businesslike. "I want it all drawn up legally, a loan like one arranged through a bank, with nothing owed to you but money. Do you agree?"

"Agreed."

"I want you to stop work—today. I don't want another board to go up until this is all legally sealed."

Zach's demeanor changed instantly. "That's a waste of time. My word is good."

"So you say."

He just stared at her from beneath the shelf of his brow; she recognized the warning and was forced to concede again.

"There is one more thing." It sounded as if she were bestowing the favors, she thought a little giddily. "I will need to increase the loan by enough for me to live until the house is completed."

"No."

"What do you mean, no?" Sparks flew from her eyes.

"It means that I will not lend you money to live."

"Mr. Madox"—her patience was obviously forced— "I came to Seattle expecting to live at Maudie's. I haven't the funds for a place to stay or for food."

"I figured."

"Surely you can afford the pittance it would cost for me to live," she said through clenched teeth.

"I can afford it."

"What are your terms?" The question was an accusation.

"No terms. I won't extend the loan."

"Why not!"

He shrugged negligently. "I have a house big enough for both of us and plenty of everything else. I can't see you getting deeper in debt when you can just stay with me."

"I should have known." She shook her head slowly.

"I can use a housekeeper and a cook. You can earn your keep."

"And at night I can warm your bed to round out my duties."

Zach's face broke into a crooked grin. "I didn't invite you into my bed, Miss Flannery, just into my house. What a suspicious mind you have."

"Then why force me to live with you?"

"It's the most thrifty way for this deal to progress. I wouldn't think of increasing your debt and living up to your opinion of me as a bloodsucker."

"You know there isn't anything else I can do."

"I know." His broad shoulders rose in a satisfied shrug, his good nature restored. "What use has a whorehouse madam for a good reputation anyway?"

Chapter 6

The clatter of the high wheels of the surrey across an arched stone bridge heralded Lauren's arrival at Zach's home. Neither of them had spoken a word since leaving Maudie's.

The buggy followed a cobbled path through lush green lawns and flower beds to an enormous clapboard house, which had been whitewashed to a spectacular brightness, its windows framed with hunter green shutters. It stood two stories high; the second level formed an overhang for a deep porch that ran the whole width of the front.

The house had the look of a family home, and Lauren half expected a dozen children to romp into view at any moment, followed by a big dog and a watchful mother. But all was quiet and deserted. Her next thought was that Zach had brought her to someone else's home. The place didn't seem to fit the man. She pictured him in a gaudy room over a gambling hall or in a rustic cabin in the wilderness, or even, more appropriately, in the garish train car—not in a big white house with green shutters. But one look at him quelled any doubts that he belonged there, for as Zach peered up at the structure his face reflected the warmth he felt for it and a clear pleasure at being back home.

"Were you born here?" Her rising curiosity over-shadowed Lauren's anger.

"Thirty-three years ago the only thing that could possibly have stood here was a tepee." He laughed and then added proudly, "I built this place."

"All of this...just for yourself?"

"I didn't figure on living in it alone forever."

"Even then you planned to force wayward women to live with you?" she asked wryly.

His eyes crinkled at the corners at that notion. "Something like that."

One step through the double front doors was enough to show Lauren that no woman had had a hand in decorating the place. There was plenty of furniture in the parlor to the right of the entrance, all sturdy and serviceable, but upholstered solely in browns and tans. There wasn't a knickknack in the entire large, square room, nor a drape to cover the two big bay windows that arched out onto the porch. Even the lamps were plain, all tarnished brass with plain cream-colored globes, over chimneys gray with soot. The walls were painted stark white, and there wasn't a picture or a square of wallpaper to warm them.

Everywhere was the debris of living: a half-empty coffee cup beside a checkerboard on a corner table; a discarded handkerchief; cigar ashes in a dish long forgotten, the butt on the hearth where it had fallen short of the firebox; and even the pointed toe of a boot peeking out from beneath the brown sofa. And over it all was a powdering of dust.

"It's been awhile since it's had a good scrubbing," Zach said from behind Lauren, seeing where her eyes were traveling. "Now you know why I need a housekeeper."

"It goes without saying, Mr. Madox."

"Have a look around and I'll get your trunk."

Lauren prowled through the house, finding a

large room that she guessed was meant to be a formal drawing room except that a massive desk hulked in the center with papers scattered all over it. She found a dining room, though there was no furniture to designate it as such; the only litter there was a soiled towel.

Finally, she walked through a far doorway to find an enormous kitchen, with a second entrance on the opposite side opening on to the staircase that faced the front door. The kitchen was bare and spotless. It was an inviting room even without decoration, dominated by a big iron stove at one end and a round pedestal table and eight bow-backed chairs in the middle.

"Lauren! Are you upstairs?" Zach shouted from the foot of the steps.

She moved across the kitchen to the hallway beside the staircase. "I'm right here. Someone besides you must keep your kitchen," she stated unequivocally.

He smiled broadly, undisturbed by her sarcasm. "My laundress comes in now and then; she cooks for me and sees to it."

"Your laundress?" One of her brows arched skeptically. His answer was only a wider grin and a nod of his handsome head toward the stairs.

"Come on—I'll show you the bedrooms." Zach hoisted her trunk to his shoulder as if it weighed nothing and took the steps two at a time.

Lauren waited until she heard his boot heel click on the top landing before she followed, two fingers trailing along the dusty banister on the way. As much as it irked her to realize her curiosity was a source of entertainment to him, she had to ask the obvious questions.

"That one's mine." Zach gestured toward the first room at the front of the house. "You can use this one at the other end."

Besides the master bedroom, Lauren counted six

others, most of them empty. Her room, as well as all
the other five she peered into, was the size of the
parlor, dining room, and kitchen combined in Harvey's house. There were no warm touches here either: a bed flush against one wall without even a
coverlet over the mattress; a tall wardrobe; a washstand with a small oval mirror above it; the planked
floor without so much as a rag rug as protection
against the cold.

"Is there a reason why you haven't any curtains in
your house, Mr. Madox?" she asked.

He kneed her trunk up against one wall, out of the
way. "Just never took the time, *Miss Flannery*." Again
his use of her name mocked her formality. "There's
nobody close enough to see in anyway, and I figured
when a woman comes to her new home she likes to
add her own touches in things like that."

"Are you expecting someone?"

"A wife, when I find one," he answered simply,
hands on his hips and a provocative grin on his face.

"Did you have no rugs or curtains put in at Maudie's as well?" she asked, changing the subject as she
realized he was teasing her.

Zach chuckled smugly. "Maudie's is all set, every
last detail. Not like this."

"How so?"

He looked at her as if she were witless, the teasing
expression gone. "Maudie's is a whorehouse. But
this"—he peered around, seeing something more
than bare space—"this is going to be a home."

Lauren did not linger in the tub that evening, and
as she dried herself with brisk, efficient strokes she
glanced around at the shelf-lined walls of the bathing
closet. Nothing took up the shelf space, and it struck
her that this was just another portion of the house
waiting to be used.

She dressed in a light cotton gown, peppered with

faded blue flowers, and then covered it with a matching robe that she wrapped tightly around herself and tied with a sash at her waist. Then she opened the door to let the steamy air out and brushed her hair in counted strokes before braiding it into a heavy plait that reached her waist.

She left the kitchen through the side door, avoiding the parlor where she knew Zach was sitting. Her bare feet padded quietly down the hall to the staircase; she was intent on reaching the privacy of her room. But the front doors stood open and the cool night air beckoned. Lauren placed her bundle of belongings beside the steps and answered the call.

The night was silent except for the rhythmic chirp of crickets in the azalea bushes below the porch, whose small flowers scented the air like sweet sachets. With her hands braced on the railing she leaned out to feel the bare whisper of a breeze on her cheeks. Closing her eyes and turning her face up to the silvery light of the nearly full moon, she basked in the soft sensations of a summer's evening.

Zach watched from one of the big bay windows in the parlor. It was nice having company, he thought, even though she was still being uppity. She looked at home, and he liked that. Lauren all fresh-scrubbed and relaxed for the night was an appealing change from her usual stiffness. He moved to the doorway then, his deep, earthy voice easing around her.

"Can I come out, or are you avoiding me?"

"It isn't my place to forbid you your own porch." Her tone was hushed so as not to disturb the peace of the night, and it softened the clipped words.

Zach sat on the smooth white railing, his back against the rounded belly of a pillar. He bit off the top of a cigar, spitting it into the bushes. Lauren heard the scrape and sizzle of a sulfur match on the banister and without looking knew Zach would puff until he had the thing lit; then he would shake out the match and fling it away.

"Still stewing over Maudie's and staying here?" he asked idly, but his black eyes were watchful.

"I do not stew," she answered simply, not opening her eyes.

"How about a nightcap then?"

"No, thank you," she answered imperiously.

One corner of Zach's mouth went up crookedly. "You're still angry, all right."

"I don't waste time on things I cannot change, Mr. Madox."

"That so?" He laughed, "What do I have to do to get you to stop calling me Mr. Madox like that?"

"Anything else is too familiar."

In the dim light he thought he saw the glimmer of that serene amusement of hers. "We're living in the same house, you're standing on my porch in your nightgown with your feet bare and your hair down, biding your time until you can take over a whorehouse that I'm paying for. But you think calling me Zach is too familiar."

"Uh-huh," she breathed. There actually seemed to be an air of mischief about her.

"A good businesswoman would make a deal. Familiarity is what you're selling, after all."

Her eyes opened slowly and she turned her head smoothly in an exaggerated movement to face him, just barely smiling. "Speaking of which, when will Maudie's be finished?"

He laughed at the diversionary tactic. "Are you in a hurry?"

She shrugged and he noticed how slight her shoulders were beneath the thin fabric. "It's inevitable, so I might as well get on with it." The temporary reprieve tamped down her fears and allowed the return of her calm acceptance.

"Is this really what you want, Lauren? Or, if you

had another choice, would you take it?" he asked more seriously.

Her eyes met his squarely. "You mean like being your housekeeper indefinitely to fill some of the emptiness in this place?"

He laughed at that. "Don't go jumping to conclusions, Irish—you'll come up short. I know what I want and just what I intend to fill my 'emptiness' with. A permanent housekeeper is not what I had in mind."

What Lauren heard in his words was that a whore's daughter was not what he wanted. It salted an open wound, and she turned back to the moonlight to hide her pain.

"You haven't answered my question. If you could do something else, would you?" he pressed.

Admitting her reluctance gave it too much substance, and so she laid out her reasoning for him. "Oh, I know, I could take at some menial job and be paid a pittance for working long hours at the whim of someone else. But that would be silly when Maudie has handed me an independent future...at least it will be when you're paid off. This is what has been left to me to do, Mr. Madox. If it was good enough for my mother and Maudie, why should I be any different?"

"Because you are, that's all."

"Am I? Brandon Bentley didn't think so." There was no bitterness in her voice; in fact, she seemed to find the doubts about her virtue amusing.

"What difference does he make?"

"Oh, he wasn't alone. My mother's reputation was handed down to me like old clothes. The assumption was that lack of virtue runs in the blood, like insanity or big feet." She shrugged and laughed just a little. "Who knows, perhaps it does. At any rate, I'm going to make the best of this."

He watched her, shaking his head dubiously, "I

don't think you have any idea of what you're getting into. You're too naive for your own good."

"I'm really not." There was such quiet conviction in her voice that he almost believed her. Then she pushed herself away from the railing. Better to escape gracefully before he raised more doubts when she had just reasoned away the last of them. "I'll need an early start tomorrow if this place is to be cleaned properly. I'd best go up to bed."

Zach's gravelly voice stopped her just as one foot touched the doorsill. "You know, Irish, blind, stubborn innocence is a dangerous combination. Turning yourself into a whore or even just pretending to might cost you more than you think."

The words scratched at her confidence again and she sought to shake them off with calm acceptance. "Perhaps. But my loss will be your gain, so count it as a merit."

"It's not a nice life, Lauren." His words gouged a little deeper.

"My mother and Maudie were happy," she hedged, and wished she believed it.

"You only saw them through the eyes of a child," he persisted.

"I appreciate your concern, but it's misplaced," she answered over her shoulder as she left, determined to get away.

Zach shook his head; she was the most damned obstinate woman he'd ever met. He answered her last statement with soft words to the darkness: "Not as misplaced as you are, Miss Flannery."

Chapter 7

Zach left first thing the next morning. Lauren set about cleaning his house with the dedication of a zealot. All was spotless and sparkling by late that afternoon, with only the master suite left in the path of the whirlwind of lye and beeswax. It was a huge space, half bedroom, half sitting room, but stark enough to house a monk.

Lauren coughed from the clouds of dust she was raising from an overstuffed chair near a small table, which was the only furniture in the sitting room. Then she polished the night tables on either side of a bed bigger than any she had ever seen, realizing that, since only one of the oil lamps was covered with soot, Zach slept on the left side.

After she scrubbed baseboards, floors, and walls, she stripped the soiled linens from the mattress. Before remaking it, she sat cross-legged in the center to polish the brass headboard.

Her back ached in unison with every other muscle in her body, and for two cents she would have pretended not to notice the tarnish. But she went at it with a vengeance, grumbling to herself, "A dozen of these blasted spindles! Why would anyone buy this bed if they weren't going to keep it up?"

"Not that it's any of your business, but there is a

perfectly good explanation for it," Zach said from behind her.

Her head snapped up, and she pushed at a string of hair with her forearm. "You frightened me to death!"

"Then we're even, because the sight of you is enough to scare the hell out of me," he retorted, crossing to sit in the newly cleaned blue chair facing the bed.

"Did you expect me to be working in a tidy little uniform, apron and mobcap, like a good maid?"

"That's more likely than finding the fastidious Miss Flannery sitting like an Indian with her face smudged. But then, of the two this is a damn sight better. It's nice to see that you're human...at least sometimes. I will admit, though, I didn't think I'd ever see you in my bed like that!"

"I am not in your bed. I am on it," she amended like a schoolmistress. "And I wouldn't need to be if you had the good sense to buy a headboard that did not require this sort of care."

"I couldn't have done that." He grinned at her. "When I bought the bed I planned to make a lot of babies in it. I figured it needed good, strong rungs to hold up to that many birthings."

Lauren stared, wondering about him. Her unsatisfied curiosity sprouted tragic images and she began to think some great secret lay behind the house's genesis. "How were such elaborate plans thwarted?" she asked softly.

Zach's boisterous laugh boomed. "What are you thinking, Irish? That I was crazy in love with some woman, built this place for her, planning to have a passle of kids, only to be left at the altar?"

"Is that what happened?" She was unperturbed by his amusement, thinking that perhaps it hid deep pain and old scars.

He smiled at her then, a warm, pleased grin. "No,

it isn't. Nothing happened. I haven't put my plans into motion yet. In fact, my grimy housemaid, your lovely little butt is the only one besides mine ever to have touched that mattress."

"Oh, I see," she answered evenly, her expression composed. "You're teasing me."

His handsome head drew back as if struck. "I am not!"

"Do you expect me to believe you're a virgin?" She laughed derisively.

"I didn't say that. But I have never taken a woman to that bed."

"Should I get off?" she asked with good-natured sarcasm.

"You doubt my word? Check the mattress; you won't find one love stain on it."

"Now that's disgusting."

"It's the truth! I would never bring my wife to a bed where I had made love to other women."

"Hence your familiarity with Maudie's."

"Hence my familiarity with Maudie's," he echoed mockingly.

"Is everything in this house planned for your wife and babies then?"

"Most of it. This chair, for instance." There was deviltry in his grin. "It's the perfect place for middle-of-the-night feedings." He curled his arms as if cradling a baby, bracing his elbows on the low arms. Then he turned his head in the direction of the big window beside it. "The view is beautiful from here; it's a good spot to sit and watch the rain or stare at the stars."

"Now I know you're joking."

"Why? Because you don't think a man can want a family? Is it so odd for me to think of where my children will be born, of looking up from my bed to watch my wife feeding our baby in the moonlight?"

Still his expression was both devilish and serious, leaving Lauren unsure.

"Yes, I think it's very odd," she answered honestly. "Why haven't you married then?"

"I'm a long way from a dreamy-eyed boy, no matter what you think, Irish. The place would be worse than empty if I brought some woman into it just to fill the space, someone I didn't love."

"I suppose you have strict qualifications." Lauren was thinking of their conversation the previous night.

"Not a one. It'll all come from gut feelings, or should I say, from heart feelings."

Lauren raised her eyes heavenward. "And I thought all blind romantics were women."

"And I thought all hard-assed cynics were men," he countered. "Don't you believe in love, Lauren?"

"No, I don't."

"Come on! Hasn't there ever been anybody you had even a little crush on? Not even Alan Bentley?"

She smiled at that. "I'm realistic. Love is a rush of insanity that drifts away like smoke. I can do nicely without it, thank you."

"You don't know anything about love."

"And you do?"

He shrugged those wide shoulders. "I know it's there. And I know I want some of it."

"When Maudie's opens you can get your share... for a price."

He stood up to leave, giving a good imitation of her own enigmatic smile, one that said he knew something she didn't, "For a smart lady, Lauren Flannery, you can be one hell of a silly girl."

"And you, Mr. Madox, can be awfully naive yourself." She met his expression with an equally knowing one. It was a standoff; each was convinced of knowing more than the other about the secrets of the heart.

* * *

Torrents of rain crashed against the big house from a blackness that was like a dark abyss.

Zach lay on his back in bed, his hands behind his head, staring at the long shadows thrown on the ceiling by the lamp he had left burning to read by. But he couldn't keep his thoughts on the pages of the book. The leather-bound volume rested on the night table.

He wondered if Lauren was disturbed by the storm. There wasn't a doubt in his mind that she would cut out her tongue rather than tell him she was. So, what if he wandered to the end of the hall just to see if her light was burning? She was too suspicious minded, he judged; she would be sure he had come to attack her. Better to leave her alone.

If only she would leave him alone.

How could a man go to sleep with his head so full of a woman? She might as well have been snuggled up close beside him for the effect she had on him. How long had he been lying here, hard and wanting her?

She wasn't like any woman he had ever wanted. In fact, she was a lot like women he had hated, the sour-tempered matrons he remembered from the place he had grown up in—an orphanage that made hell look good. But there was more to Lauren. Her straitlaced haughtiness struck him as protective more than vindictive. It was as if she put it on like clothes over bare skin, to shield an innocence and naiveté she didn't want to admit was there. Probably no one else had ever admitted it might be there either. A whore's daughter couldn't possibly be so unworldly. But he knew she was, just as surely as he knew the floor would be cold against his bare feet as he swung from the bed, pulled on tight denims, and moved to watch the silver sheets of rain beat against his window.

Opposite feelings warred within him. The need to cosset her as if she were a child, to slowly, gently make her aware of what she was headed for, using soft words that would blur some of the ugliness while still opening her eyes, collided with the desire to say to hell with it, let himself find the comfort his body craved in being the first to try her out. At least there would be some caring then, because he did care for her, though only in a compassionate way. Maybe a little more than that. But not man-woman caring. Well, not beyond bed. Hell, he couldn't explain it. He wanted to bed her and he didn't want to be the one who did. Who could understand that?

Maybe he could go just halfway down the hall to see if a light still shone from under her door.

Pure exhaustion should have put her to sleep, but Lauren lay watching the glimmer of the rain-washed windowpanes and listening to the steady downpour. It wasn't fear that kept her awake. It was the past and the future and what the thoughts of a man could do to a woman.

She pinched her eyes shut, trying to chase him out of her mind. But there he stayed. Zach Madox stuck like dried egg. Never let them in, her mother had warned, or you can never get them out again. Men were thorns in a woman's heart.

So why did Lauren feel disappointed that he hadn't done her bidding on the train? And why was she lying there all warm and tingly, wanting him to kiss her again? She knew enough to be aware that whores didn't pine for men's kisses. How often had her mother shoved poor Harvey away when he had asked for one?

Still, she could feel Zach Madox's lips. Softer than she had expected a man's mouth to be. Just a tiny bit parted and moist without being too wet; his breath held the warmth of life as it had mingled with hers.

Then there were his arms...thick, powerful arms, and wide shoulders that cupped around her and made a place for her in the curve of a chest normally bulging outward and hard-muscled as stone.

Lauren wriggled. Out, damn it, out!

But there he stayed.

She bolted up out of bed, jammed her arms into her wrapper, and yanked the sash into a tight knot around her waist. Maybe a glass of milk would put her to sleep. She opened the bedroom door soundlessly. One step took her out. With the second, she crashed into that very same bare chest that had been plaguing her. Reflex sent her hands against his bulging pectorals, and his arms shot forward and tightened around her.

"Mr. Madox!" Her outrage pushed her out of his steadying embrace, but it was something else entirely that quickened her pulse.

"Out for a midnight stroll?" his husky voice taunted her in the darkness.

"What are you doing outside my door?"

Suspicious minded, all right. "Just checking to see if your light was on. I wondered if you were afraid of storms."

"That would be silly and childish."

Of course. "Then why aren't you asleep? After the day's work you put in, I would have thought you to be long gone."

Lauren swallowed, grateful that drumming of the rain muffled the sound. "Too tired, I suppose," she bluffed.

"So you were headed to my room for a second stab at what you tried for on the train?" he concluded mockingly.

"I was headed for the kitchen and a glass of milk."

"With all the pure thoughts of a saint," he murmured derisively.

"May I pass, or is that forbidden?"

Forbidden fruit, but not milk. "Are you sure you want to?"

She drew herself up straighter than usual, but her eyes went, on their own, to the hard, bulging muscles that shaped his body and the valleys of shadow that accentuated his masculine beauty. Again the tingling sensation broke out along the surface of her skin. And again she tried to chase it away, forcing her eyes back to his face and her thoughts back to the subject.

"Actually, I'm more tired than I thought." She tried to sound bored. "I don't think I need any milk after all." She had turned halfway back before his hand closed around her arm to stop her.

"Milk wouldn't help what ails you anyway, my prudish Miss Flannery."

He pulled her back against his chest. His shadowed eyes stared down into hers and read her thoughts. Then his lips barely touched hers. The kiss was perfect—soft and sweet, a delicacy to soothe a hunger she hadn't realized she possessed. She returned it without inhibitions, and this time without calculation. Her lips met his, matched his, welcomed the warm wetness of his tongue. Her toes left the ground as his arms came around her as his embrace tightened, molding her body to his, large and powerful, just as she had so vividly remembered moments before in her lonely bed. The smouldering sparks in her blood lit up bright-hot.

Her hands slid from his chest to his shoulders to clasp the nape of his neck, where soft hair curled over her fingers. For the first time she felt passion—pure, exquisite, overwhelming sensations that wiped her thoughts away and reached something and someone she didn't know was inside her.

Zach trailed hungry kisses to her ear and down the arch of her neck as her head fell back, and breathing took a conscious effort.

"I am my mother's daughter," she whispered to herself in painful revelation.

He stopped. Everything stood suspended. Very, very slowly he straightened away from her until he was a towering shadow fighting for control with every ragged breath. "No!" His gravelly voice exploded fiercely. "Never that. Never by my hand."

He let go of her completely then. Her knees were so weak she wasn't sure she could stand, but pride locked them tightly.

"Go on back to your safe bed, Lauren, because I swear to God I won't be the one to make you what your mother was," he vowed, more to himself than to her.

She watched his broad, naked back retreat down the hall and disappear into his bedroom. His door closed with a sharp finality that roused her from her trance and sent her scurrying behind her own wooden barricade.

But sleep was again impossible; his effect on her had been too strong. What was there about him that drew her to him and out of herself? There was no denying the masculinity of Zach Madox. But was it the man himself? Or would it be all men?

The thought raised a thick, gagging lump in her throat.

Chapter 8

Lauren lay sleeping soundly, oblivious to the late morning sun pouring in through the window of her room. She rested on her back, one arm outstretched, the other curved up around her head, flattening her breast beneath her thin gown.

To Zach as he stood at the footrail she was the picture of unguarded comfort. He carefully pulled the top sheet away from the mattress until her bare feet were exposed and then ran a single finger from heel to toe. He laughed quietly as that foot drew up and out of sight and returned to the attack by tickling the remaining member.

Lauren sat bolt upright and glared at her provoker. "What do you think you're doing?"

"Making sure you don't sleep all day and miss keeping me company on my errands," he answered cheerfully.

"A simple knock on my door would have sufficed!" she snapped.

Zach laughed. "That's a lie! I've been clattering pans and slamming doors all morning and you never budged. Even my first tickling didn't rouse you. You sleep like the dead."

"Regardless, you have no business playing with my feet!" She graced him with a leveling stare and de-

cided to forge ahead as if nothing had happened between them.

"I wanted to save you from feeling all adither over
facing me after last night."

"You do flatter yourself, Mr. Madox."

Zach laughed again. "I made scrambled eggs for
your breakfast, if you can call a meal eaten now
breakfast. I'll wait for you downstairs." As he left, he
murmured just loud enough for her to hear, "Whew!
She's crabby in the morning!"

The first stop of the day was the office of Zach's
attorney, where proceedings on his claim to Maudie's
were stopped and legal papers were drawn up detail-
ing Lauren's debt. The bank was the second errand,
for on Fridays Zach paid his construction crew, and
that led to their third stop: Maudie's.

As Zach went through the long process of count-
ing out each man's earnings, Lauren quietly walked
the floors of her establishment. She admired the
workmanship Zach had demanded throughout, only
the best was going into it.

She even approved of his space allotment on the
ground floor, which was divided into a large kitchen
in back, two grand drawing rooms, and a smaller
space she could use as her office.

For a moment Lauren stood assessing the entrance, deciding where to best position the burly man
she would hire as a reminder that no rowdiness
would be tolerated. Then she strolled out the front
door and stood on the wood-planked boardwalk that
was the pedestrians' right-of-way down the street.
She turned to admire the building's facade, which
had been redone in such good taste, it could have
been an English gentleman's townhouse.

"Looking for signs of life, darling?" a rich baritone
voice asked from behind.

Lauren glanced over her shoulder, thinking to
give the stranger a dressing-down for the too-

friendly tone. Instead she wilted just a bit at the sight of a strikingly attractive man grinning warmly at her through a full, wheat-colored beard and moustache.

When she didn't answer, he went on in the most pleasant way. "I'm here to see Zach Madox. Do you know him?"

Lauren reassessed the man. His manner was so courteous and gentlemanly that it outweighed her first appraisal. In fact, there was a great deal of charm in the way his sky blue eyes looked at her with what seemed to be an innate fondness for women. She faced him with a small smile. "He is inside, but if it's dealings with Maudie's you're here about, you can speak with me."

His return smile was as smooth as silk, showing no signs of surprise or insolence at her statement. "Don't tell me I'm too late! I just heard the rumor that Maudie's was to be sold upon completion. Have you beaten me to it?"

He was impeccably groomed, his wheaten hair trimmed and combed meticulously in place, his brown suit crisp, fresh, and businesslike, yet suave. Lauren reminded herself not to stare. "I'm afraid you've been misled, sir. Maudie's belongs to me through inheritance. It is not up for sale."

Surprise finally showed in the arch of his perfectly shaped eyebrows. "The rumor mill has been lax. We all assumed Zach Madox owned Maudie's."

"Not quite. He was a friend of my aunt's. Since her death he has been overseeing it for me. But it is definitely not for sale." She had no way of knowing her secret smile was enchanting him.

The man gave a little laugh of pure pleasure and bowed slightly. "I've been remiss. My name is Mark Rossiter. If Maudie was your aunt, does that make you a Miss Flannery as well?"

"It does. Lauren Flannery." The eyes of passersby studied them and Lauren suddenly felt uncomfortable. It was hardly discreet of her to be chatting with a man on the street outside a known whorehouse. "I hope you haven't come too far out of your way because of that misleading rumor," she began, to dismiss him. "I assure you that Maudie's will not be sold any time soon."

Mark Rossiter recognized her uneasiness at the furtive glances those passing along the boardwalk sent them. "Might we step inside to talk a moment? Perhaps we can reach an agreement," he persisted gently.

"I'm afraid not."

"Then at least give me a tour of what I will be missing, won't you?" he cajoled.

Lauren stood firm, not understanding why she didn't want Zach to meet this man. "There is nothing to see yet. It isn't that near to opening."

Again he chuckled lightly, but her hesitancy made him suspicious. "I think I had better talk to Zach Madox after all. Just to convince myself that I'm not being outdone by a very clever, very lovely lady buyer."

"Are you calling me a liar, then?" she demanded stiffly, her reserved friendliness giving way to hauteur.

"I think you could be anything in the world that you wanted, Miss Flannery." He took her arm in an entirely gentlemanlike gesture and propelled them both into Maudie's. "And believe me, I don't mind a bit if you are a liar."

Piqued, Lauren pulled free and stepped away from the man. "I'll introduce you then, and prove my claim." She marched off ahead of him while his appreciative grin followed her proud back.

Zach's first sight of Mark Rossiter raised the hair on the back of his neck. There was no outward reason for it; the man had a courteous, businesslike manner and showed a respectful deference to

Lauren. Zach just didn't like the man. And he knew he would never have sold Maudie's to Rossiter, despite his friendly overtures.

"Miss Flannery was telling you the truth. She is the owner of Maudie's," Zach said curtly, backing her up. "Now, if you will excuse us, I must finish up with my men."

Mark Rossiter extended his hand to Zach with meticulous manners. "I apologize for keeping you from it."

Zach hesitated before taking the manicured hand, but in the end he did, and then he watched Lauren walk Rossiter back out. The sight irritated Zach all the more.

"You will turn it into a fine house, I can see that." Rossiter said to Lauren as he paused to glance up the stairway. He leaned his long arm against the banister, obviously intending to share some parting words with her. His tone didn't begrudge her Maudie's or judge her, so Lauren found it easy to be less curt. "Perhaps there will be another house you can buy."

He grinned at her again in a way that old and fond friends reserve for one another. "I own *The Countess*. It is a floating pleasure palace. But I fancied having Maudie's as well. Promise me that if ever you do decide to sell, you will give me the first chance to buy her; would you do that for me?"

An abrasive burst of sound from outside almost drowned out his words, and Lauren barely heard his last, soft-spoken request. She thought it strange, for he didn't act as if they were discussing the ownership of a whorehouse but rather some prized, mystical jewel. His attitude took away some of the tawdriness Zach's attitude seemed to give Maudie's. "It seems an odd promise. I'm not likely to sell. But if it appeases you, I'll give it."

"It does. I trust we will be seeing much of each other in the future, so if you do change your mind,

I'll be near at hand. I can already see we share so much in common that rivalry between us wouldn't suit at all. So we will be friends instead, won't we? None of that heathenish competition that goes on down on Skid Row between us. Rather, I put myself entirely at your service."

"Thank you, but everything is being handled quite nicely."

"Well..." He sighed a bit longingly before straightening up from the banister. With a feather-light grasp he took her hand and raised it to his lips. "Another time, then..._Lauren_," he finished with an expression of boyish mischief. Then he left her.

For a moment Lauren stared after him, not hearing the roar coming from up the street. An interesting man, she thought. Not at all like Zach. This one didn't rile her as easily. But with thoughts of the past night's kiss and the torment of wondering if suppressed within her was an unnatural fondness for men, she was easily able to shake Mark Rossiter's image from her mind. Inexperience, she decided, would be her undoing if she let it.

She finally moved to investigate the commotion that was now directly outside, still paying little attention to the words being shouted. As she reached the front door, she brushed sawdust from the same brown skirt she had worn upon her arrival in Seattle. She stepped out into the sunlight for the second time that day, her head still lowered to her task, when a booming male voice rose in exuberance.

"Who have we here, my friends? Could it be Maudie herself? The evil harlot forcing her depravity back into our midst?"

Lauren raised her head slowly to the man standing up in a buckboard. His arms were raised to the sky dramatically, a bible clutched in one hand. As her gaze met his squarely, her outward confidence inflamed him still further.

"Our maker has sent the fires of hell to rid us of her wretchedness! She is the devil's own wickedness walking among us!" he screamed, sending his voice over the murmur of the gathering crowd whose curiosity was aroused by Lauren's appearance.

She stood very still, unsure whether to turn and run back inside or brave the scene through.

"Evil! Evil! Evil! I tell you we cannot allow her to infect our decent, God-fearing women! Carnal lust is her calling! Satan is her maker!"

Before Lauren realized what was happening, meaty fists closed around each of her arms. She raised her eyes to two men who more closely resembled apes.

"That will be enough of that!" she commanded. But they ignored her and continued watching the buckboard preacher intently.

Lauren tried to pull free but succeeded only in being lifted off her feet and pushed into the mob toward the man whose voice railed on. She kicked wildly and ineffectually, losing both her shoes in the process. The pins holding her hair in its tight coil slid free and the silky soft strands fell about her face and shoulders in a heavy, gleaming curtain.

Panic surged through her. Never had she endured such rough treatment or such humiliation. The cold civility, the whispers, the stares of Dry Creek had not prepared her for this! Lauren struggled and fought, but it served only to put too much strain on the worn fabric of her gown, which ripped directly down the back and each armhole seam.

When her stockinged feet again touched something solid, she found herself standing on the wooden floor of the wagon beside the preacher. Still she was firmly held, and her vigorously renewed struggle strained the front of her gown, causing it to tear on either side of the buttons. Her worn, sheer chemise was exposed, the ribbon ties loosened to reveal the tender cleavage between her breasts.

"That ain't Maudie!" came a shout from a newcomer. "Maudie's dead!" Fresh mumblings rose from the crowd.

"If she is not the owner of this devil's lair, then she is one of the instruments of sin! She came from within! No decent woman would venture into the confines of hell! She is a harlot! Even now she tries to display herself! Damnation will come to those who allow more of her kind into our city!"

Lauren felt sick to her stomach and barely able to swallow the bile rising in her throat. Perspiration glistened across her brow and trickled down the back of her neck. She stared down into the mass of upturned faces, some condemning, some leering, some simply gawking at the exhibition. Hatred and shame pricked like needles beneath her skin.

In rapid succession three reports from a gun brought a deafening silence. All attention turned once again to Maudie's door where Zach stood, lowering a revolver to the level of the preacher's chest.

"Call them off her." His voice was deadly calm, a tone far more dangerous than a shout. It was as if he were inviting a refusal just so he could have the pleasure of shooting the man.

"She is Satan's temptation into evil!" came the answer.

Zach slowly moved the gun to the nearest man holding Lauren captive. "Either let go or meet your own maker right now."

The man glanced at the preacher, at Zach, and back again. He barely paused before dropping his hands to his sides and stepping back. But the second man, more inflamed with righteousness, maintained his grip.

"Now," Zach growled.

The man did not move.

Zach fired only once. A red stream of blood spurted from high up on the man's thigh as his legs buckled beneath him. Lauren teetered, her balance nearly upset as the man tried to pull her down with him. But her instincts were strong and she yanked herself free.

The crowd parted to allow Zach a straight path to the buckboard.

Lauren gathered the torn shreds of her blouse in a frenzy; her expression was one of bewilderment, as if she didn't know what to do beyond that.

Zach's hands grasped her waist, lifting her down. She only vaguely heard his gravelly voice say in a gentle tone, "Come on, Irish. This show's over."

Clutching her gown together like a protective mantle, Lauren moved through the crowd. She felt light-headed and clammy cold, and for the first time in her life she had to fight not to faint.

Zach took her into Maudie's and all the way back to the kitchen where they were alone. "Are you all right, Lauren? Did they hurt you?"

She exhaled a long, deflating breath as she gained control of herself. "Thank you," she said stiffly.

They stood very near each other, but Lauren was so self-contained that to Zach she seemed far away, unreachable and certainly untouchable. "Are you hurt?" he tried again, his brow creased with worry.

"No," she managed to say, so softly he could barely hear it, almost as if she wasn't quite sure herself. She wanted to run away and hide in some safe, secluded spot. But no such place existed and she told herself she had to be strong as she never had had to before.

Zach felt an outrage greater than at any time in his life. He paced off some of his anger and then stopped at the far end of the room to prop a booted foot on a sawhorse, leaning one arm across his thick raised thigh. And still Lauren stood stock still, unblinking.

"I don't understand you," he said flatly, shaking his head. "How can you stand there like a statue?"

"What would you have me do?" she asked in a raw whisper. "Shall I cry for you, or caterwaul like a lunatic?"

"It would make more sense."

"It's over now. What purpose would that serve?"

"As if it doesn't matter at all to you, is that it?"

"I didn't say that. But belaboring it won't change it." She turned away from his piercing eyes, wrapping her arms around her middle. She didn't know how to respond; she knew only that she couldn't let anyone witness how utterly degraded she felt.

He saw her shudder and knew there was more going on inside her than she let on. He sighed in frustration as he crossed back to her with hard, fierce strides. He reached out to pull her roughly to him, his arms closing around her to mold her small, tense body to him.

"Come here, dammit! I need to hold you. You want me to think it didn't bother you, but I know better. And it hurt the hell out of me to see you treated like that."

Lauren closed her eyes and bit the insides of her lips to still their quivering. She let herself relax into his big body, devouring the comfort, allowing him to close in around her like a soft, protective shell she never wanted to leave. Hesitantly she wrapped her arms around his waist and clung to him, her grip tight enough to tell him she needed his comforting, no matter what she said.

It was a long time before anything broke the bond that had formed between them. His solace was a soothing balm to her wounds. But ultimately, the sounds of construction reminded her of where they were, and she pushed herself away from him.

Zach smiled down at her a bit sadly. He wished there were more he could do, more that she would let him do, but he knew better. "Looks as if we'll have to make a stop at the dressmaker's before we go home," he said practically. "The only good thing that will come out of this is that you'll get something new to wear. That is the damned ugliest dress I've ever seen."

Her smile was wan but grateful. For just a second Zach thought he had glimpsed, down a chasm and into the center of her being, something far different than what Lauren let the world see. It was someone soft and sensitive and very, very vulnerable. And he thought it just might be what he was looking for.

Chapter 9

Dusk had fallen by the time they returned to Zach's home. Once again the ride there had been silent. Lauren took her single package upstairs and only then, in the privacy of her room, did she allow thoughts of the day to surface.

Such ugliness was foreign to her. Both Maudie and her mother had been proud women, dignified and strong. And if they had not been respected, at least Lauren had never known them to be persecuted. But she realized now that there might have been much about them she had never known.

What if this was only the beginning, what if everything she thought she knew about this life had been a false front, as Zach kept trying to tell her? Then not only had she been seeing it through the eyes of a child, she had been well removed from it.

A woman is as strong as she needs to be. How often had her mother and Maudie said that? Often enough for Lauren to believe it. Maybe that was why it had been important to them.

She forced her spine to stiffen in steely determination as she stood there remembering. Her mother had withstood the life. Her aunt had survived and prospered. Would she run from it? she asked herself bitterly. Would she cower like a frightened kitten?

68

Of course not, she told herself. She could do whatever she had to do.

But the wounds of the day were still too fresh, and she shivered at the thought.

At precisely seven o'clock Lauren descended the stairs in her new finery, her head high and her face composed, for all the world as if nothing had gone amiss.

As Zach stood at the big stone fireplace, the first thing to come into his view was a black pump with a small rosette on the toe and a slim ankle in a delicate lisle stocking with a similar rose pattern up the side. A narrow maroon-colored skirt, pleated in front and draped back to form a padded bustle, appeared next; then a sheer blouse with two rows of lace on either side of pearl buttons and a creamy veil over a feminine bit of lacy chemise that rose to a high choker collar and the face he was coming to like more and more.

He marveled at her composure; she looked like a grand dame as she crossed over to him, every hair in place. More than ever he wondered what made her tick.

Lauren held out a folded slip of paper. "This is my note for the price of the clothes. Though they're more extravagant than I would have chosen for myself."

"But worth every penny," he growled.

"Yes . . . well. Thank you," she answered uncomfortably, moving away from him to stand behind an overstuffed wing chair. She was all too conscious of him and the attractive picture he made dressed in a navy blue suit, one arm lying casually along the mantle and a wine glass cupped in his blunt fingers. "Was there any truth to the rumors about Maudie's being for sale?" she asked, changing the subject.

Zach shrugged. "I had let it be known that was my intention."

"Then why did you let Mr. Rossiter believe he had been misled?"

"I didn't see what difference it made. The fact is that it's not up for sale now. Is it?" he challenged.

"Of course it isn't, but you might have explained that to him."

"Is it any of his business?"

"You could at least have matched his good manners."

"Found him pretty appealing, did you, Lauren?" he observed gruffly.

"He was attractive, nice, polite..."

"And a man to steer clear of," Zach finished harshly.

"Why is that?"

He shrugged. "It just strikes me that your high opinion of him might be premature."

"Why?"

"He's a little too slick for my taste. In your business you had better beware of such faultless men."

"If you have a reason that warrants such a warning, please tell me what it is."

"Are you planning some future connections with him?" Anger tinged his voice and his black brows nearly met in an equally dark frown.

"Of course not. I just wondered if you had anything to substantiate your criticism."

"I don't like him," he answered flatly, "That substantiates it enough for me. I think my judgment of human nature is a little more refined than yours. You're too gullible."

Her chin tilted in defiance. "I can take care of myself."

But Zach's only answer was a sarcastic "Hah!" before he threw back a full half glass of wine in one gulp.

"Will you tell me now where we are going?" Once again she opted for changing the subject.

"It's Friday night," he said as if that should mean something to her. "I have a standing invitation to dinner with good friends."

"It isn't necessary for me to accompany you."

"They wouldn't have it any other way." He pushed away from the mantle and tossed her note into the fireplace. "And neither would I."

"Mr. Madox," she reprimanded him quietly, "I will not accept gifts from you."

"Don't worry about it, Irish. It's an investment in my eyesight." Taking her arm he moved to the door and the waiting carriage beyond, ignoring her attempts to pursue the matter.

"Hello, Winnie. You're looking as good as ever!" Zach bent to kiss the smooth cheek of the small woman who met them in the grand entrance hall of the Georgian mansion they had just entered.

The older woman extended her hand to Lauren with a warm smile. "My name is Winifred. It's only this reprobate who chooses to make me sound like horse talk," she said affectionately as she led the way into a huge drawing room awash in golden lamplight, hung with maroon velvet and furnished in Hepplewhite.

The warm family circle comprised the diminutive, silver-haired Winifred Cade; her robust husband Arthur who teased her with loving playfulness; their two sons, Will and Evan, both equally matched in size and brawn to Zach, Will on the homely side and Evan handsome and blond.

And in the center of it all was Zach, tossing a subtly ribald comment to Arthur, teasing Will with an affectionate punch in the arm, and sending a mock warning to Evan over Lauren's head as he introduced her.

He ordered his scotch whiskey and a sherry for Lauren with friendly familiarity from the Cades' butler Wendell. Then he lounged on the settee near Lauren, who kept her straight shoulders several inches from the sofa back along which his arm rested casually. He fit into the family scene as easily as the Cades' sons, and Lauren felt like a stray kitten he had brought home.

It was the kind of family she had imagined everyone else had as a child, the kind she had tried not to envy for fear of feeling disloyal. And now she felt unworthy of being in their home, as though she were somehow soiling their wholesomeness and degrading their respectability.

"Where'd you two meet?" Will voiced a curiosity the whole family apparently felt.

Lauren's face froze, but Zach answered easily, "Her aunt was an old friend. I promised to look after Lauren when she died, so when we met up in Dry Creek I brought her back with me. I guess you could say she's my ward."

"That so?" Arthur scratched his chin and grinned knowingly.

"Now behave yourself, Arty! You know our Zach would never do wrong by anyone." Winifred slapped his knee and turned to Lauren. "Then you came in on that rolling bordello of Martin's. I swear he hired one of his fancy women to decorate it." Turning back to Zach she said, "Speaking of whorehouses, what's this we heard about a ruckus at yours today?"

"I should have known you'd hear about that already, Winnie. Don't you know ladies aren't supposed to realize places like that exist?" he teased her.

"Hmph! I'd have to be an imbecile!" she snorted disdainfully. "So what went on?"

Zach laughed delightedly. "It was just a preacher looking to get himself some attention."

"Who was the woman he hauled out? I didn't think the house was ready to open yet."

Lauren wanted to fade into the woodwork; her face was almost pale enough to make it seem as if she had. Zach dropped a comforting hand to her shoulder and squeezed, aware of how distressed she was. "Lauren was in town with me to run errands. I'm afraid she wandered out to see what all the commotion was and he took her for something she isn't."

Lauren could only stare at the glass she held in her lap. Coward! she silently screamed at herself. What kind of a person would deceive nice people like these? Pretending to be something she was not went against her grain, but she could not bring herself to confess that it was she who owned Maudie's, not Zach; that soon she would be taking up just the position the preacher had denounced.

"Oh, I am sorry!" Winifred said to Lauren. "How terrible! A young thing like you. It's no wonder you're white as a ghost. Let's not even talk about it. It's better forgotten." The matronly woman stood up then and, ignoring protocol, curled her arm through Lauren's and led the way into the dining room. "You're among friends; there's no need to feel embarrassed."

But embarrassed was a mild term for what Lauren actually felt.

"Second thoughts, Irish?" Zach said halfway home. He was leaning forward in the carriage, his elbows on his knees and the reins held loosely in his hands.

Lauren knew she had been conspicuously quiet throughout the evening with the Cades, but her mind was so muddled with doubts that it was the best she could do.

Zach went on before she could answer, "I didn't

notice you jumping in with the news that you're taking over Maudie's."

"No, I didn't, did I?" she said pensively.

He turned his head toward her, frowning. "Talk to me, Lauren. What's on your mind?"

"I can't. I'm sorry if I seemed rude to your friends. I liked them, but I felt badly about being there."

"Why?"

"I don't like to deceive people."

"There weren't any lies tonight."

"And there wasn't complete honesty either."

"Like I said, you didn't offer the information. Could it be you're not as proud of it as you were on the train?"

"It's . . . looking a little different to me today."

"I'm glad to hear it."

"You seem very close to the Cades," she said, changing the subject as she so often did.

"They're good people. We've been friends and business partners for over ten years now, ever since I came here. I almost married into the family a few years back."

"Oh?" Lauren tried not to sound as curious as she was. He offered so little information about himself, and prying never seemed to gain her much either.

"I was engaged to their daughter."

"I see."

"Oh, I doubt it." Zach chuckled. He enjoyed taking his own good time to inform her of his past. "Don't go assuming she's the reason I built my house. I can see those wheels turning in your head. The house had been finished a long time by then. It was an arranged marriage; Molly was pregnant."

"I believe that's more a marriage of necessity," she amended without judgment.

"It wasn't my baby."

Lauren stared at him curiously, wondering why he was telling her this.

"The father ran out on her. She came to me for help and I figured it would damn near kill Winnie and Art, so I offered to marry her. We had the whole thing planned. I went to them and pleaded passion to excuse dallying with their daughter. Of course they were good about it and very understanding. They almost seemed pleased. It was all set, and to tell you the truth, even though I didn't love her the way a man should a wife, I cared for her and I was looking forward to being a bonafide member of the family. But two days before the wedding Molly lost the baby." His voice became softer. "Nobody could do anything for her. She bled to death while the three of us just stood there helpless." He paused a minute, as if he were again at that bedside, feeling the pain and frustration. Then his tone turned philisophical. "Funny thing, though—her folks knew from the start that it was a sham. They even knew who the father was. But until Molly died they played along, didn't want to hurt her by letting on they knew the truth." He shook his head and clicked to the horses. "Seems like people will do a lot to protect the ones they love."

"You included," she observed quietly.

He shrugged. "Me included." Again he turned his handsome face to her. "But sometimes I wonder if we do our loved ones a service by keeping the bad parts to ourselves. Take you, for instance. Maybe you should have seen more of what your mother and Maudie's lives were like."

"And that's the moral to this story." She smiled faintly at him.

He grinned back at her, raising one brow mischievously. "Could be."

"Are you sure you're not out to save the souls of fallen women?"

"Your soul doesn't need saving, Irish—not yet, anyway. And I'll tell you something else; not much gets by Winnie, so don't worry about not confessing to her. Sooner or later she'll figure it out for herself."

Oddly, that didn't comfort her and Lauren wondered if shame was the crux of what she was feeling tonight. Shame for what her mother and aunt had been, for what she was going to be. If the sisters at the convent had known, they had never said it, and her mother had steadfastly insisted that she tell the other girls only that her mother was widowed. Even in Dry Creek she had interpreted the disparaging attitude of the townspeople as petty small-mindedness. But now she wasn't so sure of herself.

The carriage crossed the stone bridge with a hollow clatter and Zach's house came into view, luminous white in the moonlight. The peace of the place beckoned. It felt too good—there was danger in that. She reminded herself that it had been built for another sort of woman. And a darker sadness came over Lauren with the thought that she could never belong to a place like this.

Chapter 10

A week had passed quietly since Zach had gone to a logging camp he owned. With only herself to tend to, Lauren had spent her time sorting through the contents of the big black trunk she had dragged with her from Dry Creek.

Her mother's things. Lace-covered corsets. Black net stockings. Gaudy garters. Ruffled gowns of satin and taffeta. Since she and her mother had been nearly the same size, Lauren did not bother trying on any of the garments and instead merely mended, laundered, and readied everything for the day she would put them to use at Maudie's.

Saturday night found Lauren and Zach on their way to a dance. It was an annual occasion, the culmination of several days of revelry to which Zach treated his loggers before the winter snows kept them from coming into the city for long stretches of time.

The two shared a tufted black buggy seat beneath a star-speckled sky as they headed for an empty warehouse on the docks, the only place large enough to hold a whole campful of boisterous loggers. The air was cool and a light breeze wafted around them. Lauren pulled a cream-colored crocheted shawl closer about the puffed shoulders of her dress and spoke to the backs of two slowly trotting grays.

"Were you ever a logger?" she asked, much too aware of the clean scent of him and the brush of his shoulder against hers.

"I was," Zach answered with a sidelong glance at her.

"And you went from that to being a timber baron?"

He frowned over at her. "Timber baron? I don't think I care for that title. And I started out owning the mountain before I was a logger."

"Did you inherit it?"

His loud, full laughter echoed from the high hemlock trees that lined the road like pillars reaching to the sky. "I was born dirt poor. But I had luck. I worked a gold claim in Montana that paid some, but it wasn't the mother lode. Then I won another claim in a poker game and bought out two more. That led me here and things have worked out pretty well here too."

"I'd say. How much of Seattle do you own?"

"Enough. When I arrived, real estate was cheap. As a matter of fact, that's how I met Maudie. She bought the land her house sits on from me."

"Then it was your business...not hers...that brought you together."

He grinned at her again, seeing the train of her thoughts. "I never slept with Maudie."

"That's none of my business," she informed him stiffly.

"No, it isn't," he agreed.

"Doesn't it go against the grain for a man to...pay for a woman?" she wondered out loud.

"I can't say I've ever liked it," he admitted. "But up here it's a matter of necessity. Even an ugly woman is snatched up and married before you know it, unless she's selling herself. And I would never knowingly bed another man's wife."

"Then you have paid for the service?" Her curiosity was suddenly intense.

"I have."

"And you knew Maudie well, though not . . . in the biblical sense?"

"In every other way but," he mocked gently.

"Did she never speak of me?" It came quietly, from nowhere.

"We didn't talk about our pasts, Irish. But now that I think about it, there were some photographs she kept in her private parlor. They were of a little girl and a gangly, awkward older one. I never looked close enough to tell if they resembled you."

"They were me," she answered sadly, not understanding why this should be on her mind tonight.

"You were close to Maudie, weren't you?"

She looked away, up to the tree tops, which suddenly seemed fascinating, and her voice cracked slightly. "I loved her very much. Maudie seemed more carefree than my mother. She laughed more easily and took everything much less seriously."

"Then you must be more like your mother."

That cut deeper than Lauren would have expected. "Yes, I suppose so."

"Maudie helped raise you?"

"Mmm. And she doted on me. Spoiled me, in fact. The day they left me at the convent, she cried as I had never seen before." Lauren's throat was tight with memories, and Zach thought it better to shift away from that subject. "Did they work on their own then, or for somebody else?"

"By the time I was born, mother and Maudie owned a house together. I lived there until I was seven, though I had a strict nanny who kept me in the nursery most of the time. I was allowed to visit the kitchen only in the early mornings when no one was up, or my mother or aunt's sitting rooms when they said it was all right. But then one night, while nanny slept, I was found sleepwalking near the bedrooms. That decided it. I was sent to a convent school in Stockton. They bought a cottage nearby and spent vacations and any other time they could there with me."

"That sounds as if it was lonely as hell," he said sympathetically.

"It wasn't so bad. Our times together were full. The real loneliness came after I was sixteen. Mother married Harvey, Maudie left for Seattle, and I went to the Boston finishing school. I never saw or heard from Maudie after that."

"They must have had a humdinger of a fight for Maudie not even to write to you."

"I never knew the details. I only knew it was bitter enough to end a lifetime of closeness. I was forbidden to contact my aunt and didn't know how to find her even had I chosen to disobey." A moment of silence lapsed before Lauren turned her head to stare at Zach's handsome, frowning profile. "Why is it that every time we begin talking about you, we end talking about me?"

He shrugged. "Does it matter?"

"It does if you're hiding something."

In the moonlight, mischief glimmered in his eyes, crinkling the corners, "Even if I were, what difference would it make to you? I'm just your banker, remember?"

"Mmm," she agreed noncommittally, thinking that he certainly seemed more than that. Her outward serenity bemused him and left him wondering again just what she was thinking behind it.

Ahead of them, the wide warehouse doors gaped open, flooding the street with yellow lantern light and the strident notes of a banjo, harmonica, accordian, and fiddle. Zach lifted Lauren from the buggy and kept his hand at the small of her back as they entered the smoky space. It was filled with loggers arrayed in their Sunday best, which for most meant a purplish blue suit.

Though Zach had invited every available woman he could round up, and wives and sweethearts were in attendance, women were still by far in the minority. Lauren was greeted with a mountainous roar and swept away into a rousing reel before she had gone two steps past the threshold. From that moment on she found herself in constant, ungainly motion while one burly logger after another took his turn swinging and clomping her around with good-natured gusto, stopping only for a gulp of rum, which they each insisted she share, claiming it would revive her.

Zach looked on benevolently, leaving the others to enjoy Lauren, but watching her with an eagle eye as she smiled and teased and flirted and laughed freely. Her hair loosened from its tightly bound knot to billow like a halo around her face, and he was surprised and pleased to find that she took no notice of it. The hazy lamplight touched her softly, and her face grew bright as a healthy peach color spread across her high cheekbones.

It was an odd kind of face he thought, one that looked stunningly beautiful at certain angles in certain lights, and then sometimes undramatically plain. But always there was the spirit and courage in her eyes that lit up sometimes like a private fireworks display. And it was hard for Zach to remember why he hadn't made love to her already.

Not until far into the early morning hours did the party end with a slow dance. For that Zach pushed aside the loggers to claim Lauren. Hearty jeers and boos met his approach, but he just grinned through it and persisted until he held her tightly in his arms.

She only smiled up at him in greeting, revealing a warm, welcoming familiarity that plucked the cord that had tightened in his gut as he watched her all evening. He pushed her head to rest against his chest, lowering his chin till it touched her hair, as they did little more than sway from side to side, curved together so closely a hair couldn't have passed between them. She smelled slightly of all the rum that had been foisted on her, and he wondered if that was the reason she so willingly melded into him. Whatever the reason, he wanted that dance to go on forever.

But end it did. Clapping and catcalls erupted for a few minutes before everyone wandered out to the docks and on to the hotel. Zach didn't want to let go of Lauren, and so for a time he held her as they were. Then she raised her face to him, smiling that serene, secret smile. "You're by far the best dance partner I've had tonight, Mr. Madox, but my feet have been trod upon and nearly beaten to death. If I don't get off them, I may have to crawl back to the buggy."

He grinned down at her, his eyes sparkling with more than sympathy. "You've won hearts here, Irish." He realized only after he'd said it that his, too, was tempted by her.

She smiled her pleasure at his words but tried to make little of it. "Or maybe they just prefer dancing with me to dancing with each other."

"That too." He dropped only one of his arms, leaving the other to curl around her neck as he pulled her face into his shoulder and pressed his nose into her hair as they, too, headed out.

When they reached the buggy, his hands pressed into her waist to lift her up, and they lingered there long after she had settled into the seat.

"Mr. Madox?" she queried quietly, and that broke his grip.

The ride home was accomplished at quick canter.

She allowed her shoulder to nestle comfortably just beneath the curve of his arm.

The big house seemed like a waiting haven. Zach pulled to a stop before the porch steps. Again his hands bracketed her midsection to swing her to the ground, and it seemed only natural for his arm to stay against the small of her back as they went in. Only when they parted at her bedroom door did the intimacy between them become slightly awkward. Lauren drew herself up stiffly. "Well...good night." She said softly, and quickly slipped behind the safety of her door.

Whether it was the rum she had sipped in steady rhythm or the numbing effects of being in Zach's arms, she found herself removing her clothes slowly, sensuously. Almost unconsciously, her thoughts drifted into a fanciful dream of belonging to a man like Zach, to a respectable life. Until his voice broke in.

"Are you decent?"

"Oh!" she pulled her wrapper on over her nightgown and tied it tightly before answering. "All right, I am now. What is it?"

Zach kicked the door open and came in with a towel over his shoulder and his sleeves rolled to his elbows. He held a washbasin in one hand and a big iron kettle in the other. "Soak your feet or you won't be able to walk tomorrow." His voice seemed more gravelly than usual.

"That's very kind." She reached to take all the paraphernalia from him, but he drew it back out of her reach.

"Just sit."

She did, pulling her gown up a scant inch above her ankles as he set the basin in front of her and poured steamy water into it. Once her feet were immersed he sat back on his haunches, resting his arms on his massive thighs and letting his hands dangle between.

He started up at her, shaking his head. "You're the damnedest woman," he said almost to himself.

She didn't know how to answer that, so she said nothing.

When Zach decided she had soaked long enough he dropped to his knees, pulled the towel from his shoulder, and laid it across his hands. "Let's have them," he ordered.

Lauren complied, watching his face and thinking what a handsome man he was. She realized with a little start that he meant to work on her feet as he wrapped them in the towel and swung her around, sitting her on the bed with her feet in his lap.

With a hasty yank, she pulled at her gown to cover her legs. "Mr. Madox," she reproved gently, "this really is unseemly."

"Just sit back and enjoy it, Irish," he advised, intent on her feet as he patted them dry and then tossed the towel to the floor.

Lauren's good sense told her she should stop him. But she was tired and it felt so good, so she did as he said, bracing herself on her forearms.

His big hands worked each foot with gentle pressure, pushing against the sole and up to bend her toes towards her ankles, his palms curling around them. His hands were warm and rough and gently firm, twisting and turning, pressing, pushing, all in turn.

"Have you made a science of foot rubbing?" she asked lightly.

One side of his mouth quirked up in a grin, but he continued studying her big toe as he worked it back and forth with slow, sensuous movements. "I'm that good at it, eh?"

"Mmm..." she murmured, letting her head drop back, eyes closed.

"Tired?"

"Bone weary," she sighed. "I like your loggers, but they're hard on city girls."

He laughed, looking at the column of her throat as it arched back. "You held your own."

Both his thumbs pushed into the ball of her foot, and Lauren groaned and squirmed. Zach watched, wanting suddenly to kiss the hollow of that ivory white throat. Dangerous things were happening in him and he was all too aware of the smoothness of her bare feet and the turn of her ankle. He felt like a hungry wolf locked in a pen with a tender lamb, and his good intentions were fast losing ground.

"Feel better?" he asked in a hoarse whisper.

"Yes, thank you." Lauren took his question as an indication that he was finished, and she sat up to tuck the hem of her gown demurely around her feet. Then a grimace crossed her face, and she moaned as she reached to rub the nape of her neck. "I feel as if I've spent hours looking straight up."

Zach laughed huskily. "You have. Lie flat on your stomach and I'll see what I can do." To his surprise she didn't argue. He moved up the bed to sit beside her as she stretched out and took a deep contented breath. Her face was turned away from him, her eyes were closed, and he knew she didn't realize what a tempting sight she made.

His hands dug into her shoulders with careful force, thumbs rubbing along her neck where the soft hair grew like down. Again and again he kneaded her back, while his own senses went into a tailspin. She still smelled faintly of flowers and rum, and she was warm and as soft as satin beneath his fingers. Her long sable lashes brushed peach cheekbones as she breathed a long, languorous sigh through parted lips.

God, what was she doing to him, Zach thought.

Lauren felt as if she were floating on clouds,

weightless, with nothing binding her to earth. She was completely out of herself, lost in the heavenly warm pressure of Zach's big hands and lulled by weariness. Her spirit was as free as air. And it all felt so right. The heavy pressure of his hands turned gentle, rubbing in ever-widening circles, teasing her with his fingertips. Her thoughts floated away like smoke, and nothing stood in the path of the pure, sensual pleasure she was feeling.

But Zach was not so easily liberated. Raw passion and desire warred with the vows he meant to keep ...if only he could remember them. He felt a last taut muscle go limp under his thumbs, and Lauren wriggled sensuously in appreciation. The pale hollow beneath her ear tantalized him. He bent to brush it with his lips, like velvet stroking her soft skin.

Her eyes opened gradually and her breath caught in her throat, but she knew she wasn't going to stop him. She wanted him too much. When he nuzzled her neck with a fiery tongue she turned her head to ease his way. His hands gripped her shoulders and his breath was hot against her skin as a new, languorous energy revived her.

With a last surrendering sigh, he pulled her by the shoulders to face him. Her eyes glittered brightly as she looked up at him. Doubt still lined his dark, handsome features and she remembered that his scruples had stopped him twice before. "Should you do this?" Her voice was a bare whisper of air.

Zach looked deeply into her wide, starry eyes and very slowly shook his head, just before he lowered his lips to hers.

It was a courting kiss at first—tentative, light, dry. And then his mouth softened, opened just a bit to envelop her lips with his. Warm honey glided across her mouth, in tiny circles, again, again, and still it was not enough. And then his tongue touched her lips, teased them open farther and leisurely tested the edges of her teeth, taunting her tongue and dancing away with it back into his own mouth. His breath was hot steam on her skin, his whiskers bristled against her face, and his arm was a muscular vice bracing her against his hard chest. And she loved it all. She reached both hands to the nape of his neck to hold him.

Zach sought the side of her throat with gentle callused fingers, his thumb tracing the curve of her chin, then lower into the hollow, and lower still, in an agonizingly lazy path until his palm closed fully around her tight-crested breast and squeezed slightly.

Her gasp of surprised pleasure sucked air into her lungs. He answered with a low rumble deep in his throat and a fierce yank that pulled her up into his lap where another hard response beneath her hip made her aware of her own newfound sensuality.

So many feelings came alive in her. Her skin seemed taut—every nerve was awake to his barest touch. Never had her breasts felt so full, so sensitive, craving so much more than the touch of his hand through the layers of her gown and wrapper; instinctively she arched her back in a movement that told him all. Such a desperate physical need tormented her that she pressed her thighs tightly together, searching for something that would ease the craving.

Zach understood. While his mouth still tasted, his hand dropped from her breast to pull her sash free and the wrapper from her shoulders. His quick, agile fingers popped the buttons down the front of her gown and cool air whispered against the tender flesh between her breasts. She felt his mouth and tongue following the same trail as his hand, down her throat to flick teasingly into the crevice at the base and along her straight collarbone, his nose pushing her nightgown open and nuzzled a free path across her shoulders and down the crease of flesh that sealed her underarm. Like the glide of a feather, his hand smoothed the gown away from her body, to then close around her bare breast, kneading, rolling, sending lightning charges through her stomach and between her thighs, which she clasped together even harder as if to keep the feeling from escaping.

Zach wondered how he could keep himself to a pace slow enough not to frighten her. She was warm, smooth silk, firm and perfect and alive beneath his hands. He felt he could spend three lifetimes lost in her body.

She felt the trail of his lips begin again. His fingers played lightly with her nipple, rolling, pinching in a way that never seemed hard enough against that straining tip. Then his hand abandoned her, to be replaced with the moist heat of his mouth, his tongue flicking wondrous torment at the achingly hard tip. Her head fell back, and one hand drifted from his nape to his shoulder. Zach reached for her wrist, pulling it inside of his now unbuttoned shirt.

She needed no more encouragement to explore his broad, solid chest. Fine hair curled across muscles that flexed beneath her fingers, and she felt the hard, fast thudding of his heart gone wild with desire. What would it feel like to meet his chest with her own exquisitely sensitive breasts? She slid her hands under his shirt, copying the same motions with which he had removed her clothes, easing the soft flannel shirt back and off. As if their thoughts were one, he nibbled his way back up to the curve of her neck into her shoulder and then pulled her to him, crushing her breasts flat against his hard pectorals. He rubbed against her, teasing those hard nubs with the hair of his chest, sending tingling delight through her. But even he could stand only so much, and he pulled her tightly against him again, finding her mouth with his and pressing his desire up into her hip in a subtle warning of what he intended.

"I need it all, Lauren," he whispered between moist, open-mouthed kisses.

Her only answer was to press back into his lap and recapture the magic of his lips.

And then the slumbering night exploded with the muted sounds of gunfire. Horsewhips snapped through the air, and exuberant bass voices good naturedly dared Zach to come out.

In Lauren's dusky bedroom everything stopped. Their mouths parted, Lauren's with a silent, labored breath, Zach's with a muttered, disbelieving curse. For a moment he held her pressed tightly to his chest while he tried to believe he could ignore the drunken revelry. But outside the house the sound of his name being called drew ever nearer, and he knew that luxury was lost to him.

He hugged Lauren tightly and then let her go, pulling on his shirt while she dragged her gown up from around her waist to cover her breasts. Her long-lashed eyelids blinked as if she were just waking from a heavily drugged sleep. She saw his usually nimble fingers fumble with his buttons. He took a deep breath that swelled his chest, closed his eyes, and let his head fall back for a moment, calming himself, regaining his self-control, and wondering how the hell he was going to leave this room.

But the sharp pounding on the front door left him no choice. "They do this every year," he explained haltingly, his thoughts muddled with passion. "I had forgotten about it." His big hands combed through his raven hair. As if just the sight of her would chain him there, Zach left the room without looking back.

The click of the door closing after him brought Lauren back to herself. She hurriedly buttoned the nightgown to her chin, crossed the wrapper twice over her breasts, and cinched it tighter than ever before. Now the ache between her thighs tormented her with the primitive feeling of being deserted.

And then her mother's voice intruded: reality dawned.

She had danced through the past hours as "Zach's woman" and had ended in his arms. Now, with his abrupt departure, she felt as though it had been some other life she had led for awhile. She could not afford to lose control like that again. She had to remember where she was headed and how much worse it would be if she left her heart behind with Zach. She knew what he wanted and she had to face the fact that she was not it. Foolish and fanciful, her mother's voice said, that was what she had been that night. It wouldn't do. It wouldn't do at all. A broken heart was all she could possibly gain if she didn't remember her place. Tonight she had learned a hard lesson.

Only half an hour passed before Zach managed to send his friends off into the night and return to her, but time seemed to have moved backward instead. Lauren sat on the very edge of her bed, facing the door, as stiff and proud as he had ever seen her.

"Is everything all right?" she asked in that distant way of hers.

Zach didn't answer for a moment as a part of him yearned to have back what he had left; but a stronger part remembered the vows he had made. He came toward her but stopped at the footrail of the bed. His voice struggled for normalcy as hard as hers had. "They're gone now. It's a sort of tradition they came up with to thank me," he explained. He eyed her tightly bound waist and rigid posture. No doubt about it, she was on guard again. "That isn't the way I left you," he observed gently, but they both knew the sad truth: he had cooled down too.

"We got carried away, that's all."

Still, curiosity about what was going on in her mind spurred him on. "Maybe this time, but you wanted this before. What is different now?"

How could she tell him that before that night he had just been a man who was kind enough to trust her inexperience to? But now she cared, and that was dangerous, that was something her mother had warned, preached, harangued against. Caring for a man was a pitfall; it was a lure of honeyed sweetness that led you into a steel-jawed trap. And afterward a woman lost everything.

"I said, how is it different now, Lauren?" Zach repeated.

"It just is." She stood up to put some distance between them, but he caught her arm and roughly pulled her around to face him.

"Why? Because before I was just the owner of a useful instrument, and now you feel something for me?"

She lifted her chin and her eyes shot out a challenge. "Yes."

He uttered a short, derisive snort. "And what if I feel something for you?"

"It will pass," she answered with conviction.

"Your mother tell you that?"

"She was certainly someone who should know."

"You're a damn fool if you believe that."

"Then I'm a fool."

"And a stubborn one to boot." He stared at her, studying her, deciding how much of what she was saying was only bluster. "You're wrong. It won't pass. Not for me and certainly not for you. Once it gets hold of you it takes root and grows."

That was what she feared most. "We've set our courses, Zach. You want another sort of woman, a fine, upstanding one who can be a wife and mother; and I'm prepared to live my life in a whore's world. We'll both be less disappointed if we stay on our own paths and don't try for what can't be."

"Is that so?" He understood what she was afraid of and knew mere words wouldn't help. Instead his gravelly voice said softly, "Have it your way then, Irish. Because as much as I want you I won't take you as a whore, and if you deny your feelings for me, that's just what you will be. Go on and bury yourself in your virgin's bed." He dropped her arm and left, closing the door with a slam.

But it was a long while before Lauren could lie in that bed again. Instead she stood at the window, staring at the full moon and wishing away the desires that were aroused just by his presence. A tremor of dread rippled through her. Never had the thought of what her future held hurt so much.

Chapter 11

While Lauren prepared their evening meal two days later, Zach sat at the big round table in the kitchen, sorting through his mail. They had made no more mention of Saturday night's passion and had instead gone on as if nothing had passed between them.

"That looks like Alan Bentley's handwriting." Lauren caught a glimpse of the letter Zach was reading as she set cold chicken and bread on the table in front of him.

One black brow rose suspiciously. "You're familiar with it?"

Lauren sat across from him, meticulously unfolding her napkin in her lap. Alan Bentley had not known she meant to run her own whorehouse in Seattle. It was something she never wanted him to know. "Then it is a letter from Alan?" she asked, hedging.

"It is. Did he write you love poems?" Zach persisted.

Lauren shrugged. "Why should it matter to you?"

"A mild streak of jealousy."

She gave him her secret smile.

"Did they teach you to do that in the convent?" His faintly ironic smile nearly matched hers.

93

"Do what?"

"Smile as if you're laughing inside or know something no one else does."

The smile reappeared. "There wasn't a great deal of smiling allowed in the convent. They're very austere, you know," she answered.

"I'll bet you fit right in," he muttered irritably, still feeling a prickling of jealousy because of her interest in Alan Bentley.

"Then you would lose your money. I spent much of my time locked in the cellar as punishment for disobedience."

He laughed out loud. "I can't believe that."

"It's true. Sometimes I thought I was never going to get out."

"What good did it do to lock you in a cellar?"

She shrugged. "It taught me to see in the dark."

His face slowly broke into a grin. "Lying again, Irish?"

Her head drew back, "Not at all. It happened so often I began hording little things to take with me, candle stubs and books and things. I'd daydream and make up a family for myself, with brothers and sisters and grandparents, to pass the time. Blessedly there weren't any rats; it was just dark and damp. But I didn't like it."

Similar memories of his own struck him forcibly, and Zach frowned as he experienced a feeling of protectiveness toward her. "Didn't you tell anyone about it?"

"Of course not. In fact, you're the only person I've ever told at all." Then she remembered how the conversation had started. "Did Alan write you about me?"

"Now who's being conceited?" His tone was brusque again. "How the hell could he have connected us?"

"He saw me get into your train car. He had only to

ask the stationmaster if he couldn't figure it out for himself."

"Are you pining for him?"

She matched his frown. "I told you before, he was a friend."

"A friend you wanted to marry."

"I never said that. I said he'd asked and that's why his father ran me out of town."

"And what am I, Irish?"

Lauren thought a moment and realized she didn't really know what he was to her. She resorted to evasion. "My benefactor."

He stared her down and then smiled lazily, "Oh, I'm more than that. One of these days I'm going to show you how good making love can be. That's being a lot more than a benefactor."

Her topaz eyes locked with his black ones. Confusion whirled inside her. She was torn between wanting him to follow through with his threat and a fear of what the consequences might be for both of them if he did. "You still haven't told me why Alan wrote to you."

Zach's smile faded, "Back to him again, are we? I can only tell you that it has nothing to do with you. It's business." He answered more curtly than Lauren had ever heard him speak, and she was taken aback.

"I didn't think Alan had any business dealings," she persisted.

"Maybe he's finally growing a spine." Then he scowled and shook his head disgustedly. "Dammit, I'm not saying any more about him." He hoped his abruptness would put an end to her questions, for he didn't dislike Alan Bentley; in fact, Zach was repaying a debt to Alan. But it rubbed Zach wrong to think the other man had had a place in Lauren's life . . . or even in her thoughts.

"I'm beginning to wonder again if you aren't some sort of outlaw."

"What?" he exclaimed in stunned disbelief.

"When I first met you on the train, wounded and all, I thought perhaps you were an outlaw. You have such an air of mystery about you, I wonder if I wasn't right," she said.

He laughed at that. "I hate to disappoint you, Irish, but there's nothing that exciting about me."

He pushed the papers aside to make room for his food, unaware that one sheet drifted to the floor near Lauren's feet. She retrieved it, but just as she was about to hand it to him, her attention was caught by the word "Maudie's" scribbled at the beginning of the note. She took it back and read on.

"Were you ever going to tell me this?" she demanded accusingly, struck most by the fact that, from the contents of the letter, it was clear that the time to leave him was very near.

Zach sighed. "Not for awhile," he admitted.

"But they say the furniture can be moved into Maudie's by the day after tomorrow."

"I read it. I wanted more time." He pushed his untouched plate away and tipped back in his chair, staring at the ceiling as he teetered back and forth. "Put it off, Irish." He spoke from deep in his chest, as if it were hard for him to ask her to stay, now that she knew.

"I can't," she said agitatedly. "It's time."

"Not if you don't want it to be."

"We've been through this before. There's no sense in delaying it."

Silence fell heavily as they both sat with their confused thoughts and feelings. Then Lauren settled the matter. "I would appreciate your help in getting started. I'm not sure what steps have to be taken."

"It's simple enough," he answered sardonically. "You set up your bribes as contributions to municipal funds, let our city officials know they'll be your guests, free of charge, so they won't have you raided, and hire a bevy of soiled doves. By now I'm sure my men have spread the word that Maudie's is just about ready for business, so there won't be much to do to attract customers. You're damn near all set." He had grown angrier and angrier as he spoke each word, and as he finished, he stood up abruptly, knocking his chair hard against the wall behind it. "I've come this far, I might as well go the rest of the way with you. We can start tomorrow, if that's how you want it." He stormed out of the kitchen and out of the house with a crash of the front door.

For the first time in years, Lauren felt the hot sting of tears swell in her eyes. But she wasn't sure why.

The bribes were paid, the furniture was moved in, the bar and kitchen were stocked, and word went out on the streets that Maudie's was hiring on Saturday morning. Lauren and Zach moved through it all with painfully intense determination, the kind one needed to accomplish the most loathsome tasks. They didn't talk much, and when they did it was only about Maudie's. Each night that week they retired early to their separate rooms, each one's door closed tightly against the other.

Lauren felt Zach's disapproval like a weighty shroud. It was an added burden to all the disparaging things she thought about herself. But she pushed on, for there was nothing else she could do.

Zach felt frustrated and as surly as a wounded grizzly. Agitation was a prickly bedfellow, leaving him awake to chew it all over in his mind until, each night, he came to the same conclusion: Lauren wasn't going to be a whore. Not, by God, if he had anything to do with it.

* * *

The Countess drifted through Puget Sound, splitting the calm night with the noise of revelry. It was, indeed, the floating pleasure palace its owner advertised, offering high-spirited whores who sang and danced and graced a man's arm with a small bit of luck at the gaming tables.

A vice ship, the authorities called her, but before the arm of the law could touch her, she would sail off to a new port, turn a profit until things heated up again, and then return to the cooler waters of the previous city.

It was not of quite the caliber as Maudie's, but *The Countess* was still several cuts above Seattle's box houses and it served a refined clientele.

It was a large vessel, her sparkling, whitewashed hull rivaled the summer clouds. The main deck held a high-staged theater, where sweet-voiced women sang bawdy songs and danced the can-can in net stockings and dresses that bared more than they covered. Three mirrored, crystal-chandeliered saloons offered drinks strong enough to loosen the tightest wallets, and the remaining space on this deck held four gaming rooms that provided every conceivable opportunity to test one's luck for cash.

The middeck was given over to a dozen prime bawdy-house bedrooms that were rarely unoccupied as the seventeen filles de joie took turns working the crowd and luring nearly every man in his turn to a costly romp.

The upper deck of the three-tiered steamer accommodated the wheelhouse and Mark Rossiter's office and private bedroom. During working hours the girls were kept too busy below to venture there unless summoned, and customers knew better than to climb, uninvited, that last stairway where overdue accounts were settled with either cash or a dunking in the Sound. So it was from a retreat somewhat quieter than the decks below that Mark Rossiter awaited the woman who attended him when he had a mind for pleasure rather than business.

A thin cheroot hung from his perfect lips, but his mind was not on the cigar as he sat behind a large mahogany desk. Instead, his sky blue eyes stared past gilt-edged picture frames but saw only what was in his head. Two knocks interrupted his musings and a woman entered, smiling her pleasure at being taken away from her job to service an ultimately more munificent customer.

"Sit down, darling," Rossiter instructed her in the tone that made every woman he employed feel special. "I'm about to fire you," he added with a smile.

Dumbstruck, the woman sat down but said nothing as she tried to hide the fear that she had unwittingly erred.

"Don't go pale on me." He laughed, and it eased her anxiety a bit. "I've got another job for you."

Her hopes soared. Wasn't it the dream of every woman on board to be selected as his private mistress, to live in the beautifully furnished provincial private rooms and tend him alone, perhaps even have a chance at winning his heart? If he had one.

"I'm sure you have heard that Maudie's is reopening." Rossiter didn't notice that she had not yet responded to anything he had said. "I understand hiring is to take place tomorrow morning. It is there that I want you to work."

The whore's bright eyes widened. "You want me to work for your competition?"

His smile was engaging. "I want you to work for me...at Maudie's." He paused a moment to let it sink in, gauging by the glitter in her eyes how much this venture would cost him. "I mean to have Maudie's, but the owner is disinclined to sell it to me just yet. I have decided that persuasion is in order."

The woman relaxed and dropped her whore's facade in favor of clipped, businesslike tones. "I would have expected Tommy to be more in line for that job."

She was a good choice, he thought. The task he had in mind required the brains for subtlety. "Too heavy-handed, I'm afraid. I need someone to eavesdrop and report every detail of what goes on in that house, someone with the slyness of a fox to wreak havoc that will seem to be just bad luck."

"That doesn't sound like you."

Silence fell as Rossiter's thoughts drifted for a few moments before he answered. "This is a special case."

"Meaning you want your hands to look clean."

"Exactly." He smiled with satisfaction. "The first job at hand is to get yourself hired on as one of the girls. That shouldn't be too difficult for you. The second is to keep your eyes and ears wide open. A woman named Lauren Flannery owns the house, but Zach Madox has a hand in it somewhere. I want to know where and how far-reaching it is."

"Their business relationship?" she asked snidely.

"Yes. And every other aspect of their relationship as well. It is important that I know what he is to her personally."

"Smitten?" she ventured, a little too boldly.

His smile turned tight, icy, and dangerous. "You don't *really* want to know too much, do you, darling?" His voice was quietly threatening.

The woman swallowed convulsively; she was smart enough to know she had overstepped her bounds and was on dangerous ground. "No. It's your business, not mine."

"Very wise of you. I'll let you know what sabotage I have planned as the need arises. We will meet on your day off each week, but I expect to be discreetly informed if you learn anything of particular or imminent importance to me. Of course, you will act as if we have never even met; keep that in mind, since I plan to frequent the place, making overtures of friendship." He waited for another comment, but caution kept the girl quiet. This time his smile was a reward for her wisdom. "It wouldn't do for us to have any known contact whatsoever. Understand?"

She nodded, afraid now to ask what this would all be worth to her.

Aware that he had easily succeeded in putting her in her place and was now properly cowed, Rossiter's warm, appreciative expression returned. He nodded toward the damask-draped bed at the opposite end of the room. "For the rest of tonight I think less tiring demands are in order. We want you at your best in the morning, don't we?"

Maudie's was alive with people on Saturday morning. Workmen were busy putting the final touches on nicked paint and woodworking; the red velvet draperies were hung, the furniture was polished, the gaming tables were set up in one of the parlors, and Zach was at work in the office off the entrance, paying the last of the bills.

Lauren steeled herself to meet the women gathered in the kitchen to decide which of them she would hire. She looked every bit as calm and confident as she had facing her ejection from Dry Creek. She was dressed now in her fine skirt and blouse, but her insides churned in cold fear and dread.

She forced herself through the swinging door into the midst of a roomful of women in various stages of slovenliness. At her entrance they remained clustered in little groups, nor did they give the alert attention she had expected. Instead their eyes raked over her disdainfully and dismissed her as someone unimportant, for how could this ramrod-straight, prim, pristine young woman be of any consequence to their purpose there? They turned their backs on her to resume their conversations among themselves, ignoring her, and Lauren's courage flagged. Suddenly everything she had planned to say sounded to her like a lecture by a mother superior to a group of recalcitrant convent students.

She turned and left the kitchen almost at a run, heading down the hallway toward the front. There she flew like a whirlwind into the office, closed the door, and fell against it, her arms straight down at her sides and her palms braced backwards. Her face was pale and her eyes were wide. For the first time since Zach had met her she looked like a panic-stricken schoolgirl.

"I've just realized," she said in a trembling voice, "that I don't know what to say to them."

Zach laughed, something he hadn't done in a week. He studied her from behind the big desk. "Who?" he asked sardonically.

"The women," she answered, missing his sarcasm.

"You want me to do it?" he asked, again sarcastically, but this, too, was lost on Lauren.

"Would you please? When I come to know them it will be easier," she said, more to convince herself than him.

He crossed the room and stood towering above her with his legs spread apart, hands on his hips, staring down at her with a challenging quirk of one black eyebrow. "Think so?"

"I'm certain of it."

"Come on then." His big hand closed around her shoulder to push her back the way she'd come. The gesture made her feel relieved, grateful, and a little foolish.

Once in the kitchen he had but to clear his throat to attract the attention of every woman in the room. "Morning, ladies." His gravelly voice penetrated their whispers. "I'd like you to meet Lauren Flannery, the new owner of Maudie's. This is what we'll be needing from you."

He outlined the basic rules for the group as a whole, knowing it would save time. First, he told them, a doctor would examine each woman hired before they began work. A fair number of them left when they heard that edict. Next, they would not be allowed to steal from the customers. Out went a few more. They were to work six days a week, the only exception being monthly indisposition. No pimps were permitted on the premises; they would be working solely for Maudie's and be paid by Lauren. There would be no free entertaining of men friends. On he went, weeding them out until the group was down to a reasonable number. Then he began to speak to each woman separately.

There was Lucy Norse, brassy, sharp-tongued, and bawdy. She had a big mouth that she used too freely, but she was too beautiful to pass up. She knew well that she was a big draw on her own, so she could get away with her bold speech. "Like to know how *you* got hold of this place, honey," she said disdainfully, looking Lauren up and down with as much distaste as any snobbish matron had ever bestowed upon the lowliest whore.

There was Matty Grimes, cultured, well spoken, an unlikely whore. "The life suits me," she informed a skeptical Zach, then detailed a repertoire that would have made a sailor blush.

Straw-haired, foul-smelling Margarite was rejected. Nan, too skinny and flat chested, as well as Betty, too plump and plain, found no home at Maudie's either. Lovely Lily London, with her flame red hair and green cat eyes, was hired readily, while nearsighted Iris, beak-nosed Melanie, and cranky Colleen were sent on their way.

When Zach came to Esther Brown, he greeted her with the familiarity of old friends. An elegant beauty, she stood gracefully straight and square shouldered, with her chin high. She was quiet, proud, and older by far than anyone else in the room. Knowing her chances were tenuous, she wasted no time. "I need the work, Zach," she said earnestly. "I'm not used up yet. You'll get your money's worth out of me, I promise you that."

Though they were unalike in appearance and age, Lauren saw something of herself in Esther Brown, and it made her as uncomfortable as if she had seen her own reflection in a gypsy's crystal ball. Zach hesitated, weighing the situation. Lauren wished he wouldn't hire the woman, but when he relented and said they would give her a try, she couldn't bring herself to question his decision. The woman nearly crumpled with relief and gratitude.

Bubbly, pert-nosed Polly Carson was taken on, while her friend, flabby Blanche, was not. Sally Flournoy was also hired, once Zach got past her false French accent by making her laugh and forget her act.

Missy Tims stood in a corner at the back of the room—too young, too sweet, too pretty, too afraid. "Where are you from, Missy?" Zach asked gently.

She smiled up at him with the trusting eyes of a child. "I was borned in Kansas City."

"What brought you here?"

"My husband come to be a logger."

"And where is your husband now?"

The girl's face was wan. "He was snake bit. We couldn't save him," she answered in a voice that was barely audible.

"Have you ever done this for a living before?"

"No, sir. But I reckon I know what it's about. I want to go back home but I got no money to get there. I heard tell this is the fastest way to make it."

Again Zach paused, studying her, judging the situation. Then he peeled off thirty dollars from a roll of bills he took from his pocket and handed it to her. "It may be the fastest, Missy, but it's a long way from the best. Go on home."

"You don't want me to do nothin' for this?" Disbelief and gratitude mingled in her childish voice.

"Just wash your face and take the first train out of Seattle."

There was round-faced Belle Bristol, buxom Helen Garret, and Edna Green. Belle and Helen were hired, but Edna's missing teeth kept her out. "There's some what don't mind," she groused before spitting a wad of tobacco onto the floor and leaving.

Statuesque, honey-haired Christine Moore was another of Zach's acquaintances, and she greeted him with a warm, inviting smile. "Looks like you've done old Maudie proud," she said in a voice as smooth and rich as butter. "She would have been pleased."

"Hello, Chris," he returned heartily, "Where have you been keeping yourself?"

"Around and about," she purred. "Did you do up my room like before?"

Beside him, Lauren bristled, but Zach only laughed. "To the best of my recollection."

"Perfect, I'm sure. It will be like old times, won't it?"

"Not quite." He laughed again. "What do you say we just go on as friends?"

The woman eyed Lauren briefly and then shrugged. "Have it your way."

"I don't think she's right for Maudie's," Lauren heard the words come out of her own mouth before she considered them.

Zach's amused glance turned her way, as did Christine Moore's cold, assessing blue eyes. "Why is that, Lauren?" he asked mockingly.

"I just don't."

Christine Moore defended herself calmly. "It was purely business, I assure you."

He bent low and whispered to Lauren so that no one else in the room could hear. "Maudie would have wanted Chris back. She was one of the main attractions," he explained with an air of challenging patience that said if she meant to live among whores she couldn't be jealous of what they did. "She belongs here," he finished.

In an effort to disprove his suspicion of her motives, Lauren conceded. "On second thought, it doesn't matter to me. You're hired," she said in a too-high voice and turned away as if the matter were forgotten.

Two more of Maudie's former employees were hired: Martha Parks and Jolene McGrath. Both were overjoyed to see Zach, and Lauren began to wonder if he had bedded every woman Maudie had ever hired. But that was the last of them.

When they were finished, Lauren knew Zach had hired the best of the lot and that the place would flourish in spite of her. What she was left fretting over was that no matter how often he had consulted her, deferred to her opinion, and stressed that she was the boss there, the women responded warmly to Zach and only noticed her as an afterthought. And she hadn't a clue as to how to change that and establish her authority among them.

They rode home from Maudie's late that night, neither speaking. Zach helped Lauren down from the buggy with his usual courtesy, but his eyes never turned her way.

"You go on in. I need some air," was all he said as he headed back down the path.

Lauren watched him stop on the stone bridge and lean his elbows on the side to stare down into the brook below. With the way things were between them, her decision to follow him was difficult. But after a few minutes she went after him.

She didn't know what to say, she wasn't even sure why she had gone to join him, except that she hated the cold formality in him. She didn't know how she could change that, so she just stood beside him, staring into the dark night and wishing he would say something—anything.

When he finally spoke, he did not look at her. His gravelly voice echoed in the stillness. "Well, you're in business, Madam Flannery."

"And you're angry because of it." She, too, spoke to the quietly rushing stream.

"I'm not angry," he said, bristling.

"You sound angry and you act angry," she observed, but he didn't seem to hear. She sighed in defeat. "I'm sorry it's like this."

Silence reigned between them for awhile and then he gave in. "So am I," he admitted raggedly. He turned his head to her then, his black eyes piercing. "I've half a mind to tumble you right here and now, did you know that?"

She swallowed thickly, she couldn't answer.

"This is one hell of a predicament you've gotten me into," he ground out. "I want to make love to you but I'm afraid of pushing you into a life of sin. Then again, sometimes I think I should do it just to stake my claim."

"The decision isn't yours alone."

He straightened up slowly, turning to her as he contradicted her with deceptive gentleness: "Oh, I think it is."

In one swift motion, he pulled her possessively into his arms and pressed his mouth down onto hers with voracious force. His tongue was a hot staff digging at her lips, her teeth, her own tongue. The length of his big body arched her over one powerful arm, while he cupped the back of her head in the palm of his other hand.

She craved him too much to fight the ache in her

stomach and the burning in her breasts. His kiss became gentle as if he knew just how to fuel her yearning. The fires burned hotter and spread between her
legs. All that mattered was the pure, raw emotion she
was feeling. She reached her hand to the side of his
face, feeling whisker-roughened skin and the tense
movement of muscle and jaw working to make
magic.

Then his lips deserted her. His face became a
frowning shadow as his eyes searched hers for con-
firmation of what her body was silently telling him.
He shook his head as he found it and chuckled. He
stood her up straight again and took a step backward, away from her. "Go in, Irish. Go up to your
virgin's bed and let me think."

She was too confused by his abrupt dismissal to do
anything else, so she left him, grateful for the cool
night air that chilled the heat of her desire.

But she couldn't get the thoughts out of her mind.
Even a cold bath could not wash the feel of him from
her skin or the tingling from her taut nipples, and
nothing else could fill the aching emptiness where
her thighs were pressed hard together.

Chapter 12

She brushed her hair. And brushed it. Slower. Slower. Her mind was with Zach...alone...in his arms....

But obviously now the time had come to leave him. She felt a wave of loneliness wash over her. How easy it had been to get used to having him at her elbow, to hear the sound of his raspy voice and robust laughter. She felt she hadn't had enough of him, as if she had been beckoned and lured only to come short of reaching what he had made her want.

It was dangerous, all right, just as her mother had warned. She could feel it. But all her hard-won defenses had slipped to a point where she longed only to give in to her instincts, and damn the consequences.

Zach's room was dark except for the pale frosting of moonlight where he stood shirtless at the window. He had one bare forearm arched up against the pane, and his brow was pressed against it as he stared out unseeingly.

Lauren stopped in the doorway, unsure of herself, fearing he would turn her away. Her eyes trailed from the moon-brightened shine of his hair down the groove of his spine to the indentation just above his jeans. His feet were bare and one arch rested over the instep of the other.

Her breath was ragged, her heart pounded in her chest, and her arms and legs seemed too stiff to move. But she had come this far and seeing him only inflamed her.

"Zach..." Her voice was a whisper.

His head jolted back and he turned to her in surprise.

She swallowed and tried to speak but failed.

One black brow took wing again. "What's the trouble?" He sounded so distant that it deflated her precarious courage.

"Maybe I shouldn't have come."

"No, wait." He stopped her in midturn, suddenly realizing that she was wearing only her nightgown, without the tightly cinched wrapper, and that her hair was unbound, long and gleaming to her waist. "Why did you come, Irish?" he asked gruffly.

She took a deep breath to gain strength. "The decision is mine too. And I need..." It was so hard to voice her desire. She tried again. "I need you...I need to be with you."

Silence fell around them, chilling Lauren. She shuddered, and when she could bear it no more, she forced herself to whisper, "If you don't want me, I'll go. But we have so little time left."

"I should send you back. I decided not to do this." His voice was hoarse. His eyes strayed tellingly down her body.

"I've realized in this past week that I never meant to be more than the proprietor of Maudie's," she said in answer to his unspoken question.

"And if I do this now?"

"That won't change. You'll be giving me something to take away, the only time I can have a man make love to me without any suspicion that I'm a whore. It will be my first and last, Zach," she promised quietly, his name soft on her lips. "When I go to Maudie's, I'll be living in a whore's world, but no matter what my background is, I'm no whore. To keep my self-respect I'll be celibate. So love me, please? Just this one time."

"You mean to be the nun in residence at Maudie's."

"It's a business and I'll run it as one, that's all."

"And you want me to deflower you so you don't die wondering," he concluded caustically.

"Or maybe I just want you to finish what you keep teasing me with," she shot back.

He raised his hands to his waist, one hip jutting out to balance himself. "I won't touch you unless you tell me you want me, Lauren, because you have never admitted you feel something for me," he said flatly, still angry.

She closed her eyes tightly and sighed in frustration. "I wouldn't be here if that wasn't true."

He stared at her, nodding his head up and down very, very slowly. "You'd better be damn sure of it, lady, because this time when I get started, I won't be stopped. And this isn't where it ends, it's where it begins. Understand that."

She didn't understand it, but it couldn't matter. There was such an aching need in her. She stepped to within an arm's length of him, and her voice was a tremulous whisper. "You said you'd show me, Zach."

He felt his insides being wrenched open, and a flood of feeling rushed out. She wasn't what he'd ever planned on. She was a stubborn, proud, willful wisp of a woman with more damn pluck than anyone he had ever run into.

She looked up at him with wide eyes and wonder on her face. He saw her lips quiver, but her body was stiff with that almighty determination of hers. "You're the damnedest woman." Then he reached for her with both arms and pulled her up against him. She buried her face in his chest, smelling his clean, masculine scent. He lifted the silken weight of her hair, letting it fall through his fingers. "God, this is beautiful. You should never tie it up." He lowered his face to the side of her neck, and the softness of his mouth tickled while his hot breath excited her sensitive skin.

She swallowed the lump in her throat and raised unsteady hands to his chest. Her fingertips seemed to feel the heat of his body, as she wound them into the hair covering his hard muscles.

"You always smell of flowers and feel too soft to be real." His slackened, parted lips brushed smoothly across her neck and up to her ear; they felt like warm satin along the surface of her skin. "But you are real and you bring out things in me I can only wonder at."

His lips trailed along her flushed cheekbone and down at last to her mouth. He tugged at each of her lips in turn, sweetly teasing them open, inviting her to come share the wine. Her mouth answered luxuriantly beneath his, meeting his tongue eagerly, sure at least of this, for he had taught her. Her hands skimmed up to his shoulders to feel the cords of his neck, the hard ridges that seemed strangely taut when his mouth was so supple, almost as if he were hiding some feeling of uneasiness.

"You have done this before, haven't you?" she whispered.

He laughed, a low rumble against her chin. "A time or two." His hands came up her sides, stopping just under her arms to lift her higher up along his brawny body. His teeth took the ends of the ribbons that fastened her nightgown and began pulling them free, one at a time, until he could nuzzle his way in to kiss the cleavage of her breasts. Then he let her slide back down the length of his body, so that her gown bunched up between them. She started at the intimate contact, suddenly feeling awkward and unsure. Should she pull the thin cotton back down, or let it stay up where it was?

His throaty laugh came again. "Just relax, Irish, and let it go for once."

He bent and wisked her off her feet with a thunderous growl and then whirled them around and around as if he would spin the inhibitions out of her. She clasped her arms around his neck, hanging on for dear life. Suddenly she was falling onto the mattress of his big bed and Zach was lying on her. Her head was spinning and he was laughing and then so was she.

"Ah, darlin', 'tis such sweet lunacy you'll be knowin'," he murmured in a good Irish brogue as his mouth came down on hers in a lusty kiss, hard and moist and demanding.

His callused palm stole underneath the opened front of her nightgown. Sweet tension claimed her as his hand closed over the hard knot of her nipple and his strong fingers kneaded her to life. She thought there could be nothing in all the world like the feeling of his hot hand on her cool, bare flesh as he slowly slipped her gown from her shoulders. Then Zach's chest crushed down on her, prickling and tickling her nipples into pinched nubs that hurt with wanting.

His mouth dallied with hers, again, again, like soft honey and warm butter. Their tongues parried, thrust, and she feasted on it greedily. But when she felt his hand fidget with the buttons of his fly, a feeling of fear shot through, dampening her hunger. He made short work of it and soon was pressing his nakedness against her side with a groan of pure, raw pleasure.

But Lauren suddenly felt very uncomfortable. How much easier it had been when passion and rum had carried them to almost the same point, but after a week of closeness. Now, after five days of cold separation and her having had to beg him, she felt it was not the same. She didn't even realize that she was holding her nightgown in a tight wad at her stomach until he reached down to close a big hand around her fist.

"What's this, Irish?" his voice rasped out between the kisses he was tracking along her jawbone and down her throat.

"I think it's panic," she whispered, angling her head back to breathe more easily.

He stroked her fist, running one of his fingers up her wrist and back again. "Let go of it."

She didn't know whether he meant her to let go of the panic or the gown, but it didn't matter, because she could do neither. "I don't know what to do."

His voice was a soft, soothing growl. "Trust me, love." The heel of his hand moved up and down her arm. He kissed her softly—the hollow of her shoulder, the side of her breast, her stomach, the gully between her breasts, her throat, her eyelids.

"What's inside, Irish?" His breath was hot on her, and his tongue left little spots of dampness to dry hot-cold. "I'll tell you what it feels like to me." His breath was a cloud-soft gust against her skin. "I'm all tight inside, coiled up and getting tighter. There isn't anything in me that doesn't feel better than good. I want to soar and I feel I could. I want to touch you everywhere and make it go on all night. I want to kiss you and taste you all over and feel your hands on me and your body up against me so close there isn't a hairbreadth between us. And then I want to be up inside of you to uncoil and soar." His tongue ran along the inside of her lips, then his teeth nipped at them. "I can feel it there in you, a tight little spring. Come on, Irish, come with me." His hand curled to the underside of her arm and glided down to push her fingers open. He pulled her hand away from her nightgown and up to his neck, patting it gently. His mouth wrapped hers in moist velvet, calling her back to the warmth they had known of before.

She was torn inside with feelings of pleasure and panic, madness and sanity, hot and cold, wanting and fear. His hand reached for her breast again and her battle culminated in a tiny sensual groan deep her throat. When his mouth replaced his hand, and lowered the hand to slide the nightgown away, she gave in to the bright shards of excitement shooting through her. It was as if a secret door had opened and pleasure surged out like hot lava. His hand traveled the path to her thighs and then between them to the place where it all seemed to gather in anticipation.

It was just by accident that her hand fell from his shoulder and found the hard kernel of his own nipple nesting in the matted hair of his chest. Realization dawned that she could do for him what he was doing for her. "Show me!" she demanded.

His hand left the secret places of her body to reach for her fingers tormenting his chest. "Anything, Irish—it all feels good," he breathed, but he pulled her hand downward. When she hesitated, his fingers closed hers around his swollen length. His deep moan of ecstacy stayed her hand when she might have drawn it away in fear. Instead she explored his size and shape and the silken texture of him. She learned the power her touch held and the aphrodisiac of igniting the same flames in him that burned in her. And all the while his searing mouth was at her breast, suckling and nipping; and his big callused hand sought her most delicate regions with the gentleness of a giant touching a butterfly...until she wondered if this was more torment than delight.

Just as the thought struck her, his exploring fingers found the entrance to her womanhood, setting off a white-hot explosion that washed over her in wave after wave of blissful sensation that left her aching to feel his full shaft inside her. She opened her legs to him, and he answered by wrapping his body around hers, probing until he found his way. She barely heard him murmur, "Hang on, love." And then a searing pain took her breath away as her flesh tore open around him and turned heaven into burning hell.

"No!" she screamed in outrage.

"Shh. I had to, Irish. It'll get better."

It did, slowly, slowly, as he soothed her with kisses and tender, caring caresses until she relaxed. Finally her body accepted his place there and the pain eased so she could bear his thrusts. She even found a contented pleasure as he stiffened above her, her name on his lips, his body one long, tempered muscle. He gave a last deep plunge home and settled down over her, exhausted.

Then he remembered how small she was and braced his weight up on his good arm, while the other smoothed a bead of perspiration from her brow. "Are you all right?"

"Is it supposed to hurt, or did you just do that?"

He chuckled and pulled a long strand of her hair from across her throat. "No, I didn't 'just do that.' I'd never hurt you. That's how it is the first time."

"Did it hurt you?"

He laughed again. "No, Irish, it didn't hurt me. And I'm afraid it's not over yet." He kissed her, seeing her trepidation. "Just a little more. Take a deep breath." She did, but the flesh that had finally accommodated him did not relinquish him easily, and once more she thought she was ripping apart.

Only when the pain subsided did she breathe again and open her eyes. She was alone in the big bed and for a moment she thought that it had all been a very vivid dream.

Then he was back, his naked body all muscle and

dark hollows, a massive tower of magnificent virility and beautiful, powerful masculinity.

"Now be still," his gravelly voice commanded gently.

But she jerked upright when the sheet she had pulled up to cover herself with slid down and a wet cloth was drawn up along the insides of her thighs. "What are you doing?"

"Taking away some of the soreness, so that a few hours from now when I want you again you'll feel nothing but pleasure." She started to protest but he cut her short. "I mean to make the most of this night, Lauren. Now lie back." He pushed her against the pillows and finished what he had begun with gentle, reverent strokes, ignoring her hot embarrassment. Then he tossed the cloth aside, lay down next to her, and pulled her into his arms and the sheet up to cover them both.

And there they slept, nestled together like two matched halves of a whole.

Chapter 13

During the night the strangeness of sleeping with another person penetrated her dreams and woke Lauren. Groggily she opened her eyes, gradually becoming aware of her hand on Zach's hairy chest, and the shock jolted her fully awake. He was snoring lightly through parted lips, undisturbed by her movements, his free arm across his flat belly where the sheet had fallen away.

Lauren eased away from him onto her back and stretched her stiffening muscles. She arched her arms straight over her head and relaxed into the downy mattress. Her slender fingers curved around two of the brass spindles of the headboard. The metal was cold and she remembered that Zach had told her that this bed had been bought with only one purpose: to bring his wife to it. She pulled her hands away guiltily, hearing in her mind his voice saying that he had never taken a woman in this bed before. She felt as if she were defiling it. A heavy weight pulled at her heart, and her self-respect and shame propelled her out of Zach's room as soon as she had pulled on her nightgown.

The sheets of her small lonely bed were cold and crisp and clean, a virgin's bed to run back to, just as Zach had said. Lauren lay there in misery. She felt like an intruder and wondered just where she did belong. Nothing had prepared her for what lay beyond the secluded world in which she had grown up. For the first time in her life she resented the life her mother had chosen for herself and for her daughter.

Where the soft warmth of a woman had curved perfectly into his side there was now a harsh chill. Zach stirred, rolled over, and flung a long arm out. But all he encountered was emptiness and rumpled sheets. A frown creased his sleep-swollen face and he opened his eyes.

He swept the sheet from his body, and his big feet hit the floor with an impatient thump. "Dammit!" he muttered under his breath. He had no doubt she had fled back to her own bed because of some misplaced sense of modesty.

From her doorway he saw her on the bed, lying like a martyr, with hands clasped over the sheet and the high neck of her nightgown tied up tightly again. He shook his head, deciding now that her conscience had spurred her to regret what passion and desire had brought her to.

"Dammit, Irish, I knew this was going to happen," he said angrily, "I warned you to be sure."

"I don't know what you're talking about," she answered quietly in that remote way she had when she was all bound up inside and out of reach.

"I suppose you're in here contemplating the joy of losing your virginity," he said snidely.

"I don't care about my virginity."

"Then why the hell did you leave me? It's just damn silliness to be embarrassed to sleep with me after I've made love to you. Or do you figure sleeping is too personal?"

"That's ridiculous." She got up like a wraith rising from the mists and pulled her wrapper on, tying the sash at the waist so tightly he thought it might cut her in half.

"Then what the hell's going on?" He stood with arms akimbo in glorious nakedness, losing his patience fast.

The sight of him stirred an uncomfortable mixture of desire and guilt in her; she moved to the window and stood there straight backed, looking out, her arms hugging her midriff. "I woke up and remembered what you'd said about your bed. I felt as if I had soiled a shrine," she spoke flatly, but with a softness that revealed she wasn't as distant as she wanted to seem.

"That's how this place seems to you?" he asked in disbelief.

"Not in a bad way. I envy the kind of woman who can fit in here. It just...made what we did seem... tainted."

"I didn't know you ever thought of it differently."

Her head snapped around to look at him over her shoulder. "What does that mean?"

"I don't believe you ever saw it as an act of love. You think of yourself in the same terms as a whore, and tonight you set me up to formalize it. Then it turned out you liked it; that's a sure sign, isn't it? Now you can be a damn martyr and banish yourself to a celibate life of atonement. Isn't that how it works? I'm surprised you weren't grateful that it hurt for awhile."

That rang with more truth than Lauren wanted to hear. "Thank you for your insights, Mr. Madox. But since you got what you wanted out of it, the rest is of no concern to you, is it?"

"That's right, Irish, wallow in it. It gives you one hell of an excuse to deny you're a woman at all, doesn't it?"

"What gives you the right?" she hissed over her shoulder.

"You did, a few hours ago when you sacrificed your sainthood to me," he shot out cuttingly. "There's nothing dirty about what we did and you slap me in the face by thinking it is. My bed isn't a goddamn shrine, and I took you to it because I wanted you there."

"You're not so all-fired perfect yourself!" she raged at last. Her fury opened another door in her, freeing her to say the things she wanted to say. "Just what makes you such an authority? You're idling away in this mausoleum waiting for some paragon of womanly perfection to appear on your doorstep, and all the while you pass up dozens of women for God only knows what minor flaws."

"I passed up 'dozens' of women for one big flaw: I didn't love them!" he raved back, pointing a long finger her way. "And that's your own silly-assed notion right there. You came in here and saw a house built for a plain, everyday wife and family and figured right off that I was looking for something that didn't exist. You don't think there's any kind of woman between a whore and a nun. That's a sorry judgment to pass on your own sex."

"Right now I'm passing a sorrier one on yours."

"Why? Because I didn't tiptoe around your self-pity? Because I expect you to see that normal urges and pleasure in them doesn't make you a whore?"

"I'm not a whore!"

"No, you're not. And you're no damn saint either." One side of his mouth quirked up in that half-smile of his, and he lowered his gravelly voice to a speaking level. "And it's about time you accepted it."

"What do you want of me?" she asked coldly but without anger.

"I want you to admit it. Along with the fact that Maudie's is more to you than a means of support and independence. Admit that you want to know what the other side of your mother's and aunt's lives were like and to convince yourself that you really don't fit into it."

"You think you have me all figured out, don't you?"

"In this, yes" he answered confidently. "Can you really deny it?"

She stared at his eyes for a long moment, though they were no more than shadows in the dark. Then she turned back to the window and spoke quietly. "I can't deny it."

"I only want to help you, Irish," he said then, just as softly. "And I won't let you spoil what we started tonight with misplaced guilt. You let me worry about my bed and my whole damn house, for that matter. You don't see me losing sleep over the fact that I made love to you here. And you won't. What we did was a beautiful celebration of life, and I'll be damned if I'll let you think of it any other way. Now come back to bed."

"With you?" She faced him again.

"Of course with me. Who else? You gave me tonight and I'm not finished with it." He held out his hand for her.

She thought it over, weighing what kind of argument he'd put up if she refused, and finally she relented.

But too many truths had been revealed that night, and she found sleep wasn't easy to come by.

Chapter 14

Dawn came in pink and saffron rays to throw a rosy glow across the bed and the two people sleeping in it, curved around each other like spoons.

Zach was awakened by his arousal as Lauren pushed against him and nestled her warm rump more snugly into his lap. Lifting only his head he peered over at her and saw she was sound asleep, her face as smooth and guiltless as a child's. He let his head fall back, leaving one arm where it rested beneath her neck and raising the other across his eyes to block out the hazy light of dawn. He found it hard to push thoughts of Lauren from his mind and sleep eluded him.

Tomorrow morning she would leave. The house would be empty in a way it never had been before; Zach could feel it already. Loneliness was nothing new to him. He had been lonely most of his life. His plans and dreams of having a family had saved him more than once in his thirty-three years. A man needed a goal, and that had been his. This house was the final step; now he only required a woman to love whom he could bring here. He had enough money so he would never have to worry about providing for her. He even had enough experience to know he could settle down faithfully with just one woman and not regret it. But he hadn't met the one woman he wanted.

Was Lauren right about his being too persnickety? Did he expect too much? Maybe so. Just a little. You didn't dream for that many years without your hopes being raised mighty high. But then, hadn't he settled once before for a whole lot less than perfection? Molly Cade, pregnant with some other man's bastard, certainly hadn't fit the bill. Yet he had been about to marry her and bring her here to live, without feeling resentful or shortchanged. No, Lauren had been wrong about that, he assured himself.

And now there was Lauren. She was sure as hell not perfect. But he was experiencing feelings for her that he had never felt before. He just plain enjoyed her, for one thing. Nothing wrong with that. There weren't many women like Lauren—independent, levelheaded, strong, not looking to be petted or pampered. She could hold her own in most things, and he liked that too. You didn't see much of that in women, or at least they didn't let you see it.

Where are you going with this? he asked himself. Thinking about all the reasons he liked her was only going to make it worse when she left. Again the thought wrenched at his gut. She could be all-fired stubborn too, he argued. And all trussed up, inside and out. And what sass that woman could give you! Cantankerous was what she was. And uppity—why, there wasn't a nun alive who could look down her nose as well as Lauren could. What kind of a woman would that be to live with? She'd have him and all ten kids in rank and file.

Was he thinking about marrying Lauren? Oh, she'd like that, wouldn't she? She would accuse him of trying to fill the emptiness of the place. She had already said it.

So what about marrying Lauren?

The idea sat pretty well. Except for one thing. The

most important thing. He didn't think she loved him. And that was what kept the rest in check. He had promised himself that, especially after Molly. To make his plans work out the way he had pictured them all these years, the woman he chose had to love him. Dammit, he was entitled to that! Other people had love in their lives; they were born with it. Why shouldn't he be allowed the same? If he asked Lauren to marry him now he would never know if she had done it just to get away from Maudie's. She didn't need saving, her life didn't depend on it. If it had, it would be different. But for now he could afford to wait. She cared for him—he believed that— and that could grow. He would bide his time, wait for everything to resolve itself—the debt, her doubts about herself, and her curiosity about her background. And when it was all settled, he would be there. He was a patient man.

He rolled over tightly against her backside. Pulling his arm out from under her, he lifted his head up and sneaked the other hand around her. His fingertips reached to untie the ribbons of her nightgown, very slowly. He grinned at the thought of how deeply she slept and how he intended to take advantage of it. He slipped the worn cotton off one shoulder and down her arm, exposing her breast and a little of the shadow of a cinnamon-hued crest. He thought it was amazing she didn't wake up from the hard thrill that pushed back at her nesting rump. Instead she wriggled up against him in search of a comfortable spot, to avoid the prodding. Zach groaned low in his throat and then silently chuckled at himself. It took a steadying breath to pursue his course with stealth; he lowered his face to the inner curve of her shoulder to blow a faint, hot breath on her neck. Her answering sigh was replete, and again Zach grinned.

Tiny kisses came next, his lips barely touching her sleep-warmed flesh. He began at the bony point of her shoulder and followed nature's line to just below her ear, where he took a gentle nip of the lobe. Then he watched her face wrinkle into a frown, her head turning toward the source of the nuisance and then falling back.

He eased up carefully, leaning well over her to drop a light kiss on her breast. Then his index finger and thumb picked at her nightgown and pulled it to expose the whole beautiful globe to his appreciative eyes and questing hand. His assault became firm enough to awaken her; his play demanded her participation now.

Consciousness came slowly to her after only two hours of sleep. She felt heavy with fatigue. But there was something warm and nicely rough at her breast, squeezing gently and sending a flicker of sensation all the way to an answering openness between her legs. Never had she awakened with such a feeling of languid excitement, and after a moment she realized what it was. She eased a protective arm between her breast and Zach's hand, rolling onto her stomach as an added measure.

"You do have a penchant for tormenting me awake, don't you?" she said crossly, pushing her hips far into the mattress to appease the odd yearning he had roused.

"But this is sweet torment, remember?" he rasped, pulling her hair away to free the back of her neck for his seeking mouth. He reached below the sheet and rubbed his palm up the back of her thigh, lifting her nightgown up and over her rump to the small of her back. Then his hand slipped around to her side where her breast puffed out.

She inhaled deeply and let it out very slowly. "You are not a kind man, did you know that?"

His lips followed his hand to kiss the small bulge of breast beneath her arm. "I never claimed to be." He pushed the gown up and over her head and pulled her forward to remove it completely. Somehow Lauren managed to roll the sheet up with her and wrap it around her like a sarong, binding her chest flat. With a serene, smug expression, she lowered her arms across the sheet and smiled dreamily.

Zach kissed her bare forearms where they crossed and then just above at the base of her throat, chuckling at the challenge.

Her fine sable brows arched over her closed eyes and she said imperiously, "I don't recall signing on for more than one trip."

"Now that would be a shame after the waters were so rocky the first time out. You're staying aboard until I've proven how much smoother the ride can be." His voice was so low it was nearly a growl, and his lips played lightly over the surface of every inch of skin exposed to him.

"But I'm so tired," she complained as his teeth and tongue teased her shoulder. A determined hand tugged the sheet free to steal underneath, stopping just below her breasts, the tip of his thumb resting in the crevice between them, while his hand curved all the way around to her side.

"That's an invitation if ever I've heard one." His thumb brushed across the tightened nub of sensitized flesh again and again. Soft as a feather, he circled the outer rim and then the kerneled tip until it was taut with yearning, setting her aquiver with desire. But still she kept her eyes closed, her face bland, her arms crossed above her chest.

"Hmmm," he mused, "If not for the goose bumps and this little pucker in my hand I might think you were dead." He gave her nipple a playful little pinch and then without warning ripped the sheet down with one fluid movement.

Lauren bolted upright to retrieve it, but Zach was quicker; he laughed as he pushed her back into the mattress.

"Alive now, are we?" he teased, pressing half his length over her, one big hairy leg across the sable triangle of her womanhood.

Lauren pushed hard against his shoulder, but he simply grinned down at her as if he felt her effort not at all. "Allow me at least a little modesty," she demanded.

But Zach only laughed. "Not in *my* bed."

"You're not only unkind but evil as well."

His black gaze was devilish. "You'll come to love it," he said confidently. He covered her lips with an open-mouthed kiss. His tongue took stock, finding smooth teeth, the ridged roof of her mouth, and the soft insides of her lips, and finally settling for a quick thrust at her tongue. The hand at her ribs rose higher and again reached her desire-engorged breast. Then he lowered his mouth to its crest, and his tongue circled it as his thumb had before.

Again his mouth possessed hers hungrily. He rolled them both to lie on their sides, pulling her leg over his hip, his own thigh nudging between. His hand slid up and reached around to trace the natural contours of her most private parts from behind with the soft, whispering strokes of two fingers. The pleasure of it took her breath away, and incandescent flames seared from that spot upward until a fever heat burned away any inhibitions and she arched against him with a driving need.

Her mouth matched his urgency, and she clasped him to her with both hands. Her palms slid down his bulging shoulder blades to his tight ribs and narrow waist. Then down further, her fingers finding the firmness of his derriere, kneading it to nudge his lower body up against her own. Hazily, she suddenly realized what she was doing and her hands flew back up.

An understanding laugh rumbled in his throat and he pushed his hips harder into her. A frenzy of desire overtook Lauren, and she feverishly searched to find a way of telling him how great her need was to feel him inside her, but inexperience thwarted her and she thought she would die without finding the release she sought.

But Zach knew. Her straining, love-moist flesh invited it, her taut body and hungry mouth demanded it. And instinct answered as his flesh and his endurance stretched to their limits. Gentleness had no place in their frenetic exploration. He pushed her onto her back with the force of his own body and mounted her. The hard length of him sought entry and only when Lauren flinched in that first opening of her body did he remember she was still new to this.

Slowly, carefully, he entered, and waited in agony so as not to ruin her pleasure. Then just a bit more ...ah, but it was worth it to feel her arch in ecstasy and invite him nearer. Another thrust and he knew the perfection of the warm velvet sheathing him. And then it began, sinewy muscle driving in again, again, deeper, deeper, until kindled flames burst into white heat, each straining, striving, aiding the other until the final explosive release brought them a step nearer to earth, clinging to each other, their bodies so exquisitely entwined that every part was eased by the meeting and mixing of its counterpart.

This time when he left her he rolled her to her side so they faced each other, never allowing the distance to widen between them. He wrapped his leg around her, keeping her up against him tightly, molding them together to continue their perfect union in every other way. Lauren's cheek turned into his shoulder, and his chin rested against her hair; there they found the exhausted slumber of well-sated lovers.

Chapter 15

The noon sun was bright and hot before either stirred again. Lauren basked for a moment in the wonderful comfort of being naked in Zach's arms. Then she moved and soreness assailed her. She stifled a moan and eased herself carefully to the edge of the bed, but was stopped short as Zach caught at a handful of the silky sable hair that fell down her back.

"Don't sneak off again, Irish. I have better plans for you." He stretched out an index finger to trace the bumps of her spine, his eyes still closed.

"Oh, no." she answered firmly. "That's all for me."

He laughed, his face half in the pillow as he lay flat on his stomach as if still asleep. "That bad, huh?"

"Worse."

He turned over, pulling her back with a gentle tug of her hair. "Then lie here a minute, and when I can move I'll fix you a hot bath."

She couldn't refuse that offer and lowered herself painstakingly to the pillow beside him, covering herself with the sheet. A few minutes passed, and she thought he had fallen asleep again. Then he groaned and arched his spine. Slowly he opened his eyes and finally braced his head up on one hand, grinning lazily down at her. His hair was mussed, his face dark with whiskers and smooth with contented pleasure.

Lauren frowned up at him. "Somehow this doesn't seem fair. You aren't the least bit sore, are you?"

"Not the least." His grin widened.

"You needn't be so smug about it."

"Actually, I'm disappointed. I had other plans for today. I wasn't going to let you out of bed at all. But since you're not up to it..." One black brow arched in question, but Lauren squelched the idea with a firm shake of her head. "Maybe a day at Lake Washington will keep my hands off you. At least until tonight."

Without waiting for an answer, Zach swung his feet off the bed. Lauren watched his firm, narrow rump as he went to the bureau for pants. She wondered at the slight disappointment she felt when she drew them on. But he was intent on preparing her bath, and she welcomed the respite.

The steamy hot water at first stung her sorely abused parts as she lowered herself into the tub in the bathing closet off Zach's room. She sank deeper so that her neck rested against the high back, with her hair piled in disarray on top of her head. She closed her eyes and let the water rejuvenate her.

Zach made no sound as he leaned against the doorway, a coffee mug in one hand. The sight of Lauren lounging in the bath warmed him. It was as good as anything he had ever imagined to wake with her in his bed, within reach, and share a lazy morning. He stood watching for a long while, wondering if he should do something to keep her from going to Maudie's after all. But his gut instinct told him to wait. With regret he left her to her privacy, without her knowing he had been there.

* * *

They took his two-seater buggy through town and
out to Lake Washington. Most of Seattle spent Sunday there, so the beaches were well populated. Pic-
nickers spread their blankets and feasted on cold
fried chicken and potato salad or purchased fresh
boiled crab, oysters, or scallops; lemonade and cold
beer could be had for a few pennies.

Children erected grand sand castles, searched for
treasures on the gray beaches, or waded in the shal-
low water at their edge, not far from their cautious
parents. Parasols shaded straw-hatted ladies, and
men took off their Sunday-best jackets, rolled up
their sleeves above their elbows, and loosened their
tight neckties to bask in the sunshine.

Zach wore a cream-colored suit that fit his lean
body with well-tailored perfection, with a matching
vest and yellow shirt. He had loosened his silk four-
in-hand tie soon after they arrived, but not until they
had been out in the sun for a time did he remove his
coat and sling it over one shoulder. He was clean-
shaven, and his hair shone with iron blue highlights;
he combed it back with careless fingers when it fell
forward, as it often did when he slanted a downward
glance at his companion.

Lauren felt an odd pride in being seen with him.
There was a radiant feminity about her that was the
direct result of his warm attention and the glint she
saw in his eyes when she peeked up at him from beneath the small brim of her straw hat.

They strolled along the beach and rested in the
coolness of the trees that grew just beyond the sandy
expanse but still within sight of the cerulean water.
Memories came back to Lauren of Sundays spent
much like this one, when Maudie or her mother
would come to Stockton and take her out of the convent to stay at the little cottage. Only now there was
Zach, his arm ever at her waist or a big hand reach-

ing for hers to slip it into the crook of his elbow. She felt complete, unalloyed joy, without once thinking that people were watching the whore's daughter. She laughed openly at Zach's teasing, letting all her self-consciousness go.

This was a new side of Lauren, and Zach liked it. She was easy and confident, fresh as a young girl but tempered with a wit all her own.

They sat on a bench to hear the band concert late in the afternoon. Lauren leaned back against Zach comfortably, liking the feel of his arm across her collarbone and his hand at her shoulder holding her to him.

Afterward they stayed on to watch the sun set in a last burst of orange and yellow that left everything earthbound looking like flat black silhouettes against it. Darkness had fallen completely by the time they reached their buggy, and only a few people were left waiting for the last cable car back to Seattle.

In town the round globes of the tall iron street-lamps glowed and, in the Sunday night lull, everything seemed to move at a slower pace. They passed people sitting on porch steps, coy young lovers searching for a moment's privacy, children chasing fireflies, and neighbors exchanging end-of-the-week gossip. All the people who, come tomorrow night, Lauren thought forlornly, would revile her.

When they finally reached the stone bridge and Zach's house came into view, they saw a carriage waiting in front. "Looks like we have company," he observed.

"Were you expecting someone?"

"Not that I know of. How about you?"

Lauren was about to answer when they drew near enough for her to recognize the visitor. All her joy in the day dissolved.

"Alan." She breathed the name so softly that Zach barely heard it, and he wondered whether it was affection or dread that caused her reaction. For himself, he was none too pleased by this particular surprise. He felt Lauren push as far back into the seat's shadow as she could and comprehension dawned.

"He didn't know why you were coming to Seattle, did he?"

"Only that I had inherited a business—not what kind," she whispered.

And he certainly wouldn't expect you to be living alone with a man, Zach finished to himself. But there wasn't anything to be done about it now, so he patted her knee reassuringly and pulled to a stop behind Alan Bentley's carriage. Lauren must have come to the same conclusion, he thought, because he felt her draw herself up straight and stiff and knew she was steeling herself to face him.

"Mr. Madox!" Alan called, waving as if he might be overlooked otherwise. "I hope you don't mind my being here." It was his nature to apologize before he was even acknowledged.

"I'll be right there, Alan," Zach answered impatiently, as if he were speaking to a child. He reached into the shadowed interior of the buggy and closed steadying hands around Lauren's waist. He had to acknowledge her courage, because she didn't hesitate to let him lift her into view.

But it wasn't until they had reached the steps that Alan recognized her; the shock threw him into a nervous dither. "Laur...Lauren? Is that you?"

"It is, Alan." She put a calming hand on his arm without thinking and then realized she had always treated Alan somewhat like a child herself.

"What are you doing here?" he asked, staring at her. He seemed to have forgotten Zach.

"I might ask you the same," she said and sent a sidelong glance to Zach.

"Oh, well." Alan cleared his throat, remembering his purpose and his manners, and turned to his host.

"I'm sorry, Mr. Madox. I know you didn't expect me for some time yet, but my father found out that I'd been dealing with you, and I couldn't stay in Dry Creek."

"It's all right, Alan. Shall we go into the house?" Zach gestured to Lauren to precede them.

She unpinned her straw hat and set it on a side table in the entrance and then began to light the lamps in the parlor. Alan watched her, noting her familiarity with the house, and found himself baffled.

Zach decided to let Lauren herself explain the situation to her former suitor. "I'll make us all some coffee and see if I can't find that cake left from yesterday," he offered and waited for a sign from Lauren that she wanted him to stay. She only smiled and nodded her assent, so he retreated to the kitchen but not out of earshot.

"Lauren?" the simple word was question enough.

She sat stiff-backed in a wing chair and took a deep breath. "Sit down, Alan, and I'll explain."

He did, and for a moment Lauren just studied the plain, smooth-skinned face across from her. He was the only true friend she had ever had. He had believed in her innocence in the face of Dry Creek's suspicions and his father's accusations. Now it seemed she would confirm what they had all thought of her and make him seem foolish.

"I came to Seattle on the train with Zach." She forged ahead with the story of her business having burned down and Zach taking her in and lending her the money to rebuild. Then she waited for the questions.

"Where are you staying?"

"Here. I couldn't ask for more money from Zach for lodgings. He was kind enough to put me up." In the kitchen Zach wondered why she was protecting him.

"I guess we're both lucky to have met up with him," Alan said obliquely. "Will it be long before your business is ready to open?"

Lauren swallowed thickly; if she had been speaking to anyone else but Alan, she would have been much more at ease and self-assured. "Tomorrow, as a matter of fact."

"Will you still live here until it gets going?"

"No; I'll be living there."

"You haven't told me what the business is, Lauren. Will you have rooms above a shop or something?"

"Don't think badly of me, Alan," she said softly. "I inherited a brothel. I'll be living there."

"Oh, Lauren, no." Disappointment and dismay were evident in his voice, and in the kitchen Zach's heart wrenched for Lauren.

"It's a living, Alan," she said quietly. "I'll be the proprietor, that's all."

"Will you really?" he asked ironically.

Lauren sighed and tilted her chin in serene confidence. "Yes, I really will. Your father was wrong about me and still is. I'm not what my mother was."

"But you're living here with Mr. Madox."

"Yes, I am," she reconfirmed simply. Zach decided it was time to rescue her, so he picked up a laden tray and left the kitchen.

"I hired Lauren as my housekeeper until her house was ready, Alan," he said as he appeared in the parlor doorway carrying a tray, which Lauren gratefully took from him. "So..." he said, changing the subject as Lauren poured coffee and served cake, and thus ending Alan's inquisition, "I haven't told Lauren about our dealings."

Alan smiled sadly but acknowledged the end of the discussion by answering, "It's not a secret anymore. There's no need to protect me now." He faced Lauren. "My father had one of his underhanded ideas to make himself more money. He was going to buy out all the minor stockholders in Mr. Madox's railroad until he controlled a major portion. Then he intended to sell out to the competitors for a stiff profit. I knew what he was planning, and I saw what he was doing to you. I couldn't help you, but I could strike back at him about the other matter. So I told Mr. Madox what he was doing."

Zach took up the story. "Alan saved us from a potential catastrophe. I needed time to warn the board of directors about what was going on in order to take steps to prevent it. I've been buying out anyone who is tempted to sell to Bentley."

Alan finished his story: "Mr. Madox offered to help me start a life of my own, away from my father, in return. That's why I'm here."

"How did the old man find out?" Zach asked.

"One of the men he approached told him to whom he had sold his stock. It was easy enough for my father to put it all together. He knew how angry I was about what he had done to Lauren."

"Was he very hard on you?" Lauren asked with obvious concern.

"No more than usual. He took a whip to me and then threw me out of his house. Luckily, I had a little money hidden away, enough to get here and pay for my room and board for awhile."

"You do have a place to stay, then?" Under other circumstances Zach would have offered Alan his hospitality, but he didn't want Lauren's last night with him ruined by Alan Bentley's presence.

"I've taken a room in a boardinghouse in town. I was going to start looking for Lauren tomorrow to see if we might pool our resources." He looked dubious about it now.

"Why don't you come to Maudie's with me?" she offered hesitantly, fearing the reaction of both men. "I need a piano player, and you're so talented at that. I couldn't pay much to start, but it would give you a

place to stay and some time to decide what you want
to do."

Zach frowned darkly. His gravelly voice inter-
vened while Alan was still weighing the suggestion.
"He doesn't have to do that, Lauren. I said I'd take
care of this, and I will."

Alan broke in, thinking out loud: "It would give
me time to consider the possibilities. After all, it's my
whole future I'm choosing. I wouldn't want to make
a mistake. I've never even been in a brothel before."

"Good point!" Zach interjected. "I have any
number of businesses you can try your hand at before you decide."

"But at least we'd be together, wouldn't we?" Alan
asked Lauren, who was aware of Zach's attempt to
dissuade him. "I think it's a fine idea!" he concluded,
and Zach's jaw worked angrily. "Just give me the address and I'll be there whenever you say."

Lauren smiled wanly but wrote out the information and then walked him to the door. Alan took her
hand, his pale eyes staring into hers earnestly. "You
honestly aren't ... one of those?"

"I'm honestly not." But it disappointed her that he
wouldn't have accepted her if she were. "I'll need
tomorrow to settle in myself, Alan. Would it be all
right if you waited to come until Tuesday?"

"Whatever you say, Lauren." He left reassured
and she watched him go, unaware of Zach standing
in the parlor doorway.

"I don't know whether to be raving mad at you for
hiring him, or at him for hurting you," he said to her
back.

"There's no need for either." She turned and went
to gather up the cups and dishes from the parlor,
keeping her eyes turned away from his.

"Why the hell did you do it?"

"He's my friend, Zach. In a way he's in this mess

because of me." She set the china in the sink and Zach doused the lamps.

"Is he more than that?" he asked angrily as he climbed the stairs behind her.

"No," she retorted, passing his room and heading toward hers. Zach yanked her back.

"In here, lady," he ordered. "You have me riled and I'd like to paddle your backside, but my anger won't last all night."

Lauren laughed a little at that. She crossed his room to stand at the window. She could just see Alan's carriage off in the distance. "I love Alan as if he were my brother. Maybe better, because we chose each other. He is my friend, my beloved friend. To say he is nothing more sounds silly, because he means so much to me. But there is no passion in it, nor any kind of man-woman feelings."

"Then why were you run out of Dry Creek for wanting to marry him?"

"I never said I *wanted* to marry him, just that he had asked. Even that was an act of friendship. He knew I was in dire straits and it seemed the best solution to my problems. Much like your situation with Molly Cade, I suppose."

"Except that his solution put you in a worse predicament. Bentley might not have run you out of town if Alan hadn't opted for marriage."

"I think he would have. Alan's proposal was just the last straw. He had wanted my mother and me both out long before she died. We soiled his perfect little town. As for Alan, he meant well. He was just never able to judge what his father might actually do. I suppose he hoped right up until the end that Bentley would prove to be less of a villian. Alan hasn't had much kindness in his life. He always tried his best to please the old man, but it was never enough. I'm glad you're going to help him," she finished.

Zach came up close beside her. One big hand

cupped the nape of her neck to pull her head to his chest. His thumb rubbed her neck soothingly and he dropped his face into her hair. "I wish he hadn't been so hard on you," he said gruffly.

"He didn't mean anything by it," she answered softly. "Besides, disapproval of the life I will be leading is something I will become accustomed to again." And gratefully she allowed Zach to comfort her and ease the old pain.

Chapter 16

Maudie's was a palace of red velvet and gold, at once tasteful and garish. Lauren took over the only space bare of whorehouse decor: the large attic room. It was an open area divided into bedroom and sitting room only by a bed and nighttable at one wall and a blue sofa and a chair before a carved fireplace at another.

Zach carted her trunk up and set it at the foot of the spool bed, waiting until Lauren was busy elsewhere to bring in another good-sized valise that he stashed on the left side of the bed. She had had white wallpaper dotted with tiny blue flowers hung on the walls, and crisp white curtains with lace ruffles framed the box windows. It was a bright haven from the dark red and gold of the rest of the house...and a room obviously meant for a lone woman. The thought made Zach grin as he went to find Madam Flannery.

Lauren stood in the foyer beneath the huge crystal chandelier, straight and stiff and quietly iron-willed. "I do not care how much money this could mean. I will not allow it in my house."

"You here alone, dearie?" asked a nasal, insinuating voice just before Zach hit the bottom steps.

"No, she isn't alone," he answered with deceptive congeniality.

Standing in front of Lauren was a dwarf dressed in a black sack coat, striped trousers, a gray double-breasted waistcoat, and a silk cravat tied high on a slack neck. He carried a silk hat and gold-headed cane. Behind him loomed a man twice his size and three times his girth, with a face that looked as if a meat pounder had been taken to it.

"Mr. Madox, isn't it?" The small man smiled around gray teeth. "I heard you were in on this place, but the lady tells me she owns it," he finished condescendingly.

"She does," Zach answered smoothly enough.

The dwarf laughed. "Well, she needs a few lessons in business. Maybe you can explain to her about how things work around here."

"I'd be happy to." Zach turned to Lauren and said instructively, "Unless I'm mistaken, I believe this is Big Jim, one of our city's leading crimps, and his muscleman, Max. Now a crimp, Lauren, recruits crews for lumber ships. You see, the twenty dollars a month and slops are not enough incentive for a man to join one of the crews of these ships, and so businessmen like Big Jim here help out. A few knock-out drops in a prospective sailor's drink and the whole system prospers—isn't that how it's done?" He smiled, but it didn't reach his eyes.

"Simple as that, and the lady gets a fair cut."

"The lady," Lauren said in clipped tones, "has no intention of complying with such a practice."

Zach shrugged and shook his head in mock sympathy for Big Jim's failure. "There you have it, gentlemen. Better luck with the next house."

"I don't think you two understand how much weight I pull around these parts," Big Jim said as the muscular Max took a step closer.

"No sir, you're wrong about that," Zach contradicted him genially, moving carelessly to the desk that was to be the bouncer's station. "Your reputation is well known. You're a shrewd man, Big Jim. You're known to be cunning and wily and deadly when it suits you." As unobtrusively as possible, he pulled a pistol from the desk drawer and then leveled it at the little man's chest. He continued in the same pleasant tones: "You serve as the unfortunately necessary middleman . . . but not in this house." He smiled amicably. "Don't come around here again or you're a dead man."

Big Jim set his hat on his overlarge head, tapping it once to angle it jauntily. He matched Zach's grin. "Your loss. But don't be too sure we're finished with this." He turned slowly and left at an awkward gait.

"Maybe I should hire you as my bouncer," Lauren said when the door was firmly closed behind them.

"Too late. I hired your cook's husband an hour ago when she came in to fix our dinner."

"Our dinner?" One fine brow arched.

"Yours, mine, his and hers," he affirmed as he replaced the gun in the desk drawer.

Lauren let it pass. She dreaded the time when he would leave to go home. The only place in the whole of Maudie's that she felt comfortable in was her attic.

"Did my aunt go along with shanghaiing?" she asked curiously.

"Not Maudie. She ran a clean house. Not much different than this." His black eyes scanned the place.

"Do you ship your lumber on boats that acquire their men that way?"

"I own my own ships, Irish, and I make damn sure to keep conditions pleasant and profitable enough to enable me to hire on all the men I need."

She laughed lightly. "I should have known." Then she paused a moment and her humor evaporated. The details she had been putting off had to be faced.

"Are you ready to teach me how my business will operate?"

"Are you ready to learn?" he asked dubiously. He had been suggesting it to her since early that morning.

"Since we open tomorrow night, I think I'd better," she said resignedly. It was the final step not only in taking control of the place; it was also the last thing she required of Zach.

They entered the office, an austere room with a big desk, wood-paneled walls, and three leather chairs. Zach had intended to use it himself, so it lacked any feminine accents or whorehouse decor. He sat behind the desk and Lauren stood beside him to be able to look into each drawer as he pulled it out and explained its contents.

"I've set it up the same as Maudie ran the place. Here are your brass checks." He opened a side drawer that held metal tokens. "Customers buy them from you and then pass them along to the girls who settle up the next morning. The house takes half, and the girls get to keep any tips. They should also get a cut on the drinks; it's incentive for them to push the liquor. They'll pay you rent and dress themselves, and you pay expenses: salaries for maids, cook, bouncer, bartender, and piano player. That's all been taken care of for a month. The account books are here." He opened drawers in succession. "Keys in this one, cash box here, and derringer in here. All you have to do is set your prices."

"I haven't any idea of what to charge," she said simply.

"Maudie's girls went for fifty to a hundred dollars each customer. That'll keep out the riffraff and the brawls to a minimum, though nothing prevents them altogether. I think the place and the girls we've hired can command that much."

"Men will actually pay that much...for this?" She was dumbfounded.

"They will here."

Lauren paced the room, her arms wrapped tightly about her waist. Now that they were down to business, she was afraid and nervous and embarrassed, and she didn't know how she was going to manage. "Did Maudie like this life?" she had to ask.

Zach sat back and watched her. "She didn't dislike it, Lauren. As you've said twice now, it was a living."

"Did she take customers herself while she was here?"

"At first, but only selectively. Then she got sick and stopped."

"I never knew what brought them both to the life. I do know there was a man my mother loved dearly when she was young and he hurt her badly."

"Money brought Maudie to it. She said she had a family to support and no other way to do it," he answered quietly.

"My mother was the only family she had...and then me." She turned to Zach, staring levelly at him, "Do you think after awhile I'll understand?"

He shook his head. "Not completely."

"It worries me, you know, the way you and I are."

"They are two separate things, Irish."

"Are they? I wonder if you're the kind of man to break fragile hearts and leave me feeling the way my mother did."

"I didn't know there was anything about yourself that you would admit was fragile."

"There isn't much."

"Not much you'd admit, but there's plenty that's fragile."

She laughed mirthlessly. "I can't afford to be."

"Tell me something, Lauren." He watched her closely. "What would you say if I asked you to marry me?"

She stopped short at that, looking closely at him to see if he was teasing her. "Are you asking?" she said dubiously.

He shrugged, not sure himself. "I've been thinking about it this past week. I didn't want you to come here."

There was no mention of his feelings for her, if he had any, and because of that her answer was different than it might otherwise have been. "I'd say that was no basis for marriage. You'd never know if I married you just to clear my debt. I'd never know if you did it to get a hold of Maudie's after all, or just out of pity. I'd wonder if you felt you had lost out because you settled on less than what you've been dreaming about all these years. You'd wonder if I did it out of guilt to prove I'm not my mother's daughter." She shook her head. "I guess I'd say no."

"And what if that broke my heart?"

Now she thought she understood. He was just postulating, probably to teach her another lesson. "Male hearts don't break."

"That's not true. In fact, it's a lot of nonsense. We're all made of the same stuff, Irish, and my heart's as fragile as yours, I guarantee it."

There it was. The point he wanted to make was that he was as vulnerable as she. But Lauren didn't believe it and only smiled knowingly.

They ate at a small table set at one side of the attic room. The new cook passed the test of her talents with a wine-laced stew and fresh bread. Conversation between Zach and Lauren was again about business —how she would settle the girls in the following morning and organize the opening to the last detail.

Afterward, when the table was cleared and the cook complimented, Lauren felt a surge of panic at the thought of Zach leaving. It brought her mother's warnings about a woman needing any man to her mind.

But instead of going, he locked up after the cook and then did the honors himself at the front door. He blew out the red glass parlor lamp, signifying the house was closed for the night, and waited for Lauren at the foot of the massive walnut staircase.

"What are you doing?" she asked, afraid to hope.

"You don't think I'm going to let you stay in this place alone, do you? Anybody could break in to get you started a night early."

"Are you sure that isn't what you have in mind?"

"I'm not a customer, lady. What's between us is not business, no matter where it happens." He gripped her arm firmly and started up the stairs. "Besides, it will help you look more human to your girls and not have them figuring you're a virgin madam."

Lauren stopped to look him in the eye. "Do you mean to take up permanent residence here?"

He grinned. "Let's just say I'm in for quite a visit." He pulled her the rest of the way up to the attic room and bolted the door securely behind them.

She felt a welling up of relief. She told herself she would worry about the future later. But for now, she would have Zach awhile longer.

He stood near the door, watching her with a slight grin. The creamy glow of the only lighted lamp touched his strikingly handsome face, deepening the hollows of his cheeks and making his nose seem narrower, his eyes blacker. He wore a plain white shirt with a short, banded collar that opened into a small V where wiry black hair curled at his throat. His faded jeans were snug over his narrow hips and massive, rock-hard thighs. He made short work of removing the shirt, baring his flat belly and broad-shouldered chest.

Lauren's eyes were on him as he crossed to where she stood beside the bed. His thick fingers unbuttoned the fly of his denims, leaving yet another V to hint at what nestled beneath in shadow, and her lips curved into a slow smile.

He sat back on the bed and extended a booted foot her way. "Give a yank, will you, Irish?" his voice rasped.

"I look like a boot jack to you, do I?" she said, pretending to be piqued.

"You look like the woman I can't wait to get my hands on. Would you rather I leave my pants around my ankles and my boots on to dirty your sheets and just flip your skirt up over your head?" He raised his expressive brows comically.

"What an uncivilized suggestion," she replied with mock hauteur.

"And not nearly as nice as what I have in mind." He raised his foot again and Lauren complied with an exaggerated sigh. While she wrestled with the second boot, he pushed his bare foot lightly against her rump and let it remain to rub up and down the firm curve. "Does this mean you want it civilized tonight?"

"How have I had it before?" she countered innocently, and Zach laughed at her unaccustomed boldness.

"Pretty civilized; want to try the other?"

She dropped his boot and turned an assessing eye his way, her hands on her hips. "If you throw my skirt over my head I'll cut your visit short."

He stood up, so close to her they nearly touched; his face laughed down into hers. "Never that."

He turned her around and gently pulled the pins from her hair, freeing it to cascade down her back and then fingering the silken fall slowly. Then, when she least expected it, swift hands gripped the collar of her gown and ripped the worn gingham down the front with one yank, baring her practical chemise and petticoat.

She gasped in shocked outrage, staring down at

herself, but Zach only laughed. "I've been wanting to do that since we met." Seizing the advantage he'd gained by his surprise attack, he finished the job with her underthings, leaving torn petticoats at her feet and her gown and chemise hanging like ragged curtains framing a patch of creamy skin and a triangle of sable curls.

Her topaz eyes widened and she reached for his open waistband with retribution in mind. But her small hands succeeded only in pulling his jeans lower on his hips and freeing his desire for her.

In turn, Zach slid his hands under her torn clothing to smooth them away from her shoulders. "Patience, Irish, patience," he teased. With a husky growl he again took her unawares, lifting, swinging, and dropping her to the bed all in one fluid motion before she knew what had happened. He pulled his jeans off in one motion, and he bounded on top of her, pinning her to the mattress.

"How do you like barbarianism so far?"

"Being a fiend comes quite naturally to you, doesn't it?"

"Mmm," he admitted with another growl as his mouth took hers in mock violence that instead soothed her with the balm of his sweet passion.

His lips were soft and wet and slippery. His hands explored her with callused gentleness, and his body surged with power contained in the long, sinewy column of his manhood.

Her mouth opened for his tongue, her teeth nipped his slackened lips, her back arched to his hand, and she was all pliant warmth and tender searching.

The bed was a cushion of down that swelled up and wrapped them in a cloud. Only their senses spoke, and their hearts joined and flew and kept secrets that cooler heads would reason away.

Chapter 17

The first day at Maudie's began with the arrival of Neddie and Josef Brown, cook and bouncer at the crack of dawn. Three housemaids set to work, the bartender checked his stock and arranged his bar, and fifteen of Seattle's loveliest ladies of the evening appeared with trunks and baggage and loud voices.

Zach disappeared with the first arrival and left Lauren to learn very quickly on her own that a madam had to be a confident, motherly figure with an iron hand. Her staff was volatile and raucous and quick to argue, and Lauren had to set boundaries and establish her authority as head of Maudie's in those first hours. She was too busy and too harrassed to worry about whether or not she did it right.

Alan was the last to arrive. He stood just inside the front door, his pale eyes nearly popping from their sockets and his mouth gaping wide in astonishment.

Lauren looked up from giving instructions to Polly Carson to see him rooted to the spot. He caught sight of her then, but his eyes traveled to Polly and suddenly sparkled. He drew himself up and made fast work of the distance between them. Lauren was momentarily stunned by his obvious appreciation of the young blond girl, who seemed a more likely candidate for an ice cream social than a whorehouse.

Alan pressed a kiss on Lauren's cheek and whispered, "Would you introduce us?"

Lauren eyed Polly Carson, seeing that she was more than interested in Alan, and she was further astonished when the girl's cheeks colored a robust pink. "Alan Bentley, meet Polly Carson," she murmured, and then, worrying that he had somehow gotten the wrong impression, felt obliged to add, "Polly is one of the girls."

It didn't seem to matter to him. "I can see that you're busy, Lauren." Still his eyes stayed on Polly. "Perhaps Miss Carson can show me to my room."

"It's Polly, please," requested the girl in a tone of voice very unlike the one Lauren had heard from her before. It was as if she had dropped her facade.

Alan's grin was crooked. "Polly, then. It suits you."

Lauren cleared her throat. "Alan is our piano player. His room is three doors down from yours on the right," she informed them. Alan finally tore his eyes away from Polly and smiled at Lauren beatifically.

"I think I'm going to like it here better than I thought. Thank you for hiring me." And off he and Polly went, chattering as if they were long-time friends.

Lauren stared after them, thinking that she had never known anyone to make such a quick and strong impression on Alan.

By late afternoon the house calmed down once more, though never again would it be as still as it had been the previous night. Each girl was given time to eat her dinner and dress for the evening, and Lauren escaped to her own refuge. She sank into her private bathtub, which was hidden behind a plain white dressing screen in a corner of the attic.

When the key turned in her lock, Lauren didn't budge until Zach flicked a fingerful of water in her face, and then she just raised one lid to stare at his crooked grin and appreciate how handsome he was.

"Serious doubt has been raised about your courage, Mr. Madox," she said pointedly. "Leaving here today of all days was a distinct act of cowardice."

He laughed. "Looks like you did pretty well on your own, Irish. Everything all set?"

"Uh-huh." Her eyelid slid shut again.

"How is Madam Flannery holding up?"

"Not too badly. In fact, it's all been somewhat exciting."

"Oh?" He wasn't pleased to hear that, but comforted himself with the fact that real whorehouse life hadn't yet begun. "I brought dinner up. Why don't you get out of there and we'll eat before you dress?"

"I'll be right there." She was so self-satisfied that Zach wondered if he should have stayed around all day and run things so that she wouldn't be feeling so sure of herself.

In fact, Lauren was now feeling not altogether bad about Maudie's and her place in it. Everything had been set into motion, and she expected it to proceed with dignity and discretion. She had it in mind to approach this evening and all future evenings as if she were the overseer of a grand, sophisticated salon, blessedly oblivious to the sporadic disappearance of girls and their guests upstairs.

"My God, Lauren, you look like the cat that ate the canary," Zach observed across a dinner she barely touched. "I take it that you're happy with life as a madam?"

"It really isn't so bad," she answered smugly.

"Isn't it?" He was getting very good at deflecting the secret smile she used on him; only one of his brows arched high this time.

"No, it isn't."

"I guess we'll just have to wait and see about it when you really get started."

"I really started today."

He laughed. "All you did was get everybody moved in, Irish. This place won't be a whorehouse until tonight, and you won't be a madam till then either," he warned.

"You want me to fail," she said accusingly.

"I don't want you taken off guard, that's all. It hasn't even begun yet. For awhile everyone will be on their best behavior, but it won't last, and if you get too cocky about it there could be real trouble."

"I am never cocky," she answered cockily. "What I am is sure I can run this house. Perhaps you were hoping I'd fail so you could take over after all. Or maybe you just want me begging at your feet for your benevolence."

He frowned up at her, the hollows in his cheeks deepening with annoyance. "I could have made you beg before if that's what I was after. Or I could have just kept the place and sent you on down to Skid Row. What I'm saying is that I want you to be careful and keep your eyes open. You still don't know what the hell you've taken on here."

"You forget my background."

"No, you do. You're 'background' is a convent, not a whorehouse."

She had no retort, so she sought refuge in sarcastic formality. "Thank you, Mr. Madox. I'm sure it will amuse you to watch me make this place thrive."

"I'm sure it'll be entertaining as hell," he answered derisively. "And if you call me Mr. Madox one more time I'm going to beat your bare backside!" he ended with a shout and they each vented their fury in dressing for the coming evening.

But the confidence that had withstood Zach's words was soon shaken.

Lauren had watched her mother pile her hair into towering curls often enough, but now, when she arranged her own hair similarly, she hated her reflection. She brushed it free again and settled on a slightly fancier version of her usual staid coil at the back of her head, which she achieved by pulling a few tendrils free and allowing them to drift coyly around her face.

The dress was worse yet. It was red taffeta, with large flounces that barely covered the peaks of her breasts; the corset beneath pushed them upward so they looked like two ripe melons ready to roll out. The hem was nearly as bad; the back didn't even reach her ankles, and the front swooped up nearly to her thighs. Black net hose with black and red ribboned garters were the clincher.

Lauren stood staring at herself in the cheval mirror and was sickened by the sight. Above that costume her face was pale and her hair much too sedate; she looked like just what she was, a woman wearing clothes that didn't belong to her.

From his vantage point lounging on the blue sofa, Zach watched the play of emotions across her face—distaste, embarrassment, and then an agony of shame for this manifestation of her mother. He kept quiet about it, fearing that in her present mood anything he said might goad her into wearing the hated, unsuitable costume.

She disappeared behind the screen a second time, and when she came out she was dressed in the outfit he had bought for her. She stood before the mirror again, smoothing her burgundy skirt and straightening the high choker collar of the sheer blouse.

He waited until they had left the room and then in

his gravelly voice he said very, very gently, "You see, Irish, you're still in for some big surprises."

Maudie's doors were unlocked to receive a large group of men, all dressed in their best, whether it was tailcoat or suede jacket and string tie. In the parlor doorways the women lounged, garbed in off-the-shoulder gowns much like the one Lauren had discarded, garish and scant, with flowers in their hair and an abundance of cheap jewelry, paint, and powder.

Lauren descended the stairs to greet a foyer full of anxious customers with dignity, elegance, and quiet poise, thus setting the tone for her house.

"Good evening, gentlemen." She addressed them as if she had been doing it for years. "Welcome to Maudie's. Our house rules are much the same as before; we run a nice, clean place here. No rowdiness will be tolerated, and you may purchase brass checks from me and drinks from the girls. The first round is on the house."

In the parlor Alan struck up a lively tune on the piano, and one of the girls picked up the melody and improvised lyrics. Maudie's was back in business.

Zach watched from above as Lauren entered the office like a duchess, amid the appreciative joviality of her audience. He shook his head at the spectacle and made his way downstairs to the bar, ignoring the bawdy invitations and long-nailed hands that smoothed the navy blue serge of his suit. He leaned against the oak bar until his scotch was served. Only after a hearty swallow of the stuff did he follow Lauren into the office, taking a place behind her chair to see for himself how Madam Flannery went about her business.

In they came, some customers cowed and embarrassed, hair mussed from snatching hats off; some

brash and bold, swaggering and flaunting large wads
of bills or plump coin purses; some arrogant, aristo-
cratic, and blasé as they all faced Lauren's desk and
paid without blinking an eye at the high cost.

"I'll take you, little honey." It happened at about
the twentieth man, a cowboy out celebrating his
birthday. He was dressed up for the occasion, his big
ten-gallon hat pushed way back on his head.

Zach come to attention, but he waited to see how
Lauren would handle the situation.

She smiled brilliantly at the man, and her low
voice answered with a pleasant firmness that brooked
no argument. "Why, thank you. But any one of my
girls will make this a night for you to remember."

The cowboy laughed heartily and left, and Zach
shook his head. That one had been too easy and
wasn't likely to instill the caution she would need
toward those who wouldn't be so easily put off.

The night wore on, the music went on without
pause, liquor was guzzled, and the maids worked in
an unobtrusive frenzy collecting empty glasses, wip-
ing spills, and keeping fruit dishes full and china spi-
toons empty. Lauren oversaw it all—kitchen, bar,
gambling salon, dancing—everything but what went
on upstairs.

Zach found a spot near the piano, and stood there
nursing a succession of scotches and keeping an intent eye on her.

"She's a wonder, isn't she?" Alan marveled, his
own gaze following her.

"She is that," Zach agreed politely.

"She's more to you than a housekeeper, isn't she?"

Zach's glance was hostile as he answered with a
warning note in his voice, "Considerably."

Alan seized what little courage he had and ventured: "Then why are you letting her do this? If I
had the means I'd keep her from it."

Zach gave a short, derisive sigh, "It's not that simple, Alan. What I am doing is sticking close to make sure she has her taste of independence, but I'm going to try to make sure that it's not too foul," he confided.

"Then it's true that you're staying here, in her room?" Alan asked so softly it was barely audible over the music he was playing.

Zach's brows furrowed in surprise. "It's true," he said flatly. "Did Lauren tell you?"

Alan shrugged. "No. I...I've struck up a friendship with Polly Carson, and she told me they're all wondering what Lauren is. No one figures she's a whore, but the cook said you spent last night here alone together. I didn't think her being your housekeeper had anything to do with that," he added wickedly.

Zach's black eyes settled on Alan thoughtfully, sizing him up. "Are we competing for her?" he asked straight out.

Alan looked sheepish as he caught a quick glimpse of Polly, and he answered, "No. But I don't want to see you hurt her, either. She doesn't belong here, and you could take her away from it."

"It was her choice, Alan. I'll grant you that I made it possible, but it's what she wants." Zach's eyes glided around the room until they located Lauren again. "She's hell-bent to do this, and until she gets it out of her system there's no sense fighting her." When he looked at Alan again it was to find Alan's pale eyes following Polly in much the same way his had searched out Lauren. "Seems to me," Zach broke in, "that you're taking up with another female. Why not leave Lauren to me?"

Alan had the good grace to laugh at himself, but he didn't back down, "I still mean to look out for Lauren," he warned Zach, although he felt it was fruitless in the face of Zach's decisive strength.

"You do that, Alan," Zach said, amused. "God knows even two of us probably won't be enough."

It was nearly four in the morning by the time the doors of Maudie's closed for the night. Lauren was too exhausted to say much about the evening, except to comment that she thought it had been a success. Even her earlier pique at Zach had vanished with her fatigue. She fell into bed, rolled into his arms, and let out one long sigh just before she dropped off to sleep.

Zach rubbed his hand up and down her arm slowly, staring up at the low, slanted ceiling. He listened to her rhythmic breathing, felt the softness of her body curve into his, and wondered how far this venture would go and how long it would take.

Chapter 18

"She must have a price." The speculation began on Friday night.

"O' course she has. We just haven't found out what it is yet," someone responded from halfway across the room, thus attracting the attention of the entire house.

"Anybody know what Lauren charges for a romp?" a burly man shouted to the room at large, setting off a murmur of negative replies.

From her office Lauren heard the ruckus and decided she had best see what it was. She motioned to Josef to follow her as she crossed the foyer.

"There she is! Let's ask her! What'll it cost for you, sweet thing?" All the men in the room turned to her, presenting a mass of eager, leering faces.

Alan didn't like the tone of the voices and stopped his playing to come stand beside her. "Where's Zach?" he whispered uneasily.

Lauren placed a reassuring hand on his arm and smiled calmly. "He isn't here, but it will be all right. Don't look so worried, Alan."

"Set your price!" someone else called out.

Lauren turned her serene smile on them. "Now, gentlemen, let's not get excited." Poor choice of words. Laughter erupted and Lauren lost a bit of her

159

confidence. But she forged on, holding out her palms to calm the growing exhilaration. "What we've assembled here for you are the best girls this side of San Francisco. Look around you—I know you'll find someone to suit your fancy."

"Come on, boys. Her highness ain't a lowly working girl." This came from tough, trouble-making Lucy, who thought Lauren was a snooty bitch who considered herself better than her girls.

"Sure she is; why else would she be here?" demanded another male voice. "Let's start the biddin' and see how much it'll take."

"I'm willing! I'd pay a pretty penny for her!"

"I'll give double the best in the house: two hundred for a night of her charms!" Whooping and yelling started at that, and above it the bidding began with raucous fervor.

To two fifty it went. Then two seventy-five. Three. Three and a quarter.

"Get out of here, Lauren!" Alan urged, feeling the growing determination that was turning the group into a mob.

She shook her head, believing she had to face down the situation. But all her efforts to quiet them failed, and Josef brought his pistol into plain sight, ready for the worst.

Three eighty. Three ninety. Three ninety-five. Four hundred dollars.

The bidding slowed, and Lauren decided there was nothing she could do until they stopped. Then she would simply refuse the highest bid and that would end it.

Four ten. Four fifteen. Four twenty-five.

Alan's face was ashen. "Please, Lauren! Run while you can!"

"I can't run from it; this is my house."

The voices grew louder, and excited tension filled the room like a balloon ready to burst. A prickle of fear made her turn to Josef. "Fire into the air," she ordered.

The big man looked doubtful but did as she asked, and plaster rained down on the group like dry snow as the bullet lodged in the ceiling.

"Looks like we hit her price!" a gleeful voice shouted. "Four hundred and seventy. Mr. Sylvester's got her!"

"No!" Lauren said firmly. "I do not have a price, gentlemen. I have been trying to make you understand that."

"I told you fellas," Lucy's snide voice interposed, "what we got here is Miss Priss. She'd show you a rotten time of it."

"We won't know that till we have a go at her!"

"What say we have some fun, boys, and settle up later?" A man shouted from near the front. His suggestion was met with cheers of encouragement.

Alan pulled frantically at Lauren's sleeve. "Get out of here now. Please, Lauren! We'll keep them at bay as long as we can!"

Lauren straightened her back and squared her shoulders. If she allowed them to drive her into hiding now all would be lost.

The roomful of men seemed to move forward en masse. She took a step backward, shouting more fiercely for control. Surely they would concede if she stood firm! But her heart pounded and her fear was a buzzing in her ears as they kept on moving toward her, and nothing she said deterred them.

Alan stepped forward, trying to reason with them, but they paid him no more attention than they would a gnat.

Suddenly Zach stepped to Lauren's side and wrapped a possessive arm around her shoulders. His presence alone halted their movement.

"Let me explain something to you, gentlemen." He waited for the murmurs and bawdy comments to die down. Then his gravelly voice rang out, tightly threatening. "The lady owns Maudie's," he said plainly. "And I own the lady. She has no price because she's not for sale. It's as simple as that." His black eyes scanned the room, looking for a challenge, but none came. One by one the men turned back to their drinks and the other women, their manner now subdued.

"Do you think you can handle closing up tonight?" Zach asked Alan, who nodded his assent while he breathed a sigh of relief.

Then Zach swooped down on Lauren and lifted her into his arms, leaving the room agape and convinced of his claim, just as he had intended.

He climbed the three flights of stairs, kicked open the attic door, crossed the threshold, kicked the door closed again, and threw her none too gently on the spool bed. Lauren bounced back up, surprised by the anger in Zach's face as he stood above her, his square fingers digging into his own hips.

"Looking to get yourself raped, are you, Irish?"

"I appreciate the rescue. To be honest, I wasn't sure how I was going to get out of it." She was not reassured by the heated look in his eyes.

"I'll tell you what Maudie would have done, or any other madam around," he said harshly. "She'd have been flattered, taken the highest bid as extra profits for the night, and given the man something to brag about the next morning."

"Is that what you're suggesting I should have done?" She didn't know whether to be angry or hurt.

"What I'm suggesting is that just maybe you don't belong here, dammit! If that had turned ugly you could have ended up raped by the whole lot of them. Did that ever occur to you? They don't come here to be teased."

"I don't tease!" she shot back. "I've never even

hinted that I would be willing to bed any one of them at any price!"

"You're here, aren't you?" he shouted, echoing the reasoning that had ruled downstairs. "Blushing virgins fresh out of convents aren't whorehouse madams! *Whores* are whorehouse madams!"

"I don't blush, and I'm not a virgin," she raved back illogically.

"And you're no damned whore, either!"

Lauren sighed and said more reasonably, "I'll be more careful in the future. Besides, I think you've put an end to it."

"What about when I'm not around? There aren't many who consider it rape if the woman is supposed to be a whore."

"If it happens again I'll run for cover. But it won't; what they really wanted was to have me because they thought no other man had. Now they'll think of me as any other madam and look for cheaper entertainment."

"Any other madam would be a hell of a lot older and used up. You look like a peach ready for the picking. If I came here I'd rather have a turn with you than with any of your girls, because you're a goddamned novelty."

"You took care of it," she persisted. "Word will get out that I'm not for sale, and no one will bother."

"For now, maybe." He shook his head in frustration at her naiveté. He found he hated her being there even more than he had before. "Tomorrow I'm hiring another bouncer, and when I'm not around I want him to follow you like a shadow. Is that clear?"

"Fine," she conceded.

He pulled her roughly up against his chest, his hands biting into her arms. "Or maybe the solution is just to keep you busy up here every night." His mouth took hers in a bruising assault that vented his

own fears for her in the game she was playing so
blindly.

She tore her mouth from his and tried to push
against a strength that was suddenly unyielding. His
gentleness and patience had blinded her to the
power he could unleash. That frightened her more
than she had been facing that crowd of men, for this
was a Zach she didn't know, driven by something she
didn't understand. "You're hurting me," she
breathed in stunned disbelief.

"I thought maybe that's what you wanted. Maybe
you weren't hurt enough just by being a whore's bastard; maybe you have some misplaced need for punishment, and that's why you're setting yourself up for
it here. Will it satisfy you if I abuse you, Lauren? Or
does it have to come from living with whores and
being treated like one?"

"No! Stop it!" she ordered, bewildered by his rage.
"What's wrong with you?"

"The same thing that should be wrong with you. It
scares the hell out of me to think that if I had been
ten minutes later I would have had to pull some rut-
ting hound off you and fought a dozen more waiting
their turn. You float around here like the hostess of
high tea, playing it so coy it's no wonder they all figure you're just waiting for the right man and the
right price."

"What should I do?" she shouted back. "I'm the
madam here! That makes me hostess, doesn't it? I
have to act the part!"

"Then play it to the hilt! Let's go back downstairs
and set your price. How about a thousand for a roll
with Madam Flannery? That ought to convince them
and leave you safe from rape, so long as whoever
comes up with the money gets the goods!"

"I suppose I should be flattered that you price me
so highly." Her Irish temper flared.

"I *prize* you too highly to want you to be here at all.

I don't want you within a hundred miles of this place!"

"What has changed in five days?"

"You have! You've turned into some damn coquette, sashaying through this house with your eyes closed."

"I'm doing what I have to do!"

"What you have to do is open your eyes before someone opens them for you ... and not too nicely."

"Like you're doing now?"

"Yeah, like I'm doing now."

As if fate was taking a hand in backing him up, a woman's screams erupted from a room on the floor below.

Zach cursed disgustedly as he released his painful grip on Lauren, and they both ran down the stairs toward the source of the sound; it was now punctuated by thuds and glass breaking amid the shrieks.

"Help! The bleedin' fool's trying to kill me!"

The door was locked from the inside and Lauren had forgotten the key, so Zach kicked it open with his big booted foot. Helen Garret ran out into the safety of his arms, her olive-hued flesh cut and bruised from the brutal treatment of an enraged customer.

The man stood naked in the center of the room, his fists clenched at his sides and his nostrils flaring like a mad bull. "I caught her going through my pockets! She needs it taken out of her thievin' hide!"

Lauren stood staring at the scene, wide-eyed and pale with horror. And the illusion she had been fostering shattered before her like a rose-colored beveled glass window, leaving her faced with stark reality.

She returned all of the man's money, including what he had paid for the brass checks. Helen Garret was fired and sent packing right then and there, both as an example to the other girls and as a reassurance to her customers that no thieves worked at Maudie's. Lauren went about it with grim determination, hoping her shock and revulsion were well covered.

Zach hung back through it all, his arms folded across his chest, never offering so much as a word of advice, a nod of approval, or an ounce of help. From appeasing the naked man and chastising the raving, battered whore to calming the rest of the girls and customers in the house, he left it all to Lauren's inexperience and stunned sensibilities.

When it was all settled, everyone was soothed and Maudie's closed down for the night. They went back to the pristine blue and white attic room. Neither of them spoke, for Zach had said his piece and Lauren was too proud to admit he was right.

And the ugliness had only begun.

Chapter 19

There was the ox of a farmer who burst through the locked front doors screaming for his sister. He threatened to kill Lauren for making Lily a whore and keeping her against her will. When the girl convinced him that she was at Maudie's because she chose to be, he backhanded her across the face and ended up being carried out bodily by Josef and Billy, Lauren's new bodyguard.

There was the irate society matron who stampeded her buxom way in one morning with a brass check she had confiscated from her meek son's room. Maudie's had been the scene of birthday revelry with his friends, but even though he had paid for one of the girls, his confidence had faltered and he hadn't been able to take the girl upstairs. The rotund mother, bedecked in furs and brocade and more jewelry than any whore would wear, demanded her son's money back and warned that if he was ever again admitted to Maudie's, she would out–bribe Lauren and have the place shut down.

There was stealing among the girls, as well as jealousy and rivalry and backbiting and sloth. There was even one who turned up pregnant. There were men who drank too much and tried to press themselves on Lauren, making her grateful for Billy and his brawn when Zach wasn't nearby. There were rows over girls and gambling for no reason anyone knew; fights among the housemaids; quarrels among the kitchen staff; and arguments with merchants who figured a fancy house like Maudie's could well afford inflated prices. The cost of bribes soared, and replacing broken furniture and glassware became a weekly expense.

There were complaints that the drinks were watered when they weren't; outrageous expectations by men with the power to close the place if their wishes weren't met; girls who claimed their monthly indisposition every other week; and some who resented Lauren mightily, as Zach had predicted.

Through it all, she came to rely on Billy's hulking presence. He was a huge man who rarely spoke and never appeared angry or impatient, but he never failed to lend Lauren support when she needed it.

Through it all, Zach stayed in the background as he had planned from the beginning and watched Lauren sink deeper and deeper into the quagmire she had created. He remained near enough to help if there were no other way out, but he never once did anything to ease the strain or sweeten the distasteful day-to-day squabbles. And the longer he waited for her to capitulate, the stronger her determination grew that she wouldn't. Each night they slept in the same bed, but it was the only celibate one in the place.

Lauren wondered why he stayed at all...and sometimes so did he.

And Maudie's was making money faster than Lauren could count it.

"He says he owns her," the whore reported to Mark Rossiter. "He's there most of the time and he sleeps in her room every night. Looks to me like he keeps things from getting too far out of hand for her."

"Then it *is* more than a business relationship," Rossiter mused darkly.

"He doesn't touch anyone else, no matter what gets offered or how many times, and believe me, there are plenty he could have. He takes his meals alone with Lauren and his eyes never leave her when things are in full swing in the evenings. If he isn't around he has a big bruiser named Billy who has orders never to leave her side for any reason. The hulk stands over her with a rifle across his chest as if he were guarding gold."

"I see." A feral sneer crossed his face. "But he doesn't own a piece of Maudie's?"

"That's what he announced to the whole place. She owns Maudie's and he owns her—that's just what he said. As far as I can tell he doesn't take enough of a hand in any of the dealings or decisions to own a part. I'd say it's her house. And I'll tell you something else: from some of the comments he throws her way, I'd say he isn't any too happy to have her there at all."

His smile was thin, but he kept his racing thoughts to himself.

After a moment, she went on: "I did all you wanted. I bragged into the right ears about all the money Maudie's is making, and her bribes doubled the next day. Lucy is easy enough to handle, and I always water the drinks I serve. It isn't easy either. The rest of her staff is loyal, and they watch out for her."

"You're doing well enough," was all the praise she got; it was obvious she was hoping for something more lavish. He could tell just by looking at her that she was angling for a bonus.

Seeing his reserve, the whore played her last card. "There is one piece of news, if you're interested."

He gave a long, drawn-out sigh that expressed his rapidly fading patience. His well-manicured hands came together and with slow, careful intent he cracked each knuckle in turn. "That is what you're being paid for."

The woman knew better than to press him. With a resigned shrug, she relented. "Madox is leaving for a week. He tried to get her to go with him—something about visiting a logging camp—but she refused."

Her reward was a Cheshire-cat smile.

Lauren sat behind her desk on the fourth Friday night Maudie's had been in business, but her thoughts weren't on the account books in front of her. Her mind was on Zach, gone, as he was every Friday night, to the Cades' home for dinner. This was the first time he hadn't tried to persuade her to go with him, and she wondered what it meant. She hoped he had just given up, since she refused each time, but she was pretty sure that wasn't the cause. Maudie's seemed to have turned him surly and short-tempered.

A knock on the door interrupted her brooding, and Alan came in. His manner was casual, familiar, and friendly. She had been surprised by how much he had come out of himself in the month he'd been at Maudie's. Polly Carson was the cause, and Lauren wondered what, exactly, was between them. His face always lit up whenever Polly came into a room, and more than once Lauren had found them giggling in the kitchen before any of the other girls had come downstairs for the day. But Alan had never spoken of having had Polly for a night, and Lauren strongly suspected their relationship was platonic.

"I think we've made a mistake, Lauren," Alan began as he sat in a chair facing her.

Lauren laughed wearily. "Now what?" She had taken to discussing things with him, and as a result

Alan frequently spent his days grappling with house problems instead of playing the piano.

"I think we acted too hastily in firing Esther."

Lauren had liked Esther Brown more than the rest of the girls she employed, but the woman had been found to be working with the crimp, Big Jim, in shanghaiing an occasional customer. Once a susceptible man was in her room she would drug him, steal his money, and then call one of Big Jim's men, who would be waiting in the bar, to come get his drunken friend.

"I don't know what other choice we had." She sighed, thinking how much of the business was distasteful.

"I found out today that she was doing it because she was desperate for the money. Her husband deserted her and left her five children and his own mother to support. I just thought that maybe we should have talked things over with her, tried to help her. Lucy says she's down on Skid Row now, working in the worst box house there and having to roll every drunk she can."

Lauren shook her head, struck by how much better Alan got along with the girls than she did. They went to him with their problems, no matter how personal, while Lauren was treated with the barest courtesy. She knew they resented her. Some showed it in quiet coldness, while others, like Lucy, were openly hostile and abusive. But there didn't seem to be any way for Lauren to cross the barrier.

"What do you think we should do?" she asked, knowing by the now-familiar look on his face that he and the girls had thought of a solution.

He shrugged. "I thought maybe we could go looking for her and hire her to do something else. Neddie needs more help in the kitchen, and Esther was good with a needle and thread too. The girls have all agreed to pay her to sew for them. What do you say?"

Two hours later Zach greeted the news with a black frown. "You'd better make up your mind whether you're going to work these women or save them, Lauren, because if you do this you'll have every hard-luck story in Seattle on your doorstep."

"I'll take my chances," she said firmly, "Will you take me to Esther?"

He shook his head disgustedly, thinking at first he would offer to go alone, that Skid Row was no place for Lauren. Then he decided a taste of it might aid his cause. "Against my better judgment," he grumbled.

It was ostentatiously called King's Kastle, and Zach paid ten cents to get into the basement dive. What lay beyond the doors was something Lauren could never have imagined. The air was thick and foul with the stench of smoke, liquor, unwashed bodies, and sex. A bar stretched down one wall with a small stage at the side of it. The piano player was caged behind a wire barrier for protection against brawls. The music was discordant, but the singer couldn't carry a tune, so the one canceled out the other, and neither could be heard anyway over din of the disinterested loggers.

Pictures of naked women were the sole decoration, though most were torn or stained with whiskey splashes. Tables and chairs cluttered the center space and box-like cubicles lined the remaining walls. When they weren't taking their turn singing or dancing onstage, greasy, half-dressed women wandered about selling drinks and themselves.

Zach glanced down at Lauren, sure she didn't realize she was clutching his arm for dear life. He bent down so she could hear him over the commotion. "Nice place, isn't it, Irish?"

"Let's just find her and get out!" she snapped, too appalled to hide her revulsion.

Zach patted her cold fingers, which were digging into his arm, and moved through the crowd to the bar. Along the way Lauren had to swallow her aversion and her outrage as meaty hands slapped her rear and one even reached out to touch her bosom.

At the bar, she stood close to Zach as he asked where he might find Esther and then described the woman. But nothing came free in a place like that; as the fat barman stared blankly at them, Zach slid a bribe across the greasy bar. The barman furtively took the money with grimy hands that left blurs on the glasses. He studied the silver pieces, pocketed them, and then raised one black-nailed finger to point to an end cubicle.

Grateful that they could skirt the tables to get to it, Lauren still kept hold of Zach's arm as if, had she let go of it, she might be swallowed up in the muck of human flesh. Her stomach churned, and disgust tightened her throat. She couldn't imagine what desperation would drive someone to work in a place like this.

They reached the box just as an unshaven, potbellied sot stepped out. The man scanned the room proudly, grinning and giving an exaggerated tug to straighten his pants.

Lauren pulled back on Zach's arm as he was about to enter the small space, as horrified as if he were about to pull her into a snake pit. But Esther stepped out just then, looking for yet another partner.

Convincing the woman to come back to Maudie's as cook's helper and seamstress was an easy task, once they assured her she would make as much money as she ever could in a place like this. But try as they might, they couldn't persuade her to leave with them right away and lose a night's pay.

Lauren rode back to Maudie's in shocked silence.

The gray pallor of her face and the still, wide circles of her eyes told Zach she was feeling the effect he intended.

But the evening's lessons were not over.

They were greeted by the crash of broken glass as a man hurtled through the parlor window, and from within came a deafening uproar that told them that Maudie's was in the midst of a full-fledged brawl.

Visiting the house that night had been three upper-class troublemakers and several loggers who had come to spend their month's earnings on a taste of what was being touted as the best whorehouse in Seattle. It was a volatile combination, and Lauren had warned Alan to watch them all carefully.

But as she and Zach rushed in, it was impossible to tell what or who had started the fight. Fists flew, feet kicked, fingers gouged, and anything not nailed down was being used as a weapon. Alan, the bartender, Josef, and Billy were all in the middle of it, working futilely to break up one group only to have another erupt. The women had climbed onto the bar and the backs of sofas and were watching with amusement or even helping things along with a well-placed kick.

Lauren stood in the doorway of the parlor watching the worst havoc Maudie's had yet seen. It seemed like a continuation of the King's Kastle coarseness and violence as one man's ear was ripped off by a logger and another man lost a chunk of skin to a clawlike hand. She felt helpless to stop Maudie's from being destroyed before her very eyes.

Luckily Zach was not so thunderstruck. From behind her, he aimed a long-barreled pistol at the glass chandelier suspended from the ceiling and shot at the thing so that it crashed down on the center of the fray.

Everything came to a sudden halt as Lauren

stared, so stunned she missed seeing the final fist that was aimed at the man in front of her, who ducked at precisely the right moment.

"Haven't you had enough?" Zach's gravelly voice finally asked. He had carried her upstairs in stony silence and sat now resignedly holding cold compresses to her fast-blackening eye. The house was quiet; it had been closed down early so the staff could clear away the debris left in the parlor.

"You could have killed someone with that chandelier," she said evasively.

"I didn't." His words were clipped and tight. "Besides, they'd have killed each other if I hadn't stopped it, and they would have wrecked more of the house in the process." He dabbed at the cut on the ridge of her brow and Lauren winced. "You didn't answer my question," he added.

"I've definitely had enough for one night."

"That isn't what I meant, and you know it." There was an ominous determination about him as he sat on the edge of the bed treating her so dispassionately. "I don't want any part of this place or this life any longer. And I don't want you in it either."

Lauren swallowed thickly, avoiding the black eyes that stared at her too intently, too seriously, and much too coldly. "I have to stay," she said simply through a tight throat.

"You don't *have* to do anything."

"I still owe you eight thousand dollars and I have no other way of making a living."

"I don't care about the damned money." He was calm and totally devoid of emotion.

"But I do." It came out a whisper. "Besides all the rest, this is a better place for people like Esther than the King's Kastle," she finished feebly.

"Then turn it into a damned mission." He covered

the whole side of her face with a damp cloth, pressing her in to the bed pillows.

"I have to see this through until you're paid off." Her quiet determination matched his.

"You could marry me," he said flatly, deciding, on the spot, that even if she didn't love him he couldn't stand her doing this any more.

"Not like this, I couldn't. I told you that before."

"Not like what?"

"Not to cancel a debt. Not to escape." *Not when you ask that way and never even mention that you want me,* she added in her mind.

"Haven't you had enough?" he repeated.

"It isn't a matter of having enough. When your loggers are hurt or fire burns the woods, is that enough to scare you away from your business? Of course not. You take care of what needs to be taken care of and go on. That's what every businessman does. Well, Maudie's is my business, not some game I'm playing at. Yes, sometimes it is ugly, but so is injury and fire, or any of the other hazards that go along with every business. I'm not running away from it. And if that's what you expected from me, you were foolish."

"I was foolish?" he spat out. "I thought that when you had a craw full of this gutter life you would be smart enough to get out of it."

"I intend to do what I can to make it better, to avoid incidents like tonight."

"Like I said, maybe you should turn the place into a mission and try your hand at being a missionary nun," he shot back sarcastically.

"Maybe if *you* can't take the life, you should stay away from it."

"Maybe I'll just do that."

Long, fierce strides took him to the door before she stopped him as the sight of him leaving cooled her temper. "Zach..." She swallowed before she could force her voice around her pride. "I didn't mean that," was all she could concede.

He turned around to her and leaned back against the door, frowning down at the floor to gain control of his own rage. After a minute he sighed and looked at her. "Well, I did mean what I said. I want you to spend this next week while I'm gone thinking about it, thinking about a whole life full of what you've had a taste of these past weeks. Because it won't get better, Lauren; nothing you do can make it better, nor can you avoid what belongs to this life as surely as ships belong in the sea. There's no changing it. It changes you. It hardens you until you don't see the ugliness or care when you do. And I can't stand around and watch that happen to you."

He opened the door before she found her voice. "Where are you going?"

"Home," he answered. "I can leave from there in the morning, and I think I'll get a better night's rest in my own bed. I'll see you when I get back."

He slammed the door on her heart.

Chapter 20

"What do you mean, no one in town will sell us liquor?" Lauren railed.

"Just what I said." Alan stood opposite her desk. "Our regular man claims we didn't pay his bill."

Zach had been gone two days, and Lauren was in sour spirits and a foul temper and in no mood to deal with Maudie's many day-to-day problems, let alone a major catastrophe. "I asked Zach to pay that bill when the last delivery came. I was firing Esther and couldn't spare the time. I'm sure he did it—he wouldn't overlook a thing like that. Did you check for a receipt?"

"Everywhere. If there is one he took it with him."

"Of course he didn't take it with him," she snapped. "We will just have to pay cash in advance until this can be settled."

Alan knew how miserable she had been since Zach left, knew she felt as if he had given her an ultimatum. If Alan was any judge, it was risky business to back Lauren into a corner. Knowing how upset she was, he didn't take her anger personally, but he chose his words carefully. "I'm sorry, Lauren. I already tried that. McGuffy controls every drop of decent liquor in the city and for some reason he's blacklisted us. I don't know what we're going to do. Maybe you had better send for Zach."

"And have him say I can't run the place without him? That would be my undoing. There has to be a way."

In the ensuing silence, a knock sounded on the office door. Lauren stormed to it and flung it open.

There stood Mark Rossiter, hat in hand, his appearance flawless, smiling his most pleasant, warm smile. He nodded amiably. "Good day, Miss Flannery. I thought it was time to pay a welcoming visit."

"Mr. Rossiter, isn't it?" she said distractedly, her face a deep frowning reflection of her disturbed thoughts.

"Have I come at a bad time?"

"I don't mean to be rude, but yes, you have. I'm sorry. Perhaps another time." She closed the door a fraction to let her intent be known. But Rossiter took a step forward into the opening, blocking her movement.

"I hate to brag, Miss Flannery, but I have operated a similar establishment for well over ten years. I dare say I have encountered every problem there is, so if the lines that mar that lovely face of yours have anything at all to do with Maudie's, it is possible I could help."

Lauren had never heard a prettier speech given so sincerely. She threw a questioning glance over her shoulder at Alan. Should they trust an outsider? it asked.

A what-else-can-we-do shrug answered her.

"Come in, please, Mr. Rossiter, and sit down."

Rossiter entered, but before sitting extended his hand to Alan. "Mark Rossiter. I own *The Countess,*" he said, introducing himself.

"Oh, I am sorry," Lauren was quick to apologize. "It seems there is no end to my rudeness today. This is my dear friend and...well, Alan does nearly as much as I do around Maudie's: Alan Bentley."

They shook hands as Alan studied the dashing Mark Rossiter, seeing in him the same appreciation for Lauren that was evident in Zach Madox. Alan's curiosity awakened. "You haven't mentioned Mr. Rossiter to me, Lauren."

Rossiter's laugh interrupted her answer, "Please call me Mark. I'm afraid I insulted her on our only meeting. I had come to buy Maudie's, you see, not realizing Miss Flannery already owned it. As you might understand, the news that she was settling in Seattle eased my loss."

"Did it?" Alan asked evenly, feeling suddenly as if Zach needed defending. But before the feeling was confirmed, Rossiter turned to Lauren, his manner more business-like.

"What calamity can I help you with?"

"McGuffy has cut off our liquor. He claims we didn't pay him and while I know it has to be a mistake, we can't find a receipt."

A handsome frown pulled his wheat-colored eyebrows together as he stroked his meticulously trimmed beard thoughtfully. "McGuffy can be an ornery devil; I know that for a fact. Did you try offering cash up front plus a bonus?"

"I did," Alan interjected. "I tried offering him double his usual price."

"Stubborn man." Then his gleeming white teeth appeared in a reassuringly confident smile. "But I don't think he'll be too stubborn. I own the warehouses in which he stocks his inventory. I think he will listen to reason. Will you come with me to talk to him, Miss Flannery?"

"I'll go," Alan offered defensively.

"Thank you, Alan, but it's best if I see to this. I'll be right with you, Mr. Rossiter."

Within an hour, the matter was resolved, though

McGuffy continued to maintain that he had not been paid. Lauren marveled at Rossiter's firm but subtly threatening handling of the intimidating, pot-bellied man. He oversaw the loading of the delivery wagon and demanded that it follow his svelte black barouche as they left the warehouse, and returned to Maudie's.

Alan helped with the unloading, eyeing Rossiter warily as Lauren turned to the man with the first smile Alan had seen since Zach had left. Apparently she was not afflicted with the same sense of disloyalty that plagued Alan.

"There is a price for my services." Rossiter grinned comfortably down at Lauren.

"Which is?" She fell easily into the flirting game.

"Dinner with me Saturday night."

"Oh, no, I couldn't." Treasonous feelings struck her at last.

"Oh, dear," he said teasingly, "was McGuffy right about your not paying your debts?"

It struck her as strange that this man's comments didn't rile her the way Zach's did. "You will have to choose another form of payment," she said, enjoying the banter.

"Your time is all I want," he said in a low, intriguingly confident way. "Grant me just an evening, that's all I ask. I'll warrant you haven't had a night out since this place opened."

"No, I haven't. But..." His invitation was too appealing.

"You said yourself that Alan can do everything you can. I won't accept less."

"I'm afraid I'm not really in a position to..."

"Don't crush my every hope with the news that you're a married woman."

"No, but..."

"Engaged? Betrothed? Bound in slavery?"

The pure, lighthearted amusement in his tone was

infectious. And it was a welcome balm to the heavy
feelings Lauren had been having since her parting
argument with Zach. "I don't actually know what I
am," she told him honestly.

"I thought you were the owner of Maudie's, a
woman to be reckoned with and one who did as she
pleased, when she pleased, and with whom. A
woman who pays her debts," he goaded with a grin.

She thought for a moment. She knew nothing
about playing this game. Her head was turned by
Rossiter's flirtatiousness. She felt a fresh sense of
femininity. "Just one dinner and we will be even?"

"Just one."

"All right then."

"After that I mean to win you into wanting to see
me again." He gave her a boyish wink. "I'll come for
you at eight."

But Lauren was to see Mark Rossiter long before
Saturday night.

On Tuesday he arrived just before lunch with a
proposal that he introduce her to his butcher. "He
will give you a better price," he told her solicitously.
Ever conscious of cost, Lauren agreed. It was only
good manners to invite him to share her private meal
beforehand, though propriety dictated that they stay
in the kitchen rather than taking it, as she usually
did, in her attic room.

The new butcher's prices were, indeed, more reasonable. Lauren hired him, commenting as Rossiter's
elegant carriage returned them to Maudie's that the
savings would help defray the weekly expense of
broken glass.

On Wednesday Rossiter introduced her to a somewhat seedy but eminently cheaper supplier of that
commodity.

Thursday he introduced her to two gargantuan
bullies with the suggestion that they be hired as sentries. Their purpose, he explained, would be to stand

guard in the parlor and gaming room, facilitating an early stifling of brawls like the past Friday night's debacle. A single bouncer posted in the entrance was nearly helpless, said Rossiter, while the addition of these brutes would keep the peace.

Lauren took them on.

Rossiter's Friday afternoon visit began with a reminder about Saturday's dinner. But by the end of his hour there his charming interest in Alan and his not overly effusive compliments had won even Alan's guarded approval. "If ever Miss Flannery no longer has a need for you, Alan," Rossiter offered, "you have a job on *The Countess*. I can always use a good, hardworking man like yourself."

His subtle comments about her single set of dress clothes, worn night after night, was the spur for her buying a new outfit, not dinner with Rossiter, Lauren assured herself as she took the new items from their parcels. It was only coincidence that the sky blue velvet skirt and delicate cream-colored blouse with its high, round collar and covered-button front arrived in time for Saturday night.

Maudie's was an hour away from opening as Lauren descended the stairs to await Rossiter's arrival. The girls had all dined and were dressing for the night. The maids had not yet lit the lamps in the parlor and as Lauren passed she caught sight of a shadowy form in the far corner.

"Alan?" she called out.

The shape divided guiltily into two, and Alan and Polly Carson stepped from their embrace into the dim lamplight from the foyer.

"Lauren!" he breathed in an unusually husky voice, "I . . . Oh, damn." He had unconsciously moved to stand in front of Polly protectively. "I . . . uh . . . I know the rule about the girls' private lives never entering Maudie's," he stammered. "This isn't actually what it seems. It's innocent, I swear it. I just—well, I care for her, you see."

So it had gone beyond admiration from afar. Lauren smiled at her friend and said mischievously, "Does Polly feel the same?"

Polly Carson stepped out from behind Alan, eyeing her employer warily. "I love Alan." she blurted out. "But I need this job, Lauren. I won't do anything that might get me sent away."

Lauren didn't know whether to feel happy for them for having found each other or saddened by the circumstances that forced them to hide in the shadows. "Alan," she ventured, afraid of meddling, "perhaps you should do something about that."

But it was Polly who answered. "He knows how it is with me. I have to keep working. I have responsibilities. My family depends on what I earn here."

Lauren saw her friend's regret and her heart went out to him. But altering her rule could only do harm. "Are you willing to accept"—she motioned to the dark corner—"just this?" she ended feebly.

"I am. For now," Alan answered without hesitation.

Lauren sighed. "Then it isn't my business. I'm sorry I barged in on you, but I do have to speak with you about tonight, Alan."

Polly took her cue and left Alan's side, but as she passed Lauren she stopped, her wide, blue eyes sincere. "I know you don't know how it is with me, but I have to have this job. Alan understands."

Lauren shook her head as if she did too, though it was a false assurance. When Polly had gone, Lauren crossed to Alan and gave him a hug of support; then she began to talk of work.

When the discussion of his duties for the evening was concluded, Alan ventured a turnabout and inquired into her affairs. "You are taking Billy along tonight, aren't you?"

"I was thinking he would be of better use here."

"Zach hired him to protect you, not the house," he reminded her.

"Do you think I am in need of protection from Mr. Rossiter?"

Alan hesitated, but in the end he opted for honesty. "I like the man, Lauren, and I know he has helped you a great deal this week since Zach has been gone. But I can't help wondering why he has bothered, unless he's after something. And I think that something is you."

So it hadn't been her imagination. "He has been a perfect gentleman," she said, hedging.

"Then give him reason to keep it up by taking Billy with you."

Flattery and admiration from an amazingly attractive man were heady things to a woman who had never known them. Mark Rossiter had a way of making her feel better about herself and her connection with a whore's life than anyone she had ever encountered. He treated her like a queen. His hands, his eyes, even his thoughts, as far as she could tell, had never strayed where they shouldn't. She sensed no threat, no danger from him. Instead, she felt respected, pampered, appreciated. And it felt good. "I don't need Billy," she finally decided. "I will rest better knowing he is here, keeping the place from ruin." Then, seeing the doubtful frown on her dear friend's face, she sought to reassure him. "It will be all right, Alan. There isn't anything to worry about."

But worry he did.

They drank champagne out of cut crystal goblets in the dim, velvet interior of Rossiter's carriage as it swayed through Seattle's streets toward the pier. Remembering how alcohol had effected her twice before, Lauren barely sipped hers.

"We will take a ferry out to a small island I own in

the Sound. The staff at my house there has prepared our dinner," Rossiter explained. Then, seeing her reluctance, he added, "We will be well chaperoned and the ferry will wait at the island's dock to take us back the moment you decide you want to go."

Lauren smiled her reply, hoping she hadn't made an error in judgment about this man. But still his manners were flawless, and by the time they stood at the ferry's railing she had relaxed again.

"That's my *Countess*." He nodded toward a huge, beautiful steamship that looked as if it belonged on the Mississippi. It glistened white and gold in the moonlight. Bright lanterns lined the decks, the paddle wheel was motionless, and no smoke came from the high black steam chimneys. Muted music could be heard from the inner rooms, and laughing people strolled the decks. It had the look of a cultured gathering, not a floating den of vice.

"I had thought of taking you there to dine," Rossiter told her. "My cook is a talented Frenchman. But I decided it would do us both good to be away from business for one evening. Henri was delighted to cook for us alone at the hideaway."

The "hideaway" was indeed that. Lamps high on wrought-iron posts lit a wooden stairway that climbed and wound through dense, junglelike foliage. The house, bathed in yellow lamplight, looked like an enormous tree house, its wooden structure built around and amidst hemlocks, pines, and oak trees; some had been left to grow through holes in the balcony that circled the entire structure.

As they climbed the stairs, Rossiter told her the story of the house. "It was built by a smuggler as his hideaway. It is indiscernible from the water but you can see all of the city from here. I understand that the beauty of the smuggler's subterfuge was that no one expected him to be so near. He could hide out here, shave his beard, and then sail across to Seattle and pretend to be an honest citizen while the authorities believed he had taken to the high seas. For me, it is a refuge I can escape to when bawdy house life gets wearing. I would highly advise you to find a similar haven. Believe me, after a while, you will need it."

The rooms were spacious and airy, with a view of the city through large windows that was quite spectacular. They dined by candlelight on the balcony, with three silent waiters watching over them, a clear night sky for a canopy, and a cool breeze whispering a soft song through the treetops just below.

The meal was a masterpiece, consisting of turtle soup, asparagus spears, duck in orange sauce, and a creamy custard flan. Rossiter kept up an easy stream of conversation that was polite and amusing, never hinting at anything Lauren might find improper, and so she put the last of her reservations to rest and discovered that her pleasure in the evening could not have been more complete—until they strolled the balcony with cup and saucers in hand and Rossiter reminded her of Zach.

"The question is impertinent, I know, but how involved are you with Zach Madox?" he asked casually enough, with just a glimmer of mischief to relieve the serious intent of his words.

Lauren didn't answer readily, suddenly feeling that what was between her and Zach was somehow tawdry compared to the elegant splendor of this place and the refined manners of this man. Finally she settled on, "We are very close."

"I was afraid of that." Mark Rossiter stopped a few feet ahead of her and turned to lean against the balcony, his long legs stretched out into her path and crossed comfortably at the ankles. Moonlight played on his wheaten hair, giving it golden streaks. He was a splendidly handsome man. "I take it he is involved in Maudie's as well?"

"Maudie's is mine." A stab of conscience pricked Lauren at the thought that she was talking about Zach at all.

"But it is Madox who neglected to pay your bill with McGuffy," he reminded her casually.

"He was doing me a service. I was otherwise occupied at the time. I'm sure he paid it, at any rate. It was all just a mix-up that Zach will straighten out as soon as he comes back."

"I hope so," he said earnestly. He allowed a heavy, doubtful pause to follow before going on. "Maudie's is a jewel among stones, you know that, don't you? It is important for you to guard it as one."

"I don't understand what you're implying."

"I'm sure it's nothing, just a misunderstanding, as you say. But you will be careful of subterfuge, won't you?"

"From Zach?" The very thought was ludicrous.

"From anyone . . . myself included," he finished, as if he were jesting. "I'm only saying that damaging Maudie's reputation with the merchants could be disastrous. Beware that it wasn't a ploy, won't you?"

"Zach doesn't want Maudie's," she said, feebly defensive. Was it possible that Zach had done such a thing on purpose? She knew he didn't want to own the place himself, but wouldn't Maudie's failure accomplish just what he wanted in getting her out of it? And then it would seem to be her failure, not something he had forced on her. Would he do that to her? She couldn't believe it. "You needn't warn me to be cautious where Maudie's is concerned. I am not likely to give up my livelihood easily."

Rossiter smiled, revealing gleaming white teeth in the full shadow of his beard. "I hope not. It would rob me of the excuse to see you." Then his teasing tone grew serious again. "You know I fancy owning Maudie's myself, or I wouldn't have made you promise to give me first option if ever you decide to sell.

But I only want it from you on the best of terms...
and certainly in the best of shape. So if ever you need
anything from me—help, advice, anything at all that
I can do for you—don't hesitate to come to me. Will
you promise me that too?"

Lauren barely paused. "You've proven yourself a
friendly ally this past week. I think I can easily promise that."

"Wonderful," he breathed a contented sigh. "You
are a very special woman, did you know that?"

"Oh, I don't think so."

"I know you don't. That is what makes it so."
There was a moment's silence that was heavy and uncomfortable for Lauren as Rossiter's words hung in
the air. Then he said lightly, "One more promise before I take you home. I feel as if we are good friends
and I know we are going to be better ones. Can't we
please call one another by first names?"

Lauren laughed, relieved at the change of tone. "I
suppose we can, yes."

He pushed away from the balcony and offered his
arm. "Then the evening has been truly perfect."

As Rossiter's carriage drew near Maudie's,
Lauren's thoughts wandered of their own volition to
her feelings about him. He was so unlike Zach, and
she felt very comfortable with him. But since their
relationship was strictly business she decided it
shouldn't warrant this much thought, and she tried
instead to concentrate on what he was saying.

He walked her to the kitchen entrance to avoid the
noise and commotion of a whorehouse still in full
Saturday-night frolic. The back of the house was
dimly lit by one lamp, and the clatter of pots was
more prevalent here than boisterous voices.

At the kitchen door, with his hand lightly at her
arm, Mark Rossiter turned Lauren to face him.
Without a word or warning he very slowly bent, lowered his face to hers and met her lips with his.

It was a chaste, dry kiss. The scent of the woods clung to his clothing. The feel of his beard was soft. His breath tasted sweetly of mint and his hands at her shoulders held her as carefully as if she were fine bone china. He lingered only a moment, not too long, not too short, and then he murmured good-night and left her. But it was time enough for Lauren to become aware of two disturbing thoughts.

Guilt assailed her with sudden severity and turned what she had so steadfastly been assuring herself was an innocent evening into something more portentous.

And the certainty dawned that, despite Mark Rossiter's appeal, her heart was not tempted from the brawny, rough-hewn man she was beginning to fear she loved.

Chapter 21

It was the poorest of luck that brought Zach back late Monday afternoon just as Mark Rossiter was leaving Maudie's. Lauren and Rossiter were standing together in the doorway of her office as Zach passed the oddly apprehensive stares of Alan and Billy the bodyguard. Then he heard Rossiter's voice.

"I appreciate this, Lauren. With four girls down sick and a big birthday celebration coming on board, I wasn't sure how I was going to make it through tonight without a loan of at least two of yours. I'll bring them back first thing tomorrow."

"Think nothing of it. I owe you, Mark." Lauren's friendly response was like a splash of cold water in Zach's face.

The two moved a few feet outside the office and came face to face with Zach. His hard black eyes locked onto Lauren's startled topaz ones while Rossiter greeted him with the same open comraderie he had used with Alan. But Zach saw through it. "Rossiter." He acknowledged the man's greeting brusquely, without pulling his glance from Lauren.

"Good to see you again," Rossiter persisted. "How was your week? Not easy, from the look of you. Hellish life, logging. You look as if you could do with a few good nights' rest."

Zach's head pivoted deliberately toward Rossiter. He stared at Rossiter from beneath ominous brows, declaring his recognition of an enemy with that one look. "Something I can do for you?" he asked frigidly.

"Not a thing. Lauren has taken good care of me." Then, with a broad smile directed at Lauren, Rossiter excused himself. "I will wait for the girls outside."

When he had gone, Lauren faced Zach awkwardly. "A hot bath is what you need," she offered.

"So I hear."

"Will you come upstairs for it?" Lauren had spent a lot of time in the past week worrying that he might not come back. She was so relieved when he stomped up the stairs, bellowing for hot water, that she thought she could face any amount of his rage.

Zach wasted no time once they were in the attic room. He turned on her with more fury than when he had left her a week past. "Want to tell me just what the hell is going on with him?"

"Business. Nothing else. He paid a social call early last week, found us in a horrible predicament, and helped Alan and me out of it. Today I returned the favor."

She was too fidgety for that to be all there was to it. "Pretty chummy, aren't you?"

"I saw a great deal of him last week. He shared some of his experience in this business. He introduced me to a new butcher, a new glass supplier, and two new bouncers to keep brawls down. Things like that." Her chin tilted defiantly. She had nothing to hide. But, at the same time, she decided now was not the time to tell him about Saturday night's dinner.

"What's his game?"

"It is purely a business association, Zach," she insisted.

"Hah!" he snorted. "You don't really believe that?"

"Of course I do, because it is the truth. McGuffy cut off our liquor supply. He said he hadn't been paid. We couldn't find where you had put the receipt and the man wouldn't even sell to us with cash in advance. I didn't know what we were going to do. Mark persuaded him to give us a second chance."

"'*Mark*,' is it?"

"Oh don't do this!" She lost her patience and shouted at him in frustration, "Yes, "*Mark*,' and I had dinner with him Saturday night and he kissed me and all it did was make me wish for you. Are you satisfied?"

Satisfied was a long way from what he was. His hands went to his narrow, denim-clad hips as he stood with his legs apart. He stared at the floor, breathing hard and fighting the feeling that a heavy fist had found his gut. "Seems as if you've had a full week."

"A full week of worrying that you weren't coming back," she answered in a hushed voice.

His eyes pinned her. "So you thought you would fill my place with Rossiter?"

"Don't do this," she beseeched again. "There isn't anything between Rossiter and me except business."

"Made himself pretty handy to have around in that area though, didn't he?"

"Did you pay McGuffy?" She didn't know what else to say. Her pride had taken enough of a beating already and she had gotten little for it.

"Of course I paid him. The receipt is in the file."

"No, it isn't."

"Well, that is where I put it."

"It isn't there," she insisted.

His own impatience sounded through gritted teeth. "Then I will personally reimburse you for whatever you had to pay him over again."

"That isn't important. It's all taken care of."

"By Rossiter."

"Zach, we're going in circles."

His bath water arrived then, which gave them both a moment to think. When the last maid had gone and they were alone again he murmured to himself, "Dammit, I didn't want to come back like this." Then he said, "I don't suppose you spared much time thinking about what I said when I left."

Lauren sighed and wished for strength. "I have to stay at Maudie's and see this through," she said softly.

He stripped down and sank into the bathtub. For a week he had told himself she was going to react this way. It hadn't been long enough yet. She hadn't had her fill. Only time would make her see that it would never improve. What he didn't know was how long he could wait for that to happen. But for now, he did know he couldn't leave her. "God, I hate this place."

"It's better now," she said, trying to convince them both. "The men Mark brought over are matching mountains. No one dares make a commotion with them around. Things have been fairly quiet, and I have weathered the worst of the bedroom crises. I know what's coming now. It isn't so odd to me anymore."

He stared at her from amidst the whorls of steam that rose around the broad expanse of his shoulders. "So in a week, with the help of Rossiter, you have not only decided to accept this life, you've decided to like it, is that it?" His tone of voice was a harsh, hurtful judgment but also implied he wanted her to refute what he was thinking.

"He didn't have anything to do with it, beyond reminding me that there is still an outside world to escape to when I need it. He is an example of a person who knows how to deal with this life with dignity."

Zach sank low in the bath water, closing his eyes. This was only a temporary setback, he decided; he hadn't lost this battle yet. "I guess we'll see how this new theory works out, won't we?" But what he was feeling was not patience. A quiet desperation was more like it.

The evening passed with Lauren tending to Maudie's while Zach stood with his back against a wall, nursing a drink and wondering how he was going to get her out of there. When the doors had closed at last and he still had no solution, he took her upstairs to bed. After weeks of celibacy she was surprised to feel him reach for her, pulling her into the cove of his spread legs where he sat on the bed. A feeling of well-being filled her, for it seemed he had accepted her ownership of Maudie's and things would go back to the way they had been between them when it opened.

She drew the tips of her fingers up his arms, tracing his bulging biceps on the way to his shoulders. "It really will be all right," she whispered.

He only sighed and murmured softly, "No talking. I just want to make love to you." He pressed his warm lips to the hollow of her shoulder as her clothes fell around her. Lying back, he pulled her with him, stretching her naked body along the full length of his before rolling them both to their sides. His mouth found hers in short, slow kisses as he shed his own clothing, taking his time as if he wanted to savor what he had denied himself for far too long.

Lauren tried to stifle the quick surge of craving that made her want to hurry him. It had been so long—so long. And she wanted him with an urgency that was revealed in the arch of her back and the aching void between her thighs.

But Zach would not be hurried. The palms of his hands smoothed every inch of her back, her arms, her shoulders. His lips brushed across hers, then moved to her cheeks and down the length of her neck. Slow, sweet torment washed through her with the full force of a crashing wave. Her hips thrust into him all on their own. He reached to her bare back-side to hold her up tightly against the heat of him, but still he refused her body's plea. Lowering his mouth he caught the taut, swollen tip of her breast instead. The rocking of his hips against hers teased her desire to a near frenzy before he at last eased her back, poised himself over her, and then thrust into her in a joining so sweetly necessary that Lauren groaned with the pleasure of finally feeling him full within her.

Again his pace was slow and steady, promising so much more with the controlled depth of each thrust. Building. Deeper. Faster. Deeper. Until his need, every bit as great as hers, exploded into fast rhythmic beats that took them closer...closer...ever closer ...to ride a wave as towering as if the sea itself had picked them up on the crest of the highest breaker and held them suspended in air before depositing them once more on the earth, soothed and sated, comforted and rejoined.

And when they were finished he held her so close it seemed he wanted to take her into his body as he had been in hers.

Lauren felt certain they could go on together now, hoping that she might even be able to win his love.

But Zach's thoughts were not hope-filled. The shadow of Rossiter loomed like an evil presence over Lauren and his determination to get her to give up Maudie's. And then the shadow lengthened to touch and remind Lauren as well.

"You honestly did pay McGuffy, didn't you, Zach?" she asked softly in the dark, a shred of doubt linger-ing.

"Why wouldn't I have?"

She hesitated and then ventured, "Maybe to ruin Maudie's."

"Rossiter say that?"

"He said maybe you wanted Maudie's for yourself, but I know better than that."

Zach, suddenly saw Rossiter's game in a flash of intuition. "What else did he suggest to you?"

"He wasn't 'suggesting' anything. He was merely warning me to protect what was mine," she answered defensively.

"Don't be a fool, Lauren. The man is no good."

"You don't know him; how can you possibly judge?"

"I know what he is. For God's sake, don't be so gullible. You're letting yourself be blinded by a charming smile and some flattery. I would expect it from a bare, blushing chit, but you're smarter than that." But no more experienced with men and their wiles, a second voice in his head reminded him.

"He is kind and friendly and helpful. Maybe you're jealous." She worked hard to make her tone sound teasing.

"The man is just what you accused me of being the day you found out I had loaned Maudie money for opium, Lauren."

"Don't you think I would see that if it were true?"

"It is true and you don't."

"He is a gentleman and I won't have you malign him."

Frustration made cords stand out on his neck, and the jealousy she had accused him of tightened his throat. "Is there more you feel for him? Is that why you refuse to see him for what he is when you're all too ready to believe the worst of me?" His grip tightened so much he almost hurt her.

"I believed the worst of you only for a few minutes. Look how foolish that was," she said trying to appease him.

"So because I proved innocent of your suspicions you've decided to blatantly trust any man who shows a little interest in you. Are you that much in need of male attention?"

She pulled out of his arms. "At least he isn't lying in wait for me to prove I'm a whore."

He glared up at her from his pillow, his voice so low it was barely audible. "You know better than to even hint that that's what I'm doing."

Lauren wilted in defeat. "Why can't you just accept that he is a business acquaintance? You accepted Alan as a friend."

"Why must you always suffer the worst before you believe what is obvious to everyone else?" he countered.

"Damn you," she breathed.

"Damn you for the hell you're going to put us both through if you don't open your eyes."

"What is all of this?"

It was a week later. Lauren had come upstairs for dinner before dressing for a usual Thursday night at Maudie's to find Zach waiting for her. A formal gown and accoutrements lay on the bed.

"It's a birthday present."

Zach's grin was mischievous, something she hadn't seen the entire time they had been at Maudie's. "It isn't my birthday," she answered tentatively, unnerved by the surprise but a little leery of driving away what looked like the old Zach.

He saw her uncertainty and laughed. "As near as anyone can tell, it's mine."

"I don't think mauve is your color, Zach, and the waist looks too small to go around your middle."

"You've been a whorehouse madam too long, Irish; it's affecting the way you think," he retorted lightly. "My gift is to see you in the dress and get us both out of this place for awhile. You did say you needed that, didn't you?"

"I have to work."

"You have Alan to do it."

"Where are we going?"

"To the opera."

"You're teasing again."

"Now don't be a snob, Lauren. I like opera."

"I don't believe you."

"Then you will have to come along and see, won't you?"

She thought about it for a moment; she was always hesitant about leaving Maudie's. But it was as if the rogue in Zach had been reborn and it beckoned irresistably. "I'll talk with Alan."

"All done. He's taking over and is glad to play boss for a night. Get dressed."

"Whose clothes are these?"

"Yours."

"You know how I feel about accepting gifts from you." But she knew it was a token protest as the exquisite gown tempted her.

"You aren't accepting a gift from me; you are giving me one by wearing it. After all I've done for you, you wouldn't refuse me a birthday present, would you?" He winked broadly. "I'd be happy to help you get into it."

"Determined to have it your own way tonight, is that it?"

"To the last."

There were sheer, lacy underthings, silk stockings, and rosette-tipped shoes, all delicate, fine, and fancy. The dress was a brocade of the same mauve that brightens the sky at dusk. The closs-fitting bodice was fastened from throat to waist with a full seventeen pearl buttons. The skirt was draped in a swag across the front and swept up into an oval pouf in back, revealing a decorative lace underskirt the color of sand. Elbow-length sleeves ended in ruffles, and a matching satin cloak finished the ensemble to perfection. Lauren felt like a little girl playing dress-up.

When she came around the dressing screen to show Zach the result of his efforts, he was gone. It wasn't until Alan came to fetch her downstairs and reassure her that he could handle Maudie's that she saw Zach for the first time in formal garb. A swell of pride buoyed her admiration as Esther brushed a final fleck of lint from his broad shoulder.

He wore a black tailcoat; under it his white shirt was stiffly starched, with a wing collar that opened in a small V just below his Adam's apple. Over this was a white satin waistcoat with pearl buttons down the front and a gold watch chain across his flat middle. At his throat was a white silk tie, kept inside the vest by a diamond stickpin. The sharply creased trousers hugged his hips like a caress. He stood before her, tall and straight and so very handsome, even without the slick perfection of Mark Rossiter, proving that the rugged Zach Madox could match and best any other man.

The lopsided grin was his alone as he extended his arm for Lauren. "We had better get out of here fast, Irish. The ladies are threatening to attack me."

A one-horse hansom cab with a liveried driver standing tall in the back waited outside Maudie's front door. They dined at Seattle's finest hotel and then went on to a performance of a Verdi opera, which Zach thoroughly enjoyed. Lauren endured it with good grace, pleased with the company, if not the entertainment. Gone was the intensity he had displayed at Maudie's. Lauren reveled in his gentle mockery and blessedly forgot Maudie's even existed.

The late night air was chilly as the evening came to a close and the hansom cab again glided through city streets. Zach sang his favorite aria, impressing Lauren with his knowledge of Italian, and she had to admit she preferred his bass rasp to the perfect tenor of the singer who had performed the roll on stage. Again her comparison of him to Mark Rossiter fa-

vored Zach. For while Rossiter was suave and cordial,
he lacked Zach's spontaneity. The proper Miss
Lauren Flannery would not have believed a year ago
that the more improper Zach Madox would appeal to
her now.

When the darkness of the country night descended on them, Lauren's attention was drawn from
Zach to their direction. "The driver has missed Maudie's."

"So he has." Zach's gravelly voice had an under-
tone of amusement. "I mean to have my own way to
the last tonight."

His house waited silently and patiently, the touch
of the moon's glow making it shine irridescently in
the blackness of the night like a welcoming beacon. A
fire had been laid in the hearth and required only a
match to set it aglow. Two snifters sat next to a crystal
brandy decanter on the table before the long brown
sofa.

"How long have you been planning this?" she
asked as he poured the amber liquid and handed her
a glass.

"Just since I came back from camp." He took her
hand and led the way around the table to sit close to
her on the couch.

"I have to get back to Maudie's," she reminded
him softly, loathing the thought of returning there
that night.

"In plenty of time for tomorrow night, I promise."
He raised his leather-clad feet to the tabletop.

"We're staying here tonight?"

"We are. It's my birthday, remember?" Still he held
her hand in his as his thumb rubbed smoothly across
the back of it.

"It's past midnight. Your birthday is over."

"The advantage of not knowing the exact day of
my birth allows some leeway. I'm claiming all night."

"Why don't you know your exact birthday?" She

willingly let the subject of Maudie's lapse. "Or is your past still a secret?"

His black brows arched in mock surprise. "I haven't kept it a secret."

"You've never told me anything."

"It isn't something I'm proud of."

"You know all about mine."

Zach sipped his brandy thoughtfully and then decided she should know the whole story. "I spent the first years of my life in an orphanage, dumped there by God only knows who. I ran away at ten, figuring anything was better than that. But I found the only difference was that I could run away from the lickings I got instead of just suffering them. I lived by my wits, but I was just barely surviving as a runny-nosed beggar and a heavy-handed thief until I met a man named Dennis O'Grady. He taught me the more refined arts of the swindler. He said picking pockets was a last resort in finding the cash for a stake in some gambit or another. We played every hoax imaginable, from selling phony bibles and stock to passing me off as a prince from some little country collecting donations to feed my people. I boxed and rigged card tricks and shell games and about anything else we could come up with."

Lauren sighed skeptically. "You don't expect me to believe that."

Zach's laugh boomed out. "It's the truth."

"How did you get from that to this, then?" she asked dubiously.

He shrugged. "The older I got the more I hated that life. I wanted to settle down, to be known as a decent man, a storekeeper or anything respectable, in a place I never had to run from. So I retired to Montana, staked out a claim on a small mine that paid off, then another, bigger one, and everything just seemed to work out after that. I made money at whatever I did and then I stopped in Seattle and decided to stay." He gulped the remaining brandy. "So there you have it. My notorious past. Satisfied?"

There was something in the gruffness of his voice and the expression in his eyes that made Lauren believe him. "That was really how you grew up?"

"Would I make up a thing like that?"

"You would if there were some lesson for me to gain from it."

He laughed again. "I'm leaving you to learn all your lessons through experience, Irish. You're too damn stubborn to learn from my stories." He ran his free hand through his hair, pulling it straight back for a moment before he let it fall into wings again. He arched his neck against the tight collar and tie. He loosened both and then looked at her slyly. "I didn't bring you here to study my past, Lauren."

She watched him, feeling a wellspring of tenderness for this man who had come so far all alone. "For what exactly did you bring me here?" she asked in a low voice that had grown deeper with emotion.

He nodded toward the stairway. "A night in a bed big enough for both of us." His arm reached across the sofa back; one hand found the nape of her neck and his thumb ran trails down it that soothed and excited her at the same time. "Come upstairs with me," he urged huskily.

He took the stem of her glass between the same two fingers that held his and set both glasses on the table. Then he drew her through the house and upstairs into the bedroom where he turned to Lauren and, with slow gentleness, undressed her. "I hated being here without you the night before I left for the logging camp." His cheek pressed against her temple as he spoke, and each word gusted in to her hair as he loosed and fingered it.

"I said then that I hadn't meant you to leave," she reminded him.

Satiny lips brushed across her forehead. "I was too angry to stay." But the words were a caress.

She kissed the underside of his chin and he groaned. She smiled against the sensitive flesh and then sighed into the hollow of his throat as he removed the rest of his own clothes and pulled her bare breasts against his hair-roughened chest.

"For a man who grew up in a sordid life you haven't much tolerance for Maudie's," she commented breathlessly.

He kissed her eyes and her nose and tickled the corner of her mouth with his tongue. "None at all and growing less by the day." His fingers kneaded the flesh of her shoulders, his thumbs pressing into the hollows in front.

"So you brought me here to remember what it's like," she guessed intuitively. She felt his lips tighten into a smile in answer. "Underhanded and despicable." She teased his nipples.

"So is that," he growled, pulling her up harder against him.

"You deserve it."

"I'll take all you want to give." He pulled her back with him onto the bed, finding her mouth with his, open, hot, slippery. His tongue thrust against hers in demanding invitation and she bit it gently.

"Did they teach you that in the convent?" He laughed, pulling little patches of her skin into his mouth on his way to her breast.

"They taught us to bite harder," she retorted, twining her fingers through the coolness of his hair. Her hands trailed down the nape of his neck to his back, feeling the firm mounds and hollow valleys of his body shift beneath her palms.

"Like this?" He nipped the hardened peak of her breast, tugging gently.

She moaned and arched and breathed, "I don't think so."

He laughed and drew the firm globe fully into his mouth, sucking and flicking a pointed tongue at the tip. He pulled one of her hands from his back and moved her fingers to slide over his shoulder, down his chest and stomach, and then lower, to that part she was never sure of. But when her hand closed around the steely rod and his whole body tensed with pleasure, she stayed to explore his silk-encased strength.

She heard him swallow hard and breathe as if the air was thick. A shiver scudded up her back at his response to her ministrations. Then his palm smoothed its way down her stomach and slipped between her thighs, where his questing fingers found her core.

Her legs parted eagerly and her hips thrust against him in yearning, ardent invitation. He encased himself in her, easing the ache inside, driving himself home in the warm velvet of her body. And then lightning struck and starbursts blotted out every sense in them both, forging them together in a universe of their own making.

A full putty moon shone through the undraped windows into Zach's eyes as they lay entwined, still holding each other tightly. He hadn't felt this way since before Maudie's had opened. His heart was full, and his sense that this alone was right was very strong. But what was she feeling? What would she say if he asked her to marry him now?

"Lauren..."

But the words stuck. She had given him her answer once before, on the eve of Maudie's opening. If it were the same now he knew he couldn't go back with her. He had to feel there was hope, that there would still come a time when she might be willing to leave Maudie's and its way of life behind, to forget her pride and all her mother had made her believe she would surrender in loving a man.

"What is it?" she asked as the sound of her name still hung in the air.

"Nothing," he answered raggedly. "Nothing."

But Lauren was too lost in her own thoughts to hear his regret. What had begun after Rossiter's kiss as the niggling fear that she might love Zach had tonight erupted into the blinding realization that she truly did. There could be no denying it now. If only he hadn't brought her back here and reminded her of how it could be between them, maybe she could have kept her heart safe. But he had, and she was in terrible peril. She knew why her mother had warned so harshly against love, for it was going to be so much harder to return to Maudie's now.

Chapter 22

"Get him off! Get him off! He's gone and died on me!" Shrill screams tore through Maudie's three nights later.

Zach and Lauren lunged from bed at the same time, his head crashing into the low attic ceiling. "Dammit! I forgot about that!" He pulled on his pants, grumbling about how he should have let the place stay in ashes.

Lauren wasted no time on his complaint. Fumbling in the dark, she found her robe, tied it around her waist, and, as she had learned from experience, grabbed the key to the bedroom doors on her way out.

When she and Zach entered the bedroom below, they were greeted by the soles of a pair of boots and the bare, fleshy backside of an inert man lying on top of the still shrieking Belle, whose arms and legs were tied to the four bedposts. Zach rushed in, rolled the man, who was indeed dead, off Belle and quickly untied her.

"He just up and died!" she wailed. "There wasn't anything I could do! He got all red in the face and his eyes bugged out and he dropped like a lump of blubber!"

Zach watched as Lauren stared in disbelief at the

whole scene. But a second later she snapped to and began giving instructions in a practical, businesslike tone that set everything back to normal as she dispatched Billy and Josef to fetch the doctor and the police.

It took about two hours to settle the matter without incident. The doctor ruled it death by heart attack and had a good laugh with the police chief about the man dying happy. But under-the-table protocol required Lauren to offer them a drink and compensation for their trouble, and that couldn't be hurried.

Zach sat at a distance, nursing a cup of hot coffee. He alone saw the pallor in Lauren's face as she smiled at the off-color jokes and endured the lascivious comments. His hands ached to wring somebody's neck and he wasn't sure whose. The dark scowl that creased his features was ominous, and it didn't change when Alan crumpled into the seat beside him.

"Welcome back," Alan said facetiously.

"It goes on and on around here, doesn't it?" The question was answered from across the room by a foul-mouthed expletive ending an obscene, raucous exchange between the two officials. Zach's head dropped back and he took a long, ragged breath. "I can't sit by and watch much more of this."

"I understand that feeling," Alan murmured softly. It was now common knowledge that he pined for Polly Carson, suffering at the sight of her climbing the stairs time after time with yet another man, and never taking a turn himself. But until now Zach hadn't seen the similiarity in their predicaments.

"How do you stand it?"

Alan shook his head. "I wonder that myself. But she sends the money back home to her widowed mother and eleven brothers and sisters. Until I can afford to send as much and support us too, what can I do?"

"Why didn't you come to me? I'll put you to work anywhere you want, doing whatever you want, and make sure you are paid enough."

"I know you would. But Lauren needs me here too."

"I'll take care of Lauren."

Alan sighed in frustration before admitting, "It isn't only that. I'm not sure Polly will have me. She's a different girl from what you see on the surface. She's driven. Too many years of nearly starving have made her determined to do whatever she has to for money. It never seems as if she has enough. I have to convince her to settle for what I can give her. Until I do, at least I'm here with her. I just have to try and understand . . . and bear it."

"I don't know about you, Alan, but understanding is coming harder and harder for me."

"Don't give up on her yet, Zach. There are hungry wolves waiting in the woods."

"Rossiter."

"I could be wrong," Alan was quick to add. "He was aboveboard and strictly proper, from what I could see."

"I've already heard how perfect he is," Zach said rudely.

"But I think he wants Lauren."

"Or Maudie's."

"You haven't seen the way he looks at her."

"How is that?"

"Like a starving man in front of a bakery window. Besides, if he were just after Maudie's he could have let us go under last week. Instead he put things right and showed her better ways to do some things. I think it's Lauren he's after."

Across the room Lauren was escorting her guests out. Zach stood up to follow. "Thanks for the warning. Keep in mind that I still owe you, whenever you're ready to call in my debt."

Alan only nodded hopelessly.

But his own words rang like a church bell in Zach's head.

"Madox is staying with her the same as before, as far as I can tell. But from the sound of the rows they've been having it won't be for long," reported the whore to Rossiter, knowing it was what he wanted to hear. Then she broached the subject of her own demands. "If I have to do anything else in the office, like stealing that receipt, it's going to cost you more. I nearly got caught on that one."

"It will all be worth your while."

"Lucky for you they don't know you own McGuffy," she said recklessly. "How much longer do you think this will take?"

"Other plans, darling?"

"I just don't what to be found out. If the other girls knew I was some sort of spy, it could make my life real hard."

"Relax. I suspect that it won't be too much longer now. If you do your job right, no one need ever know about our partnership. In fact, I think it's time we helped things along by driving the wedge between Lauren and Madox a little deeper. I'm going to have to know the next evening he won't be in the house."

The Friday-night crowd was relatively tame. Lauren greeted her guests cordially, overseeing their comfort on the first floor with the same gracious poise with which she had opened Maudie's. Her girls worked the lower rooms, serving drinks and flirting, lounging on male laps, nuzzling necks and whispering sly propositions into overeager ears before leading the way upstairs. In the parlor Alan played a lively tune on the piano in accompaniment to the ga-lumphing dancing of a handful of loggers and their hostesses while the clink of coins spoke in the gaming room.

Following Zach's firm orders, Lauren's big barrel of a bodyguard trailed her every step, towering over her in mute warning. Tonight would be profitable too, she was thinking, as always. And she felt as much of a sense of well-being as she ever could at Maudie's.

It was short-lived.

Not a breath of warning sounded before Maudie's front doors flew open with a crash. "It's a raid!" came the shout.

In swarmed the police. High-pitched shrieking whistles blew, female voices screamed, male ones cursed, and mass havoc erupted.

"Oh, my God!" Alan shouted, but Lauren only stood in a stupor.

Men in blue serge uniforms were everywhere, wielding billy clubs high, while meaty hands grabbed arms, flinging customers and employees alike back toward the entrance. Everywhere guns flashed, while people shouted and pressed and stampeded like cattle for the rear doors where more men in blue serge shoved them back again.

It couldn't be happening! Lauren's mind raged. The bribes had been paid. This was a mistake. She grabbed a thick blue arm to get its owner's attention, but before she could utter words, her hand was slapped away and she was yanked into the waiting grip of another policeman. Again and again she was handed roughly from one to another, until she felt the momentary brush of cool night air before being thrown like a hay bale up into a paddy wagon.

Gutteral curses heated her ears along with snatches of raged comments: "...Supposed to be taken care of...no house gets raided if the right people are paid...might as well be in the streets if this is going to happen...Don't you know how to run this business, lady..."

The wagon doors closed with a crash. The compressed mass of bodies swayed as one, threatening to topple before adjusting to the hard bounce of the wagon. Inside it was pitch black and hot, and the smell of too-strong perfume, liquor and smoke was cloying.

"...There will be hell to pay for this..." The outbursts of anger settled into low, threatening mumblings: "...She ought to be horsewhipped for putting us in this position...I know men in high places...Close the damn place down..."

Lauren felt lightheaded and removed, as if she had nothing to do with the scene at all. In the blind darkness it seemed like a nightmare, the crush of human flesh around her just the cushion of bed, the disembodied voices just dream rumblings in her mind.

A sharp turn sent up a fresh roar. Then as abruptly as it had started up, the wagon jolted to a stop, the doors flew wide, and they were jerked out the way they had been tossed in and then shoved into Seattle's seediest jailhouse.

All the people from Maudie's was crowded into three square cells, leaving not even enough room to sit down. Two policemen stood guard, their billy clubs swinging at their sides. With every new curse or threat shouted at Lauren, one would step up and rap furiously on the iron bars and promise to bash skulls if they didn't quiet down. But she overheard the mutterings and whispered vows just the same.

Smashed into a corner of the cell, Lauren didn't know what to do. How long would they be kept here? Would they be tried and sent to prison?

Alan's cell abutted Lauren's; he worked his way to her and reached a comforting hand through the bars. "It will be all right," he mouthed to her. But Lauren didn't know how it possibly could be.

"What about the bribes?" she whispered back.

"Zach paid them," he said, and each thought about the McGuffy incident but said no more.

After an hour the guard changed. But Lauren didn't even hear the noise around her anymore; it was just an indistinguishable drone of abuse and anger. The jail door closed after the departing sentries, and the two replacements settled into the same positions as those of the men they had replaced.

"Couldn't' a come at a better time, I be tellin' yuh." The thick Irish brogue of one of the guards caught Lauren's ear simply because of the change in accent. "Me Mary Colleen was naggin' fer a new stove, she was. Now there's the money."

The other officer laughed. "Collected from the cap'n already, did yuh?"

"Aye. I wanted me fair share before that hefty bribe was spread too thin."

"Was it a rival paid to have us raid the place, do yuh think?"

"More likely an unsatisfied customer." They both laughed heartily. "Nah. The way 'twas told to me, 'twas old Zach Madox hisself. A grudge it was. Yuh know the place was to be his. Smart money says he's tryin' to run dear old Maudie's niece right out o' the business. Sunk a fair piece o' coin into rebuildin' and then some fancy lass sashays in to take it over. 'Nuff to boil any bloke's blood, is what I'm thinkin'," concluded the speaker. "All I know fer certain sure is it was a fine fee he paid to us to close the place down tonight."

Far back in the cells Alan couldn't bear the sight of the anger and heartbreak on Lauren's face.

* * *

Maudie's was quiet by the time Zach brought Lauren back. The girls were all in their rooms for the night, consoled and compensated. Alan and Polly were clearing the mess left from the evening's entertainment and the raid.

Lauren climbed the stairs to the attic room as silently as she had spent the hours since Zach had come to the jail and arranged for everyone's release; hers had been last and the costliest. Never had he seen her back as straight, her head as high, her face as pale. Maybe he wouldn't have to play his ace in the hole after all.

Lauren crossed the room, not turning around until she was at the far wall, as if she needed it to guard her back. She clasped her arms tightly over her middle, raised her chin high, and let the full flame of her topaz eyes loose at him. Her voice was steady, firm, and as cold as a rapier. "Gather your belongings and get out of here."

Zach's head jerked toward her to be met by the hatred shining from her glittering eyes. "What the hell is this?"

"I know what you did," she hissed.

"I just paid a small fortune in bribes to get you out of jail."

Her nostrils flared with rage. "Don't stand there and lie to me. I know what you did. Two of the guards discussed what they meant to do with the money you paid them to raid Maudie's."

"Paid them to raid Maudie's?" he parroted in outraged disbelief.

"You have been found out. You want this place to fail, you want me to fail. So you decided to sabotage me. First it was McGuffy, but Mark foiled that plan, didn't he? No wonder you dislike him so much. Tonight it was the raid. That was supposed to be so ugly it would scare me off, wasn't it? Well, you should have been more careful. Now I know and you can get out," she rasped.

"Don't blame me for what this life is," he shot back heatedly. "Did you expect it to be roses and sunshine, for God's sake? Whorehouses are illegal, Lauren, and they get raided. Sometimes even if your bribes are paid they get raided. It is a risk every house runs. A new man on the beat that doesn't know you're paid up, an official who lost too much at your tables, or maybe they're just making a statement that they want to up what you're already paying out to avoid it. There are any number of reasons for a raid. If you wanted to run a safe business you should have opened a hat shop."

"You aren't listening. They said *you* paid to have me raided," she shouted.

"I wouldn't waste my money." He pulled his shirt-tails from his waistband with a vicious movement.

"I said to get out," she repeated louder still. "I don't want you here anymore, knowing my business and able to do damage when the opportunity arises. You no longer have a place at Maudie's."

"I haven't done any goddamned damage," he said through gritted teeth.

"I know better."

"You always think you do."

"Get out!"

"No." His boots made hollow thuds as he strode to the bed. He reached under it and pulled out the valise that held his belongings. When he straightened up again he held an envelope. "I didn't arrange for that raid, but I'll admit I was hoping it might work in my favor. Since it hasn't I'll tell you now what I figured to say tomorrow anyway." His black eyes bored into hers, the tension between them palpable. "I'm calling in the note." He flung the envelope onto the bed.

Lauren's eyes spewed contempt as silence fell be-

tween them. How could she have thought she loved
him? "You are everything I ever thought you were.
Every vile, evil thing I was taught men are," she spit
out, but still she didn't grasp the full impact of what
he had said.

The hatred in her voice tightened Zach's gut as if a
fist had landed there hard, but he stood stock still, as
straight and unyielding as she. "That may be, lady,
but unless you come up with seven thousand dollars
in two days, Maudie's is mine."

Lauren's grip around her waist constricted. "You
can't do that."

He nodded at the envelope. "It's all right there
and perfectly legal. I have the right to demand the
full amount of the loan any time I see fit. I see fit
right now."

"You bastard," she breathed.

"You can call me anything you want. I can't stand
to watch you sinking deeper and deeper into the
muck of this life. I gave you your taste of what your
mother and Maudie were and of the life they lived.
Now you've had it, it's time to get out."

"If you are trying to sound noble you have the
wrong audience. You're stealing from me, remember?"

"I don't care what you call this either. But unless
you have a real big nest egg stashed around here
somewhere, this place is mine and you are out of it."

"Maudie's is mine."

"You have the money?"

"You know I don't."

"Then Maudie's is mine."

"If you wanted it from the start why play it out this
far? Just to get me into your bed?"

"More like it's because you're in my bed that I
want you out of here. I care for you, dammit, can't
you see that? Do you think it would matter to me if I
didn't?"

"If you cared for me you wouldn't steal from me," she railed.

"You'll thank me for it eventually."

Her anger was like a boiling pot erupting. "Who do you think you are?" The words vibrated in the air between them, "I won't thank you because I don't ever want to see your face again."

"Fine." He thought it was her anger alone that spoke. "Just pack up and we'll work that out after I have this place closed down."

"I am not going anywhere and you are not taking over Maudie's. I'll pay your filthy money."

"How?"

"I don't know how!" she screamed. "But I will. If it's the last thing I ever do, I'll raise it and pay you off to get you out of my life!"

Zach watched her. She couldn't get hold of that kind of money so fast. He had already used his influence with every banker in Seattle against her. All that was left was to wait her out. In two days he would close Maudie's and when Lauren had cooled off, he would try to reason with her. "Then that's what it's going to be, is it?" He was calling her bluff.

She saw how confident he was that he had won, and it fueled her already blazing rage. "Get out! I'll see you in two days when I have the money!"

He grabbed his valise and crossed to the door, stopping with his hand on the knob. For long seconds he stood there, gaining control of his own temper before he spoke. "I did this because it's best, Lauren." His low, gravelly voice barely penetrated her rage.

"The best thing you could have done was to stay out of my life completely."

Ignoring her tirade, he went on in a calming tone, "We can have a future together once this place isn't between us. That's what I want." He turned his head so that his black eyes once more stared at her over his shoulder. His gravelly voice pronounced each word slowly and precisely. "I want you."

She laughed, an hysterical burst of mirthless disbelief. "I would go the King's Kastle before I'd ever come to you. You made me a whore. I may as well put it to good use."

He swung the door wide enough to crash into the wall behind it and was gone.

And Lauren was too full of rage and hatred to care.

Chapter 23

"Are you all right, Lauren?" Alan's concerned voice came from the doorway.

Lauren still stood with her back against the wall. Her head snapped up, but her mind was too full to have heard either the final slam of Maudie's front door as Zach stormed out or the approach of a worried Alan outside her room. "He has done it," she breathed, still not believing it. "He has called in the note on Maudie's. I have to pay him seven thousand dollars in two days or he closes us down." She began pacing in a frenzy.

Alan watched her in silence for a few moments before venturing carefully; "Maybe it's for the best."

"The best?" she shrieked at him. "My God, you sound just like him!"

"Let me get you a drink. It's been a night full of shocks." He was quick to appease her.

"I don't want a drink. I have to figure out a way to raise that kind of money. Think, Alan! I need help."

"He cares for you, Lauren. I think he loves you," Alan said. "If I had the power to get Polly out of here I wouldn't hesitate to use it."

She turned on him with venom in her eyes, and he was frightened by a rage the likes of which he had never seen in her before. "Don't you ever say that he

219

cares for me again, do you hear? I know what you feel for Polly and I'm sorry this is how it has to be for you both. But it is not the same, Alan, it just is not the same."

"Not in some ways. But in most it is. Try to understand how hard it was for him to see you doing all you had to here, to see you in jail tonight."

"He put us there!" she shouted in frustration.

"He said he didn't." Their argument had been loud enough for all ears.

"It was a lie."

"Why would he do it, Lauren? Think about it. If he had the papers ready to close us down he didn't need a raid to evict you. And even if he had been the one to order it done, why would he have gotten us all out of jail?"

"He probably thought it would make me accept his highhanded tactics, make him seem like a hero. He probably expected me to thank him for setting me free. You don't know him the way I do, Alan. He is a great one for teaching lessons and making points through demonstration. It would be just like him."

Alan said, almost to himself, "I don't believe that." Then he turned back to Lauren. "Try and consider this clearly. We both know Maudie's is not what you expected it to be. It goes against your grain. Wouldn't you be happier away from here?"

"Doing what?" she shot at him fiercely. "Maudie's is my livelihood, my legacy, the means of gaining my independence. It isn't as if he has bought me out and I'll come away with a little money when the loan is paid off. I'll have nothing. I'll be penniless. Where does that leave me, Alan? I'll tell you where. It leaves me in the streets. If he cared for me he wouldn't do that, would he?"

"Zach will take care of you." For a moment Alan thought she might hit him.

Instead her tone turned to cold steel. "I will never

trust any man to take care of me. I was raised to
know what that costs a woman and I will never, never
give in to that. I won't simper and whine and grovel
at any man's feet for what I need. I take care of myself."

"All right, Lauren, all right," he said, giving in
gently. "Then what are you going to do? I'm the son
of a banker, remember? No bank is going to lend an
illegal...immoral...establishment that kind of
money just for the asking. Bankers are conservative
people. Maybe if you had been here long enough to
cultivate the friendship of one of them it might have
worked in your favor, but you haven't. That way is
closed to you. If you go to the moneylenders you will
end up worse than if you concede Maudie's to Zach
now. So how can you possibly come up with seven
thousand dollars? He has you, Lauren," Alan finished softly and waited for her to explode again.

But it was as if his reasoning only strengthened
her determination. Instead of another fit of temper
she answered him with pure stubborn will. "I'll get
that money. No matter what I have to do."

The waters of Puget Sound lapped against the hull
of the sleeping steamer; a few lamps were left burning to light the way for before-dawn departures.
Mark Rossiter had described the alloted spaces
aboard his ship to Lauren as they had passed it on
their way to his smuggler's hideaway for dinner.
Lauren remembered he had said his quarters were
on the upper deck behind the wheelhouse, so it was
there that she headed.

After hours of pacing and discarding idea after
idea of how she could raise the seven thousand dollars, she had come to the reluctant conclusion that
Mark Rossiter was her only hope. Panic and the press
of time would not allow her to rest until she had approached him on the subject, and Lauren had de-

cided this was emergency enough to seek him out in the middle of the night aboard *The Countess.*

The first hard raps on his door roused only a giant of a man with the pointy-featured face of a fox. He stepped from the wheelhouse and leered down at her like an angry fate, but Lauren was too lost in her problems to feel fear of a mere ugly man. "I must see Mark Rossiter immediately," she demanded of him as he stood before the still-closed door, blocking even another knock.

"Come back in the morning," he commanded.

"If it could have waited until the morning I wouldn't be here now."

He wasted no more words; instead, he closed his ham-sized fist around her shoulder to escort her off the ship. But before he had managed to budge her, the cabin door opened.

Rossiter stood in a silk brocade dressing gown, his hair slightly tousled in a way that made him seem younger and more vulnerable. He directed a sleepy, curious smile at Lauren while he dismissed the man he called Tommy. "Just one moment, Lauren, and you can come in." He closed the door all but a crack and when next it opened Rossiter shoved a reluctant woman out. "Now, Lauren"—he ushered her smoothly into the office half of his room, which was lit by two lamps on a large desk, leaving the disheveled bed in shadow—"sit and let me pour you a brandy. You look as if you need it. Then tell me what has brought you."

Lauren breathed deeply to shore up her confidence, taking the glass he offered but never sipping from it. Ignoring his second invitation to sit, she remained standing behind a tufted leather chair that faced his desk. Her back was ramrod straight, her shoulders square. "I'm sorry to bother you like this ... at this hour."

He waved her apology away. "Nonsense. I can't tell

you how pleased I am that you came to me." He
leaned against the desk front, both of his leather-
slippered feet flat out before him. His own brandy
snifter was cradled in his palm, his well-manicured
fingers curling up the goblet to warm the fine
French cognac. There was appreciation in his azure
eyes as he watched her, recognizing her difficulty in
broaching her subject. "Out with it, Lauren—tell me
what I can do for you."

"It is a galling, awkward request."

"I'm anxious to do anything I can for you."

There was nothing to do but blurt out the facts.
Lauren couldn't look him in the face, finding the
humbling circumstances unbearable. Not until she
had finished and heard Rossiter's suave chuckle did
she raise her glance to him, fearing he was laughing
at the absurdity of her plea. Instead what she saw
was delight.

"Is that all it is?" he breathed, giving her a mock
frown. "I thought it was something dire. Sit down
and relax; of course I will lend you the money." Rossiter marveled at his own luck. He hadn't any idea
that Lauren owed Madox money. It couldn't have
been better if he had planned it himself.

To Lauren it seemed too easy, which alerted her
suspicious nature. "You understand that this is a temporary loan, that I will repay you before a year is out,
at whatever rate of interest you ask, and then I will
own Maudie's free and clear."

"Certainly."

"Haven't you any qualms at all?"

"Not a one." He saw her doubts and laughed
again. "Surely you didn't expect to have to beg me,
did you, Lauren?"

"I didn't expect it to be so simple."

"What kind of a friend would I be if I put you
through any more upset than you have obviously
suffered tonight? There isn't anything for me to lose,

is there? If you take the money and run off I could claim Maudie's. But I know you won't do that. You will pay me back before I even realize the money is gone, and I will make a fair amount of profit on top of it. So why should I bicker or barter or even hesitate? You have already said you'll pay whatever interest I decide on. I am a businessman, and what you are offering me is a sound business investment. That's all."

It sounded reasonable enough. "I only have two days to pay him."

"I will have it to you first thing Monday morning. You can take it directly to him and be done with it."

Panic gave way to pain. Lauren took a gulp of the fiery brandy, not even aware of the path it burned in her throat. Rossiter saw it all in her face—her fear, her uncertainty, but most of all her pain at Zach's betrayal. Genuine sympathy furrowed his wheaten brows and he shook his head sadly. He set his snifter on the desk and crossed to Lauren, reaching to enclose her in a tender embrace.

Lauren hadn't the strength to fight...nor the desire. She yielded to the warmth of his tall, lean body, letting him press her head into his chest. His hand stayed against the back of her head, above the tight knot of her hair; his other hand held her just firmly enough to comfort her. "He has hurt you, hasn't he, darling?" he whispered.

But Lauren didn't respond. She just stared into the brocaded sleeve inches from her face, lost in sudden bewilderment.

"I know he has hurt you badly, but I promise it will get better. We will get him out of your life, and time will do the rest—you'll see." He raised her chin with one finger and peered down at her, a gentle smile on his handsome face. "I'm here for you, Lauren, for anything you need or want. My feelings for you are very special."

His words barely penetrated the painful thoughts that shrouded Lauren's mind. She drew away from him, standing stiff and straight once more. "Thank you," she murmured.

"Let me dress and I will see you home."

"No, that isn't necessary. I have a carriage waiting ... and Billy. I'll get back on my own."

He smiled compassionately at her. "Until Monday morning then. Bright and early, I promise."

She turned to leave and made it all the way to the door before she looked back at him, feeling the need to say more in recognition of his magnanimous kindness. "Mark..." She swallowed back the swell of too many emotions. "I can't tell you how much I appreciate this. I promise you I will pay back your money as soon as possible."

"Go home to bed, darling, and don't give it another thought."

Lauren was awake, dressed, and waiting by dawn on Monday morning. She had barely slept at all in the two days past, but the stupor that had lulled her into Mark Rossiter's arms had left her completely immediately after that episode. Cold, hard anger fueled her, and nothing could ease it.

Alan, too, had found no rest, worrying about the course she had chosen to take. But still he offered her mute support and companionship as she awaited Rossiter in her office.

Over and over again he had voiced his doubts and his fear that severing all ties with Zach in favor of Mark Rossiter was not a wise choice. It would salvage Maudie's, she had argued, and that was all she cared about. It was an act of survival, no different than her leaving Dry Creek to take over Maudie's in the first place. She would not give in to a manipulating man any more now than then, and if she was going to owe any man money it might as well be one who at least understood this business. They had argued as never before, but Lauren was not to be swayed and Alan was too much a friend to desert her even when they disagreed.

"The money is all here, Lauren." Rossiter sat across from her barely half an hour after sunrise, patting a leather satchel in his lap. "But I think I should be with you when you pay off Zach. You shouldn't be going about alone with such a large sum."

"I have Billy," was all she answered. "Have you the note for me to sign?"

"We can tend to that later."

"I would rather it be done now."

Rossiter sighed patiently and spoke to Alan, who stood behind Lauren's chair. "She hasn't rested at all in these past two days, has she?" Alan shook his head slowly.

Rossiter drew a paper from his breast pocket. "All right then, Lauren. But I want your word before I go through with this that you will come directly back here, go up to your room, and sleep the day away. Do I have it?"

"I will be fine as soon as this is over with."

"Promise me. Alan can run Maudie's until tomorrow, can't you, Alan?"

"I promise," she answered tersely.

Rossiter slid the paper across the desk. Lauren barely read it, only checking to be certain the interest was fair. Then she signed it and slid it back, rising to collect the satchel.

"Take Alan with you, if not me," Rossiter suggested. But Lauren left without a backward glance.

When she had gone, Rossiter turned to Alan and faced a black scowl. "I advised her against this." Alan confessed quietly.

Rossiter was noncommittal. "It gets her what she wants," he said tonelessly.

"I wonder if maybe you are after Maudie's for yourself. If she is going to lose it, I would rather it be to Zach. He would at least make sure she doesn't come away with nothing."

Rossiter sized him up. Alan's courage was only a result of desperation. Harmless, he judged. "I will admit I wanted Maudie's when it was up for sale before. That is, after all, how Lauren and I met. But I want Lauren even more."

"I think you want her, all right, but I don't know that I believe you want her more than Maudie's.

Rossiter shrugged one shoulder and smiled in that winning, friendly way he had. "Consider this, Alan. If Maudie's was what I wanted I could have refused Lauren the money. Madox had the word out that he wanted to sell the place before Lauren ever came to Seattle. It stands to reason that he would still be willing to sell, and Maudie's would be mine. What I want is Lauren . . . happy, independent, and free to choose between us. If my helping her to own Maudie's makes that possible and wins a little for my side in the bargain, it is a good investment. Simple as that." He stood up to leave then. "I can see that your loyalties are with Madox and I respect that, Alan. But he isn't the only man in the world for Lauren. In time you will come to see that I am better for her."

Alan truly didn't know whether Rossiter was right or wrong.

Lauren didn't question how Billy knew where to find Zach; she was too absorbed in how she was going to get through the meeting with him. She sat in the buggy seat just behind her big bodyguard, but her spine did not touch the seat back. The money satchel rested in her lap, her hands in a white-knuckled grip around it. She felt so odd, so removed from herself, as if she were hiding in a shell, only temporarily protected from pain.

The Cades' house was quiet in the early morning hours. Winifred alone was up and about. Showing no surprise at finding Lauren on her doorstep, she greeted her warmly, if a trifle formally, and led the way to the drawing room.

"I have come to see Zach. Is he here?" Lauren managed to say in a soft voice.

The older woman ignored the question. "We must have tea first, don't you think?" she asked and, without waiting for a reply, left Lauren. She returned with a steaming pot and two cups. "Sit down, dear." It was more an order than an invitation.

Lauren obeyed but perched on the very edge of her chair. Her back was rigid, her chin high, and her face very, very pale.

Winifred poured tea and handed Lauren a cup before sitting down across from her on the gold sofa and taking up her own cup. The older woman was solemn but gracious. "We've asked Zach to bring you to Friday supper, but he never says much about it," she said pointedly. "That's his way. He jokes and teases and before you know it he has skirted around the issue. He speaks so highly of you that I assumed it wasn't because he didn't want to bring you that you didn't come. Was it because of your working at Maudie's?"

Lauren's face grew even more ashen. She drew herself up stiffly and had to clear her throat before she could speak. "He told you that I own Maudie's?"

Winifred clucked. "Of course not. Zach doesn't tell tales out of school. But I hear the gossip. He's always a good subject for tongue-wagging women hoping to catch him. And a place like Maudie's doesn't go unnoticed by a long shot either. Put them together and you two have been the best gossip stirred up in years."

"I see. Then I should apologize for coming to your home and involving you in it. The busybodies

will have a field day with you for this. If I could just
see Zach, I will be on my way."

"Nonsense. I just said I had invited you, didn't I?"
The silver-haired woman stared Lauren up and
down. "I don't believe you're a whore, anyway," she
said bluntly, ending the subject. "Zach didn't mention
that he was expecting you."

"We have business."

"Couldn't it have waited until later in the day?"

"I'm afraid not." Lauren thought she would burst
with tension if she didn't get this business over with
soon. "It is important that I see him now and get
back to Maudie's."

Again Winifred stared at her, and Lauren had the
feeling she was facing a very protective mother bear.
But in the end the older woman relented and went
upstairs. She returned alone, poured herself more
tea, and settled calmly back in her seat, all without a
word.

Frustration tensed Lauren's already taut nerves.
She opened her mouth to question the other woman
impatiently, but before the words were voiced there
came from behind her the familiar gravelly tones;
their effect was like salt in a wound.

"Well, well, what have we here but Miss Irish Pride
herself." His voice was rougher than usual.

Lauren turned her head his way and was taken
aback by what she saw. Zach leaned against the door
frame, his thumbs hooked in the waistband of his
snug denims. He wore a wrinkled shirt buttoned only
at the bottom and nothing at all on his feet. His hair
was a tousled mess falling over his forehead, his face
was whisker black, and his eyes were the color of un-
dercooked beefsteak. He looked as ill as anyone she
had ever seen, but he had obviously inflicted it on
himself, and Lauren tried hard not to care.

"It should be no surprise to you," she answered

him coldly. "Two days have passed and it was, after all, the deadline you set yourself."

Zach leered at her, ignoring her words, and eased away from the doorjamb to sit beside Winifred, his every movement painstaking. "God, I hope that's coffee you have there, Winnie."

"It isn't. But there's some coming."

Zach's face flinched in agony, and he pinched his eyes shut as he sank back, groaning as he rested his head against the back of the sofa.

"What's wrong with him?" Lauren asked the other woman impersonally.

Winifred glanced sideways at Zach. "He has a monumental hangover—haven't you, dear?"

Zach growled in answer and Winifred explained to Lauren, "He has been this way all weekend. Will and Evan have taken to following him around just to keep the crimps from getting him. Then the boys bring him back here, pour him into bed, and when he wakes up he starts all over again. Around here we think he's heartsick, but he won't say much."

"You have a big mouth, Winnie," he grumbled.

After her own misery Lauren wondered why she didn't find this revelation satisfying. But her feelings were too heavy even for that.

His coffee arrived just then and his tone softened. "Do a dying man the service of handing me the cup, eh, Winnie?" She did and he took a swallow as if it were the elixir of life. Then he glared through eyes that were barely slits and said irascibly, "Come out with it, Lauren. Why are you here at this ungodly hour?"

"This should be done in private," she answered curtly, adding, "no offense, Mrs. Cade."

"There isn't any reason for Winnie to leave her own parlor. Unless it has something to do with your damned pride and then she can stay anyway."

"Suit yourself." Lauren refused to be baited by his

foul temper. "I have your money." The words fell like lead.

For a long while Zach's stare—hard and dark and inscrutable—pinned her. He had told himself this wouldn't happen...couldn't happen, and yet somewhere in his gut he had known it would. Where the hell could she have gotten the money? But she didn't look as if she were bluffing. "You have seven thousand dollars with you right now?" he asked finally.

Lauren stood up and placed the satchel on the table in front of him; then she sat down again. "Please count it and return my note." Where had the lump in her throat come from?

Zach's eyes ignored the satchel and bore into her. His voice was quiet. "You're going to do it, aren't you? You're going to put us both through unholy hell."

"I'm going to do what I came to Seattle to do. Run Maudie's to support myself."

Neither of them noticed Winifred discreetly leave the room.

"Oh, it's more than that," Zach spat out. "You're going to act out your mother's vendetta against men by turning on me."

"You called in the note. The choice was yours," she reminded him, wishing she felt as aloof as she sounded.

"I don't want you there!" he shouted then.

"It is none of your business what I do with my life," she stated coldly.

Barely controlling himself, Zach spoke through cleanched teeth. "Where did you get the money?"

She told herself she should have wanted to fling the truth in his face. Instead she was suddenly ashamed to say it. Her admission was barely audible. "It was a loan from Mark Rossiter."

Lauren expected a violent explosion. But as if the wind had been knocked out of him, he breathed,

"Oh my God," and pressed his eyes closed with his thumb and forefinger. "I didn't know there was that much between the two of you. You're a damn good liar, I'll give you that. You really had me convinced he was no more than a business acquaintance—certainly not a source of that kind of cash."

His abhorrence did more to unnerve her than any amount of rage could have done. "Just return the note," she said in a small, lame voice.

He lowered his hand from a face still creased with disbelief. "How could you have gone to him?"

"It is strictly a business arrangement. He will charge me interest until I can pay him off. Unlike you, he won't take his profit out of my soul," she defended herself harshly.

"And what did you take out of mine?" he shot back.

Lauren clasped her hands in her lap to still their sudden trembling. If he had cared, she told herself, he would have found another way of getting her out of Maudie's, a way that left her pride and dignity and independence intact. If he had cared he would have told her, offered her a brighter future with proof that love existed. But he only wanted it his way, just as her mother had warned—he wanted her crippled by dependency while he offered nothing of his heart. The reminder strengthened her will and her shoulders with it. "Count the money and give me back the note," she repeated, thinking that if she didn't escape from those black eyes soon she would turn into a raving lunatic.

"Take the money back to him, Lauren. Nothing is worth what Rossiter will want in return," he predicted.

"He will get nothing but the money owed him. You have taught me that lesson very well."

"Don't be a damn fool. He is not like anyone you have ever dealt with before. He'll swallow you alive."

"You're wrong."

"Or you're blind."

She stood up abruptly, waiting like a stone statute for him to comply with her demand. "The note," she said yet again.

He stared up at her, silently damning her pride and stubborness. And then he shoved the satchel across the table. "Forget the note. Take this back to Rossiter. I won't close the place, and you can pay me off when you have the money on your own."

She hadn't expected this. Temptation pulled at her, but her pride yanked her back into stony determination. "No," she said flatly. "You and I are finished. I can't trust you not to close me down without warning." *And I can't have any connection with you and manage to free my heart too,* she added to herself.

"I give you my word that I won't do that. I won't come near the place."

"No. I don't want anything to do with you."

She said it with such cold, hard finality that Zach knew with a sudden searing flash she couldn't love him as he had hoped; she couldn't feel anything for him. It was as if everything that meant anything to him had shattered before his eyes and there was no avoiding the stark reality that was left. Everything else might be worked out if she loved him as he was coming to realize he loved her. But there was no hope if she didn't. "Just consider it exactly the same kind of business deal you would have had with Rossiter," he said, making one last attempt to protect her from the other man no matter what the cost to his own pride.

But Lauren felt that for her own sake she had to be strong...and free of him. "I said no and that is what I meant. Nothing will change my mind."

A palpable silence kept them both immobile. Zach wanted to push time back, to shake her until her teeth rattled. Instead he muttered, "Dammit," and left her standing alone in the room.

Lauren took a deep breath to steady herself for just a little while more but it caught in a small gasp. Then he was back again, his tall, brawny body just inches in front of her, holding the papers out for her to take.

Her hand was unsteady as she grabbed them, and without even looking at them she hastily stepped around him to leave.

One of Zach's blunt hands grasped her arm to stop her. "Think about what you are doing," he exploded.

The fight against the tears welling in her eyes made Lauren lift her chin high, and her voice came out in a raw, whispered command: "Don't . . . please."

And she was gone.

Chapter 24

"He's here again, Lauren. Don't you think you should come downstairs tonight?" Alan asked in his most cajoling voice, feeling a bit panicky as he sat on the settee in her room.

It had been a week since Lauren had paid Zach off, and in that time she had not come out of her attic. It was as if she couldn't face the place without him and Alan was worried.

Just before Maudie's opened that first night, Mark Rossiter had come to see how she was faring. Finding her in a near trance, he had led her like an invalid to her bed, assuring her he would see to Maudie's until she felt up to the task again. Even though Lauren had repeatedly thanked him and said he needn't do that, and Alan had assured him that he could handle Maudie's alone, Rossiter persisted in playing host in her absence.

Alan had decided the only solution was to force Lauren out of her apathy.

"Is there a problem Mark can't handle?" she asked impatiently from a wing chair in front of the fireplace.

"No, of course not. There isn't anything he or I can't take care of. I just think it would do you good to take charge again."

"I have to collect myself, Alan. Then I will get back to work. In the meantime I feel fortunate to have Mark's help."

Alan looked dubious and tried a new tack. "You might as well have let Zach take the place and sell it to Mark if you're going to give it up to him like this. Zach has beaten you again, hasn't he?"

Surprise made Lauren turn her topaz eyes on her friend. Never had Alan spoken to her like that. "I am not beaten."

"Then why are you hiding up here like a mole in a hole, letting someone else neglect his own business to tend to yours?" he asked, trying to bait her before storming out.

An hour later Lauren descended Maudie's stairs and entered her office. Two latecomers were purchasing brass checks from Rossiter and only when they met Lauren in the doorway did he notice her.

"Lauren!" His tone was warm and bright and so pleased that Lauren was glad she had decided to end her seclusion. Alan was right, she decided; she would be letting Zach and her feelings for him win if she couldn't go on here. It was time to put him and the past behind her.

"Are you feeling better?" Rossiter asked eagerly as he rounded her desk and led her to one of the two chairs facing it, sitting himself in the other and keeping his hold of her hand.

"Alan has been scolding me because he feels I have imposed on your friendship long enough, Mark, and I fear he is right. Though I am grateful for your help. I just wasn't ready to face all of this until now."

He smiled handsomely, but his brows creased slightly with a doubtful frown. "Lovely as it is, there still isn't a drop of color in your face, darling. Are you sure Alan isn't pushing you too soon? I don't mind standing in for you at all."

"I am fine, really," she assured him, as proud as always, every sable brown hair in place, her high-collared blouse and blue skirt as crisp as her words. His endearment grated on her, but how could she reprimand him for the familiarity after all he had done for her?

"I'm delighted to hear you're improved. If you are up to it, I propose a little wine and business talk then. Are you?"

He seemed genuinely anxious to hand her back the reins of Maudie's. Lauren smiled, put at ease as always by his courtesy. "Business talk perhaps, but not wine." Her stomach was still in knots, and not even food appealed to her. "But please have it without me."

"If you are sure," he said as he released her hand. Lauren was surprised to see him walk to a small table in the corner behind her desk. The table, decanters, and glasses had not been there before. When he had poured his drink, he returned to sit beside her, settling in with a contented, comfortable sigh. "Maudie's is a marvelous place. I commend your talents and taste, Lauren. I hope you won't think me presumptuous if I voice an idea or two I've had while here."

Lauren laughed lightly. "Not as long as they are just suggestions and not unalterable decrees by an investor."

"Oh, Lord, no." He was quick to refute her charge, laughing easily with her. "Maudie's is yours alone. I respect that completely. I just thought a little of my experience might be of use to you. It occurred to me that with a house this size you could double the number of girls. It would work well enough as long as you organized certain signals between them to rotate the usage of the rooms. You rarely have a full house of overnighters, so sleeping arrangements could be dormitory style for those girls who weren't working after closing."

It seemed a tawdry idea and reminded Lauren of the arrangements at King's Kastle. She knew her girls would hate losing their own rooms, and she was a little shocked that Mark would have considered it. But she hid her reaction well. "I don't think so." She smiled to ease her rejection of his suggestion. "Things are chaotic enough around here without complicating matters. And I prefer keeping Maudie's a bit more elite."

His admiring expression did not alter as he studied her for a moment, stroking the wheat-colored beard. "It was just a thought. But of course you are right. It is that special touch you bring to the place that makes it a cut above the ordinary"

For some reason his scrutiny unnerved her. "Well," she said, "I have kept you from *The Countess* for far too long. I can take over now."

As if on cue a loud, angry voice boomed from the gambling room, answered by another that sounded even angrier. Rossiter stood up quickly, reaching to pat Lauren's hand reassuringly. "You just rest and take care of things here. I'll deal with this. Too much too soon isn't a good idea, darling."

Lauren started to refuse his offer as he headed out, but the sight of Zach standing in the doorway forestalled her.

Rossiter's composure was unshakeable, "Madox," he said, greeting Zach cordially enough but adding as he dashed confidently past, "Couldn't stay away, is that it?"

Tension filled the room as fast as smoke. Lauren's eyes met Zach's and hardened in answer to the steely anger in his. "Cozy," he ground out sarcastically. "He seems to have settled in with the slither of a snake."

A vise tightened around Lauren's heart and threatened to stop its beating. "Why are you here?" she rasped out.

Zach's glance dismissed her as if she were inconsequential. He crossed to her desk and tossed a handful of coins onto it. "This is a whorehouse, isn't it? I came for a night's romp," he said harshly.

Lauren's skin turned clammy cold, and she thought she would be ill. How could she watch him pick one of her girls and go upstairs? "There are other houses in Seattle. You are not welcome in this one."

He nodded back over his shoulder. "But he is."

"He is a friend who has granted me considerable assistance."

"And I'm just the poor bastard who..." He stopped himself from revealing feelings that were as painful as thorns. "And I'm a paying customer," he amended. "I had enough offers while I was here. I thought I might try some of them out. From what I saw when I came in, you're well enough occupied not to mind what I do, where I do it, or who I do it with." He hadn't intended things to work out this way when he had decided to come here tonight. He had just wanted to make sure she was all right, but seeing her with Rossiter and hearing him call her darling were too much for his already tortured mind. He felt driven to hurt her as badly as he was hurting, and he was so blinded by his own torment that he failed to see to any signs of the same feeling in her.

"I don't want you in my house." Her voice was toneless.

"He still lets you call it *your* house, does he? I wonder how long that will last? Not much longer would be my bet." Still he didn't look at her, couldn't look at her. He railed at the wall, "Come on, Lauren. I'm paid up, hand over the brass checks. Or can you admit you care enough to be jealous and that you don't want me with one of your girls?"

Lauren saw the ploy for what it was but could not admit anything to him. She rounded the desk, pulled open a side drawer, and counted out his tokens. Zach took them and began jingling them in his hand, keeping it up until she thought she would scream. But all he saw was the stiffness in her back, the proud denial that she cared.

The sound of glass crashing in the other room shattered Zach's will to go on with his charade. He gave a derisive, mirthless chuckle. "I hope all this was worth it to you." Then he stared up at the ceiling for a moment before lowering his black eyes to her again. He dragged his empty hand through his hair as he gave up. His voice was gruff, gravelly, and no longer taunting as he said, "I didn't come here for this tonight." He held the brass checks out to her.

Lauren swallowed thickly and for the first time let her own eyes touch the face she had been working so hard to forget. "Why did you come then?"

"To tell you that if you need me, need anything, not to let your damned Irish pride stand in the way. I'm still here for you." He let the brass checks fall onto her desktop in a metallic rain and left Lauren sitting in her chair deflated and awash in a fresh surge of misery.

"She needs the work and I can't use her, darling." It began two days later with Rossiter bringing in a slovenly girl named Tilly. "I told her you have a good heart."

Lauren eyed him warily, determined not to let his charm override her good judgment. "You know Maudie's is full too, Mark. We discussed this very thing the other night," she reminded him.

"I know we did, but actually this is a different matter altogether. One girl is far from what I suggested, darling. Wouldn't one of your girls double up? It would be a favor to me."

How could she refuse him such a small thing in the face of the great favor he had done for her? In spite of her reservations, Lauren hired Tilly.

Next it was, "You need the variety, darling. I talked with all of your girls while I was here and not one of them performs this girl's particular specialty. Take it from an old hand; hiring her will be well worth the trouble."

Then, "...paired up with Sally's fairness they will make quite an attraction. Have I led you wrong yet?"

Before Lauren realized it the number of girls at Maudie's had grown by half, all brought in by Mark Rossiter who visited daily. Grudgingly, Lauren admitted that profits were growing, and as the girls learned to follow Mark's organization of signals and cues, there was no more confusion than before.

His hand became evident in the very appearance of the place. Maudie's began to teem with flowers, red and yellow roses for the parlor, white for Lauren's attic. All sent by Mark Rossiter. "Just to brighten your spirits," said his first card. After that he wrote, "Fondest affections, Mark," until two weeks had passed and he graduated to "Love, Mark."

Lauren fought her growing suspicion. He was the most proper gentleman she had ever met. His attentions were all perfectly correct, polite, and flattering. With Billy lurking in her shadow every waking hour there was no reason to feel unnerved by Mark, she lectured herself.

He began sharing her evening meals on a regular basis, lingering well into the night, lending a hand with the nuisances, offering advice and suggestions and showing the wisdom of his experience in a most unthreatening way. Since everything he said proved valid or profitable, Lauren could not take offense. But she *was* naive, and when he approached her with another proposal midway through the third week she was taken aback.

"Let's get away for a few days, go out to my smuggler's hideaway on the island. We could both use a little respite...alone together," Rossiter suggested over a late nightcap.

Lauren nearly choked on the cognac that had somehow come to be stocked at Maudie's. Her eyes widened as she stared at him. "I could never do that," she informed him firmly.

His sky blue eyes twinkled with delight. "Isn't it just possible that Alan could run the place well enough without you?" he asked easily.

But Lauren sensed even through the smoothness of his sudden jest that he had not expected an instant refusal. "Business is only the second reason, Mark."

"You are quite unique, darling, did you know that?" His smile was perfect, his eyes warm and devouring. "You have managed to retain a certain innocence even here. I think that is part of what draws me to you. And make no mistake about it, Lauren, I am drawn to you like a thirsty man to water."

"Please don't say that."

"I must. I know it hasn't been long enough for you to have fully recovered from your emotional wounds, but I have to tell you how I feel. I'm a patient man. I can wait for you to come back to yourself, but when you do, darling, I don't want to be overlooked. I've wanted you since the first time we met, here, when Maudie's was just a pile of boards and plaster."

Zach was lost in the past, everything between them ended, and here sat an undeniably attractive man, generous, kind, and caring. Lauren felt flattered but unmoved. Her mother would have been proud of her but for the intense pain that still wrapped her heart. "No, Mark, I can't..."

"Stop! Don't even say it. I won't have you crush my hopes with words. You will feel differently in time. One day you will wake up and be amazed by what you feel for me—I know it." He finished his brandy and stood up to leave, pulling her hand into the crook of his arm and keeping it captive as they walked to the kitchen door.

"I know he has soured you on romance for now. You have good reason to shun the very thought," he assured her once they stood outside in the cool night air. "Tender hearts like yours must take care around men like that. They want only one sort of wife and no other: dour-faced dams with big dowries and pristine pasts. He has brutalized you and you have understandable reason to beware of that happening ever again." His hands closed over her upper arms, drawing her directly in front of him and very close. His tone was soothing and sincere. "We are not alike, he and I. You will come to see that. I want to share your life, every part of it, not change it."

He kissed her then, gently, with only fleeting passion, before releasing her mouth to press his lips to her brow. "You and I are two of a kind, Lauren; we don't belong to the world outside this life, yet we are so much better than those we live among. We have to carve out our own niche here, deal with it strictly as a business, make it as clean as we possibly can to keep ourselves from being soiled by it. There isn't another person in the world who could understand this in either of us. We are a bit like Adam and Eve," he concluded, laughing at his own analogy, "the only two of our sort, alone in a dubious garden of Eden. But together we can create a wonderful place just for the two of us, where we will be unmarred by the thorns that surround us."

The words were more than flowery. They made sense to Lauren. "I don't want any more entanglements," she said softly.

"No entanglements. I promise. I will be straightforward with you at all times. And when we finally do get together, your eyes will be wide open and you will know exactly what you have in me."

He kissed her again and was gone, leaving Lauren wondering if they were, indeed, kindred spirits and if some sort of personal partnership might fill the gaping hole left by Zach's defection.

Chapter 25

It was just over a month since Lauren had last seen Zach, but it seemed so much longer. When would the feelings go away—the desperate wanting, the need just to see his face. Soon, she hoped. It was eating away at her energy, even at her will.

Many insidious changes had occurred at Maudie's in that time, all brought about by Mark Rossiter. He was there more often than not these days, arriving for breakfast and not leaving until the place closed for the night. He had such a talent for rechanneling the workings of the house from Lauren to himself that one by one even the iceman, the butcher, the fruit vendor, all began to submit their bills and to be paid by him. Then he would present the receipts to Lauren for reimbursment.

"Just lightening your load," he would say to explain it away, and Lauren was too emotionally drained to argue about it. Besides, it was much too difficult to find fault with his reasoning or requests for favors or with circumstances seemingly beyond his control.

"By the way, darling," he had informed her with regret and apology, "I had a disagreement with your bartender and I'm afraid he has quit. Completely my fault; I shouldn't have put my nose in where it didn't belong. But don't fret over it. I insist on making amends. I have already sent for *The Countess*'s barman. None better. He is so adept at watering the liquor no one is ever the wiser."

"I don't do that here," Lauren had reminded him.

"I know you haven't up until now, but it's time you started. It saves a small fortune and keeps some men from dragging out their visits upstairs for too long. You'll see. He will make the world of a difference."

And so Maudie's had a new bartender.

Rossiter's way always proved more efficient, smoother, more profitable. How could she dispute it? Especially since his presence was a constant reminder of the greater service he had rendered by lending her money.

Their personal relationship had altered just as insidiously but less drastically. He was an attentive suitor, alert to her every mood or whim, always courteous and proper to a fault. Even though his intention to seduce her had been thoroughly explained and discussed, he still made no overt move that might frighten her. Instead, he wooed her gently, carefully, with well-controlled kisses when they parted each night, a light hand at her arm or waist as they walked through Maudie's, and only the most fleeting of embraces. Again, there was no cause for complaint, and so Lauren's uneasiness about Mark Rossiter seemed to be nothing more than unfounded, unreasonable suspicion.

She was left doubting herself, her own wits, at times, for why should she have these elusive misgivings about him? Why should his kindest attentions cause her such uneasiness? Why was she growing more and more uncomfortable when she was with him when just the opposite should be happening? He was beyond reproach, his actions and motives never secret.

Yet Lauren could not shake the feeling that something more was happening. With some doubt about her own sanity, she nonetheless cautioned Billy not to leave her side or venture out of earshot when Mark Rossiter was at Maudie's.

"Are you all right?" It was Alan who spoke. He had come to her attic room after Rossiter's departure for the day. It was nearly three o'clock in the morning, but with Mark in constant attendance or at best lurking nearby, Lauren and Alan found no time to talk together of anything other than business. But the sight of her gaunt, pale face and the catlike wariness in her topaz eyes had stirred his concern for her.

"Oh, Alan." She smiled warmly at him. "It seems as if we haven't seen each other in such a long time. It must sound silly since we are together every day, but I have missed you."

"You're so taken up with Mark," he said, cautiously critical. "Is it what you want, Lauren?"

"He means well," she hedged weakly. "And he has shown me how to double Maudie's profits."

"But are you happy?"

A short, mirthless laugh answered him better than words. "Maudie's is a thriving business. That is all I wanted."

"What about yourself?"

She knew what he meant. "I'm getting over him, Alan," she lied. "But I do need a confidante. Would you mind coming up like this every night, just for a few minutes' chat before going to bed?"

Never had she seemed so pitiful to him, and Alan said instantly. "You know I will. I've always been your confidante. We can't let Mark Rossiter change that too, can we?" But Alan feared Mark Rossiter had already changed too much.

"How can that be?" Lauren shouted at the bad news Alan had been forced to bring her first thing the next morning. "I locked the cash box in the safe myself."

"I know you did, Lauren, but the safe was broken into last night. Everything is gone."

"My God, Alan, that was the whole month's profits. That was everything!"

"I was afraid of that." Alan shook his head, reluctant to go on. "It gets worse. The police were here an hour ago. They found Sally Flournoy dead on the docks. The empty cashbox was nearby. It looks as if she planned it with an accomplice and was then killed for the money."

"Oh my God," she groaned again as she paced the attic, her arms tightly cinched over the robe belted at her waist. She suddenly felt as if she were drowning in muck.

Alan watched, feeling overwhelmed by helplessness. "I don't know what to do for you, Lauren. Maybe Zach . . ."

No! She turned venomous at the very mention of his name. "I will work this out. Are the police suspicious of Maudie's in any way because of the murder?"

"No. It was their theory that she had been in cahoots with someone else and that is who killed her."

"Do they have any idea who it might have been?"

"None. And you know not much time will be spent in trying to find him. A whore dead, a whorehouse robbed—neither of them warrant much official concern. There isn't a hope that the money will be returned."

"And that's our biggest worry now, isn't it? The bills are all due and I haven't a dime."

"What I have saved won't help much, but you are welcome to it."

She worried her bottom lip. "It might be enough to stave everyone off until we can pay the rest. I'll give it all back to you, Alan, with interest."

"There's no need, darling." Rossiter's silky voice came from the open doorway. He stood regally perfect, smiling consolingly. "Would you excuse us please, Alan?"

Alan's glance went uncertainly from Lauren to Rossiter and back again. His sense that she needed protection from this man was strong. But as if Lauren knew what her old friend was thinking she gave him a lamely reassuring nod that dismissed him.

Rossiter closed the door after Alan and crossed to Lauren, taking both her arms and pulling her into an embrace meant to comfort her. But comfort was not what she felt. Finding that he could not ease her stiffness, Rossiter retreated to a wing chair near the hearth. He sat casually, with his legs crossed, stroking his beard. "Be calm, darling; everything is taken care of."

Lauren frowned down at him from where she stood. "You know what happened?"

"The dock was alive with police before dawn this morning. Of course *The Countess* was under scrutiny. They call her the vice ship, and we are always the beneficiary of their first suspicions for any wrongdoing. With the empty cash box near the body of one of your girls, Lauren, it was hardly difficult to guess what happened. I arrived just after the police had spoken to Alan. Your cook filled me in on the details and I realized what this would mean to you. So I took the initiative before rumors could fly that Maudie's was unable to pay its debts. I knew how upsetting this would be for you. I wanted to do what I could."

Lauren's back stiffened as she said sternly, "I wish you had consulted me before doing anything so rash."

"I've offended you. I am sorry, darling." He sounded genuinely contrite. "I was only thinking of you and Maudie's. I assumed that since you came to me for the money to pay off Maudie's in the first place, you would naturally let me help you out of this. I wanted to spare you having to ask."

Lauren was coming to doubt his intentions no matter how convincing he was. "I appreciate your help, Mark, I truly do. But I can't go on accepting so much from you. Better that I had dealt with this in my own way." But his smile was so open and friendly, so understanding that it was unnerving to her to feel suspicious and ungrateful.

"Sit down and let's talk. I promised to be totally honest with you and I am about to be just that."

Lauren remained standing, the tilt of her chin questioning. Rossiter merely grinned broadly at the defiant stance.

"Oh, dear, I have made you angry, haven't I? I didn't mean to. It is the last thing I would ever intentionally do. Come out with it then. Tell me just what is boiling inside you."

Lauren hesitated only a moment, and then, with a measure of her old spirit, she did just as he asked. "You assume too much, Mark. I don't like having decisions taken out of my hands. I know you mean well, but you must remember that Maudie's is my house to run and the problems are mine to solve."

"Of course, darling, that is not in dispute. I understand perfectly your pique. But..." He sighed elaborately. "How should I put this?" he asked himself, stroking his beard in a slow, methodical rhythm, "I consider ours a partnership of a sort, born not so much from the money I have invested in Maudie's but from my deep and abiding feelings for you."

Again he hesitated as if choosing his words. When he continued, it was with unquestionable sincerity. "I am in love with you, Lauren. There you have it. Deeply, deeply in love with you. I had wanted to postpone telling you because I know you don't yet feel the same for me. I accept that, darling. I nurture the hope that it will change, but for now I understand and accept it. But you must see that because I feel so much for you, because we are so alike, because I believe with all my heart that destiny has chosen us to be together, I consider us partners in Maudie's. It doesn't even occur to me to pause before doing what I know is best for the place, just as I would for *The Countess*, but never do I question your ownership, your ultimate place here, and your absolute, total control of all that goes on. My thought is only of assisting you with the reins, like a fine pair of gloves; never, ever of taking them from your hands."

There didn't seem to be anything to disbelieve. And yet Lauren didn't believe him. "I don't doubt your intentions, Mark. I just think perhaps it would be better if you concentrate more of your efforts on *The Countess* and leave Maudie's to me," she said as kindly and tactfully as one could who suspects her own judgment of being wrong but must abide by it nonetheless.

"No, darling, quite the opposite. This is what I propose." He launched into a full-blown plan. "A firmer hand is needed around here to ward off incidents like last night's. I think we should strongly consider a better living arrangement. *The Countess* can do without me, but Maudie's has the potential to be so much more, if only I can be here to guide you. I thought Alan could run *The Countess* for me. Piano players are easy enough to come by, but Alan is a born manager. He handles the girls well, and once everything has been established, as it is there, he can run it perfectly. I can take his room for my private use, and by my being here all the time the girls will feel my presence and not even consider repeating what Sally got away with last night. We could accomplish so much more, for Maudie's and for ourselves. Together, Lauren, we can make this place legendary." He suddenly turned rueful. "And it would allow me the time I crave to be with you. That, I confess, is the crux of it. I just want to be with you."

Lauren was speechless. Mark Rossiter's machinations were suddenly clear. First had come the suggestion, with only the most offhand reminder of her debt to him. A short time would elapse while he would act as if he had forgotten the debt, and then he would do what he had outlined in his plan anyway, regardless of her refusals and opposition. But now, faced with the worst incursion by him yet, how was she to break the pattern? And how could she accomplish that without rousing the vindictiveness in Mark that would call in her note and cost her Maudie's? She had to keep her wits and her temper. "Alan wouldn't consider leaving me," she said cautiously.

"He would for the right price, darling," Mark assured her.

"He wouldn't leave Polly."

"We could send her to *The Countess* as well and replace her here with one of my girls." Again he had thwarted her.

"Please don't take offense, Mark." She only prayed that at least part of what he had said was true and that she could use his determination to win her through patience against him. "I do care for you, but as you have said, it isn't love. I need more time to sort out my feelings, my thoughts, and your being here would hinder that. I want things to go on as they are. Now is not the time for you to move into Maudie's. If you love me as you say you do, give me this."

"I understand, darling. I am only trying to do what is best for you. Let's both give my idea some thought though, shall we? I know you will see the advantages to it." He stood up and came to press an affectionate kiss on her cheek before leaving. "We will be so wonderful together. You'll see."

Lauren was left in a cold sweat, knowing that the strength of her determination was no match for his. Her only hope was to play for time, to do all she could to keep him from moving into Maudie's until she could scrape together every penny to pay him off and be free of the threat he now presented.

The Cades' Georgian mansion was brimming with guests, all arrayed in wedding finery. Knowing the financial straits of Evan's bride's family, Winifred had insisted she and Arthur be allowed to host the celebration.

It was a maudlin Zach Madox who attended the festivities, trying hard to be pleasant and polite, to call up his usual repartee as a defense against the ladies there who saw him as a likely matrimonial target. He nursed a single glass of champagne, having lost his taste for alcohol because of overconsumption in the past two months.

How much worse it was to watch other people's happiness, he thought, and misery washed over him like acid. Was she happy without him? he wondered. Had she learned to weather bawdy-house life with aplomb? Had Rossiter taken his place? Damn her all to hell! Why couldn't he get over her? Damn himself for not just biding his time until she was ready to leave the life on her own. Fool mistake. He should have known better than to back her into a corner.

A feminine hand slipped through the crook of his elbow, and Zach plastered a semblance of a smile on his face to greet yet another woman he would rather have cursed. But when he lowered his black eyes to the hand's owner he found Winifred tugging at his arm. "Come and dance with me, my friend," she commanded gently.

The music was slow and soft enough for conversation to be carried on over it, which was just what Winifred Cade had in mind. "Still no better, are you,

Zach?" She cut right to the heart of what was on her mind.

He grinned lopsidedly down at her. "I'm fine, Winnie, fine."

The silver-haired woman laughed derisively. "You know I can spot a lie every time you tell one."

Zach just chuckled. "Is that so?"

"Had your fill of women yet, or is that going to take longer than the whiskey did?"

"Just what do you know about my fill of whiskey or women?"

"I know you finally stopped trying to drown yourself in the first, and I know you have spent this second month trying to immerse yourself in every woman that would have you. You will never know the bragging I've heard. A night spent trying to win you over has become the sport around these parts. I decided I had to do something about you. Otherwise I will never be able to have another dress fitted without my face burning with embarrassment from listening to what is being said about you behind the next curtain. Why, I've never heard such things discussed in a public place—those women, comparing their experiences with you that way!"

"Favorably, I hope," he said teasingly.

"Oh, you're showing them all a good time, all right. I just wonder what you're doing to yourself."

"Just passing time, Winnie."

"Passing time my foot. It isn't working, is it, my friend? No, never mind. I can see another lie coming, so don't bother. You're brokenhearted, Zach, and I know it."

"I see a lecture on the horizon."

"How long since you've seen her?"

"You know that too." He dropped all pretense and let his face relax into the somber lines that were natural to him now.

"I wasn't certain if you had seen her at all in these two months."

"I haven't."

"Then you don't even know how she is faring?"

"I've seen Billy Bartlett a few times. He's the man I hired as her bodyguard. He doesn't say much beyond reassuring me that he is taking real good care of her." His voice was ragged.

"So what are you going to do about yourself?"

"Ride it out."

"Did you ever tell her you love her?"

"Who says I do?"

She ignored his question. "I would say she loves you too."

"You would be wrong. She doesn't," he answered flatly.

"Did you ever ask her?"

"Don't be silly, Winnie. I expect more from you."

"But you'll never know for sure unless you do."

"Somehow I think we have taken the long way around to get to what you wanted to say when this dance started. Let's have it."

"Go and see her, Zach, now that you've both had time to cool off. Swallow your pride and see what happens."

Chapter 26

Maudie's was at the height of its nightly revelry when Lauren trudged up the stairs to her attic room just past midnight. Bone weariness had turned her feet to lead. She had falsely pleaded a headache and left Alan and Mark Rossiter to finish out the evening. Never in her life had she felt so exhausted so much of the time, but her days had become so fraught with tension it was not hard to understand. Warding off Mark's increasingly overt and distasteful advances and keeping him from moving into Maudie's had become a ceaseless chore; added to this was the financial maneuvering she was doing behind his back, it and all these unpleasant activities were taking their toll of her spirit and her flagging energy.

Big, mallet-faced Billy followed her all the way to her room. With Mark's more avid pursuit, it had become necessary for the bodyguard not to leave her until she was safely behind her locked door. These days, if not for Billy or Alan's persistent intervention, she would find herself too often in Mark's unwanted embrace, his still chaste kisses repulsing her.

With her hand on the doorknob she turned a wan smile on Billy. "Go on to bed for the night. I'll see you in the morning."

The big man nodded mutely, watching her go into her room as he did each night, after which he would retire to the small alcove just next to it where he slept. She pressed the door closed behind her, careful to lock both latches before turning and stopping cold. She couldn't believe her eyes. Her ever-stiff back fell against the door for support. There sat Zach as if in answer to some silent, unconscious plea.

He was slumped on the settee, his raven-winged head against its back, his hands clasped over his chambray-clad belly. His long legs were stretched out and crossed at the ankles, their denim covering pulled tightly across his massive, hard thighs and ending in the sharp tips of leather boots pointing like arrows to the ceiling.

He didn't look her way at first, just sat staring into the fire he had started in the hearth, his handsome profile a perfect silhouette, clean shaven and utterly masculine. It gave Lauren a moment to assimilate the fact that he was actually there and to decide how she felt about it.

Reason told her she should be enraged, that she should show her contempt for him and then have him forcibly evicted. But her life had turned so ugly that she could feel only relief and unbridled joy. Forgotten for the time being was the pain of their parting. She remembered only how he had been when she had paid him off, looking like death as he experienced the after effects of his drinking binge and suffering as much as she with what had come between them.

"What are you doing here?" Her whisper betrayed her presence.

He turned his head her way. Slowly he leveled those black eyes at her. "Sass starvation," he said so gently it took away any sting. The sight of her, looking as tightly prim as she had been on the train when they had first met, relieved him, as if it were a sign

that she hadn't changed, hadn't succumbed the life
. . . or to Rossiter.

The teasing in those two small words lightened
Lauren's heart as nothing in the past two months
had. Still, she cautioned herself against feeling hope.
She forced her voice to be cool, calm, removed.
"How did you get in here?"

"The back way, with a little help from Alan and
Billy." He realized he had even missed her uppiti-
ness.

It wouldn't do to seem overeager, she lectured
herself, and so she tried to sound disdainful. "Then I
suppose it won't do me any good to call Billy for
help."

"None at all." He paused, and then the need to
test her pushed him on. "But I'm sure Rossiter would
be more than happy to toss me out if that's what you
want."

"Is it dangerous to be alone with you?"

He shrugged, and her eyes went of their own volition to his shoulders, lingering there until she
dragged them back to his face.

"Could be; I've been a long time without you," was
his provocative answer.

Her heart pounded wildly and she knew she felt
far too much for him, but she couldn't stop it.

"Are you going to stand there all night, or will you
come sit with me?" he beckoned in those husky tones
she couldn't resist.

Her fatigue left her completely as she pushed herself away from the door. She moved to the hearth
rather than allowing herself to be too near him. His
being there was heady enough, but of course she
permitted none of it to show in the composed lines of
her face. "Why are you here?" she repeated.

"Winnie told me to come." His lips twitched with a
suppressed smile. "She said I was a damn fool to stay
around worrying and wondering about you . . . and

wanting you." He, in his turn, had to pull his gaze
from its lingering glance at her body back to her
face. "So here I am. But I'm having a hell of a time
remembering what I came to say when all I seem to
be able to think about is making love to you." He said
it too offhandedly to sound serious. "Did you miss
me, Irish?"

His gravelly voice wrapped around her and took
her away to a time and place much easier than the
present. When she came back to herself, he was
standing beside her, clasping one of her hands gently
and rubbing it with his callused thumb. "I said, did
you miss me?"

"No," she lied feebly, not even trying to retrieve
her hand.

There it was! The smile. He had missed that secret
smile of hers. "Not even just a little?" He kissed her
palm, the inside of her wrist, the tender flesh in the
crease of her elbow. "I missed you. More than you'll
ever know."

His breath was hot on her skin and she nearly admitted what he wanted to hear...the truth. But in
the end she couldn't. "What do you want, Zach?" she
asked softly of the mantle.

He moved to stand behind her, his arms whispering around her shoulders to pull her back against
him. When he met no resistance, he kissed her ear
and the side of her neck. "I want to make love to you.
And then I want to fix the rest of this misery between
us," he answered from deep in his throat.

"I can't," she breathed partly in denial, partly in
surrender. "Then I would be a whore, wouldn't I?
Sleeping with you when you just happen by." But her
need to be with him, held by him, kissed by him,
comforted and protected by him, was so great.

As if he read her thoughts, he rasped against her
cheek, "You would be a woman who needs me right
at this moment as much as I need her. That's all,

Irish. For just a little while let's forget the things that have kept us apart, soothe what we both need soothed, and then talk about the rest afterward. What was between us was never anything but good and beautiful."

She shook her head back and forth, but even she didn't know if it was in denial of what he was saying or of what he was awakening within her. Why couldn't she resist him even when she knew she should?

Reaching from behind her, he undid the buttons of her blouse as carefully as if they were eggshells pulled through the lace. He kissed her neck gently, slowly, warmly, nuzzling her ear, nipping her lobe. He pulled the linen blouse free of her skirt, slid it down her arms, and then tossed it onto the sofa. His hands came back to her upper arms, squeezing, rubbing and then turning her to him. He tilted her face with a finger under her chin and saw her doubts like a hazy mist over her desire. An open, loving smile answered her, and then he lowered his mouth to hers in a chaste kiss.

His hands loosened her skirt and let it fall to the floor and Lauren stepped out of it. Her mother's voice was silent within her; all of Rossiter's carefully planted defamatory claims against Zach evaporated, and only the racing of her own blood and the tingle of her wide-awake senses ruled her. She yielded to him and to what she herself wanted.

His arms were hard, bulging muscles as her hands glided up them, his shoulders so thick she couldn't span them. His back was bent to her, broad and taut, his neck like the bole of a tree, corded with tendons of steel. Her fingers threaded up into his hair, soft as down, and she looked into a face that was all rugged beauty and gentleness.

Her lips parted in wonder, and Zach's caught them in an open-mouthed kiss that searched for a response and received one in the teasing of her tongue. And as their mouths met, tasted, and enjoyed, he raised his hands to the coil at the back of her head, bound up as tightly as she was, until he applied the magic of his fingers to free the heavy curtain of sable hair and the passionate spirit of the woman.

Lauren never fumbled as she undid his shirt, slid it from his powerful torso, and dropped it to the floor. She reached to his jeans and freed the buttons and him, pushing down on the stubborn denim until it, too, joined their things. Then, with his rumbling chuckle vibrating in her mouth, he untied her petticoats and let it slide down her thighs, leaving nothing but a sensible chemise between them, but not for long. His hands moved from her thin shoulders to her tiny waist and lower, cupping her backside to pull her up against his seeking hips, branding her his with the press of his long, hot staff.

His mouth was wide open and so was hers as fever heated their desire, and their tongues played. She let her hands move slowly down, across his sharp collarbone and into the curling hair that masked the sinewy mounds of his chest. Then they traced their way down the hard, flat sides of his middle to his iron, bulging thighs and around and up again to press his tensed derriere more tightly against her.

Zach groaned and tore his mouth from hers. Without knowing how she got there, Lauren found herself pressed backwards onto the bed, with him astride her and his hot tongue at the pinched crest of her breast, sucking, nipping, and tugging her into a world of warm desire and tingling delight—never had her breasts been so sensitive. Her small hands held his head, her back arched in response to the wetness of his mouth, and little shards of white-hot light flickered across her skin.

"Love me just a little, Irish," he breathed, wishing out loud.

His words awakened everything she feared most. If she revealed her feelings for him, she would be left weak and wanting and hurting more than she could bear. She pushed him away and sat up on the edge of the bed, naked and angry and confused by a body and heart that betrayed her reason.

"What is it?" he asked, stunned.

"Don't talk to me of love, do you hear?" she ordered and begged at the same time.

He sat up and eased behind her, pulling her close to him. He took the silky mass of her hair and gently lifted it. Then he pressed his mouth to her shoulder and folded his arms around her again. "Then I won't; just let me love you," he said gruffly.

It wasn't the emotion he meant then, she thought, but just the act. And that hurt as much as the emotion she fought.

But Zach was the only possible comfort for the pain she felt, and Lauren let herself curl back into the shell of his body, fighting sudden, surprising tears and a desire for him that overwhelmed her. "I'm so afraid of you," she whispered to herself.

His breath was hot on her shoulder as he kissed her with the velvet delicacy of a rose petal. "Shh. Never that. Never."

They stayed there for a long, healing time and then Zach lay her back over one of his thighs and moved to hold her, so they were facing each other again. His hands rubbed her back, soothing, easing, gentling, while his breath stirred her hair and his body hardened all over again for want of her.

Little by little her fears were eased away, and with them her worry and caution. Her desire took over once more, for she loved him too much to win this battle.

Zach knew she was once more his when she raised her hand and placed it tenderly against his cheek. He peered down into her topaz eyes, now wide and vulnerable, and closed his arms around her like a vice. One of his hands cupped the back of her head, and his mouth took hers with renewed ardor that rekindled flames in her like hidden embers under ash. He fanned them carefully, lovingly, soothing, with his hands and mouth and tongue and body, the pain they had unknowingly shared, until each forgot the pain, and frenzy tensed every nerve and muscle.

He eased over on top of her, and she opened and freed the way for him to slide up into her with exquisite perfection. All heat and wetness and rigid sleekness in motion together, one thrust into the other again, again, building, growing, hotter, hotter, sparking to an explosion of white heat that then eased...slowly...slowly...relaxed...and they lay molded into one, as they were meant to be.

Then he left her, to lie on his back, crooking the arm that lay beneath her and bringing her up to snuggle next to him.

But his thoughts turned against his will to the unpleasant exchange that had interrupted their lovemaking, and it was like the kick of a mule. She didn't love him. Between Winifred's urging and his own hopes he had convinced himself that Lauren might have the same feelings he did but had left them unvoiced out of some misplaced need to protect herself. But he had asked her, begged her, and she had turned to ice in his arms.

She didn't love him.

Lauren looked up to find his face tight and angry. "Zach?" Her low voice came as if from a distance.

She didn't love him. The words sounded again in his mind.

"Zach?" she repeated, the question more urgent.

She didn't love him. She would never love him. It was the cold, clear, harsh truth. He had to get out of there before she could see what that was doing to him. "I shouldn't have come here tonight."

The words rumbled beneath her ear like an earthquake. Lauren sat up suddenly, pulling up the lacy bedspread to cover her nakedness. "Then why did you?" she demanded defensively.

But he didn't answer her. He bolted from the bed as if it were covered with spikes, crossed to the hearth in three fierce strides, and began yanking his clothes back on.

Lauren watched in total confusion, her hopes shattering with every movement of his hands. "Why did you come?" she demanded again, her tone nearly hysterical.

"Because I'm a goddamned fool," he ground out. He pulled on his second boot and swept up a forgotten sock and then stormed from the room with a final crash of the door that splintered the doorframe.

Lauren's strength dissolved and she wilted into a heap on the bed. Betrayal and lies. Had he come just to hurt her? How could he have been so cruel, how could he promise to talk it all out, to end this misery, and then leave her, naked and crushed? She squeezed her eyes shut, clamped her arms tightly around herself, and wished she hadn't let him re-open the door to her heart.

"This is the last you'll get from me. I want no more dealings with you." The whore had intercepted Mark Rossiter two blocks from Maudie's. He stood tall, peering over her head as if she didn't warrant his complete attention. But she ignored that and continued to speak, softly and urgently. "I know it was you who made it look like Sally robbed Maudie's and then had her killed. It's one thing to spy, but I want nothing to do with what you're about now."

"Brave girl," he breathed. "Want to join Sally?"

"I've written it all down and sent it in a letter to a friend far away from here. Anything happens to me and she knows to send it to the governor. Touch me and you'll hang." She let her own threat sink in for a few seconds before adding, "I'm willing just to put an end to it all between us. You keep your secrets and I'll keep mine, and we forget what we know about each other. What do you say?"

He knew her plans for the future, knew what she wanted. She had as much at stake as he. "All right, darling. Fair enough, so long as you remember how much healthier silence is. Now, what last bit of news have you?"

"There are two things; one, I've been trying to tell you for weeks now. Lauren persuaded all the girls to go without most of their money for two months. She's scraping together everything she can to pay you off."

Rossiter laughed carelessly and confidently. "Do you expect that to disturb me?" he asked sarcastically.

It made her second revelation all the sweeter. "Zach Madox is back." She dropped it like a brick from a high window and relished the sudden demise of his pleasure.

"Out with it," he ordered through clenched teeth.

"He spent last night with her. Billy snuck him in the back way." She failed to add that from the sound of his leaving and the look on Lauren's face that morning it hadn't been a happy reunion.

"Anything else?" he demanded with a ferocious sneer.

"That's all. Just remember, we're quits."

Rossiter left her on the street, but he didn't go directly to Maudie's as he had originally planned. Instead he walked off some of his rage. He wanted Lauren, but he didn't want her by force if he could help it. And he knew that had he gone directly to

see her he would have taken what he felt was his
fair share of that which she gave so freely to Madox.

By the time Rossiter entered Maudie's doors he
was once again in command of himself, shored up by
the thought that he would make sure Lauren never
saw Madox again.

Chapter 27

Two days later Lauren was awakened by the scraping, thudding sounds of furniture being moved in the room beneath hers. Lunging from her bed, she hastily donned her robe and descended the stairs to find Mark Rossiter overseeing his belongings being moved into Alan's room.

"What is all of this?" she asked, holding down on rising panic, for it was obvious the man was following the same pattern that had increased the number of girls at Maudie's, watered the liquor, lowered the quality of the food, and any number of other undesirable alterations he had so insidiousy managed.

"Good morning, darling." He greeted her with a smooth, handsome smile. "I'm sorry if we woke you."

"What are you doing?" she persisted.

"I'm afraid Billy has left, Lauren," he answered obliquely.

"Billy is gone?" Confusion clouded her thoughts. "What do you mean?"

Rossiter's expression turned artfully sympathetic. "In the night, I'm afraid, darling."

"Why would he go?" Her tone was accusing. "I trusted him. He swore never to leave my side. He was one of Zach's most loyal men."

"Perhaps that is your answer. If he was one of

Madox's men he was probably called off." Rossiter's words seemed so sincere. "I am sorry, Lauren. I know you were fond of your bodyguard. You must feel abandoned. Madox's continued torture of you must be stopped. The man is ruthless, selfish, and uncaring. I see how he hurts you even now. That is why I am moving in, just as we discussed. When I came in early this morning and discovered Billy had deserted you, I knew it was time to put our future plans into motion. With Billy gone and Madox bent on tormenting you even at a distance, I cannot stay away. I have set Tommy to guarding you in Billy's place, and I will be right here for you as well."

"No!" Full-fledged panic overtook her. Billy had been a comforting presence, making Lauren feel safe and protected. He had been on her side. The sly, weasel-faced Tommy in his place seemed like a jailer. "I don't want you here, Mark," she blurted out.

Rossiter merely smiled, unaffected by her bluntness.

"Where is Alan?" she demanded in the face of what was beginning to feel like helplessness.

"As you thought, Alan has refused a generous offer to run *The Countess*. His loyalty to you is admirable, darling. Even when I suggested that Polly might be moving there without him, he refused to go. But he has agreed to take a room behind the kitchen, that I might be nearer to you."

"Stop this right now, Mark! Come up to my room; our business together is finished." Lauren stomped back to the attic with a pleasantly calm Rossiter at her heels. From beneath her bed she pulled a box, tied like a gift in twine. She thrust it out to him. "I am only short a thousand dollars. I'll have that to you next week and you can return my note then. For now, you will have your things moved out immediately. I want nothing more to do with you."

Rossiter tucked the box under his arm, still smiling at her. "You're overwrought, darling. What can you be thinking?" he asked patiently.

"I want you out, Mark!"

He sighed elaborately. "Darling, I know what has been troubling you these past two days. I know Madox came here the other night and upset you all over again. You aren't thinking straight."

His appearance was merely a facade; Lauren knew that now. What she was seeing and hearing was not what it seemed, not what he really was. Her mouth was dry with fear and frustration, but she forced herself to be calm. "I know exactly what I am doing. Most of your money is there; the rest will be paid next week. Get out of my house; we have no more dealings." She repeated it all very slowly, very precisely, very firmly.

"I am afraid that just isn't true, darling. I long ago adjusted the wording of your note to allot me half ownership of Maudie's for the price of seven thousand dollars. We are truly partners, you see. But it isn't only Maudie's that I want. It's you, Lauren. I have told you that before." He patted the money-filled box. "What you need now is rest. I will make sure all of this money is returned to your girls, including the bonus you promised, and finish settling in downstairs while you give yourself some time alone to think about our future together. I know you will see how right I am. Tommy will be just outside your door."

"How did you know where the money had come from and about the bonus I had offered the girls?" she shouted at his retreating back.

Rossiter turned halfway toward her with a smug expression. "I know everything about you, darling. We have no secrets."

* * *

Lauren spent all of that day and night pacing her attic room, all too aware of how right she had been in thinking of Tommy as a jailer. Each time she opened the door to leave her room the tall, fox-faced man stepped to block her path. "Mr. Rossiter says you're to stay in and rest," he told her as he closed her in each time.

It wasn't until long after she heard the sounds of revelry downstairs that Rossiter returned, carrying a tray of food for them both. His expression was warm and confident.

"If you are so sure of yourself, why am I being kept prisoner?" Lauren shot at him the moment he entered.

His perfect eyebrows arched in surprise. "Prisoner? Whatever made you think that?"

"The fact that every time I try to set foot out of here Tommy blocks the way."

Rossiter laughed easily. "He can be overzealous at times. I merely instructed him to be certain you rested today," he said smoothly, reiterating what the fox-face guard had said. "Of course you are not a prisoner."

"What exactly is going to happen from here on?" Lauren stood straight and stiff in the center of the room, fiercely proud even now.

Rossiter set their meal on the small table to which he had never been invited as he spoke. "Everything will go on as it has, Lauren. We are partners. You will continue with all you have done in the past and I will do as I have . . . as well as initiating a few projects that will bring Maudie's up to its full potential. I have already told you—together we will make Maudie's legendary. It wouldn't be all it is without you, darling, without your special touch." He eyed her still-stubborn stance. "You are upset about my part ownership. I know it was despicably underhanded, and I expect you to be furious with me for some time to come. But you will discover that there is absolutely no change in your position here and very little in mine. When you see how much better and more profitable Maudie's will become, you will know I was right to do it. Now come and eat, darling."

Lauren stared at him through narrowed eyes. "Maudie's is mine."

"Absolutely."

"Take the money I owe you and leave."

"Never."

"I will force you out."

Again he sighed elaborately. "Oh, Lauren, let's not be silly. I hadn't wanted to put it bluntly, but I see I must. Legally I have proof that you sold me an interest in Maudie's. I own enough officials in Seattle to uphold that claim. I have a virtual army of men in my employ against whom you would be like a gnat attacking an elephant. As you saw today, I can keep you prisoner if I so choose, to gain what I want from you personally as well. I know you for the practical, sensible woman you are. Let's have no more of this foolishness and go on to a better future together. I am here to stay and you will benefit as much or more than I by the alliance. You haven't lost any of what you had before, you have only gained an able, willing, and appreciative partner. Now come and dine with me in the civilized manner we both deserve."

His azure eyes glittered, his handsome face turned hard and implacable. It was then that Lauren saw the other side of Mark Rossiter. The side she had only suspected—feared—existed. Gone was the quiet patience, the even temper. All a sham. For here, she thought, was an evil, powerful determination that would follow its course at any expense. Here was danger. Here was hell's fire raging, and she was standing in its midst.

Keeping her wits, Lauren decided there was nothing she could do at that moment. She would comply to throw him off guard and bide her time until she could find a solution, a way to push the devil out of her house and regain what he had taken from her.

"There isn't anything I can do." Lauren whispered to Alan in the pantry. Her life was at once unchanged and unbearably altered. Allowed to move as freely about Maudie's as she had before, Lauren was never more than three steps in front of Tommy's dogged pursuit. She performed the same duties, held the same authority and responsibilities, but never did she have access to money or freedom from Tommy, and if, once outside Maudie's, her path ever appeared to veer from that which Rossiter decreed, a weasel-claw hand steered her right again.

"I'll go to Zach," Alan offered in a matching hushed tone. He knew all too well Lauren's predicament, for he was still her confidante in the moments they managed to snatch alone, and now he had become her ineffectual protector as well.

"No!" she insisted in answer to his suggestion. "Never Zach! I will find a way out of this. I just need time."

Alan spared her a dubious glance before leaving to answer a summons in the parlor. Lauren closed her eyes for a moment, wishing she felt as certain as she sounded. But after the way Zach had treated her, she knew the one solution she would never choose was asking Zach Madox for help.

Steeling herself once more, Lauren headed to her office. Charging through the doorway in a frenzy of frustration she came up short. The dwarf, Big Jim, paced before her desk on stubby legs.

"What are you doing here?" she asked disdainfully, wasting no effort on courtesy.

The little man merely granted her an ugly grin.

"Get out! I told you before that there would be no

shanghaiing in my house and I stopped it when I discovered it. Don't ever come on my property again, do you hear?"

Still he smirked . . . and stayed where he was.

"Lauren?" Rossiter's questioning voice came from behind her, "What's the problem?"

"This man is not allowed here. Have him thrown out."

"Calm down, darling," he said soothingly. "I have asked Big Jim here. We have an appointment."

Lauren turned on Rossiter. "I won't have his shenanigans in Maudie's."

"Leave this to me." A bare threat underlay his words.

"There is to be no shanghaiing in my house," she reiterated firmly, uncowed.

"Of course not," he agreed. "But Big Jim and I have business to discuss anyway." He nodded for the ever-present Tommy, who suddenly stepped up to her elbow. "Go on with what you were doing. We will be finished with the office in just a little while."

She was led away like a recalcitrant child.

And shanghaiing came to Maudie's.

"You can't charge them rent for the rooms and fees for laundering sheets and even part of the household staff's salaries. You're making them pay to work here." It was Lauren's next cause when Alan repeated the new policy behind Rossiter's back.

"Of course we can, darling. It is a privilege to work at a place like Maudie's. You have been far too soft on these girls until now. They are not leaving in rebellion, are they?"

"I won't have it."

"It is already done, Lauren. Don't waste your time being concerned. They are just whores, after all."

There was cheating at the gambling tables, too subtle to be detected. Prices were raised on food, and its quality was lowered even further. Rossiter hired more girls with even less adherence to the standards Zach had set, and the house grew crowded. But profits soared and Rossiter considered himself vindicated.

On the surface Maudie's remained as before—cultured, sophisticated, attracting a well-bred, high-paying clientele, but beneath the veneer it had become as treacherous and seedy as the King's Kastle. Lauren waged futile battles against all Rossiter did, but she began to realize how really helpless she was.

When she learned that he was supplying some of the girls with opium, she thought they had sunk to the lowest limits any bawdy house was capable of. What more could he do? she wondered. And then she found out.

Maudie's had been closed for an hour and all was quiet. Lauren slept fitfully as she had since Rossiter had moved in, so with the first frightened scream she bolted upright in bed, listening intently. Silence. It must have been a dream, she decided. But then another, tortured shriek sounded.

She flew from her bed, pulling on her robe as two more screams ripped the night stillness. No one but Lauren stirred. The halls were empty. Every door remained closed, their occupants ignoring the continued cries from Belle's room. Lauren ran, feeling sick to her stomach from the sounds that assaulted her. She threw the unlocked door wide in time to see Tommy's fist raise and pummel the woman's already bloody face as she cowered in a corner.

From the center of the room came Rossiter's smooth voice as he watched. "You are holding out on me, darling. You know the new rule. All tips are turned over with the brass checks. Now where are they?"

"My God!" Lauren shouted from behind him, charging into the room. "What are you doing?"

"Go back to bed, Lauren," he advised gently.

"Get your hands off her!" She ignored Rossiter's instructions and spoke to Tommy, fighting mad and sickened at the same time. But the fox-faced man merely awaited Rossiter's command.

Tension was thick, the only sound that of the sobbing woman. Lauren's topaz eyes burned defiantly into Rossiter, who paused as if weighing the situation. Finally he nodded to Tommy. "I think she has had enough of a warning. Get the money from her." Then he took Lauren's arm and led the way back to the attic room, where he softly closed the door and leaned back against it with a weary sigh.

"I am getting very tired of your interference, Lauren," he breathed. "We are going to have to get a few things settled between us, aren't we?"

Lauren stared at him, wishing she had a gun, for at that moment she would rather have shot him than look into the mask that was his handsome face.

Rossiter went on to lecture her with forced patience. "In the future, what I decide to do here is not to be questioned by you. I know what I am doing. I know what needs to be done to produce the results I demand. I'm sorry if you don't agree with my methods, but I won't tolerate your storming in as you have so often in these past weeks. You forget that this place is a whorehouse, that these...women...are whores, lowly, disgusting creatures who do not deserve your tender concern. Don't force me to use more drastic measures with you as well."

Still she stared at him, too furious and yet too aware of her own helplessness to speak.

He smiled brilliantly at her, an expression meant to console and mollify her. His tone eased in to the same one that had convinced her so long ago that he was genuinely good and kind. "I think a portion of our problem is our relationship. I have been so busy settling in at Maudie's and getting everything established as it should be that I have neglected to woo you properly. We have both suffered from it." He came toward her, ignoring Lauren's backward steps, stalking her without seeming to. "We haven't paid attention to strengthening our special corner of this life, to keeping that clean haven we each can provide for the other. We've let the tawdriness in, haven't we, darling? And it's taken its toll. Now it is time to pay attention to our private lives together. After all, it is so very much more important than business."

Lauren had backed herself against a wall. Her eyes widened as he stopped just inches in front of her, smiling down in the way she had once thought so pleasant. She was speechless and frozen with fear.

He raised his hand and tenderly brushed her cheek with the backs of four fingers. "So cold. So pale. The ugliness has disturbed you tonight, hasn't it? Come, let me soothe it away." He forced her stiff body into his arms, his palm cupping her head to turn it and press it into the soft nook of his perfectly tailored coat. He whispered into her hair, "It's time now, darling, time we seal our partnership here in the room we will share from now on."

Fear turned to powerful terror and Lauren tore from his arms, lunging away. "Don't touch me, Mark," she hissed.

His patience was already stretched to its limits. "I want you, Lauren. I want to be with you in the last way that separates us. You will see how much better it will make everything. I know best in this just as in all else. I have proven that to you."

"No!" she shouted, grabbing the fireplace poker to protect herself.

Rossiter eyed her calmly. He took a deep breath that raised his chest, and gone was the last of the sham. What Lauren faced again was his cold, unrelenting determination to have what he wanted. Still his voice was even and steady, but it lacked all pretense of cajoling or soothing. "I want you willingly, Lauren," he conceded. "I see how upset you are by tonight's incident; you're appalled and I am the villain. That will excuse you for now. But I won't wait much longer to have you. And have you I will; make no mistake about that. I leave the choice to you and a day in which to ponder it. But in the end you will be mine. Willingly, lovingly, we can share the joy I want us to have. Or I will force you."

He turned and left.

And now Lauren knew she was burning alive in hell.

Chapter 28

Pregnant. How could it be? On top of everything else. But there it was and Lauren had to face it. The suspicion had been lurking in the back of her mind for some time, but with so much else to think about and to work out, she had pushed it from her thoughts. Four months. That meant she had probably conceived on Zach's birthday, the night they had gone back to his house. And the time since had been the most bitter months of her life.

The fleeting butterfly movements now forced her to acknowledge what her natural slenderness had helped conceal. Zach's baby. Zach, who had tried to steal Maudie's from her. Zach, who could never accept her life and what she was. Zach, who was everything her mother had always warned her against and the man who owned her heart, her soul . . . and who didn't want her. How could there still be so much pain at just the thought of him? But that was there too. Heavy misery that had dragged her spirit down and left her easy prey for the likes of Rossiter.

Rossiter. Dear God. What was she to do about him? There was but one solution, and Lauren had finally reached the point where she was willing to act on it. It was time to give up Maudie's. She had loved her mother and her aunt regardless of what they

278

were, but she knew now that she could not bear this life. At best, it was ugly; at worst, it was what Maudie's had become under Rossiter's hand. Never would she bring her baby into this corner of the world. She would walk away from everything for the sake of her baby—Maudie's and Rossiter and Seattle and all her dreams.

Dawn found Lauren up before anyone else in the house. She had opened her door to find Tommy had spent the night in a chair outside her room. Taking two steps out into the hallway, she wondered if she would be allowed to leave. When he did no more than follow her, she hurried to her office. "When Mark rises, would you please ask him to come to me here?" she asked the homely guard before carefully closing the door against him. Then she sat behind her desk to wait.

Her fear of Rossiter had receded behind her resolve, and the Lauren Flannery that awaited him was the woman he had met initially, strong-willed, independent, and more stubborn than possibly he realized.

A scant half hour passed before he entered her office without a warning knock to announce himself. He strode in, his smooth smile in place, and sat down confidently opposite her. The perfect, handsome illusion of his face held not a trace of the threatening man who had given her his final ultimatum only hours before. Instead, in his sky blue eyes was the appearance of warmth, admiration, and kindness.

"So serious, darling?" he said sweetly in the face of her solemn stare. "Is something troubling you?"

His audacity was galling, but Lauren fought against responding to it. Anger would not serve her in the face of his calm control. "I am not troubled at all, Mark. In fact, I feel better than I have in a long time. You see, I have reached a decision."

His mouth stretched into a knowing grin. "You

really are wonderful, Lauren. I have never known a woman with so much sense."

She ignored his pleased assumption and pushed on with a steady, firm tone. "I want you to buy me out of Maudie's."

Very slowly his grin disappeared, his eyes became hooded, and his joy subtly altered into a brick wall of determination. Still, he was able to assume an innocent, shocked mien. "What do you mean?"

"I know you have wanted Maudie's all along and now I am willing to relinquish it to you. I want no more of this life. I will sell the remaining half to you for a reasonable price and leave Seattle." Her topaz eyes met his evenly, never wavering, never cowering.

For a long moment he returned her stare as if she were mad, smoothing his beard with precise, methodical strokes. And then he laughed. "I believe you're serious."

She answered him with an expression of unrelenting resolution and a stiffening of her posture.

But Rossiter only laughed again and then began speaking in his most pleasant, most confident, most steely tone of voice, the one he used to explain irrefutable facts to recalcitrant whores. "I have exactly what I want right now...or I will have by tonight. Owning Maudie's on paper isn't really all that important to me. I own enough of her that way and the rest—well, it's hardly yours, is it, darling? Her profits are all mine, control is all mine, Maudie's is all mine. But it isn't just Maudie's that I want. It hasn't been since the day we met. That should be clear to you by now. I was quite serious when I told you I wanted you, Lauren, not just to get my hands on Maudie's as you seem to think. I've had my heart set on having both you and Maudie's. And that is just what I now have. I wouldn't even think of buying you out and letting you leave me, darling. On the contrary, tonight we are going to consummate our partnership and finally begin what I have so patiently waited for." He stood up and moved to the door, as if his brief amusement had worn thin. "Think well today, Lauren, on how you will have it between us." He opened the door and spoke to Tommy in a voice loud enough for Lauren to hear. "Make certain she doesn't leave here today for any reason. And from now on she is not to go out at all unless both you and I accompany her."

The fox-faced man stepped into the doorway, legs spread wide and hands behind his back, closing the way against any escape.

The hours seemed to at once drag and speed by as Lauren's mind searched frantically for a way out. Never would she submit to Rossiter, but the new knowledge that she carried a child spurred her on more fiercely. One clasp of her waist would reveal the thickness there, and her baby would be doomed. She knew all too well how he handled this problem among the girls, and she swore she would never become the victim of his abortionist's knife.

She could not risk Tommy overhearing her plea, and so she scrawled her desperate need for help onto a piece of paper and slipped it to Alan in the guise of a receipt. But still the day wore on and Alan gave no sign of acknowledgment of her plight. Not until she entered her attic room to dress for the evening did she receive any response from him. Once she had closed and latched the door against the bodyguard, Alan stepped from behind her dressing screen.

Lauren became shaky with relief, but she wasted only a moment before pulling Alan back behind the screen to talk in hushed tones lest Tommy overhear. "Thank God you've come!" she breathed. "I hated to involve you, Alan, but I have no choice."

His smooth-skinned features were bleak. "The only reason I've stayed on here is to help you, Lauren; you know that. What has happened?"

"I have to get away from here tonight. Hard as it may be to believe, I'm in worse trouble than you know. I'm going to have a baby."

Alan's face drained of all color. "I thought Billy and I had kept him away from you."

"He hasn't touched me. It isn't Rossiter's baby," she whispered miserably. "And that's all the more reason to get away from him. He has threatened to rape me, Alan. We are to 'consummate' the partnership tonight. I tried to sell out to him and thought maybe he would just take my offer and let me go, but he won't. Maudie's has become a prison and I have got to escape."

"I'll go to Zach."

"No!" She was vehement.

"He has the right to know, to help you and save his own baby," he insisted.

"He is to have no part in this, do you understand? You don't know how it ended that night he came here. I would stay with Mark before I would ever ask him for help. Swear, Alan, swear you won't go to him."

"What else can we do?"

"I know some of the girls use knockout drops to shanghai whoever Rossiter decides is an easy target. Can you get some?"

He hated to admit that Polly had done the deed on several occasions. "I can," was all he said.

"I will plead illness just after Maudie's opens, and that will put Tommy just outside this door the way he is now. If you can put the drops in a drink and bring it to him I can sneak out before Rossiter comes upstairs."

"What will you do then?"

She worried her bottom lip. "Have you just a little money I can borrow?"

"I have offered it to you before."

"I will take only what I need to get out of this city."

"You make it sound easy, Lauren, but you know Rossiter is not a likely dupe."

She grasped both his arms in a hard, fearful grip. "There is no other choice, don't you see that? A few hours is all I have to get away from him!"

Alan nodded his agreement, but his fear for her was a tangible thing.

It was a raucous Saturday-night crowd. For the first time Lauren realized that even the clientele had deteriorated. While there was still a fair share of well-dressed gentlemen, they were vastly outnumbered by the rougher element of Seattle's newly rich.

As if her desire to abandon the place had opened the floodgates of her deepest, most honest feelings, Lauren at last admitted to herself how much she hated Maudie's. Her efforts at pretending it was better than it was and overlooking the worst of it didn't change the fact that it was a whorehouse, a place where women sold their flesh like sides of beef to be used in any way a man with the price decided. It was a life without morals, without ethics or scruples; but worse still, it was a life without human dignity. She wondered if she would ever again feel clean of the filth she had tried so hard to deny existed.

She realized now how far Zach had understated all his warnings about what this life really was, and how right he had been in not wanting her to be a part of it. If only she could call back the past, and believe him this time, if only she had sold the place when he had called in the note, then she could have paid him off and gone on to something else. But her pride and stubbornness had ruled her reason, and she had been so bent on proving she was not somehow better than her mother or her aunt and that she could live their kind of life and know that their pride had not been just a sham to conceal what they really were. She had been blindly determined to prove that everyone else was wrong to be contemptuous, and that Maudie's was just a sensible means of survival, that it could be made just as respectable as any other kind of business.

But now, with the future of her own child to think about, Lauren knew she could never have any part of a whore's world. Never would this legacy touch her baby. She would make sure of that.

She claimed a headache after dinner and climbed the stairs with Rossiter's eyes boring into her back. "It won't work, darling. I will be up later," he had answered her plea, but she ignored him. Her stomach was a hard knot and her heart beat so fast she could feel the reverberation in her neck and the pressure of it in her head. But her back was as rigid as ever, her chin as proudly held. Rossiter would not get the best of her. No man would.

She closed her bedroom door and locked it. Fighting the urge to pace, she sat in the wing chair, facing the door, her fingers drumming on each of the velvet arms. Please hurry, Alan, her thoughts begged. Perspiration moistened her brow, and for the first time in her life the high collar of her blouse felt as if it was choking her. Would Alan have had the time to get the knockout drops? she wondered. Would the girl who secured them tell Rossiter? Would Tommy be suspicious of the proffered drink and refuse it?

She felt the fluttery stirring of her baby beneath the now-tight waistband of her burgundy skirt, and the reminder nearly drove her into a hysterical panic. She had to get out of here! She took one deep breath and then another. No good could come of losing control. A woman was as strong as she needed to be, she repeated to herself like a litany.

Finally, Alan's voice sounded in the hallway. Tommy answered congenially enough. They talked for a few minutes until Lauren thought she might be sick, and then she heard a muted thud.

"Lauren?" Alan whispered urgently.

She flew from her chair, her icy fingers fumbling with the door's latches until she flung it wide. Alan's face was rose red and beaded with sweat as he bore the full weight of the unconscious Tommy. Lauren helped him drag the man just far enough into the room to clear the door and they lay him on the floor.

Alan pulled a roll of money from his pocket and thrust it at her. "There is a buggy waiting out back, on the south side of the stable so no one will see you leave. Get as far from here as you can. Promise me!"

Lauren swallowed a sudden rise of emotion and pushed the money into her skirt pocket, for she could not chance the encumbrance of even a reticule. "What about you?"

"I'll stay around Maudie's until I'm sure you are safe from him and then I'll leave too. Polly has agreed to come away with me. Just be careful, Lauren, and think of yourself."

She planted a hasty kiss on his cheek. "Thank you, Alan." Before she had moved more than a step away from him, he stopped her with one hand at her arm.

"Go to Zach, let him help you," he beseeched one last time.

But Lauren only shook her head in refusal and hurried from the room.

The back hallway was dimly lit and quiet. She walked as fast as she could without appearing to be hurrying, should she be spotted by one of the girls or the servants. A low, guttural laugh stopped her on the second landing, but Mattie Grimes didn't seem to notice her and continued to lead a staggering man into her room.

Lauren held her breath as she descended the second flight of stairs to the kitchen. The room was warm and brightly lit by cooking fires and lamps. The steady chatter of voices and the clank of pans kept up a din as kitchen workers busied themselves with their tasks at the stove or at the work tables. The savory scent of meat roasting, stew simmering, and pies baking threatened to gag her.

She paused, weighing whether to try and sneak out behind the cook and her helpers or to simply pass through as if she were headed to the outhouse. The second choice was better, she decided. Forcing herself to adopt a slower pace, she made it through the room without so much as a curious look in her direction, and then the cool evening air cleared her nostrils and chilled the moist collar that perspiration had glued to her neck.

The yard was dark and quiet. Lauren spared only a furtive glance all around to be certain no one was watching, and then she picked up her skirts and ran for the stable. The earthy tang of horses, manure, hay, and leather assailed her as she entered. She could hear one of the stable boys playing a lively tune on a mouth harp. The slosh of her foot in a puddle seemed to shout her presence, but nothing happened, and she slid around the corner of the big gray barn.

Just as Alan had said, there stood the small buggy he used to run Rossiter's errands, a single horse waiting patiently with the aid of a pile of fresh hay before him. Bless you, Alan, she thought as she hiked up her skirt and climbed into the buggy without a hitch. She leaned forward and closed one sweaty palm over the reins and lifted the straps to slap the horse into motion as she released the brake.

But leather never met horsehide.

A big, cold hand clamped her wrist and yanked her back into the tufted buggy seat. And then Mark Rossiter stepped from the shadows.

"Very foolish, darling. Very, very foolish," his smooth voice cut through the night.

Lauren tried to wrench free, but Rossiter nearly jerked her arm from the socket as he pulled her from the buggy to fall in the mud at his feet. His other hand snaked into her hair, which had fallen loose in the struggle, and raised her to her feet with a painful yank at her scalp. He spoke into her ear, his breath hot. "Don't make me show you how I teach intractable whores to behave themselves, Lauren. You wouldn't like it."

Lauren dared not fight. With every step back to the house, he ripped more hair from her head. As they passed through the kitchen, all hands stopped, all faces turned to gawk in stunned silence as he forced her up the back stairs to the attic from which she had just escaped. There stood two of Rossiter's burliest bullies, flanking Alan where he had crumpled to the floor. He looked up slowly, dazed from the blows that had already swollen his left eye and bloodied his nose. "Oh Lauren, no . . ." he groaned at his first sight of her, her head wrenched back with Rossiter's fist still holding her long sable hair.

"I ought to have you killed," Rossiter said cordially to Alan as he staggered to his feet. "Had she succeeded in getting away, I would have."

"He had nothing to do with it," Lauren cried.

Rossiter only laughed, yanking her head to the side to view the still unconscious Tommy. "You didn't do this by yourself, darling."

"Let her go, Rossiter," Alan said feebly. "Why would you want a woman who doesn't want you?"

"Oh dear, this from a fool in love with a whore." Again came the laugh that sounded so evil now. Then he spoke to his henchmen. "One of you throw him out. He really is a harmless little annoyance. And one of you can get Tommy to bed to sleep this off."

Lauren could barely see Alan as a punch in the stomach doubled him over and the smaller of the two bruisers dragged him from her attic room. Only when the door had closed on all four men did Rossiter let go of her with a shove that sent her to the floor.

"Clean yourself up, darling. When Maudie's closes for the night I will be back and we will settle this between us. Pity you didn't choose the pleasurable route." He left the room as casually as if he were taking a summer stroll and locked the door from the outside. With cool, clipped orders he instructed two more of his men not to let her out for any reason and then the precise click of his measured steps took him away.

And Lauren knew all was lost.

Chapter 29

Zach plopped down on the brown sofa in his parlor, pulled off his boots, and sank back with his head on one tufted arm, his feet crossed at the ankles on the other. Everything was finished. The house was ready to be closed up, his bags were packed, his businesses all turned over to his most competent foremen and managers. He knew it would be a long time before he could face this city and this house again. He only hoped leaving would help ease the agony that still tortured him.

Damn woman.

Damn love.

He had expected a life of quilted warmth, proceeding at the pace of slow maple syrup in a world of cut-crystal prisms. Instead he had gotten an ice-water dunking, a hot poker in the gut, and a world too gray to wake up to every morning. It had never occurred to him, in all his plans, that he might fall in love with a woman who didn't love him back. That just wasn't how it worked. But there it was. She loved a damned whorehouse instead.

Try San Francisco, Winnie had suggested. Maybe a change of scenery would pull him back into the world of the living. So that was where he was headed, determined to leave all thoughts of Lauren behind.

Hide away and hope to God he would heal. That was all that was left now that everything else had failed.

Company was the last thing Zach expected, but the sound of horse's hooves coming fast across the bridge and toward the house made him bolt up from the sofa. He went out onto the porch in his stocking feet. Whoever his visitor was, he was racing at a reckless pace on a seat that was none too steady. For a second Zach didn't think the horse was going to stop, so he moved quickly to the side of the porch as horse and rider seemed about to enter his parlor through the front window. But with a last scudding of mud from the animal's hooves, the horse reeled about and Alan Bentley half fell from his mount. Zach ran to him as his knees buckled.

Alan grabbed the stirrup and made it to his feet just as Zach reached and steadied him. Alan smelled of sweat and blood, and the glow of the full moon was enough to illuminate the bruised, distorted mass of his face.

"Good God, what happened to you?"

"She needs you, Zach," Alan rasped between hoarse coughs. "Hurry!"

"Looks like you need me more. Let's get you into the house."

Zach practically carried Alan up the front steps, lowering him gently to the sofa he had just vacated. "Who did this to you, Alan?" He grimaced at the cuts and bruises and open gashes that left the boyish face almost unrecognizable.

"Rossiter." Alan grasped Zach's arm with surprising strength. "You have to get Lauren out of Maudie's."

"I tried that, remember? It didn't work," he answered bitterly.

"You don't understand!" Alan shouted hysterically, spewing forth the story of her botched escape. "He means to have her...rape...her," he breathed at

last, but seeing the hesitation still lingering on Zach's
features, the small man knew he could no longer
hold anything back in his efforts to convince him.
"Rossiter only did this to me because I helped her.
You have to get her out of there before he does anything. She's pregnant, Zach!"

Zach's posture had grown more and more taut
with each revelation, but one doubt had to be erased.
"Whose baby, Alan? Will I be pulling her out of her
lover's arms?"

"No, no, no! The baby is yours. He has never gotten to her. Lauren wouldn't have him, and until now
Billy and I have made sure he abided by that. But he
will do it tonight unless you stop him!"

"Will you be all right?"

"Go! Now!"

Zach yanked his boots back on with murderous
vengeance. He grabbed his revolver from a cupboard drawer, loading it before he jammed it into his
waistband. The big hooves of his stallion chewed the
muddy turf as he pushed his fastest horse relent-
lessly, not knowing how little time he actually had.

Lauren sat in the same wing chair in which she
had awaited Alan's help so short a time before. She
faced the door, her hair hanging in tangled disarray.
She still wore the soiled skirt and blouse, and her
shoes were encrusted with mud. Her face was composed and blank, trancelike, as if she didn't quite believe her life had come to this.

She had tried the door first thing. Then she had
thrown open both small attic windows to see if there
was a ledge. But there were no ledges, nor any other
way for her to climb out safely. For a brief moment
she had considered jumping, but even her badly
beaten spirit could not give in that far.

With no possible way to escape she had turned to
searching for a weapon. All she could find was a

long, sharp hat pin, now hidden in the pocket of her skirt with the money Alan had given her. Could a man be killed with a hatpin? she wondered, but she knew it wasn't likely. Still, she had something to defend herself with, and she vowed she would not be taken without a fight.

She heard Rossiter's approach from far off as the sounds of Maudie's quieted and then grew still. Her mind shunned all thought.

His steps were measured, perfectly spaced, one never varying from another. Like heartbeats. Closer. Louder. They stopped just outside the door. He dismissed the guards and turned the key in the lock on the attic door.

Lauren did not spare him a glance but sat stony-faced. His appearance was an illusion, and she would never be fooled by him again. The door closed. The inside locks clicked into place. His steps sounded hollowly as he crossed the planked floor to stand before her.

"I have had this time to reconsider, darling." he said smoothly. "I was very angry with you earlier and had every intention of forcing you to give in to me tonight. But anger cools, doesn't it? And then the truth comes back to us. The truth here is that no ugliness should be between you and me. That is what we have both wanted all along—to protect ourselves from ugliness with the haven each can provide for the other. Let's not mar that now. Let's just forget the unpleasantness that forced its way between us and go on as we were meant to."

She raised her eyes very slowly up the long length of him. Perfect. Immaculate. Tailored. Suave. Handsome. Evil. "We are to go on as before, then?" Her voice was flat.

"Much the same, yes. Except, of course, that I will be moving up here with you and we will be sharing a bed." He slid his jacket off and folded it meticulously,

brushing a stray hair from the sleeve before laying it
carefully over the back of the settee. His long, manicured hands loosened his tie and unfastened the buttons of his vest, draping both over the coat. He freed
one button at his throat before rounding her chair
and stopping just behind it.

Lauren didn't so much as twitch. "No," she said
simply, plainly, and firmly.

"Think about it, darling." His voice glided
through the air like silk. "Don't let your anger rule
your reason. Your only choices are to yield what I ask
willingly and enjoy the result just as I will . . . or rape.
I must warn you that if you force me to choose the
latter there is the danger that I shall never feel the
same about you." He reached one hand to her
shoulder, fingering her hair. "I have in my life ini-
tiated virtuous, though reluctant, women into whore-
dom, used them in every way imaginable, taught
them obedience, and then turned a fine profit from
their sale. That, of course, always required force.
When I was finished I quite loathed the ugliness that
had soiled me. If you persist in this foolishness, I will
still have what I want from you. But our future will
be tarnished beyond repair and you will be nothing
more to me than another turned profit. Let's avoid
that, shall we?" He drew the tips of his fingers across
the inch of her neck that showed above her collar.

Lauren lunged away from him, feeling the threat
of his hand at her throat. Once on her feet she
whirled to face him, her blood coursing with fear
and the anticipation of the fight she knew was to
come. Her topaz eyes burned with hatred in her
ashen face. "You will never have me at all," she
hissed.

Rossiter's sky blue eyes were calm beneath one
arched brow. He shook his head sadly. "Think,
Lauren," he entreated as he stepped casually around
the chair toward her, stalking her as she backed away.

"Think very, very carefully. I offer you my love to fill the only corner lacking in your life. Together we will own so much and so many, we will sit like royalty over that which will make us wealthy and free of the mundane rules that guide everyone else. Together we will have everything. But deny me, darling, deny me and you will be just what you set yourself above, the lowliest whore. With me you will have all you ever wanted from Maudie's and more. Without me you will have nothing. Take my love, Lauren—be wise."

Slow step by slow step he came, and she retreated before him. Then he grabbed for her with the speed of lightning, imprisoning both her arms in a biting grip and crushing her into his chest.

"No!" she shrieked again, writhing and kicking with every ounce of her strength, pummeling his shins again and again with her foot.

He growled through clenched teeth, "Always remember that I gave you the choice," and the back of his hand slammed into her face with a stunning blow that sent her crashing into the wall behind.

Before her head stopped reeling, he had yanked her across the room to the bed and flung her onto the lace coverlet. Again he slapped her. But Lauren had regained her wits. She groped in her pocket for the hat pin, grabbing it just as Rossiter fell on top of her. She plunged the long pin into his side, striking bone that deflected what might otherwise have been a more deadly thrust.

Rossiter screamed in surprised pain and reared back just long enough for Lauren to bolt from the bed and grab the china water pitcher from the washstand. This time her aim was perfect. She threw it forcefully at his head, shattering the porcelain against his skull and dazing him.

Lauren seized her opportunity to dash to the door. But her hands shook and her fingers were clumsy and much too slow. She had two locks undone, but Rossiter reached her before the third could be moved.

Viciously grabbing a fistful of her hair, he wrenched her back toward the bed. Heedless of the pain that brought tears to her eyes, Lauren swung her fist at his stomach. But this time he was waiting for her attack. He caught her wrist and twisted it behind her back, shoving her before him onto the bed face first. With a knee in the middle of her spine he held her in a killing grip. The soft down of the mattress billowed up around her face and cut off her air supply. She gasped for breath, wriggling fiercely, but Rossiter pressed her down with the full force of his weight. Her lungs burned for air. Horrible panic gripped her throat, but her limbs grew too heavy to fight.

The door suddenly flew wide open and Zach stormed in. He grabbed Rossiter by the scruff of the neck and pulled him from Lauren, throwing him against the wall as if he weighed no more than a feather. For a moment Lauren knew only that someone had turned her over and that she could breathe again, and then she realized the two men were fighting wildly.

Fists flew and hammered into flesh. Zach pummeled his adversary ferociously, as if the floodgates of pent-up violence had been unleashed. He battered the other man mercilessly until the debonair Mark Rossiter lay unconscious, his handsome face a worse sight than Alan's had been.

Zach stopped then. Sitting back on his haunches, he made certain Rossiter was out cold, and then he stood up and went to Lauren, who was sitting on the very edge of the bed.

"Is he dead?" she managed to croak.

Zach only shook his head, stunned at what he had been feeling, at the fact that he was not only capable of beating another man to death but that he wanted to. But with a half dozen of Rossiter's men in the house he knew there was no time to waste. "Let's get out of here."

He took Lauren's hand in his and pulled her with him. They made it down the back stairs to the second-floor landing, but there they met two of the brutes, each wielding a gun.

Lauren froze, knowing they were done for. One big bruiser raised his pistol without so much as a wasted word. Zach surprised him by drawing his own revolver. Gunfire exploded in the narrow stairwell, filling the space with acrid smoke. Then through the haze there was a heavy thumping sound as the two hulks fell end over end down the stairway to lie in a heap at the bottom.

Again Zach pulled Lauren behind him, leaping over the bodies to sprint through the kitchen and outside. Behind them Lauren could hear the sounds of commotion. It seemed as if her earlier, foiled escape was being replayed to torment her. She kept pace with Zach, but her eyes searched the darkness, fearing Rossiter would lunge out at them at any moment.

They skirted the stable and fled down the alley. Lauren's breath was a wheeze in her swollen throat, her heart drummed in her ears, and stabs of pain knifed her sides. But still they ran without slackening their pace, dodging down alleyways, between buildings, and across yards. Her head jerked with every turn, her arm was stretched from its joint, her hair streamed behind her.

The shrill whistle of a train tore through the air. The train station. For a moment Lauren expected to be thrust up into one of the cars, in another repetition of the past. Instead Zach pulled her with him up into one of the hired hacks waiting there. He shouted directions to the driver and shoved a handful of bills into the man's hand as incentive for the speed he demanded. And then they were both jolted back into the seat of the hack to catch their breath and let the horse finish the last leg of their escape.

Chapter 30

Not a word was spoken as the carriage raced through silent streets and across country roads. Too many emotions were being jumbled together, and both Lauren and Zach were awash in their separate worlds of turmoil.

A single lamp in the parlor silhouetted Alan's slight form standing in the undraped window as the hack approached Zach's house. Until Lauren saw him, it hadn't even occurred to her to wonder how Zach had known to come to Maudie's when he had.

Without waiting for Zach she rushed to her friend's side, seeing now what he had endured after Rossiter's henchmen had taken him from the attic room. Alan tried to smile at the sight of her, but pain stopped the effort. "Are you all right? Did Zach get there in time?" he blurted out, meeting her in the entrance.

"I'm fine. Nothing happened," she assured him as Zach joined them. "What about you? You don't look as if you should be up."

"There's nothing that won't heal." He shrugged off her concern in turn and then asked the most important question: "Rossiter?"

"We left him unconscious." Zach said, which drew a regretful frown from Alan.

"But not dead?"

Zach shook his head.

"Too bad."

The venom in Alan's words surprised Lauren. In all the attacks he had suffered at his father's hands, with all the injustice and mistreatment meted out to him, she had never heard such hatred from him. "Alan?" she said his name as if only barely recognizing him.

"He deserves to die, Lauren. Don't deny it. There isn't a more evil, treacherous man alive. I would rest better, and it would be best for everyone's sake, if he were dead right now." Then he turned to Zach, speaking with new confidence. "I have to get to Polly. Rossiter will know I sent you, and he is likely to take his revenge on her."

"You can't go anywhere near Rossiter, Alan." Lauren was appalled. She hadn't so much as looked at Zach, but now she spoke to him, staring at the center button of his shirt rather than let her eyes touch the face that affected her so deeply. It was difficult to be obliged—to owe her life—to a man who had hurt her so badly, whom she believed felt nothing but revulsion for her. "Don't let him do this. Rossiter will kill him."

For a moment Zach stared down at her, believing her reluctance to look him in the eye was because of the contempt she felt for him. "Go to Billy," he said to Alan, his words clipped. "He's been itching to get even since Rossiter trumped up that accusation of stealing and had him beaten and thrown into the Sound. He will get Polly off *The Countess*. I'll give you the address of some friends who will hide you safely until I can work something out for you." His boots pounded hard into the floor as he left them in search of paper and pen.

When he was out of earshot Lauren said urgently, "I'll go with you. When Polly is safe I'll take the train out of Seattle." The statement brought to mind more practical matters. Lauren felt in her skirt pocket for the money Alan had given her earlier. Her fingers only came in contact with cloth, and a groan of frustrated defeat threw her once more into a panic. "It's gone! I must have lost your money in the struggle with Rosstier."

"Good," Alan asserted. "Stay here and give Zach a chance."

"I can't do that."

Hollow boot thuds warned of Zach's return before Alan could say more. He took the slip of paper Zach offered and thanked him brusquely.

Zach shrugged it away. "I owe you another debt, Alan. I'll be in touch to settle up both of them when everything calms down. Take the two-seater out back and be careful."

They shook hands and Alan stepped around Zach to leave. Lauren started to follow him when Zach's hand grasped her arm and stopped her. "No, you don't, lady. We aren't finished, you and I." His black eyes bored into her. "Go on, Alan. I'll tend to this one."

"I want to leave with him," she said stiffly to the wall.

"He has enough on his hands without you." Zach knew she couldn't refute that.

Alan looked from one to the other, and decided to side with Zach for Lauren's sake. "He's right, Lauren," he said tersely, and then he said to Zach, "Take her away from here until you can find a way to get rid of Rossiter."

"I don't run from scum like that."

Alan shook his head. "You don't know how bad he is, Zach. Get her out of harm's way."

"She will be fine, Alan. I won't let anything happen to her."

"Think about it." Alan tried again. "Rossiter is devious. He won't come at you from the front; he'll wait until your back isn't covered."

"I appreciate the warning. Just take care of yourself and Polly."

Alan hesitated, wishing he could find the words to convince Zach of the real danger he knew surrounded them. But in the end he could only take his leave.

The back door banged shut, and silence fell around Lauren and Zach like a shroud. Still his hand at her arm stayed her. When his voice broke the quiet it was a husky repetition of Alan's query. "Are you all right, Lauren?"

Her face turned up defiantly now, her topaz eyes glittering with anger. "I would be better if I were gone from here."

As she faced him he saw the darkening bruises along the high crest of her cheekbone and jaw. He tilted her chin to get a better view, and his rage intensified. "Alan was right, I should have killed that dirty bastard."

Lauren yanked her face away, ashamed of the proof of how she had been treated. "Let me leave," she said in a small voice, not even thinking of her lack of means.

He gave a reluctant sigh, seeing in her pallor and the effort required to keep herself rigid the terrible toll her recent experiences had taken of her strength. Thinking only of her and the baby she carried, he delayed the inevitable. "We will talk this out after we've both had some sleep."

"I don't want to be here," she insisted, knowing even as she said it that she lied. Weariness overwhelmed her, and, deny it though she might, she felt safer than she had in many weeks.

"You've made that clear enough. Now go up to bed, because your only other choice is to be manhandled a second time tonight if you don't go on your own."

Her eyes shot fire but she relented and, resigned, climbed the stairs to the back bedroom she had used when she had first come there, to fall exhaustedly onto the bare mattress of the virgin's bed.

Lauren dreamed that Rossiter's hands were tight around her throat and jolted awake. Terror stricken, she scanned the room. Finding herself alone, she realized the choker collar of her blouse was constricting her throat and had caused the nightmare. Her heart pounded in her breast, and the very thought of sleeping again was frightening, so she got out of bed.

All was quiet, and as she passed Zach's room she peered in to see him sleeping, his arms crossed up under his head, the sheet and blanket just over his belly. Two hairy armpits gaped up at her, and for a brief flash Lauren longed to be using his broad, hard chest for a pillow. Then she drew herself back and left his doorway, silently rebuking herself for being a hopeless fool of a woman.

The sky was a low-hanging, ominous gray that obliterated any sight of the sun. Lauren was shocked to find the time on the big grandfather clock in the entrance to be nearly midday. Half the day wasted, she thought. She should have been long gone by now. A good, strong cup of tea was what she needed to bolster her still weary spirit and rouse her determination. So she headed for the kitchen. The pantry was bare of anything save a few stale biscuits and a piece of moldy cheese. Lauren shook her head in disgust. How could the man live like this? She closed the door again.

Just leave, she told herself. Walk out that back door, take one of his horses, and go.

But she sought the bathing closet instead, meaning to freshen her soiled and slept-in clothes.

Wouldn't it be foolish to leave without a cent in her pocket? another part of her mind reasoned. She was too likely to end up back in Rossiter's clutches. Better not to make a hasty dash into even worse trouble.

With as much done for her appearance as possible, and having made the decision to be patient, Lauren walked from room to room of the lower floor, sorting through her thoughts.

The house was as big and empty as she remembered it...and as homey and inviting. What she would have given to grow up in a place like this. But she shoved the thought away. Dangerous. Her baby would never know this house...or any like it. She consciously renewed her determination to leave. It hurt too much to be with him, here, knowing she revolted him. She had to get away even if it meant stealing the money to do it.

She was sitting stiff-backed on the sofa when Zach came down a short time later. Her hair was twisted into its usual tight knot and the soil had been cleaned from her clothes, though brown stains still shadowed the places where mud had been. Her hands were folded primly in her lap, her face was composed, her eyes were serene. And all about her like a glow was pride, confidence, and that almighty stubborness.

"Morning," Zach greeted her and crossed to the decanter-strewn cupboard to slosh a finger of brandy into a glass. He drew it into his mouth, swished it from one inflated cheek to the other and then threw his head back to swallow it. With a slight shiver of his bare shoulders he fell into a leather chair near Lauren and crossed one ankle over a denim-clad knee and sat scratching the bare sole of his foot.

They were again the two strangers on the train, he surly and detached, she straight, stiff, removed, and oh-so-formal.

"Well, where do we go from here, Irish?" his gravelly voice rasped.

At last Lauren raised her bruised face to him, wishing she could be unaffected by his tousled hair, his angular, handsome features, the sharp jaw shadowed with black whiskers, and even that big foot poised before her. But her pride stood firm, hiding it all. "As much as I hate to admit it, I am in need of money."

"Some things never change."

She ignored his sarcasm. "Would you consider buying out my part of Maudie's?"

"Your *part?*"

"Rossiter altered the note I signed to make the seven thousand dollars an outright purchase of that much of the place. Will you buy out the rest?"

"Sorry. I'm too likely to set fire to it and burn Seattle to the ground again. I'm surprised you are so willing to let it go after everything you've done to hang onto it."

Her glance wandered uncomfortably. "Yes. Well— I am." She stammered slightly before the scrutiny of his black gaze. "Perhaps, then, you will consider extending me another loan...much smaller than the first, of course."

"No."

"I only need train fare."

"To where?"

"Stockton."

"Nice place, Stockton. Do you plan to beg in the streets?"

"I plan to go to the convent where I grew up. I know they will take me in until I can get back on my feet again. Maybe I can hire a lawyer from there to handle the sale of Maudie's for me." Something in the feel of his eyes on her made her voice trail off. It was as if they burned into her, and Lauren forced herself to look back at him to see why. His face bore an ominous expression, his black brows nearly meeting over the bridge of his nose. The silence stretched on as if he were waiting for something.

When he finally spoke again, his voice was a low growl in his throat. "You aren't going to tell me, are you?"

Her hot topaz eyes turned to ice. "I have nothing to tell you," she lied softly.

"Haven't you?"

She answered him with a defiant tilt of her chin.

"You would do it, wouldn't you? Knowing how I feel and how much I want it, you would actually take my money and leave without telling me about my own baby."

Lauren swallowed the lump in her throat. "I know only too well how you feel," she said to herself, and feeling the pain of it, she retaliated. "No one said it was your baby."

His black eyes scorched her from beneath the shadow of his brows. "That's the cruelest thing you have ever said. The more so because it's a lie. Would you brand your own baby a bastard out of spite?"

He shamed her, but only the white line around her lips revealed it. "Leave me be," she implored.

"No, I won't." Still he stared, pinning her back with the look on his face. "Don't punish me like this. You know you can hurt me more with this than with anything. But don't do it."

"I didn't know I could hurt you at all."

"Then you're blind."

"Don't pretend." She shot from the sofa, pacing as though her movement would make her a more difficult target for his contempt. "You let me know much too clearly what you felt the last time we were together. You couldn't get away fast enough. I made the mistake of thinking you had come back because you cared, that everything would be all right. I won't go through that again." She fought and failed to keep the raw pain from her voice.

"What the hell did you expect? I asked you to love me and you went cold in my arms. Did you think I could stand that kind of slap in the face? I had to get away."

"Well, now you can stay away," she whispered and then forced the strength back into her voice. "I only need train fare. You will have it back as soon as I resolve things at Maudie's. But Alan was right, I can't stay in Seattle. Rossiter won't let this go. He will wait patiently until my guard is down and then he will strike like the snake he is."

He ignored her talk of Rossiter and went back to the pain of their last parting. "So you thought I cared and everything would be all right; you just wouldn't admit you felt anything for me, is that it? Or was it what I thought then, that you really didn't care for me in return?"

Too much had happened for her to admit to any feelings for him. "I need the train fare, that's all."

"Answer me, dammit!" he shouted, lunging from his seat to spin her around to face him. His hands bit into her shoulders as he shook her just once. "What was it? Were you taking your mother's advice and protecting yourself, or did you just not care?"

"Leave me alone, Zach." Her voice quivered.

"I'm not going to leave you alone! You crucified me that night and I want to know why."

"What did *you* expect?" she screamed back. "You sabotaged Maudie's, had me arrested, and tried to force me out. Did you think I would accept all that meekly and still fall at your feet with love because you happened by one night? You proved to me that everything my mother ever said about men was true. You think you're better than Rossiter, but I see it differently. You're just alike, except that I never cared about him, so he couldn't use that against me. From where I stand that makes you worse."

"I couldn't have used something against you that I

didn't know existed. I didn't sabotage Maudie's or
have you arrested either. But I damned well did try
to force you out because I did care about you! I
wanted you out of that hellhole!"

"You just wanted to own me."

He threw his hands up in disgust. Now he turned
his back, his fingers digging fiercely into his own
hips. But rage spun him around to her again the
next minute. He poked a blunt finger at her.

"You tell me, lady, which of us tried to own you.
All I did was try to pull you out of that muck before
it swallowed you alive. And Rossiter stripped you of
everything and made a possession out of you."

She couldn't deny the truth. "Just help me get out
of Seattle and we will both be free."

His finger speared her middle. "*That* keeps us
bound tightly and *no* baby of mine is going to be
hidden away in a convent."

"It is my baby and my choice," she hissed.

"It is *my* baby and *my* choice." They faced off, one
as stubborn and angry and hurt as the other.

"So you saved me from one prison to lock me in
another. How are you better than Rossiter?"

"If that's what it takes."

Lauren turned her head and pleaded softly, "Let it
die, Zach."

"I won't let it die!" he exploded. "I want you to
marry me."

"You don't want to marry me! You just want to get
possession of the baby."

Fear that she would throw it back in his face kept
him from denying it, from admitting he loved her.
"Can you ruin both our lives and deny the baby its
own father just to get even with me for something
that was as much your fault as mine? Our getting
married is just plain practical."

The omission of his feelings was once again con-
spicuous. And Lauren had been hurt too much to

concede to practicality. "No. If you won't lend me the money, then at least tell me where Alan is. He won't refuse me train fare."

The silence stretched out as Zach tried hard to read her. Then he vented his frustration into the air. "I won't let you go, Lauren. And I'll never let you take that baby away from me. It's your choice whether we stay together respectably or not, but from this minute I'm not letting you out of my sight, not to eat or sleep or go to the privy. Understand that."

But months of feeling betrayed had left scars like grooves and a contemptuous look was his answer.

The lack of food in the house, Zach informed Lauren tersely, was the result of his intention to leave shortly on an extended visit to San Francisco. She tried not to analyze why the thought of his leaving Seattle bothered her so much as she sat mutely beside him in the two-wheeled gig on the way into town for supplies.

In the general store, she stood as woodenly as a cigar store Indian while Zach put in his order for foodstuffs and then rummaged through the rack of ladies' dresses. He chose two in Lauren's size, both feminine, flowered, and full around the waist. Lauren made no comment but swore silently never to accept his gifts.

His eyes never left her for long, and Lauren knew it was no use trying to escape him, nor was she brave enough to chance fleeing, penniless, through a city in which Rossiter and his bullies roamed. She had to bide her time once more until she could leave safely.

Outside again, she couldn't help nervously scanning the street up and down, fearing Rossiter would appear at any moment. Zach noticed her skittishness as he handed her up into the buggy and reassured her quietly: "I won't let him get anywhere near you again."

Before she could deny her concern, Winifred Cade called to Zach from the boardwalk in front of the dressmaker's shop two doors down. Lauren grew rigid. Wanting to spare her the older woman's curiosity, Zach met Winifred halfway.

"What is going on?" She wasted no time in getting to the heart of the matter. "You should be in San Francisco by now. Instead here you are with Lauren, of all people."

Zach explained the circumstances briefly, knowing from the look on his old friend's face that Winnie's quick mind was leaping ahead of him.

She gave him a sly glance. "It's been a long time since I saw Lauren last, and I will admit I was far away when she got into your buggy, but she looked a little thick around the middle. Shall I have my eyesight checked?"

Zach let out a breath like a sigh, studied the bakery across the street for a few minutes, and then admitted reluctantly, "Your eyes are as keen as ever, Winnie."

"Yours?"

"Mine."

"Not much happiness between you from the look of it," she said compassionately. "Are you fixing to do something about it?"

Zach gave her a half smile. It seemed so long since his face had eased even that much that it felt strangely relaxing. "I'm doing my best to try."

"I've seen too much of your temper lately, my friend. Did you go at her like a bull at a red scarf, or did you try some sweet talk?"

"The first, I'm afraid."

She patted his arm like a well-meaning mother and advised kindly, "Try the other. It works a whole lot better on proposals." She gave him a little wink, a peck on the cheek, and left.

Zach thought over Winifred's words as he and Lauren shared a silent dinner at the hotel and saw too clearly just how fearful Lauren was of being back in Rossiter's vicinity. He felt strongly protective of her, and he vowed to try to resolve some of his harsh feelings about the past.

Darkness enfolded them on the way home and made the awkward silence seem more natural. For the first time in months Zach began to feel he could make the mess they were in come right again.

The leaden clouds above finally grew too burdened. What began as drizzle grew into a heavy winter rain while they were still a mile from Zach's house. It drummed on the carriage roof so loudly that neither could have heard if the other had spoken. Twin lamps swung from the carriage sides, throwing some light against the solid wall of water sheeting against the horse's rump.

Lauren huddled into a laprobe and pulled the shawl Zach had forced her to accept close around her shoulders. But she could not blanket out the chill, and her teeth chattered like wild castinets. Just as she began to doubt they would make it to the house at all, the wooden wheels splattered across the cobbled bridge. Seconds later they pulled to a stop a few feet from the porch steps.

Zach ran around to help her out. By the time they reached the safety of the porch they were drenched to the skin; water ran down Zach's back from the brim of his hat and plastered Lauren's hair against her skull like paint. The house smelled musty but felt welcoming all the same as Lauren stood dripping in the entrance.

"Go on upstairs and get out of those wet clothes," Zach barked. "Put my robe on and then come back down. I'll have a fire going by then." Before she could answer he had disappeared out into the storm again to drive the carriage around to the stable.

Lauren had worn the same clothes for nearly two days, and it felt good to peel them away. She dried off briskly and searched through Zach's wardrobe for the heavy woolen robe she had seen him wear once. How good it felt; it was warm and dry and hung soft and loose around a stomach that was growing much too rounded for the waistband of her skirt. Without thinking that she was complying too easily with his wishes, she took towels from the bureau and padded downstairs as he had ordered. It didn't occur to her that somehow during the journey home in the rain she, too, had softened a bit.

She found Zach kneeling on one knee before the hearth, the other bent to prop up his forearm. The yellow glare of new flames lit his face as he fed them with his breath. Her eyes glued themselves to his broad back as tightly as the sopping shirt that was molded to him like skin. Then she resolutely turned her gaze to the fire.

Fool of fools, she consciously reminded herself, she had trusted two men and she must not let it happen again. One had stolen her inheritance, everything she had worked for at Maudie's, her sole means of survival. Worse yet, the other had stolen her heart and badly bruised her spirit. A muscular back was not enough to make her forget that. Still unsure of what she was going to do to get away from Zach, she reassured herself that the time would come and she would seize her opportunity.

He had pushed two big wing chairs up close to the fireplace. Without a word Lauren set towels on the seat of one and sat with stiff-backed poise on the other. She unfastened the coiled braid at her nape, flipping it over one shoulder to squeeze it dry in small sections of her towel.

When the fire was blazing Zach sprang up, giving

an exaggerated shiver. Without at first realizing it, Lauren watched him peel away the soggy shirt to bare his hairy chest. She followed his movements as he dried his hair with a brisk rub of the towel in his big hands, then his belly, chest, and bulging biceps in turn.

Anger had obscured her memory of his masculine beauty, and as he unfastened his jeans and stripped them off she felt distinctly uncomfortable and pressed her knees tightly together. She forced her errant eyes to study the fire again until he pulled on another pair of pants that must have been the ones she had seen hanging in the bathing closet that morning. But still his chest was bare, gilded by the fire's glow. His hair was a wild tangle smoothed only with his fingers, and his face was shadowed with the day's growth of beard. He was much too much man to leave the woman in her unaffected, no matter how much she would have preferred it.

Then he plopped down low in the chair, his big feet stretched out to the heat of the fire and his hands clasped behind his head so that she looked at his profile through a hairy web.

"Oh, that's better," he sighed, paying no attention to her rigid formality. "How long are we going to keep this up?" It was his old, patient tone of voice telling her the Zach who had captured her heart had returned.

Lauren's whole body tensed. "I suppose until you see there is no future for us and let me go."

"Or until you believe I won't ever do that and give in," he countered calmly, not in the least deterred.

"I'm not likely to give in to such high-handedness," she said high-handedly.

"That so?"

"It is."

"Then what would it take?" he asked with a crooked smile.

"I am never going to, Zach," she stated firmly.

"The way I have it figured, Lauren, is that I couldn't have hurt you so much unless you cared an almighty lot for me. How do you figure it?"

"I don't."

"You don't figure it or you don't care for me?"

"Both."

"You're a liar."

"And a whore." The words she believed he meant to add just slipped.

Zach's features sobered as he turned his face toward her. His tone was quiet and devoid of any teasing. "That isn't true."

"It's what you think."

His black eyes were shadows that devoured her, and the depths from which his voice came showed her the difference between true sincerity and Rossiter's ruses. "I know better than that. There was one second when Alan told me you were pregnant that I was afraid the baby wasn't mine, and even then I didn't think of you as a whore. Living at Maudie's should have proved you aren't even to you."

She couldn't bear his disappointment and sought to divert his attention from the subject by bending over and trying to tug the hem of his robe around her icy feet. Catching her unawares, Zach shoved his chair opposite her and then spun hers to face him, flinging her back like a rag doll. Before she could form the inevitable protest, a big bare foot landed on either side of her. He pulled both her feet up to his chest, crossing his arms over them to give them warmth. "Brrr!" He shivered again, easing the tension that had grown between them with the reminder of the old, sore subject.

When she tried to yank free he just tightened his hold, his chest hair curling up between her toes. "God, I'm dying to feel that belly of yours," he said to himself. Then his black eyes singed her once more.

"Tell me what it is you want, Irish." His fingers stole around her feet, rubbing gently.

"I have told you that a dozen times today."

"No, you haven't. You've told me what your mother would have expected you to say, what pride forced you to say. But the truth is that you have finally given up on Maudie's, you're willing to be rid of it at any cost; you have learned too well that you don't belong in that life and now you're carrying my baby. There must be something you want for that baby, some idea of how you want it to grow up. So what is it?"

"Quietly," she clipped out.

"In a convent, lonely and outcast the way you were, never knowing its father or a house or a normal life?"

"This isn't going to gain you anything," she observed caustically, her glance touching the sheen of his naked shoulders. The arches of her feet fit into his hard bulging pectorals, and the heat of his body seeped into her soles and slowly up her legs. It made her feel weak, and she tried again to pull free.

Zach's big hands clamped her ankles and held them. "I like them here."

She did too. That was the problem.

"Be honest with me—be honest with yourself—this is where you both belong; but more than that, this is where you want to be."

"Not with you."

"With Rossiter?" he shot back sarcastically.

She swallowed convulsively at the mere mention of the man's name. "No, not with Rossiter."

"With whom then? Whom would you choose to raise my baby?"

No one. No one but you, her fickle mind shouted, but instead she said, "Can't you leave me alone?"

"No. I won't," he answered, but he saw that she was wavering and he eased up on her.

He rubbed his hands gently across the tops of her feet, up her ankles and back again.

Where were all the logical reasons to deny him? she asked herself. How could the simple warmth of his hands soothe away so much pain?

The rain still drummed outside, but inside it grew still. Zach watched her silently argue with herself and knew he was winning ground. Then, without her realizing it, her toes burrowed into his chest and tickled him.

He removed his feet from her sides and hers were suddenly on the floor, and he was hauling her up to stand before him. He raised his hand gently to the side of her neck, tilting her face with a thumb beneath her chin so that all she could see was his handsome features bathed in fireglow. His thumb slid along her jaw, and when he spoke his deep, rough voice was like warm honey. "I'll never let you go, Irish. I love you enough for the both of us."

Confusion furrowed her brows. "What do you mean, for both of us?"

"I mean it doesn't matter that you don't love me. I built you a house and I've waited a lifetime for you to come fill it. Don't leave me all alone here anymore."

Her whole body shuddered at his words, but he just kept stroking the side of her face with his thumb. The baby inside her kicked so hard that even Zach felt it vibrate through her body.

"We're already a family, Lauren," he barely whispered. "We owe our baby the life you and I never had. Marry me and let me make you happy. Marry me and grow old and wrinkled with me, and neither of us will ever be lonely again. Marry me because you want me, Irish. Just because you want me." His hypnotic words trailed off.

The heat of his body enfolded her. Oh, how it hurt to love him! She had locked her feelings away to protect herself and now they welled up to burn like acid.

And her mother's voice was oddly still within her.

And the baby kicked and moved about and reminded her.

And all she really wanted was to lean into that big body, just inches away, and be able to trust him.

Chapter 31

"What therefore God hath joined together, let no man put asunder."

It was a sunset wedding the next day in the Cades' parlor. Alan gave the bride away, Winifred and Arthur stood up as witnesses, and an unusually subdued Polly looked on.

Afterward, the talk turned to the revenge Rossiter might be planning and Lauren's baby, due in only five months.

Polly and Alan both shared Lauren's worry about what Rossiter might do. He wasn't a man to accept being refused anything he wanted, they all agreed. What he wanted, Zach felt sure, was Maudie's, and Zach thought he saw a solution.

"I think you're wrong, Zach," Alan said with new aggressiveness. "Rossiter wants Maudie's, all right, but he wanted Lauren along with it."

"He's a greedy beggar. He'll settle for clear ownership of the place as consolation for losing Lauren to me," Zach assured them confidently.

"I hope you're right, but I would still feel better if you took Lauren away from here."

"She will be fine, Alan. I'm not going to let anything happen to her." To himself Zach judged that their fear was an understandable reaction to the power Rossiter had wielded over them all, but he felt it was not a realistic assessment of the man. And Zach was too happy to worry about it.

Lauren moved through her wedding day with mixed emotions. Four months of feeling betrayed and reviled by the man she loved, of being convinced that her mother had been right about the treachery of men, were not easily shed in two short days. There lingered in her the need to keep just a bit of herself in reserve, and because of that she had not refuted Zach's false assumption that she didn't love him.

Was it terribly wrong of her? Her conscience prickled, but still something held the words in check. The ceremony cloaked her with respectability, but beneath it her doubts still lingered and left her with the irrational sense that it was all a ruse to color a blacker truth.

You were with Rossiter too long, her heart rebuked her. Don't give too freely, her head reasoned in return. And Lauren was caught in the middle.

The short notice didn't diminish the bountiful wedding dinner. They feasted on glazed ham, sweet potatoes, baby carrots, and home-baked bread. The champagne was Arthur's donation, along with his specially chosen gift: an overlarge painting of cows grazing in open countryside.

"Put it in your barn," Winifred suggested as she gifted them with her mother's silver tea service.

Lauren and Zach were showered with wheat as they left the celebration to ride home in silence. She was feeling awkward, and he wondered why. They got to the house just seconds before another fierce storm hit, leaving Lauren dry but catching Zach on his way from the stable.

All he wanted was to pull her upstairs with him, peel off his wet clothes, and take her to bed. But she was so quiet, still so formal and removed, that he tamped down his desire and took the stairs two at a time to change.

Take it slowly, he advised himself. A whole lifetime is what you will have, and the months you have both missed are as nothing compared to that. So he buttoned up his trouser and went looking for her.

Lauren was standing at the porch railing just as she had been her first night there, staring at the wall of water rolling off the overhang. She had wrapped herself up tightly in a shawl, and for a minute he stood looking at her slight, narrow back, thinking how she was all trussed up inside again and how much he wanted to free her.

In his mind he had a picture of how it would be; she would be the stern, prim, and proper wife and mother, and he would be the lenient husband and father who spoiled his wife and child. No one would ever see the side of her he had found beneath that iron will, the side that emerged when, behind a locked door, she became a different woman with the passion of a wanton. He grinned crookedly at that thought. He loved being the only one who brought that out in her, even if she did make him work for it most of the time.

His boots thunked hollowly across the porch so that she wouldn't be startled when he came to stand beside her. "You're going to catch your death out here," he warned, looking down at her profile against the silvery raindrops. Her chin was tilted and she was smiling that secret smile he loved.

He wanted to pull her close but knew he would be wiser to move slowly. She had a right to set the pace on her own wedding night. So he plunged his hands into his pockets, his thumbs hooked into his belt loops.

"It feels good out here tonight," Lauren explained simply. "I heat up faster now than I did before. I suppose it's part of the ... condition."

He swallowed a comment on how much he would like to see an example of that! Instead he said, "Tell me about the baby. When did you know?"

"I should have realized long ago, but things being what they were, it just didn't occur to me at first. I was never really...regular...anyway," she finished, embarrassed. "Then for awhile I think I knew but wouldn't let myself face it. But things with Rossiter got worse and I couldn't ignore it any more. I was feeling life and I realized I had to stop denying it to myself and protect the baby from him."

Not wanting the ugliness of Rossiter to enter the first tranquil, companionable time they had yet shared, Zach directed his questions only to her pregnancy, wanting to know every detail, sorry to have missed even the first few months of it. "Then you weren't sick?"

"Not a day," she said simply. It sounded so easy, when it had really been so hard and had hurt her so much to discover she was pregnant in the middle of the most wretched despair she had ever known.

Something in her face told him of her inner anguish; the serene smile had gone and a kind of remote sadness had taken its place. "Did you cut my heart out a hundred times in your head?"

She turned to him, one brow arched. "Nothing that nice," she answered honestly, and he couldn't help grinning, even though he felt bad that it had been that way for her.

"I'm sorry, Irish." His gravelly voice was soft and kind and amused all at once.

"So was I."

"And now?"

"Mmm," she mused, facing the rain again. "I'm getting used to it."

His next words were difficult for him to say. "Don't you want the baby, Lauren?" It was something he hadn't thought about until then.

Her pause weighed heavily on him before she answered, "I do now." It was only as she said it that she realized it was true. "Before, it was just another problem on top of so many others."

Again he changed the subject from the grimness of the past. "When did it happen, do you think?"

"It was your birthday, here," she answered, and the secret smile flitted by again to warm his heart. "You wouldn't have had it any other way, would you?"

"My babies have to be made in my bed. That is the rule, all right." He laughed that barrel-chested boom of pleasure of his and reached up to squeeze the back of her neck.

The touch of his hand was warm and set off light sparks in Lauren's veins. She leaned her head back in his hand instinctively, but she stifled the purr that rose in her throat and said. "Do you always get everything you want?"

"I did this time," he answered, with an amused, heartfelt chuckle. He ran his thumb up and down the taut side of her neck. When he spoke again his voice was a rough caress. "When did you first feel it move?"

"Just a few weeks ago," she whispered back, deeply affected by his emotion.

"How long are you going to make me wait? Let's go upstairs so I can tell for myself that this isn't some scheme to trap me."

"Trap *you!*" she squawked "Impertinent is what you are."

"Is that all?"

She shook her head. "Not hardly."

"Does that mean you aren't going to let me take you upstairs so I can feel my baby?"

"That's what it means." She affirmed.

"Punishment?" he queried, not knowing how near the truth he had come.

Lauren suddenly felt small. He was giving to her freely, openly; he had proved himself by wanting her and marrying her, and she was still feeling the need to be niggardly in expressing her emotions. "I'm sorry," she said softly, surprising him.

"What are you sorry about, Irish?"

How could she explain it without revealing more than she was ready to? "I ... I care more for you than I have let you believe, and that was wrong of me," she said feebly. "It's just that I'm ... I haven't quite forgiven you yet."

"I know."

"Doesn't that make you angry?"

He gave a rueful chuckle. "Everything has happened too fast for you. It'll come." His arm went around her shoulders, drawing her against his side. "But I won't deny I'm disappointed." He maneuvered them back into the house and started up the stairs. "For now, I guess we will just sleep back to back and I'll try to forget this is our wedding night."

Her unacknowledged hopes were dashed. Foolish, fickle heart, to contradict reason. Halfway up the stairs she sighed in disappointment.

"Did I misunderstand?" He laughed hopefully, stopping at the landing and letting his deft fingers unpin her hair before steering her into his room.

"No. I think I did," she said to herself and made him laugh again.

"You haven't forgiven me for all the hurts I let you suffer but you want me just the same," he guessed.

"It's shameful, and I don't understand it." The back of her knees came up against the edge of the bed.

"Shame has nothing to do with it." His gravelly voice was slow and smooth as his fingers unfastened her buttoned front. "Feelings don't always agree." He slid the dress over her shoulders and dropped it to the floor with a relieved sigh. "Thank God," he finished with a smile in his voice. He kissed the highest arch of her shoulder. "Just let yourself go, Irish, and see if a little nip here..." He bit her earlobe. "...and a little tickle, a little tease, a little blowing, a little nuzzling..." He finished at the base of her throat, having skimmed off her chemise and petticoat and let them fall in a heap on top of her dress. "...can't make you forget all about everything else."

"Oh, I don't know..." she murmured dubiously, but her head fell back, and she arched her neck to meet his lips. He pressed light, chaste kisses from the hollow up along the curve and all the way to the tip of her chin, divesting himself of his shirt and pants while he did.

Lauren sighed once more and with the sigh went the pain and the memories. When she breathed in again, it swelled a desire she had made herself forget existed. The only thing that mattered was that she wanted him and he was there for her.

When both stood naked, Zach moved Lauren a half turn so that the profile of her body was silhouetted against the silver rain. He studied what he had been so hungry to see, the gentle protrusion of a pregnant belly. Only when he had memorized it did he ease her on to the mattress and lie beside her with a long, muscular thigh across hers.

Their mouths played and courted and renewed their old acquaintance. They feasted together, each on the other, in warmth and wetness, smoothness and pointed probing. His hand slid its way to her breasts, all taut satin fullness with the crests pinched into hard nubs that admitted desire and longing. To her they were the tight, sensitized ends of a cord that stretched down to that spot between her legs, a cord that vibrated with every squeeze in a way she had never felt before; the sensation was intense and sharp, as if the nerves of each nipple were exposed and waiting at the surface. And when his mouth lowered there like hot honey, she arched so fiercely he thought he had hurt her and drew away with a jolt. She pulled him back with a breathy yearning sound that made him chuckle as he realized the true reason for her reaction.

And then he moved one palm lower, down her side and then up and around to climb the small mound of her stomach. He splayed out his big hand there, kneading slightly, testing and learning and reveling in his first touch of his child. His mouth followed to kiss her raised middle reverently and then, with a growl, he nipped her gently and felt the baby dart away from him. They both laughed at that, the first sharing of pleasure in its antics.

"I love you, Lauren," he whispered up into her hair as his hand played a little longer with her belly.

Suddenly the words came so easily to her own lips that she let them spill out. "I love you, Zach," she whispered.

His happiness was uncontainable. His eyes filled and he breathed a long, long sigh into the silkiness of the hair beneath his face. "You wouldn't lie to me at a time like this, would you, Irish?" he asked in a ragged, hushed voice.

"No," she answered huskily, "I wouldn't lie to you. I do love you, Zach."

"It's been a long time coming." He sighed and held her so close she was crushed into him, but even that didn't seem close enough. For a long minute his heart beat into her ear and she dampened his chest with her tears.

When he could make himself let go of her he cupped both sides of her face in his hands and kissed her again, gently, taking away the salty dew on her cheeks. Then his mouth took hers, first softly, chastely, then more firmly. His lips were barely parted, his tongue flicked just the pointed center of her upper lip, and then his full open mouth took hers with intense desire.

She filled her hands with him, skimming her palms over his hard, muscular shoulders, down tensed, rolling biceps, across sinewy pectorals to the hard male nubs in curly chest hair. Then up they went again to his thick, taut neck, to the whisker-roughened blade of his jaw.

Their tender emotions were replaced by passion so hot it threatened to burn them both alive. Each stroke of her palm grew more frenzied, down once more, to his flat, ridged belly, narrow hips, and thighs massive enough for her hands to stretch wide and still not reach end to end around. And when the feel of him was branded into her flesh she closed around nature's scythe and felt his whole body stiffen with pleasure and groan from deep in his soul.

Her mouth smiled beneath his until his hand traveled a similar path down her body, his knee nudging her legs apart. His fingers combed through her tangled sable curls to slip below into the warm cleft of flesh, thrumming the chord there until she could hardly breathe with wanting him.

He rose above her then, and came into her as carefully as his driving need allowed. Her legs curled up around his waist with a will of their own and each thrust was like touching her fingertips to a star, closer, closer to grasping it. And when she did it exploded inside of her with white light and fiery sparks that ignited him as well, and he plunged into her to spend himself in what must surely have been a little death and a little rebirth.

Their taut muscles slowly eased and relaxed, and their breathing slowed in concert with sighs of perfect splendor, and their hearts were at last laid bare.

That night they slept front curving into side, where hollows met curves and curves, hollows. Their arms were wound tightly together, and their hands drank in the reassuring feel of the other's skin. And in between them their baby did a little Irish jig and went unheeded.

Chapter 32

Maudie's wasn't the same. It was still well kept and miles above a box house or a skid road bawdy house, but Zach sensed that its dignity had been destroyed. Beneath the surface now was something every bit as seedy, sordid, and ugly as the worst Seattle had to offer.

Zach casually strolled through the place, observing all that Maudie's had become on this Friday night, not quite a week after his wedding. He awaited a meeting with Rossiter, while Lauren was in the safe-keeping of Winifred and Arthur.

Maudie's had indeed changed; he would have known it even without Lauren and Alan having told him the details. The corruption was apparent in the type of men Rossiter had chosen to stand about to keep peace. Henchmen, if ever there were any. It was apparent in the leering bartender whose squinty eyes shifted too quickly to make certain no one saw what he did below the bar. It surrounded the dealers at the gaming tables with their cold, blank faces. It even showed in the girls now, whose light fingers did more than caress. If Maudie could see it now, she would put a match to it herself, Zach thought. Thank God Lauren was out of it.

A tall, broad man with the pointy face of a fox

summoned Zach and led the way to the office. Rossiter sat calmly behind the desk, watching Zach through hooded eyes over spired fingers. The fox-faced man closed the door and stood sentry on the inside, behind the chair Zach took without being asked to sit.

"Rossiter," he said, greeting the man genially enough.

"Madox," came the equally amiable response.

"I see your hand all around the place," Zach observed noncommittally.

Rossiter sized him up for a moment. "What is it you want?"

Zach smiled slowly, crossing his ankle over his knee. "You might say I am here as Lauren's representative."

Rossiter's still puffy, discolored left eye twitched, a reflex of the memory of their last meeting on her behalf. But his voice was smooth. "I miss her. When is she coming back?"

Zach laughed unpleasantly. "That is what I am here to talk about. It seems she has had enough of this life. She has decided to sell the place."

"She did mention that to me earlier. I advised her against it." It was a veiled threat.

"Well, I've decided to back her up and handle it for her."

"I would like to talk to her. I'm afraid we parted under unhappy circumstances and a terrible misunderstanding that I would like to straighten out between us."

Zach played along with the farce and sighed understandingly. "I'm afraid she won't see you."

"We were much too close for me to believe that," Rossiter insisted, his insinuation clear.

One corner of Zach's mouth lifted knowingly. "Well, it's me she is close to now. We were married on Monday night." The news didn't faze his adversary.

"Congratulations. Why don't you tell me why we are having this meeting then."

Zach shrugged. "I know about the altered note that gives you part ownership in Maudie's. Were it me you swindled I would fight it, get you out of here altogether, and sell the place to someone else. But Lauren isn't interested in revenge. She is willing to let that lie and offer you the first option on buying out the remainder."

Rossiter's eyebrows arched loftily. "What makes you think I haven't altered the note to give me full ownership already?"

"I checked the deed. It's still in Lauren's name. Besides, that really would have been foolish of you, and you aren't a foolish man, are you?"

"I see." Rossiter ignored the question. "This is not easy for me. I have always wanted Maudie's, but I wanted Lauren along with it."

"That is out of the question now, isn't it?"

"Yes. Isn't it?" he said with the perfect mixture of regret and innuendo.

"Of course, if you aren't interested, we will sell to someone else and you can work out a partnership with a stranger."

"No, of course I wouldn't want that." Again Rossiter weighed his decision. "I suppose if Lauren is lost to me there is no need to forget business. Shall we discuss price?"

Rossiter was so amenable, it raised the hair on the back of Zach's neck. "We think another seven thousand would be equitable."

"That sounds fair. When will you be wanting the money?"

"I will have my lawyers do the paperwork; you can pay them on Monday and receive the deed then. There isn't any reason we have to meet again."

"Fine." Rossiter's mouth spread into a deliberate

smile. "Give Lauren my apologies for our parting and my best wishes for your future together."

"Oh, I will." Zach stood up and rounded the chair to leave. Then he paused and, as if it was an after-thought, said cordially, "I probably don't need to say this, but if you ever so much as talk to Lauren on the street I'll kill you myself."

Rossiter stared back, seemingly unaffected, and then waved the very thought away. "No need for threats. I have lost Lauren but gained Maudie's. It is fair compensation. I wouldn't think of causing her discomfort."

"Good. I'm so glad to hear it." Zach moved to the door, facing off against the fox-face for a long mo-ment before the man stepped away.

Zach walked out of Maudie's into the night air with a confident stride, to return to the Cades' house to fetch his wife.

Tempting fate, that was what Lauren had accused him of. But Maudie's and Mark Rossiter were not going to circle over his head like vultures. He wanted to be rid of the place before it could do more damage between him and Lauren or, God forbid, before she had second thoughts and decided she wanted it back. He didn't take Rossiter as seriously as did Lauren and Alan, but then it was one thing for the man to bully a woman and a weak, powerless soul like Alan and quite another for him to deal with a man of equal or greater stature.

Still, Zach had to admit there was something un-settling about Rossiter, that same sense of evil he had felt when they first met. Jealousy, he had thought then, had added to his dark feelings. But now he wondered.

Maybe it wouldn't do any harm to take Lauren up to his logging camp for awhile. He had no fear of Rossiter for himself, but there was no use risking even a subtle type of retaliation against Lauren. He would let the lawyers handle the sale and get Lauren away from the last unpleasant association with that place and that man. Besides, the mountain air would do her good and give her a chance to forget the whole mess once and for all.

Winter rain again impeded their ride home, and because Lauren had had no desire to air the stench of Maudie's around the Cades, it was not until they reached the house that she asked about the evening's business.

"What did he say?" she questioned the moment they were inside, the fear in her fine features convincing Zach that his decision to get her away from Seattle was a good one.

He untied her new gray wool cloak and hung it on the hallstand as he answered in a calming tone, "He was agreeable." But it was enough to send Lauren into a frenzied tirade.

"Of course he was agreeable! That's his way, don't you see? It's worse than I thought."

"Be reasonable, Lauren."

"You don't know him," she interrupted.

"If you will recall, you said that to me once before and my opinion of the man proved right."

"This is different. I didn't know what I was talking about then. Now I have experience. He sits with that god-awful sincere smile and agrees with your reasoning and even gives you his rationalization of why he is amenable. And the whole thing is a ruse. I'm telling you, Zach, he doesn't give in this easily."

Zach stopped her pacing with his hands at her shoulders. "I know you have good reason to be afraid of him, Irish, and I know you're speaking from experience. But this is not the same as it was while you were at Maudie's; the stakes here are high and he is no fool. The law looks away from the goings-on at whorehouses, and anyone who deals with them takes their chances. But it is a piece of very valuable property that he has tried to steal from you, and he knows that if I push it he could be burned by that fact alone. He is not going to risk losing everything in a fight with me. You and Alan had no defense against him, but I have plenty and he knows it."

"He isn't afraid of anything or anyone. He has too much arrogance for that."

He stroked the side of her neck in an effort to smooth away her agitation. "He is smart enough to know when to accept a good deal and back away from his losses. And no matter what he might be thinking, I won't let anything happen to you. What do you say to a week or two up at the logging camp? By the time we get back everything will be taken care of and Rossiter and Maudie's will be completely out of our lives."

"I think you are shortsighted," she persisted in frustration.

"And I think you are reacting to what he has done in the past. But he can't do any more to you now. Besides, he is hardly coming out of this empty-handed, is he?"

Lauren shook her head stubbornly. "Would you turn your back on a coiled rattlesnake because he had already been fed a mouse?"

"It will be all right, Lauren. We'll be far up in the mountains by the time he even wakes up tomorrow morning. And then he will own Maudie's, which was what he wanted all along, and the whole thing will be over with."

"This isn't just vanity," she said, making one last attempt.

Zach laughed. "Vanity is the last thing I would ever accuse you of. I just want you to believe that you have seen the last of Rossiter."

"I only wish I could."

They climbed the stairs to their bedroom, each shedding damp clothes in the chill darkness. Zach could feel the tension in her, and when she raised a new flannel nightgown to slide over her head he slipped himself between her arms instead. "I wouldn't take any chances where you are concerned, Irish." His gravelly voice hinted at other things on his mind.

"It isn't only myself I'm worried about," she whispered back huskily, lowering her arms to his shoulders and letting the gown fall down his back to the bed.

Zach laughed as he nuzzled her neck. "I don't think I ever figured in his plans."

"But you could be an obstacle to them now." Her awakening senses made her draw her words out lazily.

"I just handed him Maudie's at a more than fair price. We may become great friends." He turned and whisked her up into his arms, around to the bedside, and onto the mattress.

"I don't think you have much in common," she breathed beneath a gasp of pleasure as his tongue teased the outline of her nipple and left moisture to cool-dry and tighten her sensitive flesh.

"That isn't what you said a week ago. We were just alike except that I was worse, as I recall."

"A week ago you were." She groaned and arched her back to his sucking mouth and fingers gently exploring between her thighs.

"How do I rate this week?" His teeth tugged at the crest of her breast, released it like a stretched spring, and then took the other.

"This week you talk too much."

Again he laughed and ended the conversation with his lips over hers.

Together they glided like feathers on a warm summer breeze, one flowing with the movement of the other. She above him, then he over her, with a dancer's grace. Their hands lightly skimmed and squeezed and caressed, their mouths met and parted, sought and tasted and left lightning to build in their wake.

Thoughts and fears were laid aside, and their senses sang a lover's song. As if his body was the arc of a wheel he slid up into her and completed the perfect circle of their joined bodies. Her legs lifted weightlessly to twine with his like ribbons around a maypole and then lock them tightly in an ecstasy that stood every nerve on end only to fall like dominos to one central point, to the core of each of them.

In that euphoric aftermath Zach pulled the sheet and blanket up over them as Lauren lay on her back with him close beside her. His heavy thigh came across both of hers, his arm rested below her breasts and held her in the cove of his broad chest. They each slept deeply, contentedly . . . for just an hour.

The steady din of the rain was the only sound. The room was filled with the charcoal shadows of a moonless night that left even creamy flesh and Lauren's white nightgown, lying in a pile on the floor, barely visible.

It was a dream, she thought at first when she was startled awake with the thought that someone stood at the footrail, looming over the bed. Were her eyes open or not? She blinked wildly to focus and see through darkness only an owl could have pierced. Was it the armoire that, through the unreal reality of a dream or some trick of the pitch-black darkness, seemed to have moved closer to the bed? Was there a shape? Movement? There couldn't be.

There was!

Two hands pinned her wrists to the mattress; another was clamped over her mouth. A stifled cry of terror died feebly in her throat. Beside her, Lauren heard Zach moan a complaint and stir, but the air above him rippled with sudden motion and the heavy thud of a club kept him still.

No nightmare: it was Rossiter's voice from the shadow at the footrail, hushed and calm as if he were taking care not to wake anyone. "Yes, it's me, darling. So good to see you again." Then, commanding, "You men know what to do with him. And remind Harrow that after he has worked him to the bone he is to be fed to the fish."

Squirming and writhing, Lauren fought the hand that pinned her head to the pillow, but to no avail. The dark masses hauled Zach from their bed and dragged him from the room.

"You didn't really think I would give you up, did you, Lauren?" Rossiter said conversationally. "Not after I took so much time and care to win you. I don't lose what I invest in to anyone."

She saw his arm rise like a devil's spear in a signal. The hand over her mouth came away to pinch her nose in an excruciating vise. She opened her mouth in agony, but before she could make a sound a wad of damp cloth was shoved into it. Bitterness gagged her. She gasped for air, fighting frantically, only to draw more of the vile stuff out of the cloth down her throat. Everything became hazy; she could no longer see even the masses of shadow. Rossiter was speaking, but she couldn't understand his words. Her tortured mind ordered her body to keep up the fight, but she couldn't tell if it responded. The rain seemed to roar all around, enclosing the room like a tomb.

And then the darkness came from within.

Chapter 33

The stench of rotting fish was a pungent reviver. Zach awakened enough to realize the smell was coming from beneath his nose and turned his face away. Shards of pain tore through his skull. He couldn't think straight. He only knew that the stink was fierce.

Then his mind came to fully awake with the consciousness of how uncomfortable he was. He lay on a hard, damp surface and a chilly drizzle moistened his naked chest. Where the hell was he? He opened his eyes in slits, careful not to move his head again.

The deck of a ship.

The deck of a ship! His eyes came wide open. Lauren. What had happened to Lauren? He remembered seeing Rossiter at Maudie's, going home with Lauren, making love, falling asleep. So how had he gotten here?

Voices drew closer, louder. Zach closed his eyes again and lay still.

"Hasn't come to yet, has he, Max?" came the nasal tones of the dwarf, Big Jim.

From behind, a heavy foot nudged Zach, but he kept himself limp.

"Out cold," grumbled the mallet-faced Max, and Zach heard his foot come to rest just inches from his back.

"I'd get him locked up soon, Harrow," advised the dwarf's voice again. "He won't be out much longer, and Mr. Zach Madox here ain't going to take kindly to being shanghaied. Thought he was too good to have anything to do with it, let alone get caught himself." A snorting chuckle followed his words.

Harrow? The name rang in Zach's mind. Harrow had captained one of his ships a few years back. Zach had discharged him for just this...shanghaiing his crew so he could pocket what he was suppose to be paying them. If ever there was a man with an eye toward vengeance it was Harrow.

"It serves the bloody cur right." The barrel-chested growl confirmed Zach's suspicion—it was indeed Harrow. "I've a score to settle with him. He'll wish his mam had never let him out o' the hatch before I'm through with him."

Again Zach peered through slitted eyelids. The deck before him was empty except for Harrow and Big Jim. Bearings...the ship was barely moving, which meant it was still docked, so how far was he from the gangplank? Not far. But how many stood watch? He was in no shape to take on an entire crew. Muscular Max was going to be difficult enough. Then the dwarf's words caught his attention again.

"Just don't forget what Rossiter wants. Madox shows his face in Seattle again and it'll be you that gets fed to the fish. He's taken the woman, and he means to have her for good. She suits that fancy notion of his that he's something better than the rest of us. You're to drop Madox here overboard at sea before you get back. Understand?"

Adrenaline surged new strength through Zach. Rossiter had Lauren! How much time had passed? Was it the same night? It must be. He had to get off this tub.

"Aye, I know what he wants," Harrow grumbled.

"If he's so worried that I won't do the job, why didn't he just let one of his usual boys do it?"

"Madox has too many friends in high places. The body would bring down too much heat and Rossiter would be the first person they'd come looking for. You know Rossiter. Has ears in all the right places. He says Madox here was all set to leave town— headed for San Francisco, he was. If he disappears everyone'll figure he just went on his trip. By the time anybody thinks to look for him the trail will be too cold to bother with. Besides, Rossiter didn't want it too easy for Madox. Has it in his head that he owes Madox some misery before he dies."

"Smart man, Rossiter." Harrow chuckled. "Uses them girls of his to get his information, is what I think. As for getting a little of his own back, it's like I said, I can understand that. Let's talk money."

"First things first, I'm telling you. Lock him up and then we'll talk."

Now was the time. Zach forced himself to lie limply. Harrow shouted instructions to Max and the two headed toward the companionway to go below. The muscular man bent to yank Zach up by the arms. The element of surprise worked in Zach's favor. He swung around, landing a heavy fist full force in the ugly face, knocking the man off guard.

"Hey!" Big Jim shouted.

Zach heard the other two racing toward him. Knowing time was precious, he clasped both hands into one fist and swung his arms like a club into the big man's belly; then he leapt over the doubled-up body and ran for the gangplank. A bullet whistled past his ear, but he didn't pause. Another sailor stood watch near the off-ramp. Again Zach used the fisted club of his arms and knocked the man overboard.

Down the plank he charged like a bull, with gun- shots exploding in the dark, drizzly night near enough for him to feel them cut the air as they passed.

Across the dock. Into the shadows. Between two warehouses. Then the shots stopped; they had lost sight of him. Still Zach ran, the too-short, too-tight hopsack pants that were not his own binding him. He spared not a backward glance to see if anyone was following as he raced through the quiet streets in bare feet. The blood pounded in his abused head, but one thought pushed him beyond the pain. He had to get to Lauren. Rossiter had her.

Billy's house was near the pier, and Zach went there. His hammerlike pounding roused the big bodyguard from sleep. Zach appropriated clothes, shoes, a horse, and a gun, and both men burst out again just as a gray dawn broke.

Lauren woke with a sickening lurch of her stomach. Her eyes flew wide open as her gorge rose, and the only thought she had was to find something in which to vomit. An ornate oriental urn became the receptacle. When she was finished she wilted against a silk-covered wall and slid weakly to the floor.

The room was large and perfectly appointed with a mixture of Chippendale mahogany and Ming dynasty porcelain. Immaculate. Meticulously detailed. Rossiter. The word came into a head too heavy with sickness to lift itself from the wall.

Lauren looked down at herself. Her nakedness was covered only by the sheet from the big brass bed in Zach's house, from which she had been torn so brutally. It was wrapped toga fashion around her slim body. Then she bolted back to the urn for a second turn at misery.

The door opened with her last retch, but Lauren could do no more than sink back to the floor, a weak mass against the sheer silk wall covering. Highly polished leather shoes stopped just inches from her, and

Lauren peered at the crisp crease of what could only be Rossiter's trousers. Very slowly her eyes traveled up the sleekly tailored suit to his dashingly handsome face and precisely groomed hair and beard.

"I am so sorry you're ill, darling," he commiserated in the sincerest of voices. "No doubt it was the knock-out drops. I have known them to have that effect on some. It will pass though, I promise you."

Lauren could do no more than stare up at him through a haze of disbelief and agony.

He continued conversationally, "But in the future please use the chamber pot rather than the vases, darling. Much more suitable." He reached a hand down to her. "Let me help you to bed."

Lauren did not accept his hand, but neither did she shrink back. "What do you think to gain by this?" she managed to say in a raw-throated whisper.

His smile was warm and understanding. "I have gained you, Lauren, and with you comes Maudie's, so I would say I have gained everything I want."

Her topaz eyes bathed him in hatred. "What have you done to Zach?"

He smiled pleasantly. "You are in no condition to discuss that now. When you're up to it I will be happy to tell you everything. For the moment, take heart in the fact that I have forgiven you, darling. As soon as you're well again we can go on as we should have. Though I do caution you not to repeat this unattractive show of stubbornness. I find it quite grating. Remember that I have already explained to you how distasteful I find having to force people to behave properly. Don't try my patience further than you have." The hand she had refused gently smoothed her hair. "You must rest now, darling. You will be fine again soon if you do." He bent and carefully lifted her to her feet.

Lauren tried to struggle, but her strength had totally deserted her. All she could manage was to hold

the sheet around herself as he got her to the high
bed and tenderly helped her into it.

"Maudie's suffers without your influence,
Lauren," he said casually. "It needs your touch. I,
too, have missed you. You are a respite from the tawdriness about me. But we will have to refurnish the
attic room. The bed is much too cramped, and I
crave more sophisticated beauty around me. Much
like you, darling, now that I think of it. Some would
overlook your special loveliness, but my eye is keen
and refined. There, now." He covered her with a
cashmere blanket. "Only spend a moment thinking
about how unpleasant it would be if you forced me to
drug you into compliance more often." He kissed her
brow and drew the knuckle of his index finger down
her cheek before he left.

As the door closed after him Lauren fainted from
a sickness no drug alone could have caused.

The early hour served him well as Zach approached Maudie's. With the revolver in his hand
and Billy guarding his back, he kicked open door
after door with a heavy-booted foot. Bleary-eyed
whores and hungover customers shot up from their
beds like innocent spooners from haystacks, one
after another. Rossiter's men came running, but they
stopped short when they met Billy's gun barrel.

But Zach found neither Lauren or Rossiter.

"Where is he?" he demanded in a frighteningly
feral snarl.

But the men were more frightened of Rossiter
than of Zach, and no one spoke.

Back to the docks Zach and Billy went. They
boarded *The Countess* and were soon engaged in a
swashbuckling fight as two of Rossiter's bullies
blocked the way. Again Zach crashed doors open, the
splintered wood flying high, but not a sign of Rossiter was found.

Once more Zach demanded information and once more he was judged the lesser of two evils, and only silence answered him.

Injured and too frantic to think straight, he took Billy's suggestion that Alan and Polly might have an idea of where Rossiter would have taken Lauren. Zach left the bodyguard to watch *The Countess* in case Rossiter came aboard and tried to sail off with Lauren, and he headed toward the place where Alan and Polly were still hiding from the man's treachery.

Zach pushed his horse mercilessly through the puddled streets of Seattle to his furniture factory just outside the city. He charged into the small cottage that housed his foreman and was now a haven for Alan and Polly. Zach gave Alan the news while the foreman discreetly left them. Alan's healed face blanched, and he could only stare, dumbfounded.

"Think, man, think!" Zach shouted. "Where could he have taken her?"

"I don't know!" Alan shouted back in horror. "I had nothing to do with him outside of Maudie's. It was the only place I ever saw him. My God, what will he do to her?"

In the doorway stood Polly, roused by the commotion. Her bright eyes were fearful and she worried her bottom lip. Zach caught sight of her, realizing she had overheard his tirade. "Do you know of any place Rossiter might take Lauren?" he demanded, none too gently.

She stared at him, torn between loyalty and fear. Then she said in a small voice, "He'll kill me like he did Sally."

Alan's head jerked up at her in surprise. "Do you know something?" he shot at her.

"You don't know him!" she said, appealing to them both. "He said he would kill me, and he will."

Zach lunged at her, but Alan's hand stopped him. "We won't let Rossiter do anything to you, Polly. If you know something, you must tell us. Lauren's life is in danger."

"He wants her. He loves her in his way. He won't kill her."

"You owe it to her, Polly," Zach ground out furiously.

"I don't owe anybody anything!" the whore shot back viciously and then looked apologetically at Alan. "There's things about me you don't know."

"No matter what it is, it isn't important...it won't make any difference to me," Alan assured her gently. "Just tell us."

"Don't hate me, Alan," she pleaded.

"What is it, Polly?" Zach demanded urgently, feeling every minute she delayed was an eternity.

"Whatever it is, Polly, tell him," Alan urged.

Her eyes lingered on Alan a moment longer, as if this glance would be her last. Then she turned to Zach. "I've done her a real bad wrong. I was working *The Countess* when Maudie's was getting ready to open. Rossiter sent me to work for Lauren, to spy on her and tell him everything that went on there. It was me that let him know when you were gone that first time so he could come court her. It was me that stole the liquor receipts and robbed the safe and done the damage around the place so he could fix things and look like a hero. It was me that told him Billy had gotten you up into her room that night, so Rossiter got rid of him and moved in. I told him everything that was going on, even about when all the girls agreed to wait for their money so she could pay him off. But when he had Sally killed, I said I was finished with him. I wanted no part in murder. That's when he said he'd kill me the same way if I ever told anything." Her voice rose defensively. "I needed the money. My family starves unless they get what I send. I know what it is to be hungry. I've done worse in my life for less."

"Where is she, Polly?" Alan asked calmly, wanting to stop her confession before Zach lost the tight control that barely held him from venting his mounting rage.

But Polly went on explaining to Alan, too afraid of what she saw in Zach's face to look at him. "I didn't know he would go this far. I thought he would settle for Maudie's. I stopped helping him when I said I did, Alan, and I never once linked you to any of it so he wouldn't hurt you. And I gave you the knock-out drops so Lauren could get away from him."

"I know you did, Polly. Just tell us where he has taken her."

"I don't know for sure, but if he isn't at Maudie's and he hasn't taken her aboard *The Countess*, there's only one other place left. He owns an island out in the Sound. Calls it his smuggler's hideaway because that's who built it. He might have her there."

Heavy velvet curtains were pulled open, flooding the dark room with dusky morning light. Lauren came awake with a jolt and sat up straight and stiff, her hand pressing the sheet tightly to her breasts even though it was knotted too firmly to fall. Her hair hung in strings down her back and over her bare shoulders and her mouth was dry and tasted stale, but the nausea had gone and rage had replaced it.

Rossiter tied back the heavy drapes, fixing the folds just so, and then came to the bedside in measured, casual strides. "From the look of fire in your eyes I would say you are feeling better. Are you, darling?"

"What have you done with Zach?" She spat the words at him.

"Yes, we might as well have done with that subject." He flicked a piece of lint from the sleeve of his white coat. "Your least favorite of the facts of life around here has disposed of him, I'm afraid. He was handed over to Big Jim last night."

"Shanghaied? You had him shanghaied?" she breathed in horror, and disbelief.

"Onto a ship captained by a man who despises Madox because of an old grudge. He will work him until he is useless and then throw him overboard. I watched the ship sail at dawn this morning. You might just as well consider yourself a widow already, Lauren, and not waste time harboring hopes of a second rescue. I have effectively wiped him from both our lives."

Lauren could do no more than stare at him, not wanting to believe him and yet knowing how all-encompassing and powerful his evil was.

He sat on the edge of the bed, wrinkling his brow at the sight of her. "Let's talk no more of him now, shall we? This is what I have planned for you. First of all, a detailed toilette is in order and I have sent for gowns from the city. The boat has just docked below, so they should be brought up any minute. I am sure by the expression marring your lovely face that we will have to spend a fair amount of time here on the island while you learn to accept the situation, but once you have we will go back to Maudie's and carry on with all I have planned. Before long, Lauren, we will own every business that deals in vice in Seattle. A far more valuable empire than other fools aspire to. Railroads, lumber, even gold mines don't make the kind of profit we will."

"You will have nothing from me," she said, so low it was nearly to herself.

Rossiter laughed smoothly. "Don't let's start that again. It is inevitable. Make the best of it." He stood up and sauntered to the window to peer out above the treetops. "You are a sensible woman, Lauren. I know you will come to see..." His words stopped short, his spine snapped straight, and she saw his profile freeze into a frown. "What have we here?" he hissed viciously.

Lauren's heart raced with hope. "What is it?"

"For some reason your friend Alan has just come ashore. Could he know you are here?" he asked. Then with a sigh of resignation he turned back to Lauren, taking a small derringer from inside his brocade vest. "It is time we begin our charade then, darling. Come along and we will persuade your friend not to try heroics."

Rossiter's other hand closed around the bare flesh of her arm and pulled her from the bed. The sheet was wrapped so tightly around her that her knees felt hobbled, and she had to struggle to keep pace with him.

Not Zach, her mind screamed. Alan was no match for Rossiter. He would only get himself killed.

Rossiter shoved Lauren down the hallway and out onto the balcony that circled the house. He held her close to him, standing against the railing. Far below, in the dense forest of pine trees, she could see Alan walking slowly up the lamp-lined path.

"Call to him," Rossiter ordered. When she hesitated he jammed the derringer into her side, and she called out Alan's name.

At the sound of her voice Alan stopped and peered up at them. "Lauren! Are you all right?" he asked urgently.

"Tell him to go back to the city; convince him you are where you want to be. The story is that your dear husband had a change of heart about taking a whore as his wife and has deserted you. Tell it well."

Lauren did as she was ordered.

"Very good, darling, very goo…"

Before either of them realized what was happening Rossiter was torn from Lauren's side. She spun around to see Zach's fist pummel Rossiter's face. The derringer dropped and skidded across the wooden floor to stop precariously near the edge of the balcony as the two battled. Lauren tried to reach it but she couldn't; she fell back against the wall of the house, her eyes searching for some way to help Zach.

Rossiter's cultured face fell away to reveal a fighter every bit as dirty and powerful as his henchmen. But Zach battled for everything he valued in life, higher stakes than Rossiter ever dreamed of. Zach had the upper hand and Rossiter knew it. Breaking away from Zach's crushing grip he lunged for the derringer. But the rain had left the planked wood slippery. Lauren watched in wide-eyed horror as Rossiter slid as if on ice, his tall body crashing through the railing to fall with a scream of terror that died away eerily and stopped as he hit the ground.

For a moment Lauren and Zack stood motionless, staring at the empty space where Rossiter had been just moments before. Then Zach stepped to the broken railing and peered down at the other man lying sprawled and still. Then he turned and closed the distance between him and Lauren in two long strides and enfolded her in his arms.

Chapter 34

They spent February snowed in at the logging camp, and during the stormy days of March they finally hung draperies and curtains over every window in the big house on the outskirts of Seattle. April passed in making preparations for the baby, and May culminated in endless hours of waiting. Zach was so jumpy Lauren wanted to throttle him. No matter how many errands she devised to get him out from underfoot he either rushed through them or delegated them to their new housekeeper, Mary.

When the time came it was a Friday night and Lauren and Zach were at the Cades' house. Lauren had barely picked at her food as everyone around her gorged themselves. She felt a sudden gush and found herself embarrassingly wet. Except for the inconvenience, she felt perfectly fine and so rather than alert the other people in the room, she merely waited through the remainder of the meal, her expression calm, her posture straight. When everyone retired to have coffee in the drawing room afterward, she stayed where she was, her serene smile giving not a clue to what was happening to her. In fact, Zach didn't even notice, absorbed as he was in a rousing conversation with the other men on the merits of Washington's statehood, granted that past November.

But Winifred realized something was amiss and waited until they alone occupied the dining room. "It's time, isn't it?" she said simply.

"It must be, because I'm sitting in a puddle."

"How do you feel?"

"Not a pain. Is it possible there won't be any?"

Winifred smiled knowingly. "I'm afraid not. It will start any time. We'd best get you settled in upstairs so you'll be ready when it does."

Lauren returned her smile, her tone as matter-of-fact as the older woman's. "I appreciate the offer, but as long as you're reasonably certain the baby isn't going to be born in the next half hour, I'm going home. It is important that it be born there, in the brass bed. Zach has such plans, you know. If I can avoid disappointing him, I mean to."

"Then let's get to it. There's no time to waste prattling about it; your labor could start any time. I'll call Zach and get a blanket to wrap around you."

The first sight of Zach's face was like the vision of a ghost, so pale was he. "We're staying here," he insisted before Lauren had said a word, apparently having been informed of the situation by Winifred.

Lauren gave him the smile that said her immovable stubbornness had taken over. "With the exception of being a bit soggy I feel no different than I ever have. I'm going home." Her tone brooked no argument. "I'd rather you brought the buggy around back though. I don't relish parading around like this in my present predicament."

Zach opened his mouth to argue, but Winifred's voice interjected, "There's no sense fighting it, Zach. Just do as she asks. She'll be fine, and I'll come along just in case. We can send Arthur for the midwife."

They'd both gone mad was what Zach thought,

but he ran for the buggy rather than debate it. The drive was an exercise in agony for him. He was torn between wanting to race for home and keeping the horses to a bare walk, not sure which was in order—speed or care. It was a mild spring evening, but perspiration dampened the back of his shirt and left half-moons of wetness under each arm. He couldn't tell whether panic or excitement made his blood pound in his ears. And there Lauren sat beside him, behaving as if he were taking her to a lazy Sunday picnic and chatting casually with Winifred. Dammit, didn't they know this was an awesome occasion?

Never had he known Lauren to dawdle, but it seemed to him that that was just what she was doing. She insisted on putting things to rights in the kitchen, sponging herself down standing in the bathtub, and setting out clean towels and linens and baby blankets so that everything was ready. When he could stand no more of it Zach picked her up bodily and placed her in bed, swearing that he would tie her to it if she moved and that he didn't give a tinker's damn *how* she felt about it.

Then it began, a surprisingly hard pain way down low in her abdomen. It was like nothing she had ever felt; it took her breath away and replaced her calmness with a surge of tense excitement.

The midwife arrived, a stern woman who looked more like a bald-faced man in a dress. Zach scandalized her by announcing that he had been there for the start of it and by God he'd be there till the end. Lauren was grateful, she felt she hadn't the extra stamina to fight such an intimidating creature alone.

Now it was Zach who took over tending to details, calm and purposefully, as if he had been through this a dozen times before. He tied strips of old sheets to the brass spindles of the headboard, knotting the ends into grips. He stayed with Lauren, bathing her brow in cool water, encouraging her and soothing her with husky-voiced words and rubbing her back or belly when that seemed to help.

They nearly lost the midwife altogether when it came time to push, for Zach climbed up behind Lauren on the bed and straddled her with his long legs. He didn't care that the hatchet-faced woman was appalled; he proved the validity of the position. He could support Lauren's back when the pressure pushed her to a near-sitting position and then help her rest back in his lap in between. Only Winifred's powers of persuasion kept the midwife with them, snorting her disapproval.

And then at dawn their daughter slipped into the world with a gusty wail, all blotchy red and flailing. She owned a thatch of black hair like her father's and a stubborn will like her mother's.

Only Lauren's urging could get Zach out of the room while she and the baby were cleaned up. The moment that was completed, back he came. To the final horror of the midwife, the big brass bed held all three of them then, for Zach sat propped beside Lauren, holding the baby every minute she allowed him to. He stared down at his daughter as if he had caught a cloud and couldn't quite believe it. He cooed to her when she cried and laughed when she wet him and kissed her over and over and over again.

"When can we have a few more?" he whispered to Lauren not two hours later, a glint of warm mischief in his black eyes. His face was darkly shadowed with beard, his hair mussed from the long hours of strain and hard work.

She looked up at him from her pillow and smiled that secret smile. "Did I sign on for more than one of these?" she teased him.

"A full baker's dozen, as I recall." He gave her his crooked grin, happiness glowing on his tired face.

"We may have to renegotiate." She closed her eyes wearily.

He bent to kiss her forehead, rasping softly, "I'll just have to sneak them into you when you aren't looking, eh, Irish?"

"Is it a brood mare you want, Zach Madox? If you aren't careful you'll have me thinking you never come to me in bed for any reason other than baby making," she chided thickly as the excitement settled at last and sleep crept in.

His answer was a rumbling chuckle as she drifted off; the last words she heard were his teasing, "'Tis daft ye are if ye believe that, me lovely. Daft indeed!" And then, without the brogue, he said softly, "I love you, Lauren."

Chapter 35

July, 1890

She stood at the porch railing letting a summer breeze cool her love-heated skin. All around her were quiet night sounds: crickets chirping, the burbling of the meandering brook, and leaves gently rustling in the treetops. The air was flower scented and light against her face, and the moon was a full custard ball.

Zach followed her out of the house. He propped a hip against the banister and pulled her between his legs. His big hands played with the long, loose fall of her hair while he nuzzled her neck. She laughed lightly, a rich aftertone, sounding so fresh from the rapture of his arms. He wore only jeans, half unfastened, and Lauren teased the hard wrinkles of his belly.

"Mmm. This is much better," she breathed, her head back to free the arch of her throat to his kisses.

"That's what you get for heating up the bedroom," his gravelly voice rumbled in the stillness.

"I was just standing here wondering why you chose me to fulfill your elaborate plans. You could have had anyone."

"Because you taste so good." He nipped her. "Because you're such a damn bundle of contradictions that I knew I'd never get bored."

"Do you think I'm a hypocrite?" She feigned offense.

"Never that." He settled his chin on her head. "But you're part naive and part wise; part strong and part vulnerable; part proud and part doubting of yourself enough to ask me damn-fool questions like why I picked you."

"When we first met on the train, did you believe I was a whore?"

"Not for a second. I had you figured for a bible toter and a virgin if ever I had seen one." He kissed the top of her head, thinking back to their first train trip. "I forgot to tell you—you were right about it being Brandon Bentley who shot me as I was leaving Dry Creek."

"How do you know?"

"Alan told me. The old coot would have killed me if he hadn't been so nearsighted."

"Let that be a lesson to you," she teased haughtily and made him laugh. Then her mind wandered back to the present. "Alan seems happy enough with Polly. They are doing well with Maudie's too. It was very generous of you to buy it and give it over to him."

"I owed him more than that. Besides saving me from his father's treachery he helped me save you twice. And you didn't drive too hard a bargain when you sold Maudie's to me."

"I got enough to set Sara up to do anything she wants when the time comes."

"Anything but owning a whorehouse," he amended. "What if we have all daughters? That money will get spread pretty thin."

"They will have to go into business together."

"Oh, Lord," he moaned elaborately, "there is only one business I know of that twelve girls could all work at in the same place."

"I guess you had better hope for boys." She

paused a minute in thought. "Alan doesn't seem to feel the loss of his father."

"Polly has filled the gap."

"I still don't understand why you don't like her. You criticized her so harshly when he said they were getting married that I was afraid you would drive Alan away from us for good."

"Mmm." he murmured noncommittally. Though Zach was determined that Lauren should never know of Polly's betrayal, he couldn't find it in himself to forgive the woman fully. Maybe in time, he conceded, since she was genuinely trying to mend her ways and be a good friend to Lauren and a loving, faithful wife to Alan. But it wouldn't be easy.

He nuzzled his wife's hair, but she paid him no heed. The mention of Brandon Bentley had set Lauren to thinking of fathers—good, bad, and unknown. "I'm glad Sara has you, Zach. You're a good father. I always wondered who mine was, what he was like, if he would have loved me. I would have hated for Sara to have to wonder the same thing."

"That's not what you said in January. Then you wanted to make an orphan of her."

"I was almighty angry at you." She smiled at the memory now, grateful that it had turned out as it had. Then she said, "Besides, she would have been a bastard, not an orphan. I wouldn't have abandoned her. I always felt bad for the orphans at the convent and grateful to belong to a family, no matter how irregular it was." She hesitated and then went on cautiously, "Do you remember any family at all?" It was a subject she often wondered about but had avoided bringing up, thinking it might be difficult for him.

But Zach answered easily, undisturbed by something so far behind him. "They told me I was abandoned right out of the hatch. I couldn't have been more than two or three hours old, the story goes. No one ever came back or even asked after me, so far as I know, and there were no clues. I was a naked, squalling parcel left in the alley behind the orphanage. I don't think you can get any more orphaned than that."

She raised a soft palm to his cheek, looking up into eyes that were just shadows. "I'm so sorry," she whispered.

"It stopped mattering to me the day you set foot in this 'big, empty house,' as you put it. Strange, but I just realized that. Through everything else I always felt adrift, even when I was planning to marry Molly Cade. And then you came, all tight inside and haughty as hell, the whore-to-be in the high-necked gown, and you fixed it." His laugh was like a deep rumbling in the earth.

"I do love you, you know." The serene smile that had first intrigued him played across her mouth at his description of her.

"I knew it before you did," he lied.

"Is that so?"

"It is. But I was going to have you whether you did or not. I meant it when I said I loved you enough for us both, if it had to be that way."

"And are you disappointed? Now that you finally have a wife and family for this place?"

"I'll have to think about that," he said jokingly "I never pictured a sassy, stubborn, stiff-backed little baggage as my wife, that's for damn sure."

"I trust Sara suits?" She asked coyly, proving the sassy part. He placed two hands over her derriere and squeezed as playful punishment.

"I don't know," he countered dubiously. "She's a lot like her mama. A temper straight from hell and a will stronger than iron." His crooked grin came then. "Guess you just have to know how to soothe them." He ran his big, warm, gentle hands smoothly up her thinly clad back.

"And you think you're good at that, do you?" Nevertheless, she responded to his actions by rolling her shoulders sensuously beneath the firm, kneading pressure of those hands on her back.

"Who can quiet Sara better than me?" he bragged.

"Me," she stated simply.

"That doesn't count." His teeth teased her earlobe and his voice grew huskier. "And who does her mama moan for except me?"

"Mmm," she murmured, conceding his point as she drew her hands through his silky hair just the way he did to comb back the wings.

"Think the room has cooled off by now?" His gravelly voice was ragged against her skin.

"Oh, I doubt it." She dashed his hopes only to rebuild them. "But the grass looks like a possibility."

He laughed and swung her up into his arms. Down they went to the lush green lawn, rimmed in pale moonglow, cool and prickly smooth.

"You're the damnedest woman," he breathed just before his mouth captured hers with a heaviness that belied passions spent a scant hour before.

They came together in love, soft, tender, frenzied, explosive—perfect love, shared freely on a warm midsummer's night. A cool breeze feathered their naked skin, and the moon laid a golden gossamer blanket over them while they played and petted and pleasured each other.

Each was at once sated and renewed as they went back to their big brass bed and curled up together to sleep at last. Their arms and legs entwined, their breaths met and mingled, and their voices quieted to the silent reassurance of touch.

"I love you, Lauren," he whispered into her hair as his eyes closed.

"I love you too," she whispered back with a replete sigh.

"You damned well better," he said, grinning in the dark.

And in that last snatch of thought before sleep came, Zach knew that he had everything he had ever wanted.

And Lauren knew she had always wanted just what she had now.

Authors of
exceptional promise

Historical novels
of superior quality!

MIDNIGHT'S LADY   Sandra Langford
75018-X/$3.50US/$4.50Can

SAVAGE SURRENDER   Lindsey Hanks
75021-X/$3.50US/$4.50Can

THE HIDDEN HEART   Laura Kinsale
75008-3/$3.50US/$4.50Can

BRIANNA   Linda Lang Bartell
75096-1/$3.50US/$4.50Can

DESIRE AND SURRENDER   Katherine Sutcliffe
75067-8/$3.75US/$4.95Can

TENDER FORTUNE   Judith E. French
75034-1/$3.75US/$4.95Can